A
STORM
IN
EVERY
HEART

ALSO BY KATE KING

ENCHANTED LEGACIES

A Thorn in Every Heart

A Storm in Every Heart

A Holiday in Every Heart: An Enchanted Legacies Christmas Novella

WILDE FAE

Lords of the Hunt

Lady of the Nightmares

The Last Heir of Elsewhere

A Kingdom of Monsters

THE GENTLEMEN

Red Handed

Thieves Honor

Damned Souls

THE BLISSFUL OMEGAVERSE

Pack Origin

Pack Bound

Pack Bliss

STANDALONES:

By Any Other Name: A Deliciously Dark Romeo and Juliet Retelling

ENCHANTED LEGACIES

BOOK TWO

A STORM IN EVERY HEART

USA TODAY & INTERNATIONAL BESTSELLING AUTHOR

KATE KING

First Cover edition September 2025

Paperback: 979-8-9917934-9-0

Hardcover: 979-8-9917934-7-6

Cover design and typography: Flowers and Forensics

Edge Design: Painted Wings Publishing Services

Proofreading: Emily in the Archives @emilyinthearchives

Published by Wicked Good Romance

To the marvelous and talented Pat Carroll, the original voice of Ursula.

Thank you for kindly explaining to four-year-old me that Ursula was not real and would not come to my house and eat my dog. I'm sorry I cried.

DYASPORA
THERMIA
VERNALLIS

ELLENDER
N
W
E
S
SOLISTINE
HYDRATTA

ODESSA

I'm barely aware of my body changing as I dive beneath the frothing waves.

The cold water embraces me, and I almost don't notice the scales coating my legs and torso or the webbing stretching between my elongating fingers. My body knows this is where I belong in a way that my racing mind cannot, will not, comprehend.

Not now, while my only focus is finding the prince.

He's here somewhere. He must be.

The water is like a dark abyss, and I turn my head back and forth, blinking against the salt.

Finally, out of the corner of my eye, I glimpse a flash of a tattooed forearm and the sleeve of a black shirt. My heart races as I kick my tail, propelling down, down, down, deep into the dark.

Along the sandy ocean floor, the unconscious prince floats just above the sand.

Kastian's body has gone limp. His dark curly hair is a weightless halo. His eyes are closed, and bubbles escape from his parted lips. A heavy iron chain, weighted at the end, clamps around his ankle.

A spark of panicked rage shoots through me as I grip the chain in both hands, pulling with all my strength. The iron links snap as easily as twine, and I drop them onto the sand. My heart races with hope as I wrap my webbed fingers around Kastian's arms and pull him toward the surface.

Again, something moves on the edge of my vision, but this time a creeping dread crawls up my spine.

I turn, and out of the swirling water, three ethereal figures emerge. Their forms shimmer with an eerie glow, reflecting phantom light. I recoil, and the hope in my chest stutters and dies.

Mesmerizing and terrifying all at once, the sirens have the torsos of women and the bottom half of ocean predators. *"Monsters."* I've heard them called. *"Demons. A curse upon men."*

Each of their faces is angular with enormous pupil-less eyes and tight, and greenish skin pulled tight over their skulls with no flesh between skin and bone. Their hair flows like ropes of swaying seaweed, and rows of needle-like teeth fill their wide mouths.

The two in the back have sleek and powerful fish tails, while the leader's hip bones end above a mass of writhing black tentacles. On her head, she wears a familiar crown of coral and pearls atop her green hair.

A whirlwind of fear and fascination churns within me, but I pull my gaze from the sirens in time to watch the last of the air bubbles rise from Kastian's lips.

I open my mouth to shout that I do not have time for this. We must return to the surface! But no words escape me. The water distorts my voice into a chilling blend of melody and anguish, echoing like a song entwined with a scream.

The tentacled queen stiffens at the sound of my voice rippling through the water. She raises a hand to her companions, and they fall back, swimming in wide circles around us like sharks stalking prey.

The queen glides through the water with effortless grace, her undulating tentacles propelling her closer. Her mesmerizing eyes lock onto me with unsettling intensity. Her lips don't move, but her ghostly voice whispers in the back of my mind: *What's this? Another man lost to the siren's lure. Unfortunate...and tragically predictable.*

I shake my head. *No, that's not what this is. I've already seen that happen once. I won't let it happen again.*

The queen drifts closer, and her voice in my mind answers as if she can hear my thoughts. She sounds almost amused. *You won't have a choice. You won't reach the surface in time, and even if you did, your prince is dead anyway.*

As much as it kills me, she's right. The sirens will never let us leave. Even if they do, we've been in the water far too long. It's too late.

I can't keep my thoughts from leaking out for the siren to hear. *Please help me.*

The siren's expression does not change. She doesn't blink, or even open her mouth, but somehow, I know she's laughing at me. *Help you? What would you give me in exchange?*

Anything.

1
THE PAST

ODESSA, AGE 8

"Do you know what she looks like?" I ask, my eyes scanning the crowded harbor.

Mercer, my father's steadfast first mate, shakes his head. "No."

"Then why bother looking?"

Mercer's mouth twitches beneath his beard. "Because there's nothing else to do while we wait, little miss."

I sigh. It's the waiting in general that's upsetting me.

Hydratta's royal harbor buzzes with the cries of seagulls and the lively conversations of merchants and sailors. The fragrance of saltwater and spices permeates the air, and the dock sways beneath our feet with the rhythm of the waves. Behind me stands *The Adella*, my father's grand trading ship, its sails furled and rigging creaking in the gentle breeze.

It's the only home I've ever known, and after today I'll never see it again.

"We don't have to wait for my aunt," I say hopefully. "We could get back on the ship."

Mercer glances down at me, pity and exasperation mingling on his face. "You know that's not going to happen."

"But I don't understand *why*."

"A ship isn't a suitable place for a girl."

I squeeze the heavy brass key in my hand until the metal prongs dig into my flesh. "It seems there's nowhere interesting in the world suitable for a girl."

He laughs. "True enough, little miss, but there are better places than aboard a ship, aye? The crew wouldn't know what to do with you now that your father's gone."

He says the word "gone" with gravity, as if some great illness or accident took my papa. As if it wasn't his own choice to throw himself into the sea with no care for what he'd leave behind. With no care for me.

"I could work, you know. I know how to do every job on board. Wouldn't it be—"

"That's enough," Mercer grumbles. "You'll be happy living with your aunt. I know your papa was already thinking about sending you to live with her before—" he coughs "—well, you know."

I nod automatically. Of course I know, but thinking about it makes the backs of my eyes burn. I brush angrily at my eyes with my free hand, refusing to let a single tear fall.

This is the first I've heard that Papa wanted to send me away, but I'm not surprised. There aren't many children on merchant ships, and even fewer girls, but the sea is the only home I've ever known.

I've lived my entire life on the decks of *The Adella*. While other children attended school, I've never spent more than a week at a time on land. My schooling was in navigation and astronomy, how to barter with merchants in every port in Ellender, and how to curse like a sailor. I doubt any of that will be useful in the household of my aunt, Beatrix.

My father's only sister lives with her husband and son in the eastern kingdom of Vernallis. I've never met her, and I dread what it will be like in her house. Will I have to go to school? Will they treat me as a servant or as a lady? I'm not sure which would be worse.

Sighing, I turn my gaze back to the bustling harbor street beyond the docks. Being a noble Fae lady, I can only assume my aunt will arrive to collect me in a grand, horse-drawn carriage.

I'm half right.

Within the hour, Aunt Beatrix arrives in a worn relic of a carriage, with faded paint and wheels that groan and squeak with every turn. The driver, a bored-looking Fae male, guides the carriage to a slow, creaking halt at the end of the dock. With a roll of his eyes, he leaps down from his seat and holds open the carriage door.

A beautiful, dark-haired Fae woman appears in the doorway, taking the driver's hand to help her down. She's wearing a tailored lavender silk gown that shimmers in the afternoon sunlight and looks almost ethereal against the backdrop of the battered old carriage.

My stomach sinks, and I lean closer to Mercer. "Is that her?"

He lets out a grunt that might be a "yes" or it could mean, "I'm not sure."

"She doesn't look like Papa," I observe.

Mercer chuckles under his breath, but before he can answer, we're both distracted by another figure in the carriage's doorway.

A skinny boy with messy coppery-brown hair jumps down to stand beside Aunt Beatrix. He can't be any older than twelve, but he's already taller than his mother by several inches. Mouthy, too, by the look of it, because he cranes his head back and says something to the carriage driver that makes the grown man's face redden.

Seemingly unbothered, Aunt Beatrix strides toward us, her head held high. Her son trots after her, looking somewhere between sheepish and annoyed.

Mercer straightens his shoulders and steps forward to meet them halfway. "Are you Lady Ashwater, Ma'am?"

"I am!" Aunt Beatrix's face breaks into a wide smile as she stops in front of us and looks from Mercer, to me, to the ship behind us. "And you?"

"James Mercer, Ma'am. Recently appointed captain of *The Adella*."

Her smile turns tight. "Pleasure to meet you. I hope you haven't been waiting long."

"Not long at all," Mercer lies.

Aunt Beatrix nods politely, then steps around Mercer. She pulls off her lavender gloves and bends down to my eye level. "You must be Odessa."

I blink at her, a wave of discomfort washing over me. Now that she's closer, I can see my aunt has the same blue eyes as my papa, and the sight of them makes my throat so tight I can't speak. I squeeze the key in my hand until it hurts.

"I'm so sorry about your father," Aunt Beatrix says kindly. "And I'm sorry that we're meeting like this. I wrote to Gabriel so many times over the years, asking him to bring you for a visit."

There's a long silence where I can feel all eyes on me. I swallow the lump in my throat, willing myself not to cry.

I will not cry in front of these strangers who are going to take me away from my home and everyone I've ever known. The humiliation would be unbearable. And worse, I can already see the pity on my aunt's face.

The only thing worse than humiliation is pity.

Aunt Beatrix sighs, her brow furrowing with concern. She glances at her son, who has been silent until now. "I need to go speak with Mr. Mercer. Wait here with Odessa."

Her son nods, and Aunt Beatrix steps away, leaving me alone with my cousin in the middle of the dock.

"What have you got in your hand?" the boy asks as soon as his mother is out of earshot.

I glance at him, realizing that I don't know his name. Aunt Beatrix didn't introduce him, and although I'm sure Papa mentioned my cousin's name at least once, it escapes me now. Not knowing what to say, I wrap my fingers tighter around the brass handle of the antique key.

My father gave me this key, promising to reveal the treasure it opened, but then he took his own life, leaving me forever uncertain of where the key fits.

"You're very quiet," my cousin observes. "Too bad. I've been looking forward to hearing about what it's like to live on a ship..." He trails off, widening his bright green eyes in an invitation for me to join the conversation. When I don't, he just shrugs. "...but I guess you're going to turn out to be boring."

I bristle, an immediate denial springing to my lips. "I'm not boring."

My cousin grins. "Could've fooled me. I'm Daemon, by the way."

My temperature rises as fast as my indignation. My papa always said I had a temper like a stormy sea. One moment it's smooth sailing, and the next the tide is so rough it could swallow an entire ship in one gulp. "Perhaps I simply don't want to talk to you."

"Or perhaps you can't carry on a normal conversation," he says, in a tone of mock contemplation. "Don't worry, I know it's not your fault. Mother told me you'd never been to school."

As quick as a blink, I almost forget my sadness as anger takes over. "How dare you? M-my father just died!"

Daemon's grin widens, and he shoves his hands into his pockets, rocking back on his heels. "Mine too."

I jerk back, startled. I don't know what I expected him to say, but it wasn't that.

Before I can think of how to respond, the sounds of commotion drift toward us from the adjacent street. Daemon grows distracted, craning his neck to watch, and I follow his gaze. At the far end of the cobblestone street that runs alongside the dock, a group of sailors has gathered in a circle. In the center, two men are beating each other until their faces and fists are bloody.

"Who do you suppose started it?" Daemon asks.

"Are you joking?"

"No. Why? Do you know them?"

I scoff, finding myself pleased to know something my cousin doesn't. "They're not fighting out of anger. Haven't you ever seen boxing before?"

He shakes his head. "No. The only fighting allowed in the court of Vernallis is magical dueling."

My eyebrows raise. My father was Fae, and all Fae have magic, but magic isn't good for much unless you train to use it. I've never met anyone with training. "Do you use magic, then?" I ask. "That's something I'd like to see."

In answer, Daemon flicks a hand toward a nearby lamppost. It promptly explodes, and I duck, raising my arms to shield my head from the spray of glass. "What was that for? You could have just said 'yes.' You didn't have to smash anything."

Daemon swears under his breath, looking crestfallen. "Sorry. I meant to light the lamp."

"I take it you're not winning many duels?"

His face breaks into another grin. "No, not yet, which is why I've got to learn other ways to fight. Come on, let's go."

I blink in confusion, still shaking broken glass from my long red hair. "Go where?"

"To watch the fight," he says, like it's obvious. "You know, to pick up tips."

I shake my head. "But we have to wait for your mother."

Daemon scoffs, walking backwards toward the end of the dock. "No, we don't. She's afraid you won't adjust well to coming to live with us. She won't come back until she thinks I've gotten you to talk...and you're talking. So, let's go."

I shift between my feet, my mind spinning. I'm not allowed to go wandering through the ports on my own...but then again, that was Papa's rule, and he's no longer here to enforce it. Making a split-second decision, I dash after my cousin, nearly tripping over my long skirt and the end of the dock in my haste to follow.

Looking pleased with himself, Daemon slows to half speed so

I can walk alongside him without having to run, and leads the way down the busy street toward the sounds of fighting. We pass by the shabby carriage, which is parked beside a low stone wall. The driver is sitting on the wall smoking a pipe, and he glares at us as we pass.

"What did you say to the carriage driver when you arrived?" I ask the moment we're out of earshot.

"You saw that?" Daemon laughs as we walk past the rows of merchant stalls and mingling sailors. "It's a borrowed carriage. Mother lent hers to a friend just before we heard about Uncle Gabriel, so we hired this one in a hurry. The driver is a lecherous ass who wouldn't stop staring at my mother. I told him to keep his eyes to himself or I'd cut them out of his head."

"But you said you don't know how to fight."

He shrugs. "It can't be that hard."

I look sideways at my cousin. "How old are you, anyway?"

"Eleven."

My eyebrows raise. "Do you often threaten men twice your size and ten times your age?"

He grins in a self-satisfied way. "Only when they deserve it."

I haven't spent a lot of time with other children, so I can't be sure, but I'd guess my cousin is unusual. I can't tell if he's messing with me. "Did your father really die, or were you just saying that?"

He nods. "Last year."

I squeeze the key in my hand. "I'm sorry."

"Don't be. I'm not."

I can't imagine what his father could have done for Daemon not to miss him, and I'm not sure I want to know. Instead, I ask: "Does that mean you live alone with your mother?"

Daemon shoves a grown Fae male out of the way before the male steps on my dress. Then he answers as if there were no interruption. "Yeah, just me and her. And the servants, of course." He raises an eyebrow. "And now, you too, I suppose. I've always wanted siblings. I pictured brothers, but a sister would be fine too, I guess."

"I'm not your sister."

"May as well be, right?"

I shake my head as Daemon and I make our way to the end of the narrow cobblestone street. The street buzzes with excitement, and the shouts of men watching the fight echo over the harbor, growing louder and more fervent with each step we take. We stop at the edge of the throng of onlookers, craning our necks and straining on tiptoe to glimpse the fight beyond the wall of towering men.

Daemon turns in a circle before his gaze catches on the barnacle-covered stone wall that runs the length of the harbor, holding back the ocean waves from splashing onto the street. He bounds across the street in three steps, and hoists himself up, then extends a hand to pull me after him. I pause for only a second before shoving the brass key into my pocket and taking Daemon's hand.

From atop the wall, we have a clear view of the boxing match taking place in the center of the enthusiastic crowd. The fight that we saw from the dock has ended, and two other men are preparing to enter the ring. From their cheap clothing and over-long hair, I assume they're deckhands. The taller of the two is Fae, but the other has rounded ears.

"Is that man human?" Daemon asks incredulously. "That's absurd. He's going to get himself killed! I thought you said it was just for sport."

Before I can answer, another voice sounds behind us. "I'd take that bet."

I crane my neck to see who's talking and nearly lose my balance. Daemon whips out a hand to steady me before I fall backwards into the harbor, and makes no comment about it as he turns both of us toward the voice.

My gaze lands on another boy, leaning against the wall to our right. He appears to be about Daemon's age with curly midnight-black hair, sharp cheekbones despite his youth, and warm golden-brown skin. He's wearing a forest-green cloak with the hood pulled up, despite the warm weather.

"What was that?" Daemon asks cheerfully.

The boy pushes off the wall and turns to face us. "I said I'd take that bet. Fifty gold says the human will win."

Daemon looks the boy over, then glances back at the fighters. He shrugs. "Done."

My mouth falls open in surprise. "Do you have that much?"

Both Daemon and the boy ignore my question, neither of them seeming the slightest bit bothered by the enormous sum of money. I can't even comprehend where an eleven-year-old would get fifty gold until I remember that Daemon's father was a baron. If his father recently died, then my cousin has already inherited more money and land than I've seen in my life. That still doesn't explain where the strange cloaked boy got so much gold.

Daemon waits for the boy to climb up the wall beside us, then reaches out to shake his hand. "I'm Daemon Ashwater, and this is my sister, Odessa."

"I'm Kastian," the other boy introduces himself.

I scoff in disbelief. "Sure you are."

The boy leans around Daemon to look at me, his brow furrowing in confusion. "Excuse me?"

"The crown prince of Hydratta is named Kastian. It's written on the side of that ship over there." I jerk my thumb over my shoulder. "If you're going to lie about your name, at least make it convincing."

The boy tilts his head up, looking past me toward the row of ships. Sure enough, the vessels flying the king's green-and-white flag are all docked alongside the merchant ships, and the ship nearest to us reads: *HMS Kastian Stormbreaker*.

Daemon laughs. "She's got you there, mate."

The boy shoots me a reproachful look, his cheeks flushing amber. Before he can say anything else, the surrounding crowd erupts as the Fae soldier launches himself toward his human opponent. For a moment, it seems as if the boy claiming to be called Kastian is going to lose his money in less than ten seconds. Then, the human steps out of the way far faster than should be possible. The Fae man can't stop his momentum, and with no one in the way, he dives straight into the cobblestone ground. Beside me, Daemon winces.

The Fae man, looking dazed, struggles to his feet. He charges the human again, and once again the man waits until the last second before dodging out of the way. This time, the Fae plows into the crowd, causing an eruption of shouts and swearing.

I grin for the first time in weeks as I look over at Daemon. "I think you're about to lose your bet."

His eyes narrowing, Daemon turns to the boy in the cloak. "How did you know?"

The boy shrugs, a smug smile on his face. "I've seen him fight before."

"But how?" I ask, "He's human. There's no way he should be able to move that fast."

"He *looks* human," the boy corrects.

I glance back at the fight just in time to witness the so-called human spring forward, his muscles tensing as he launches himself at the Fae man. With a feral intensity, he pummels his face with relentless fists, each strike landing with a sickening thud. Blood spurts in vivid arcs, splattering the pavement in crimson droplets. As he draws his fist back, I can almost see a ripple across his otherwise ordinary human face.

"He's a doppler," I say on an exhale, finally understanding. "A shapeshifter."

Daemon cocks his head, looking more curious than annoyed by the deception. "Dopplers don't have any increased strength or speed, though. Just that of the average Fae."

"Yeah, but they have the element of surprise." The other boy grins smugly. "There's an enormous advantage in being underestimated."

A ripple of whispers passes through the crowd. The fighting abruptly ends as people scatter left and right.

"What—" I begin, but break off as the answer to my question becomes clear.

Six armed soldiers dressed in green military jackets are pushing their way through the crowd. They look at every face as if searching for someone.

"Damn," the boy in the green cloak swears and leaps down from the wall. "Got to go."

"Where are you going?" Daemon demands. "You won the bet. I won't have anyone thinking I don't pay my debts."

The boy grins up at us from the ground. "You'll have to owe me one."

Daemon's brow furrows. "But we're from Vernallis. We'll be leaving soon."

The boy shrugs as if to say, "It is what it is," and takes a step backward into the crowd.

"Wait!" I yell before I can stop myself.

The boy pauses, looking over his shoulder at me. I reach into my pocket and grab the brass key, and toss it at the boy. As if on instinct, he raises a hand into the air and catches it. His face twists in bewilderment.

"To cover the debt," I explain. "I don't like leaving things unfinished either."

The boy's black eyes meet mine, but then the crowd shifts, swallowing him up as the soldiers keep shoving people out of their way. I stare at the place where the boy disappeared, a sense of satisfaction washing over me. We might never see that boy again, but my father promised the key leads to treasure...and it's not as if it'll do me much good now that I'm leaving Hydratta.

Daemon turns to me, looking baffled. "What the hell was that about?"

I press my lips together, looking from the king's soldiers to where the boy disappeared. Finally, I glance at the *HMS Kastian Stormbreaker* bobbing in the harbor. "I think that might have been someone who prefers to be underestimated."

ODESSA, PRESENT

"Fifty gold coins."

"Absolutely not!" I scoff. "It's hardly worth five."

"Fifty," the shopkeeper repeats, "or I'm not selling."

I let out a whine of frustration and have to resist the urge to stomp my foot.

I'm standing in front of a lengthy wooden counter in the middle of a cluttered shop. The shop itself is cozy and packed to the brim with an eclectic array of treasures. Shelves upon shelves groan under the weight of timeless antiques, vibrant fabrics, and tarnished jewelry. Sunlight streams through the grimy shop windows, casting a warm glow that dances through the motes of dust suspended in the air.

In contrast with the warm atmosphere, the shopkeeper seems carved from ice.

The austere Fae male stands on the opposite side of the counter, glowering at me. Just above his head, a miniature ship inside a green glass bottle sits upon a shelf, tantalizingly out of reach. It's barely worth five gold on its best day, but to me it's nearly priceless.

"Ten gold," I offer almost desperately. "That's twice what anyone else will pay."

The shopkeeper looks down his long nose at me, his expression apathetic. "Don't act as if you don't have hundreds of gold spilling from beneath every cushion in that mansion you live in. It's fifty, or no deal."

"Oh, I see what's going on," I bite back a humorless laugh. "You know the ship isn't worth anything close to fifty gold, but you think you know who I am and you're trying to extort me."

"Sorry." He gives me an unapologetic smirk. "It's not every day I have the king's sister in my shop. May as well try to recoup some of the useless taxes I've been paying all these years."

He turns away, dismissing me, and I sigh, leaning against the counter in defeat. Part of me wants to argue with him—to point out that he's mistaken. The taxes he's referring to were imposed by the previous King of Vernallis and have nothing to do with my brother—but I know better than to waste my breath.

It's been just over a year since Daemon and his soon-to-be-wife, Alix, ended the curse on Vernallis and ascended to the throne. Since then, they've become popular rulers. They haven't charged the citizens a single cent. More importantly, they've been working non-stop for months to help the kingdom recover from the century-long curse inflicted by the last king.

Unfortunately, you can't ever please everyone. Some Fae—especially the older ones—are still wary of the new court. This shopkeeper is obviously one of those who dislike royalty on principle. I should probably take that as a sign to give up on the model ship and leave, but I can't.

"What's so important about a ship in a bottle anyway?" the shopkeeper asks, still with his back to me.

"I like to collect things from the human realm," I answer shortly.

There's far more to it than that, but I don't need to tell the shopkeeper that the ship looks just like the one I grew up on, or that I've always had a weakness for beautiful things and I like the way the green glass glitters in the afternoon sunlight streaming through the shop window.

I reach into my pocket and extract a collection of treasures. There's a thimble, three shiny stones, a piece of blue glass that caught my eye shimmering on the road just outside this shop, and five...ten...fifteen gold coins. I pick out the coins one by one, then return the rest of the items to my pocket. "Fine, fifteen gold. That's literally all I have at the moment, and three times what it's worth."

The shopkeeper sneers. "Are you still here? Run along and come back with more money or don't come back at all."

Alright, that's it.

My eyes narrow, and my famously quick temper sparks. Perhaps I should feel guilty about what I'm about to do, but I don't. Here on land, and with no ill intentions, it's a harmless trick. Anyway, the shopkeeper tried to scam me first, and all is fair in love and shopping.

I plaster on a smile, smooth out my dress, and lean over the counter, letting my long hair drape over my shoulder. "Listen," I begin, infusing my tone with a persuasive lilt.

As expected, at the change in my tone, the shopkeeper immediately swivels around to stare at me. His stern expression falters, and his gaze goes unfocused, flicking lazily back and forth between my eyes and my chest as if he can't help but look. A pink flush tinges his cheekbones and the tips of his pointed ears.

I might not have magic like the full-blooded Fae, but my mother was a siren. Thanks to her, I've rarely encountered a man whom I couldn't persuade to see things my way.

"Give me the ship," I request, still infusing my voice with the siren song. "You want to give it to me. Nothing would make you happier than to have my gratitude."

"As you wish," the shopkeeper says dazedly.

I smile, but before I can claim my victory, a bell tinkles behind us as the door opens. I glance over my shoulder and my face falls. An all too familiar figure has entered, his broad shoulders filling the entire doorway. Our gazes collide, and I stiffen as if an icy wind has entered the shop with him. "What are you doing here?"

Kastian steps further into the shop, letting the door swing closed behind him with a thud that rattles through my bones. "I was looking for you. You're needed back at the house."

My eyes narrow. "And they sent *you* to find me? Really?"

"Something like that."

For a moment, all thoughts of the ship in the bottle and the shopkeeper flee my mind, replaced by mingled annoyance and worry. Everyone knows Kastian and I don't get along, and neither Alix nor Daemon would ever send him after me unless it was an emergency. "Is something wrong?" I demand. "Is Jett back, or—"

Kastian puts a hand up to halt my questions. His gaze has fallen on the silent shopkeeper, and he looks startled, as if he only just noticed there's someone else in the room. "Morning. You alright, mate?"

The shopkeeper blinks a few times, his eyes sliding in and out of focus, seemingly unable to form words. I bite back a groan. *Dammit, I hate weak-willed men.*

Actually, I hate pretty much all men, but the weak ones are by far the worst.

Kastian's dark eyes narrow at me. "What did you do to him?"

"Nothing! Why do they need me at the house?"

He completely ignores my question, all of his attention now focused on the swaying shopkeeper. "That doesn't look like 'nothing.' It looks like you cooked him."

Heat rises to my cheeks and I scoff. "I barely did anything. How was I supposed to know he had such a weak mind?"

Kastian's black eyes flash, and he shakes his head, his expression somewhere between exhaustion and bemusement. "Just tell me if it's going to wear off or if we have to do damage control."

My eyes narrow. I don't want anyone doing damage control

for me, especially him. I bite the inside of my cheek and try to remain calm. "It'll wear off a few minutes after I leave."

"Good." Kastian wraps his fingers around my upper arm and begins tugging me toward the door. "Let's go."

I yelp in protest. "No, wait! Just let me get my ship!"

He ignores me, his fingers tightening. I struggle, but the effort is pointless.

His majesty is the only man in Ellender who's ever been able to ignore me.

T he day that Daemon returned from prison with a pack of criminals and a kidnapped human woman in tow was also the first time I'd seen Kastian in over a century.

Until that day, my life had been in ruin. The curse on the kingdom of Vernallis was raging, and the court was in disarray. Daemon had been gone for ninety long years and his absence, combined with my secret melancholy, had driven a wedge between myself and Aunt Beatrix. I was working in the palace while she remained living at the Ashwater Estate. Our entire small family was spread thin across the continent, and with the curse looming, I never expected to see any of them alive again.

Then, everything changed when Daemon received a pardon from the king and reappeared in Vernallis—and he wasn't alone.

Besides Alix—the human woman he'd accidentally kidnapped who would later become his soul-bonded mate—he'd brought three friends he'd met in Dyaspora Prison: Jett, an entertaining trickster from the desert kingdom of Solistine; Fox, a strong and silent soldier from the snowy kingdom of Thermia; And Kastian, the source of all my problems for the last one hundred years.

It had been decades since I'd last seen Kastian and I'd half-convinced myself he was dead. Except, there he was, standing beside my estranged brother and wearing a Vernalli military uniform, looking at me as if we'd never met before. I was so shocked I hardly recognized him.

On that day, he looked exhausted. His curly black hair was chin-length and his usually dark complexion was ashen, like he'd seen little of the sun in decades. Now, a year later, his hair is cut short, only slightly longer than the hint of a beard on his square jaw. His bronze tan has returned, and he's dressed casually with his black shirt open at the neck to reveal the edge of a large tattoo that I know extends down his right forearm. I have to admit he looks good, but that's the only good thing I'll acknowledge about him.

Every moment since Kastian Stormbreaker reappeared in my life has been slow torture, and my only comfort is knowing that at every opportunity I torment him right back.

"Let go of me!" I screech, as Kastian drags me out of the shop and onto the street.

"Fine," he snaps, as the door to the shop swings shut behind us.

He lets go too quickly and the force of my effort to break free causes me to stagger backward a few steps. Mercifully, I don't fall. I don't think I could stomach the humiliation.

I straighten, smoothing my dress, and glare up at him. "You're such an arrogant prick."

He crosses his arms over his chest. "And you're a prissy little princess, but I'm polite enough not to scream about it in public."

I toss my hair over my shoulder with a sniff. He's exaggerating; this is hardly public.

The village of Storia is alive with activity. Sunlight bathes the thatched roofs and timber-framed homes in a warm, golden hue. Villagers fill the cobblestone streets, but not a single one of them pays us any mind.

"Are you going to tell me what you're doing here?" I demand. "I assume if you had to be the one to come get me then someone is dead."

His dark eyes widen. "No, nothing like that. It's not urgent, Alix just needs to talk to you."

"And she sent *you* to find me? I don't believe that for a second."

"Believe whatever you want, Princess."

My scowl intensifies. "Fine. I'll be home shortly. I just need to wrap things up here."

"Wait!" He steps in front of the door, blocking my way. "You can't seriously be thinking of going back inside."

"Don't tell me what to do, *Your Majesty*."

His eyebrows twitch, betraying a hint of annoyance. "Don't call me that."

"You're lucky I didn't shout it for the entire street to hear. Now, *move*."

Kastian crosses his muscled arms, refusing to move an inch. "What happened in the shop to make you bewitch the owner?"

"He refused to sell me what I wanted," I say irritably, attempting to sidestep him.

"What was it?"

"Nothing you'd care about. Now move before the compulsion wears off and I never get what I came for."

Kastian ignores my agitation and my attempts to push past him, a smile spreading across his ridiculously handsome face. "I didn't know you had magic," he says, his tone shifting from irritation to curiosity in the blink of an eye. "What else can you do?"

"None of your business," I snap, even as my chest gives a painful squeeze. It feels something like anguish, and I wish I could pretend I didn't know why.

There was a time when Kastian knew all about my magic because I told him.

There was a time when I would have told him anything.

That dark thought morphs my frustration into rage. I'm so over this little game of keep-away. I'm so over him. "Fine," I snap, turning on my heel and stomping away down the cobblestone street. "Fine! Block the door all night for all I care, I'll just come back tomorrow."

I'm displeased but not surprised to hear Kastian's footsteps following me down the road. I shoot him a glare over my shoulder, which he apparently interprets as a cue to quicken his pace and walk beside me. My frown deepens even further.

"I know you can walk faster than this," I grumble after a long seething silence. "Don't walk slowly on my account."

"I can't let you walk back alone."

"You can. In fact, please do."

He grins, as if trying to counteract my scowl. "But how would I explain it to everyone if you got lost? You have to admit it's possible, you get distracted walking from the kitchen to the garden."

"Don't act as if you have the right to pretend you know anything about me."

His eyebrows pull lower, displaying a hint of frustration, but when he replies his tone is almost impossibly calm. "Fine, not lost, then. You could still be kidnapped."

I scoff. "Why the hell would anyone want to kidnap me?"

"Besides the obvious?"

"I don't know what you're talking about."

I feel his eyes on me. "Yes you do. Besides the fact that you're the most beautiful woman in Vernallis, you're the king's sister and the queen's best friend. If I was going to hold anyone for ransom, I know who I'd choose."

My cheeks heat, but I refuse to give him the satisfaction of backing down. "That's funny, because if I was going to hold anyone for ransom I'd say you're a far better choice, *Your Majesty*."

He stiffens. "You really need to stop calling me that."

"Why? Afraid someone will finally realize who you are?"

He shakes his head. "Because it's not true anymore."

Startled, I meet his eyes. Over the past year, ever since Kastian fled Dyaspora with Daemon, Jett, and Fox, he never once acknowledged that there's any truth behind my taunting, or admitted that I'm aware of his identity before he was imprisoned.

I want to needle him about it, but that would require more talking...and honestly, even if he were to talk about "*before*," I don't want to hear whatever warped version of history he believes is true.

"I won't get lost or kidnapped," I snap. "It's a five-minute walk back to the manor."

"Ten minutes with how slowly you walk."

Out of spite, I slow my pace even more. His legs are so much longer than mine he's forced to take comically tiny steps just to keep in pace with me.

I almost smile.

"I see you want to prolong our time together," he says over the sound of his shuffling feet.

The smile slides off my face.

I like to play this game with myself where I have to go as long as possible without thinking about *His Majesty*. It works surprisingly well. Except that I've long suspected that Kastian is playing a similar game. He likes to get under my skin, and every time I react it's like he's tallying up the points I've lost and hoarding them for himself.

I'm not sure how, but I think at some point we began playing this game of hatred together.

And he's winning.

ODESSA, PRESENT

I'm still furious by the time Kastian and I arrive at the end of the lengthy road connecting Ashwater Manor to the village of Storia.

The Ashwater estate is a large and impressive castle-like mansion, dropped on top of a sloping hill. On our right, at the base of the long driveway, stands the new soldiers' barracks, and beyond that, the vast field where the guards are engaged in sword training. Behind the house, a sprawling rose garden hides the portal to the human realm.

Evidently deciding that he's done enough to torture me for one afternoon, Kastian falls out of step with me and resumes his normally long strides. "Thanks for the lovely walk, Dessa," he calls over his shoulder, his voice carrying as he heads toward the barracks. "We should do it again sometime."

I can practically feel steam coming from my ears. *Arrogant asshole!*

What was the point of that? If there's nothing urgent going

on at the manor then why would Kastian waste his afternoon looking for me?

I continue to curse under my breath as I walk the last few yards up the driveway. I need to go find Alix. If my best friend really sent that self-satisfied prick to ruin my shopping trip I'm going to give her a piece of my mind. She might be the queen, but that won't save her from my wrath.

I reach the heavy wooden front door of the manor and push it open to reveal a grand entrance hall. Directly across from the door, a sweeping wooden staircase descends onto the mosaic tiled floor, and at the top of the landing, an enormous arched window casts sunlight down in golden beams. To the right of the stairs is the formal dining room. On the left, a closed door leads to the former sitting room which has recently been re-appropriated into a sort of makeshift throne room.

The Ashwater Manor has always been a magnificent home, but it was never meant to serve as the official palace of Vernallis. Having spent most of my adult years working in the palace, I'm still amazed by how Daemon and Alix's casual court contrasts with King Thorne's. It feels less like a royal court and more like a chaotic family business.

As if summoned by my thoughts, my Aunt Beatrix's loud voice echoes out of the kitchen. "I'm simply suggesting that you pick a date!"

Oh no. I stride across the entrance hall and through the dining room, already sure I know what this argument is about.

"We have other more pressing things to deal with first," Daemon's low voice replies, the annoyance so obvious in his tone that I can picture his scowl.

"What could be more important?"

"I didn't say more important, I said more pressing. Please, Mother, not now. Alix and I have to go—"

"Fine, fine! Just tell me a season, then?" Aunt Beatrix replies. "Alix, please! Just consider the time it will take to plan!"

Before anyone else can speak, I push open the door to the large kitchen and all eyes swivel in my direction.

Aunt Beatrix is standing by the kitchen window, glowering, her dark hair pulled back in a tight bun and her flour-coated hands on her hips. She's wearing a frilly purple apron and in front of her on the counter is an unfinished pie crust. It looks as if she's ambushed Daemon and Alix on their way out the door, because Alix is standing in the open door to the back garden, one foot inside and one out, and Daemon is right behind her, carrying an enormous stack of papers and craning his head over his shoulder to talk to his mother.

"What's going on here?" I ask, forgetting my anger for a moment as my gaze darts around the busy room.

Alix's face splits into a grin and she leans around Daemon to talk to me. "Oh good, you're back!" she says brightly. "I was just going to ask a servant to look for you."

"Come on, Peaches. We have to get to the meeting," Daemon grumbles, cutting me off as he ushers Alix further outside. He glances back over his shoulder at me. "Come to the barracks with us, Dessa. We'll explain on the way."

"Wait!" Aunt Beatrix squeaks. "I'm not finished."

"We'll discuss this later, Mother," Daemon growls, jerking his head for me to follow them.

I sigh, and shoot my aunt an apologetic glance before trailing across the kitchen after Daemon and Alix.

"What was that about?" I ask, momentarily distracted as the door swings shut behind us.

"We got a shitload of letters from the other courts," Alix answers, gesturing at the pile of papers in Daemon's arms.

I crack a smile. "Is 'a shitload' a technical term?"

"It is now," she huffs. "I have such bad mail anxiety this is like torture, but until we can appoint an emissary we have to go over every letter ourselves."

I nod. By "we" she means the semi-official council of Vernallis. Herself and Daemon, me, Kastian, Fox, Jett and sometimes

Aurelia, when she feels like turning up to the meetings. We meet at least three times a week, but today isn't a usual meeting day, and Jett isn't even in the country.

"I don't mind an extra meeting, but that's not what I meant," I say as we exit the garden and trek back across the courtyard I just crossed to reach the house. "What's wrong with Aunt Beatrix?"

"She wants us to pick a wedding date," Alix answers with a sigh.

I glance between the two of them. "Well...you have to admit, it wouldn't kill you to choose a date."

Daemon glowers. "We're bonded. That's better than getting married. We don't need to have a fucking wedding to prove that."

I narrow my eyes. "I mean, you do if you want to secure Alix's position as queen. She can't officially hold the title until you're married, even if she's doing the job already."

Alix rolls her eyes. "He knows that. Don't listen to him, we're definitely getting married. I just don't want my wedding ruined by some invasion or uprising or some shit like that."

My brow furrows. "Is that likely?"

She looks pained. "No idea. I never realized how hard it is to run a country—I mean, obviously I knew it was, but *woof.* There's so many tiny disasters all the time, and with the mess that Thorne left us...I just want everything to be more stable first so we can enjoy ourselves and not spend the entire wedding worrying that the guests from Thermia will murder the ones from Solistine."

"Is that what this meeting is about?" I ask. "Thermia and Solistine?"

"No. The King of Hydratta sent another damn letter this morning," Daemon replies grimly. "And at least half this stack is from him."

I groan. There are four Fae kingdoms on the continent of Ellender, and although there hasn't been any major inter-court conflict in centuries, all four courts have their own internal problems.

Thermia, the snow-covered kingdom to the north, is notoriously isolated from the rest of the continent. Barely anyone goes in or out of the country, so it's hard to know how seriously we should take the rumors that no one has seen their queen in years.

The desert kingdom of Solistine is the closest thing Vernallis has to an ally at the moment, but all the information we've been able to gather about them says that their king already has one foot in the grave. He has seven children, but refuses to name any of them as his heir. If the king dies without a clear successor, there's likely to be a civil war.

Since becoming king and queen, Alix and Daemon have had friendly diplomatic chats with the elderly King of Solistine, and they've met twice with a cagey but unthreatening emissary from Thermia. They've also received numerous letters from the island kingdom of Hydratta, but anything to do with that kingdom is complicated at best.

"Is Hydratta angry that you haven't responded to any of their letters?" I ask.

"'*Angry*' isn't quite the right word," Alix laments. "More like 'suspicious,' I think?"

"The standard thing to do if we don't want to meet with the Hydrattan king would be to send an emissary to their court," Daemon says. "But there's no one to send."

"Jett?" I suggest half-heartedly.

Daemon shakes his head. "No. The situation in Hydratta is precarious and Jett's not a diplomat. He's far too busy right now, anyway."

I bite my tongue—literally—to keep from commenting.

Over the last year, everyone has easily fallen into their new roles. Daemon and Alix might act as if they're overwhelmed, but in reality they're handling governing shockingly well.

Kastian naturally fell into the role of advisor and second-in-command, handling anything Daemon is too busy—or too temperamental—to handle himself.

Fox, who was a career-soldier back in his home country of

Thermia, has been turning the hundreds of guards we inherited from King Thorne into a brutal and efficient army.

Jett, who was a thief in his former life, has turned out to be an extremely effective spy. Between his charming personality and surprising affinity for deception, it's due to him that we've gathered so much information on the other three courts of Ellender.

Meanwhile, King Thorne's illegitimate daughter, Aurelia, is a talented enchantress. She spends nearly every hour of the day locked in her tower working on various spells and potions, but when she does emerge, it's always with something useful—a healing tonic for the army or a spell for accelerated crop growth.

It's easy to notice that I'm the only one who hasn't found a natural role within the court. I've been tempted to suggest that I would make a good emissary. I enjoy talking to people, but more importantly I used to be a lady-in-waiting in Thorne's court and therefore I'm all too familiar with royal politics. My affinity for persuasion could also be useful in a diplomatic role, but since neither Daemon nor Alix has brought up the idea on their own, I have to assume they don't think it's a good suggestion.

"Is this meeting why you sent Kastian to find me?" I ask, circling back to the reason I sought them out.

Alix looks sideways, her brows raising. "What do you mean?"

"Didn't you ask him to find me in the village?"

She shakes her head. "No...I told you, I was going to send a servant to find you."

I start to respond, but a sudden, sharp shout pierces the air above us, drawing our attention upward.

A huge dark shape in the sky hurdles toward us, growing larger by the second. I gasp, when he draws close enough that I can make out a familiar dark-haired man, his wings a breathtaking span of deep indigo, cutting through the air like a dart.

Jett lands ungracefully in the center of the courtyard, the force and speed of his landing kicking up a cloud of dust. He skids across the ground, his feet carving shallow grooves in the earth, while his massive wings unfurl dramatically behind him.

My eyes go wide. Except for once when we were in mortal danger, I've never seen Jett's wings. It's not normal to see any Fae's wings unless you're threatened or mated.

"The fuck is going on?" Daemon curses angrily. He drops his stack of papers on the ground and takes off running toward the center of the courtyard.

Loose papers fly around us as Alix and I chase after him, but he's much quicker, and by the time we catch up Jett is already mid-explanation.

"—came from the harbor. A ship just arrived from Hydratta," Jett coughs, out of breath.

"So what?" Daemon replies. "Merchant vessels travel to Hydratta all the time."

"Yeah, but—" Jett breaks off, clears his throat and spits into the dust near his feet.

Daemon claps him hard on the back. "Take a breath, mate."

Jett wipes sweat from his face before continuing. "This wasn't just any ship. It was flying the flags of the king."

Before Daemon can react, Kastian's voice erupts across the yard like a thunderclap. "Which king?"

Summoned by the commotion, Kastian is striding toward us from the opposite side of the grounds, Fox right behind him. The amusement that was in Kastian's face earlier is gone, and if I didn't know him I'd take his expression as a sign to find cover.

Jett grimaces at Daemon, and waits for Kastian to reach us before answering. "The current one." His face screws up as if bracing for impact. "But that's not all. I talked to some of the crew and listened in on a few conversations…"

"And?" Daemon prompts.

Jett glances behind Daemon at Kastian and then, oddly enough, at *me*. "Maybe we should go into the barracks and sit down to discuss this."

My eyebrows raise. Jett isn't usually the type to notice or care about silly things like tact or decorum.

Unfortunately, Daemon isn't either. "Spit it out," he demands.

Jett sucks in a breath. "The King of Hydratta sent an emissary to speak with you. The word among the crew is that he's decided to take a wife."

"Fuck," Daemon curses under his breath. "I suppose I should have seen that coming."

Beside me, Alix reaches out and grips my fingers. "You don't have to do anything," she mutters under her breath.

I startle, tearing my eyes away from Jett to meet her gaze. "What do you mean?"

"You don't have to do anything," she repeats, her pale-blue eyes widening earnestly. "Fuck the king of Hydratta and his emissary. We'll go to war with them if that's what it takes."

"Hold on," Fox says roughly, his expression tight as it is every time he's forced to speak. "We're not ready for a war."

Alix glares daggers at him. "*We'll go to war if that's what it takes*," she repeats slowly, her voice turning low and dangerous. "Right, Daemon?"

"Right, Peaches," Daemon echoes without hesitation. "But let's hope it doesn't come to that."

"Wait!" I blurt out, pulling my fingers from Alix's grasp. "I don't understand what you're talking about. What don't I have to do? What war?"

A heavy silence falls over the group. I blink at Alix, and only when I take in her tight, serious expression does realization dawn.

The king of Hydratta has been writing letters to Daemon and Alix for months because he wants an alliance and now his representative is here to announce the king intends to take a wife.

Royal marriages are only ever about land or alliances, and somehow, against all odds, I've found myself in the center of a royal household where the only eligible marriage candidates are Aurelia, who most people don't know exists, and *me*.

It feels as if a blanket of shock has fallen over me. My heart pounds relentlessly against my chest, and I can't quiet my racing thoughts long enough to think of anything to say.

Without really meaning to, I seek Kastian's gaze, searching for...*something*. I don't know what.

And I'll never find out because Kastian doesn't even glance in my direction; all I can see is his rigid shoulders and the back of his head as, without a word, he turns on his heel and strides away toward the barracks.

ODESSA, PRESENT

Daemon orders everyone to reconvene in the barracks in half an hour, but I can't think of a single thing to do with myself in the meantime. How am I supposed to wait an entire thirty minutes to hear about this hypothetical alliance I'm being thrust into?

With a frustrated huff, I march straight to the barracks intending to wait in the meeting room. Clearly thinking the same thing, Jett follows. He speeds up to walk beside me. "Sorry to fuck up your afternoon."

I look sideways at him. His wings have disappeared again, but his coal-black hair is still windswept and his equally black eyes are bright with adrenaline. Between his dark hair and eyes and the head-to-toe black clothing he's wearing, he's really leaning into his namesake.

I huff out a breath. "Don't worry about it, it's not your fault. Are you alright?"

"Of course, why?" he asks.

"Because of the wings. Were you threatened?"

"It was nothing, I was fine." Jett grins, but it doesn't quite reach his eyes as we reach the entrance to the barracks.

The building is a recent addition to the estate, built to house the hundreds of soldiers who take it in turns to guard the king and queen. It's a long rectangular structure, mostly filled with dormitory-style bedrooms. There's a large dining room and several areas to store weapons, as well as a few empty rooms on the first level that still have no purpose. It's one of those rooms that has become our meeting place. A long dining table and eight mismatched chairs are the only furniture.

I file into the room behind Jett, and find that Fox has beaten us there and is already sitting at the table. He raises his blonde head and nods at us in silent greeting.

Without waving back, Jett grimaces and sinks into the empty chair. After a moment he slumps forward and puts his head down on the table. I glance questioningly at Fox, who unsurprisingly says nothing.

"Are you sure you're alright?" I ask, walking around the table to my usual seat. "I know you're not this exhausted from flying back from the harbor—even if you did go faster than usual. What's wrong with you?"

Jett lifts his head slightly to meet my eyes over his folded arms. "Do you have any idea how much sailors drink?"

I bark out a startled laugh, my memory immediately casting back to hearing the sounds of merriment coming from the deck of my father's ship while I lay awake in bed wishing I was old enough to be included. "As it happens, I do."

"Well, let's just say I wouldn't have been able to get half the information I gathered without hanging around the right taverns."

"Did it ever occur to you to pretend to drink?"

Jett's brow wrinkles. "No."

I hide a smile. "Well, maybe next time it will."

The door swings open and Alix walks in, clearly flustered. It looks as if she went back to the house to change her clothes because she's now dressed in a mishmash of Fae and human clothing, with a corseted top that looks to be from Ellender and a pair of stretchy leggings from the human realm. Her long brown hair is pulled back in a messy ponytail and her smudged mascara has turned into a smokey ring around her eyes that looks almost intentional.

"I see you all wanted to get started right away too." She looks around, seeming confused for the first time. "Where's Kas?"

I don't answer.

I also noticed that Kastian was missing the moment we entered the room. He's usually the first one to these meetings—always the overly responsible golden boy—now, I can't help but wonder what he's doing.

The door opens again and I look up, expecting to see *His Majesty*. A biting comment is on the tip of my tongue, but it's not Kastian. It's Aurelia.

Like Alix, she's also dressed in a mix of human and Fae clothing, with a purple gown and a gray hooded sweatshirt on top. Her dark hair is tied back in a slightly messy braid, showing off the row of gold and silver hoops that decorate her pointed ears. "Morning," she yawns, blinking blurry eyes at us.

Alix reaches down the front of her corset and pulls out the large gold watch that Daemon gave her when she kept complaining that the time change between the human realm and Ellender was giving her something called "Jett's lag." She smiles at Aurelia. "It's nearly 2:00 p.m."

"Oh, is it?" Aurelia frowns. "I wouldn't know. I've been working all night...and the morning too, I suppose."

"Are you joining us for the meeting?" Alix asks.

Aurelia shrugs and sits down across from me, next to Fox. "I thought I might."

"What have you been working on?" I ask.

"Weather," she says cryptically, a spark of wicked excitement in her eyes.

Sometimes I forget that Aurelia and I are similar in age, and that she's decades older than Alix. There's something about her petite frame and excitable personality that gives the impression that she's in her early twenties. Now, sitting next to tall and muscular Fox, she looks especially tiny.

Jett raises his head off the table. "What kind of weather? Controlling it, or…"

"That's a dangerous idea," Fox says flatly.

As always happens when Fox speaks, all eyes turn to him. He talks so little that everything he says holds so much more weight than it would otherwise.

"Why do you say that?" Aurelia asks.

He just shrugs, looking away from her. I frown. If anyone else reacted that way I'd assume there was something wrong, but with Fox's silent nature it's hard to tell.

Before anyone else can speak, the door opens for a third time and Daemon walks in. He stops in the doorway and looks around, his brow furrowing. "Where's Kas?"

"I said the same thing," Alix replies, gesturing for Daemon to sit down.

Daemon's frown deepens. "I don't want to have this conversation without him."

"We won't," Alix soothes. "You said half an hour, it's only been fifteen minutes."

Daemon grumbles under his breath, but circles the table to sit down in his usual seat on the far end. Now, the only empty seat is Kastian's.

A heavy silence blankets the room, interrupted only by the rhythmic tapping of my foot against the hardwood floor beneath the table. Each tick of Alix's pocket watch sounds deafening. My fingers drum on the edge of the table, each tap echoing my growing frustration. The heat of impatience crawls up my neck.

Finally, unable to bear it any longer, I swivel in my chair to face Daemon, my voice slicing through the quiet like a knife. "Are you really going to make me wait for him? This meeting is supposed to be about me, isn't it?"

Daemon's brows knit together, casting a shadow over his eyes as his lips press into a thin line. He lets out a deep, resigned sigh. "Fine. Hydratta has sent several letters through courtiers and from the king himself. They're interested in meeting you."

"And by 'meeting me' you mean they want to organize an engagement."

"Yes," Daemon says flatly.

I narrow my eyes. "And you didn't think this was worth mentioning to me? How long have you known?"

He flinches. "The first explicit mention of a marriage contract came about two months ago."

"You should have told me!" I snap, my temper rising.

"Well I see that *now*," he admits, and has the decency to look guilty. "I didn't think it mattered because obviously it's not going to fucking happen."

"Here's what I don't understand," Jett chimes in. "This king wants to marry you without ever meeting you?"

"You say that like it's unheard of," Daemon grumbles.

"For me it is," Jett replies, a hint of his usual light heartedness in his tone. "The rest of you might have grown up royal, but I'm just a street rat. I don't know shit about royal marriage customs."

Alix throws him a sympathetic look. "I don't get it either."

"It's not unheard of for a king to send emissaries to screen brides for him," I chime in warily. "And, not that it matters but I have actually met him before. Once."

"Wait, when was this?" Alix asks, glancing between Daemon and I in confusion.

I bite my lip. "Around a century ago?"

"And you were there too?" Alix asks Daemon. "You never mentioned that."

He runs a hand over the back of his head looking flustered. "I didn't know they'd ever met. Maybe I forgot, it was a long time ago, before Magnus Von Bargen was king and...fuck," he breaks off, glancing angrily at the door. "Where the hell is Kastian? I don't want to be the one to explain this."

I frown and sink back into my chair, feeling slightly guilty.

Daemon didn't forget anything. He doesn't remember that I met Magnus because I'm lying. We never met directly, but I can't explain what really happened. This is as much as I can say.

"I think the only important question here is do you want to marry the King of Hydratta?" Aurelia asks, her voice cutting through the uncomfortable silence at the table. I jump, startled as much by her voice as her question. Suddenly all eyes are on me and they're waiting for me to answer.

"No!" I blurt out. "Of course not. I don't know why he would choose me."

The silence presses on, and finally Jett breaks it. He grins at me and gestures at my face. "Come on Dessa, you know why."

My cheeks heat. "That's not it. Anyway, I'm not...*unusually* beautiful." I internally cringe.

Alix snorts. "Oh, please."

"I'm not!"

I absolutely hate this topic. There's no polite way to talk about it without sounding conceited, and I despise talking about it in the first place. Even when I asked Kastian why anyone would bother kidnapping me and he said "Besides the obvious?" I would have been happy for the earth to open and swallow me. At least he's not here now, that would make this all so much worse.

"All sirens look like me on land," I add, trying to take the focus off me.

"Yeah, but you should see them in the water." Jett gives an affected shudder. "It's nightmare fuel. No offense, Dessa."

The corners of my mouth tip up. "None taken."

Jett grins at me before he puts his head back down on his hands. I've always appreciated Jett for somehow understanding that I don't like being stared at, but I would rather die than complain about it and appear to be begging for pity.

"I doubt it's because of your appearance," Fox says, interrupting my thoughts.

"Care to elaborate?" Daemon asks.

Fox looks pained, the same way he always does when he has to explain anything. "She's essentially your sister. It's obviously about an alliance."

"There hasn't been a land war between kingdoms in centuries," Daemon argues. "Why the fuck would Hydratta need an alliance like that?"

"Everyone knows that Thermia is becoming increasingly isolated," I say slowly. "No one really knows what's going on up there and Vernallis is physically between Hydratta and Thermia. Maybe they're thinking long term "

Daemon looks contemplative. "That's possible. Not that it matters. You're not fucking going."

My back stiffens at his statement, not because I disagree but because it's so final. As if it's not my choice to go...not that I would.

"What's so wrong with Hydratta?" Aurelia asks.

Rather than answering, Daemon looks annoyed at the door. "Where the fuck is Kas?"

"Come on Ashwater," Jett says with a roll of his eyes. "You don't need Kastian to be here to explain the problem—not when nearly everyone already knows."

"Fine," Daemon growls. "Kastian is the last remaining member of the former royal family of Hydratta."

A silence follows his statement and I glance around the room judging everyone's expressions. I'm only a little surprised that hardly anyone looks as if this is news. Alix is examining her nails, Jett looks excited, and the only person who looks confused is Aurelia—and perhaps Fox, but it's hard to tell.

I suppose it makes sense. Daemon and I have always known Kastian's secret, and at some point I assume Daemon told Alix. I understand that Jett and Fox were unaware the entire time they were all trapped in Dyaspora together, but since then Jett has become the court spy and if no one told him, he obviously worked it out on his own.

"Well with that out of the way..." Alix shrugs awkwardly.

Daemon puts both his palms on the table and leans forward, his gaze intense. "The current King of Hydratta used to be an advisor to Kastian's father. Decades ago, Magnus Von Bargen staged a successful coup and his soldiers killed Kastian's mother and three sisters. His father, the king, was kept alive and tortured as a message to anyone who might oppose the coup, but he eventually died too."

"How did Kas survive?" Fox asks without inflection.

Daemon shakes his head. "No one knows, but for some reason they spared Kastian and sent him to prison instead. I always assumed it was because he was the youngest."

"Why would that matter?" Alix asks, her brow furrowing.

"Because killing children is extremely taboo," I explain.

Alix holds her hands up, counting on her fingers. "He wasn't a child though...right?"

"Not technically," Daemon replies, "But we live so long that socially you're hardly considered an adult until around thirty. It's definitely possible that's why he was spared."

Everyone around the table nods in benign understanding, except for Alix whose brow furrows. "So murder is all fine and dandy but you draw the line at killing teenagers?" she asks sarcastically.

"Yes," Daemon says flatly, throwing her a sideways glance. "You know justice is handled differently here than in the human realm."

"I know, but it just seems a little trivial. If he was thirty would they have killed him without thinking twice about how honorable it was?"

"It's not about honor," I cut in. "It's more of a superstition. Fae believe killing a child will curse you with decades of misfortune. The belief probably comes from the fact that we don't have many children to begin with. Kastian had sisters, but that's very unusual. Most Fae only have one child."

I glance around the table. No one contradicts me which I

assume means that everyone here is an only child—well, except for Daemon and I, but we're not really siblings.

More importantly, no one seems surprised that I know so much about this. Perhaps they assume that Daemon told me, or perhaps it simply hasn't occurred to anyone. I'd like to keep it that way.

"So this king let him live due to superstition?" Alix clarifies.

"That's not why."

The door creaks open behind me and I stiffen as Kastian's presence fills the room. Everyone looks up at him.

"Then why did he let you live?" Daemon asks.

"Because he's a fucking coward and couldn't look me in the eye while he did it." Kastian closes the door behind him and leans against it, crossing his arms. "My entire family were powerful magic wielders. Magnus was only able to attack them because he used accomplices and ambushed them in their sleep. I happened to wake up as Magnus and his guards were entering my room. They restrained me before I knew what was happening, but Magnus couldn't kill me while I looked him in the eye. He ordered I be banished to Dyaspora instead."

A ringing silence follows his explanation. My breath catches in my throat and I can't keep myself from staring at him. As much as I knew about his life before, I've never actually heard him explain how the court of Hydratta fell. My chest constricts. I can't breathe.

"That's fucked," Jett bursts out, helpfully breaking the tension. "But if that's who we're dealing with then why are we still just sitting here? Let's kill the emissary. Or better yet, maim him and send him back to his king with a warning that we're on our way to take back Hydratta."

"Both have occurred to me," Daemon grumbles darkly. "But emissaries are peaceful messengers, if we kill him it would give Hydratta an excuse to start a war with us and we can't handle that right now unless we absolutely have to. We're still recovering from the curse."

Fox cocks his head to the side. "We're not far off from being able to handle a war...give me six months."

"No," Kastian says flatly. "There doesn't need to be any war and we're not going to take back Hydratta."

"But it's your kingdom, right?" Alix asks.

Kastian shakes his head. "Not anymore. I don't want to go back to Hydratta. Most of the continent has believed me dead for decades, I'd rather keep it that way."

I can see the confusion on everyone's faces—they don't understand why Kastian wouldn't want to be the king even to take revenge. I understand; I understand perfectly, but I can't say anything even if I wanted to.

"We're not talking about overthrowing Magnus right now," Daemon says, sinking back into his chair. "I'd like to avoid a war with Hydratta, not start one...at least not for six more months." He nods to Fox in acknowledgement.

"I didn't hear anything about you while I was hanging around the ships in Hydratta," Jett says to Kastian. "I don't think this is about you, Hydratta probably hasn't even realized you're here."

"Right," Daemon agrees. "As far as Magnus is concerned, he's been ruling unopposed for decades. I don't know why he'd want an alliance with us but it's likely unrelated."

"So, we're back to the marriage issue," Alix sighs, turning to me. "Obviously, he can ask all he wants but you don't have to say yes. Magnus seems to think we're operating like it's the 12th fucking century over here and have the authority to sell you to him for six cows and a duck."

I can't help the corners of my mouth tipping up. Half the time I have no idea what she's talking about, but the sentiment is clear in her tone. "Thanks, I think."

"I think we should wait for the emissary to arrive," Daemon says. "We'll tell him a marriage isn't going to happen and send him home. If Magnus knows what's good for him, he won't press the issue."

"We should probably accept that we'll need to send our own

representatives to Hydratta," Alix says to Daemon. "For diplomatic relations or whatever."

Once again, the urge to say that I could be the ambassador is almost overwhelming. I know I could handle it, even with the added complication of a rejected proposal.

But for some reason, I can't get the words out and before I've worked up the courage to ask, Daemon is standing up and signaling the end of the meeting.

Jett pushes his chair back and stands, intentionally bumping into my shoulder as he does. "Don't look so moody, Dessa."

"I'm not," I say quickly, standing as well.

"Don't worry, if that prick in Hydratta really pushes it I'll marry you instead."

I choke. "Oh really?"

"Sure, why not?" He grins. "Just picture how beautiful our kids would be."

I start to laugh, but it quickly fades away when I turn around and find Kastian glaring at us. His glower pierces through me with a ferocity that far exceeds any anger he showed when discussing the death of his family.

My tumultuous temper rises, and I can't help myself. I flash him a brilliant smile as I flounce out of the room.

KASTIAN, PRESENT

*D*eep breath in, deep breath out.

There is nothing. Fucking. Happening. There's no need to react.

Deep breath in...

Odessa throws me a wicked smirk and brushes past me on the way out of the room. I unintentionally breathe in a lungful of her intoxicating scent.

Fuck.

She smells like the ocean and something sweet and floral, like the tropical flowers that cover Hydratta in summer. It's hypnotic and simultaneously infuriating. I shouldn't be looking at her, shouldn't be interested in her, and yet I can't stop.

I clear my throat and begin again. *Deep breath in...*

Jett leans against the table, smirking at me. "You alright, mate?"

I yank my gaze up to his. We're alone in the room, everyone else having already left to go back to whatever they were doing before a bombshell fell in the middle of our afternoon.

I clench my jaw and do my best not to launch myself across the room at him in a fit of inexplicable rage. "I'm fine," I grunt, then turn on my heel and leave the room before Jett can say anything else. The last fucking thing I want—aside from picking an unjustifiable fight with my friend—is to be reminded that I'm acting irrationally. I'm all too aware.

I march down the long hall and outside into the courtyard, all the while trying to keep my breathing even and my heart rate down.

The breathing is a tactic I learned quickly in Dyaspora, where the only way to survive was to choose your fights wisely and otherwise keep your head down and your mouth shut. In the beginning, it was almost impossible. Every single flat expression and even response was a hard-won battle, but eventually it became second nature not to react. I'd almost forgotten what I was like before self-control became my own personal deity.

Until *her*.

Odessa makes it impossible to remain calm even in the face of the tiniest, most insignificant interactions. She makes me do insane, out-of-character things like spend all afternoon searching the village for her or pick fights with my friends.

Jett flirts with everyone—female, male, old, young, married, single—it doesn't matter. He even comes on to Alix now and then. If Daemon, with his notoriously short temper, can handle his friend being overly friendly to his bonded mate, then there's no excuse for whatever the fuck I'm feeling right now.

Except that he made her laugh, and the best I can ever get out of her is indifference, and at worst, outright hatred.

Deep breath in...

"Kas!"

I turn instinctively at the sound of my name and see that Daemon is striding out of the barracks behind me. He's alone for once. Lately, he's never alone—either Alix is with him, or he has a pack of guards trailing him wherever he goes. We both find the guards annoying, but it's an occupational hazard of being the king. I know that better than anyone, because I spent the first twenty-ish years of my life dodging my own guards.

"I thought you went back to the house," I say as he strides toward me.

"Not yet." Daemon stops in front of me, his expression searching. "You alright, mate?"

"Yeah, of course I'm fine. Why the fuck does everyone keep asking me that?"

"Who else asked?"

I shake my head. "Never mind."

Daemon raises an eyebrow. "Maybe because that was a heavy conversation? Sorry about that. I wanted you to be the one to tell the story."

I blink in confusion. "What?"

He looks equally confused. "About your family."

Realization dawns, and I immediately feel ten times as stupid as before. We're not talking about the same thing at all.

Daemon is asking if I'm upset about discussing my long-dead family while I assumed he was talking about Odessa and this insane proposal.

"I'm fine," I grunt again.

Daemon grumbles in acknowledgement and runs a hand through his coppery-brown hair. Neither of us is exactly chatty about anything, let alone feelings, but I can tell he knows me well enough to know I'm not actually as fine as I'd like him to believe.

"Want to get a drink?" he asks, jerking his head vaguely toward the village.

"It's the middle of the day."

"So what?" he claps me hard on the shoulder. "That just means there won't be as many people in the pub to stare at us."

I shrug and then nod. He has a point. Anyway, a drink—or five—sounds good right now.

We make an unspoken agreement not to invite anyone else to come with us, and set off together down the winding cobblestone road into the picturesque town of Storia. The villagers and merchants milling around the main street all stop whatever they're doing to smile and call greetings at us as we pass. Going anywhere with Daemon in Vernallis means tacking an extra hour onto the journey so he can stop to kiss babies and wink at old women, all the while insisting that he isn't suited to being king.

At the end of the short street, just past the trinket shop from earlier, is a thatched-roof pub. We duck inside, and I'm pleased to find that it's as empty as Daemon promised it would be—only a few older Fae playing cards in the corner, and a group of mouse-like pixies chattering away at the bar.

I make a beeline toward the unoccupied end of the long, weathered counter, and Daemon and I take a seat. The elderly tavern owner bustles over and plops two full tankards in front of us before we've even flagged her down.

"Good afternoon, Your Majesty." She beams at Daemon before turning an equally wide smile on me. "And Lord Kastian. Can I get you anything else?"

Daemon pulls a handful of gold out of his pocket and tries to hand it to the woman. "Nothing else right now, Madam Magdalena, but you can take my gold this time."

"Oh, no, I couldn't do that, Your Majesty," she gushes.

"You'd be doing me a favor, really." He gives her a stern expression. "I won't have anyone saying I don't pay my debts."

"I'd take that seriously," I tell her with a wink. "He once tracked me down in Dyaspora to pay off a decades-old wager."

Her eyes go wide, and finally, she opens her hand and takes the money. "Oh...alright then, but I'm going to bring you some-thing to eat at the very least."

She walks away, and Daemon shakes his head. "I wish the villagers would stop trying to give us things. It should be the other way around."

"You're giving them enough, just be grateful," I reply, taking a sip of my drink. "Or at least, don't stop accepting gifts until after she's brought over the food. We missed lunch."

Daemon nods in agreement before taking a sip of his own drink. "Fuck, I needed this."

I don't bother asking what he means. It's been around-the-clock work for all of us to pull Vernallis out of the free-fall that Daemon's half-brother, Thorne, sent the kingdom into.

"You need to take a break," I comment.

"Maybe," he grunts. "As if this week wasn't busy enough, it never occurred to me that anyone would ask my permission to marry Odessa or that we'd have to have fucking council meetings about it."

Deep breath in, deep breath out...

I refuse to overreact to this. I should be able to talk casually about Odessa without letting her completely invade my thoughts —not least because Daemon is practically her brother and every time I've ever had a hint of an impure thought about her I feel as if my best friend somehow *knows*. It's both horrifying and helpful because it keeps me from letting my fascination grow into an obsession.

"Would you have let her go to Hydratta if she'd agreed?" I ask calmly.

Daemon barks a laugh. "I don't think I'd have much of a choice in the matter. Odessa doesn't need anyone's permission to get married, least of all mine."

"Not if she wanted to marry someone average," I say through gritted teeth, "But this would be an alliance and you actually would have to weigh in on that."

He looks unconcerned. "I hadn't really thought about it. I think if I tried to tell Dessa what she could or couldn't do, she'd do the opposite just to spite me. But it doesn't fucking matter, anyway. Obviously she's not going to go."

"True." I suck down another large sip of my drink.

"I think these royal marriage customs are bullshit, anyway. Do you remember when Thorne went to Hydratta to meet your sister?"

I shake my head, grateful for the change of subject. "Only vaguely."

He looks at me sideways. "Really? I remember it vividly."

I shrug. I remember the event he's talking about in principle. I was perhaps seventeen or eighteen when the then-Prince Thorne began his tour of Ellender searching for a royal bride. He'd set his sights on my oldest sister, Serena, looking for a similar alliance between the kingdoms as Magnus is looking to create using Odessa. Thorne brought a large group of courtiers with him, including Daemon and his mother, but it's been so long that I hardly remember the details. "A lot of the years before Dyaspora are a blur. I remember only flashes from before the coup. I think I must have blocked it out."

Daemon's eyes flash with understanding, and he clears his throat. "Right, of course. Sorry, mate."

I shrug and take a sip of my drink before clearing my throat uncomfortably.

Every part of that meeting seemed designed especially to torment me. First, talking about my family, whose memory I go out of my way not to dwell on. Then, Magnus, the fucking bastard who betrayed all of us and murdered them. And finally, there's Odessa...who I really shouldn't be thinking about at all.

"Magnus makes me fucking nervous," Daemon muses, clearly following his own train of thought. "He's calculating, and it's not as if he hasn't gone out of his way to conquer a kingdom before."

My stomach lurches unpleasantly. "You think that's what he's doing?"

"Do you?" he asks, turning the question back on me. "You actually know him."

I take a long sip of my drink and actually think about it, because I know Daemon wouldn't ask unless he was seriously concerned.

Daemon and I have never spoken at length about my family or my past. Even in Dyaspora we didn't talk much about how or why we'd gotten there. At the time, we both knew with absolute certainty that we'd never be leaving the prison. Who we were before Dyaspora didn't matter anymore.

Even when we escaped a year ago, it still didn't feel as if it mattered much. The Crown Prince of Hydratta isn't who I am anymore, and looking back on my life feels like half-remembering a story I heard once. Like my memories belong to someone else.

Before today, only Daemon and Odessa knew for sure who I used to be.

Daemon knew because we'd met once or twice in my previous life. I don't know how Odessa knows, only that she's from Hydratta and not much younger than me. I always assumed she'd seen me at a parade or something as a child and remembered. She obviously didn't care for royalty because she'd disliked me from the moment we met in Alix's room, and honestly that was part of the reason I never wanted to claim my original identity. If Odessa's reaction was anything to go by, I was far better off starting over.

"No," I say after a few minutes. "I don't think Magnus would start a war with you. From what I remember of him, he was always calculating. A war wouldn't make financial or political sense, so he's unlikely to start anything."

"I hope you're right," Daemon replies. "We're weak right now. Fox is doing a damn good job with the army, but it will take years before I believe we could actually win any battles."

I nod. "You're right."

"I fucking hate this," he growls, taking another sip of his drink. "I never wanted to be responsible for anyone else."

I grin and clink my glass against his. "Likewise."

Daemon frowns. "Is that why you said you don't want to go back to Hydratta?"

"Yes," I reply flatly. "I don't want to be king. I never did."

He laughs harshly. "And you think I do?"

"No, I know you don't, but you're actually good at it. You delegate well, and the people like you."

"The people like Alix," he argues. "They're afraid of me."

I shake my head, hiding a smile. This is an argument we've had countless times.

Daemon is wrong. The citizens aren't afraid of him; they respect him. And whatever he believes, he's a good king. Anyone who was there when Thorne died and he was forced to take up the mantle would say the same thing. "In my experience, bad rulers don't worry that they're bad rulers."

"Then why are you worried?" he grumbles. "You should go take back your own crown. We could control half the continent, and then we wouldn't have to worry about any wars."

His eyes glint with excitement as he contemplates it. I need to head this off now. "No, it wouldn't work. I don't delegate well."

"You could get over that."

"No, I couldn't," I say flatly. "I could never entrust work to anyone else, unless maybe it was you or Fox or Jett."

"Maybe—"

"No, I'm serious. The ability to delegate is an essential quality for a king. I would know; I watched my father run himself into the ground for years trying to do everything himself until he was so exhausted he didn't even notice that his own advisor was plotting against him." My voice has turned bitter by the end of my sentence and I take another long drink, composing myself.

I'm not being self-deprecating the way Daemon is, and I'm not delusional. I know that if things had turned out differently, and I'd become the king after my father died, I would have made it work, but I also know that I'm not suited for the job. It's not just that I won't delegate; I *can't*. My self-control—control in general —is too important to me.

I wouldn't be a leader; I'd be a dictator. A well-intentioned one, but still.

"I don't want to go back to Hydratta alone," I say when I'm sure my voice will come out even. "I'd much rather stay here and be an emissary for Vernallis."

"Unfortunately, that's just about the only job I can't ask you to do," Daemon says. "I need a diplomat so badly I'm tempted to let you do it, anyway. If it were anywhere else, I would, but it would just be stupid to send you to Hydratta.”

“I know.” I knock his nearly empty glass with mine again. “Why haven’t you asked Odessa to be your emissary?”

He sighs. “Because I don’t know if it’s fair of me to ask her to do anything. She’s my family, but she never signed up for any of this—running a country, that is. You and Fox and Jett are different—”

I nod. We’re different because we bonded in prison, and none of the four of us would be here without the others. Daemon knows that even if he told us all to abandon him, we never would. I don’t think Odessa would leave Daemon and Alix either, but I see why he’s worried about demanding too much of her.

Privately, I hope Daemon doesn’t ask Odessa to be an emissary. Not because she wouldn’t be good at it, but because that would mean she’d have to travel to other kingdoms nearly as often as Jett.

Daemon and I fall into companionable silence for a few minutes. Madam Magdalena returns with steaming plates of roast meat and vegetables for both of us and puts them down on the counter.

“Another round?” Daemon asks, looking sideways at me.

I start to answer but never get the words out. Out of the corner of my eye, I spot a familiar tall, thin male. My back goes straight, and I turn slowly to look.

Yes, that’s definitely him. That’s the shopkeeper I saw Odessa bewitch earlier. That was the most amazing and terrifying damn thing I’ve ever seen.

When I first walked in and saw her leaning over the counter, I barely even registered that anyone else was in the room. Immediately, my mind flew to all the things I could do to her over that counter, and I was about to break my vow to myself and say something about it when I realized we weren’t alone.

For a split second I saw red, thinking that she was flirting with this random shopkeeper, but then I got a look at his unfocused eyes. What was it she said? He was weak-willed?

"Did you know that Odessa has magic?" I blurt out.

Daemon startles and gestures to Madam Magdalena to bring us another round before turning to me with a furrowed brow. "No, she doesn't."

I frown. That doesn't make any sense.

All Fae can use magic, but how useful it is comes down to training and luck. While natural talent exists—Aurelia being a good example—access to good tutors is the best predictor of how powerful a child will grow up to be.

Both being born into noble houses, Daemon and I were each trained since early childhood, but we're the outliers.

From what little Fox has said about it, he had some early magic instruction before being sent off to apprentice with the army. Being an orphan, Jett wasn't trained at all, so any powers he has are purely instinctual. Perhaps that's also what happened with Odessa? I don't know much about her life before she went to live with Daemon and Beatrix, and I'm not sure I can get away with asking about it without inviting too many questions.

"Didn't Odessa train with you as children?" I ask, trying to sound casual.

He shakes his head. "She didn't come to live at the estate until she was eight, and you know that's too old to start training."

"But she has magic...right?"

Daemon's mouth twists into an amused smirk. "Why do you want to know?"

"Earlier I saw her do...something...to that man over there."

He glances over his shoulder, and when he turns back his posture has relaxed. "Oh, *that*. She turned him into a puppet, yeah?"

My brow furrows. "So you do know about it."

To my surprise, he laughs. "Yeah, but that's not Fae magic. It's not really magic at all. It's the siren song."

"What?"

"You know, the siren song. You must have heard it in Dyaspora. It's how they would get men to walk out of their beds and into the freezing fucking ocean."

I frown, trying to think back to all those cold, miserable years in Dyaspora. I remember the wailing coming from the ocean late at night, and I knew there were men who walked into the water and never came back, but honestly, I wasn't all that surprised. It never occurred to me that they were compelled by anything other than their own misery.

"I suppose I never really noticed," I say finally.

"Really?" He furrows his brow. "I assumed it just didn't work on you. It doesn't work on me either."

"Why not?"

Daemon narrows his eyes, still looking amused. "Why are you suddenly so interested in this?"

"I was just surprised. I've never seen her do anything like that before."

"She's never liked using it. There must have been something she really wanted from that shopkeeper."

I stiffen. Well, now I won't be able to stop thinking about it until I know what she wanted.

I get to my feet before I know what I'm doing. "Can you wait a second? I'm just going to go..."

I trail off, not waiting for Daemon to answer as I stride across the pub toward the shopkeeper. He sees me coming, but there's no spark of recognition in his face. "Can I help you?"

"You're the shopkeeper from next door."

"And what of it?" he asks snidely.

I clench my jaw. I guess I should just be grateful his brain isn't coming out of his ears, but I still have to restrain myself from reaching out and teaching him some manners. "There was a woman in your shop earlier. Red hair...unusually beautiful?"

His eyes spark in recognition, and his lip curls. "Yes, the king's sister." He glances behind me, and his eyes lock on Daemon before he looks back at me. "You're one of them too?"

I don't know exactly what he means, but it doesn't matter. "Yes," I say roughly. "What did you talk to the woman about?"

"Why?" he drawls.

My jaw clenches even tighter. "Watch your tone."

He sneers. "No, I don't think—"

Before I know what I'm doing, I slam a palm down hard on the bar beside him. The man jumps, and I lean so close I can smell his breath and see his eyes dilate in fear. "Listen, I don't want trouble. Or, more like you don't want trouble with me. Understand?"

He nods rapidly. "Understood."

"Just tell me what you talked to the king's sister about. What did she want?"

"A ship in a bottle," he says quickly.

My eyes narrow. "Was there anything special about it?"

He shakes his head. "No, it was practically worthless."

What the fuck? Why would Odessa want that enough to use her siren powers on this man? There must be something special about the ship that the shopkeeper didn't notice.

I reach into my pocket and extract a handful of gold and count out five coins, passing them to the man across the counter. "I could just demand that you give me the ship, but this is for your delivery fee."

"I don't deliver," he says in a quaking voice.

"You do now. Go back to your shop, get the ship, and bring it to me. It shouldn't take you more than ten minutes. If you're late, I'll come over there myself...and you don't want that."

He scowls, but doesn't seem willing to gamble on whether I would actually hurt him. He just nods and walks out of the pub, my gold clutched in his shaking hand.

"Do I want to know what that was about?" Daemon asks when I return to the bar.

I shake my head. "I don't think I could explain it to you even if you did."

He gives me a shrewd look, then goes back to eating his lunch. I lift my fork, but I'm thinking so hard that I can't taste the food.

What was that about?

Much like everything to do with Odessa, I have no idea.

I clutch Odessa's ship, carefully wrapped in brown paper, as Daemon and I make our way back to the manor.

The sky has turned dark, and the air is thick with the sounds of chirping crickets and humming beetles from the nearby meadow. As we reach the courtyard, a distant splashing drifts toward me from the lake. I pause in my tracks as an uncomfortable throbbing, like a phantom heartbeat, begins pounding in my chest.

"You coming?" Daemon asks, jerking his head toward the house.

I shake my head, casting around wildly for a good excuse. "I need to talk to Fox about something."

Daemon lifts an eyebrow in disbelief, and I realize too late that I should have said Jett. No one ever *talks* to Fox about anything. *Shit.*

Daemon shifts his gaze from the package in my hand to the field behind me, beyond which is the lake. His forehead wrinkles, and I know he can hear the splashing too.

"You know what? I don't want to know," he grumbles. "See you later, mate."

I shake my head, watching Daemon's retreating back for a second before I turn and stride across the meadow toward the water, already knowing it's a bad idea. If I were smart, I'd turn around and go back to the house, but lately I've turned into a fucking idiot.

It's an undeniable fact that Odessa does not like me.

It's also an undeniable fact that I'm obsessed with her. I can't stop thinking about her—can't just leave her the hell alone.

It sounds pathetic even in my head, and completely out of control in a way that makes me want to strangle something. I can't rationalize why I've developed this fixation on the one woman in the kingdom who seems to truly hate me, or why I keep inserting myself into her path when she obviously doesn't want me there.

Especially when I shouldn't want her either; when it should be impossible.

I'm still yards away when I see Odessa's silhouette in the center of the lake, lit up by a shaft of moonlight.

She's floating on her back, eyes closed, almost like she's sleeping. Even at a distance, I can tell she looks like her normal self—legs and all.

She must hear my footsteps because as I grow closer she lifts her head up and the serene picture shatters. Quick as a blink, Dessa flips over and sinks into the water until only her eyes are visible. After a moment, her eyes flash with recognition, and she rises just enough to speak. "I should have expected it would be you."

"Why, were you thinking about me?" I ask before I can stop myself.

She scowls. "I've just grown to expect that you'll try to ruin everything I enjoy."

I cock my head. Do I do that? I don't think so.

Admittedly, I enjoy teasing her, and I might have used my magic to splash her a few times. I can't seem to stop myself from trying to get a reaction out of her—even her contempt is preferable to indifference—but I haven't ruined anything except my pride.

"Your definition of 'ruining' could use some work."

"Oh really? Alix never asked you to find me earlier," she accuses.

Fuck.

I keep my face expressionless. "Why do you say that?"

"Because I asked her, you ass. Why would you ruin my afternoon?"

That is a good fucking question, and one I have no answer for. I can't tell her I just wanted to know where she was because then she'll ask why, and I truly don't know how to explain it.

Dessa swims toward me, stopping where the water is still deep enough that I can see her arms moving just beneath the surface as she treads water. "What are you doing here, Kastian?" She calls, annoyance in her tone. "Whatever you came to say, spit it out."

I open my mouth to tell her about the ship in the bottle, then stop, realizing what a painfully stupid idea that is. If I give it to her, I'll have to explain how I got it. Somehow I doubt Odessa will take: "I don't know why I did it, it was like a compulsion," as a reasonable explanation for threatening the local shopkeeper—even if he is a prick.

I shove the small paper-wrapped package in my pocket and cast around for anything else to say. "Just wanted to see if Jett was right."

Her eyes narrow. "Excuse me?"

"Everyone knows sirens are monsters in the water, but I've never actually seen one."

Her glower intensifies, and she swims closer. When she reaches the edge of the lake, where her feet must reach the bottom, she stands straight, water raining down from her in waves.

For the love of the fucking gods.

Odessa is unusually, overwhelmingly beautiful. It's not an opinion, just an undisputed fact.

She's wearing a long white nightgown, which is soaking wet and sticking to her curves in a way that leaves no question that she has nothing beneath it. Her skin is practically glowing. Her long hair—which sometimes looks red and sometimes blonde depending on the lighting—is soaked to a dark cherry red and hangs down over her chest, barely hiding her nipples from view.

Her hips swing as she walks out of the lake and stops in front of me, close enough that I could reach out and grab her in an instant.

She looks up at me from beneath her eyelashes. "Do I look like a monster to you?"

I blink and shake my head, mostly to clear the fog suddenly clouding my rational mind. Odessa misinterprets the motion as my saying "no," and sneers at me. "Then you're not nearly as smart as you think you are. Be careful, Kastian, or one of these days I won't be able to resist drowning you."

"I'd like to see you try."

"Don't tempt me."

"Back at you."

Dessa stops and glances over her shoulder at me, but instead of being annoyed, her expression is hard to read. She looks conflicted before she turns back around and walks away without another word.

I have to physically hold myself back from chasing after her. I feel bewitched. Possessed. Insane.

This isn't like me at all, and I have no idea what it means.

Of course, Odessa is beautiful, but I don't think that's the reason for my fixation. If her appearance were the only draw, I would have gotten over it months ago.

I think it must be the fact that she's a mystery.

Despite knowing each other for a year, I don't really know Dessa that well. She won't let me know her, because she's been standoffish from the very moment we met. With literally everyone else in the kingdom, she's all smiles and sunshine, but with me it's like a storm suddenly rolled in.

Yet, I don't care. She can be as sullen and ill-tempered as she likes, and I can't get enough.

Usually, there could only be one explanation for this sort of inexplicable fascination: *A soul-bond.*

Soul-bonds are unbreakable connections that only form once. There's debate among the Fae whether the connections are predestined or form organically. Some believe that they are fated connections, but most think that bonds are triggered, usually in a moment of heightened emotion or trauma.

Everyone agrees, however, that once a bond forms there's no breaking it.

If one partner dies or is somehow lost, the other often dies. Males tend to feel the connection first, and once bonded they will never leave their partners—ever. That's why there's nearly no such thing as infidelity among the Fae.

At least, that's how it's supposed to work.

If things were different, I would assume that my inexplicable obsession with Odessa was a sign of a bond forming, but I know that's impossible.

Odessa can't be my soul-bond because a bond only forms once, and I already found mine. I found her years ago and lost her just as quickly before the bond was ever able to flourish.

It's still there, though. I can feel it in my chest, taunting me, making sure I never forget.

As if I ever could.

Bonds are supposed to be permanent and unbreakable. I shouldn't want anyone else—I shouldn't be *able* to want anyone else.

So what the fuck is wrong with me?

6

THE PAST

ODESSA, AGE 16

My stomach churns with anxiety and a hint of motion sickness as the carriage trundles along the bumpy road.

Across from me, my Aunt Beatrix sits up straight, just as prim and proper as she was eight years ago on the day we traveled from Hydratta to Vernallis for the first time. To my right, my cousin Daemon is bent over the heavy leather-bound book in his lap. I envy him. My own book lies abandoned on the seat beside me, as reading it made my stomach churn all the more.

"What are you reading?" I ask, more out of boredom than interest.

Before he can answer, our carriage rolls over a bump, and Daemon swears loudly as the top of his head smashes against the roof. I bite back a sarcastic comment. It's my instinct to needle Daemon as much as possible, but at the moment I almost feel bad for him.

In the last year alone, Daemon grew nearly a foot and now barely fits in our carriage. He's sitting slightly hunched over, yet still, every time we roll over a bump, the top of his head smacks against the roof. I've been watching his expression grow moodier with every painful bump.

"Fuck this," Daemon bursts out, snapping his book shut as his head knocks against the roof for the third time in so many minutes. "I'd rather get out and walk. It would probably be faster."

Aunt Beatrix sniffs, clearly annoyed by her son's outburst. "We're almost there. It won't be much longer."

"It better not be," Daemon raises his voice so that the driver will undoubtedly be able to hear him. "If the driver can't avoid flinging us around like this, I'm going to go out there and smash his damn head against the carriage."

"No, you're not," Beatrix says firmly. "You are not going to draw attention to yourself by stopping the entire procession."

Daemon's eyes flash with anger, but for once he doesn't say anything.

Aunt Beatrix is always going on about Daemon drawing attention to himself—and rightly so. It's been almost ten years since the 11th Baron Ashwater passed away, and now that he's gone, hardly anyone bothers to keep up the pretense that Daemon is truly his son. Everyone in the court of Vernallis knows that while my cousin inherited the title of 12th Baron Ashwater, his true father is King Florian.

King Florian's legitimate son, Prince Thorne, is only a few years older than Daemon and me. He just turned twenty this past summer and began to take on more responsibilities in running the court. Largely, those responsibilities consist of raising taxes and throwing costly parties for his noble friends. Additionally, the prince is now in search of a wife, which is how we all found ourselves trapped in this carriage procession on the way to the neighboring court of Hydratta.

"I hope he picks this one," I mutter. "I don't want to keep traveling all over the continent."

"We're lucky to be included in the entourage," Aunt Beatrix points out.

I furrow my brow. It doesn't feel much like luck to me; it feels like a punishment.

Thus far, Prince Thorne has met with half a dozen royal and noble women of Ellender. Each "meeting" lasted several days and required both courts to socialize while diplomatic meetings went on between the royals. I'm starting to believe that these extended spousal selection summits are more political than anything else, and give the royals the opportunity to plot together under the pretext of a potential engagement.

We've been traveling in this carriage, along with one hundred or so other noble Fae, for the better part of a week. It's ridiculous, since the railway that runs between Vernallis and Hydratta takes only a day and a half, but for whatever reason Prince Thorne insisted on a "grand" royal procession.

"Aren't you excited to return to Hydratta?" Aunt Beatrix asks.

I shrug. "I guess. It's not as if I ever spent much time on land to begin with, and I know it's too much to hope that *The Adella* might dock while we're visiting."

My aunt nods sadly and changes the subject. "I've heard Princess Serena is lovely. An alliance with Hydratta would benefit both kingdoms. I believe there's a good chance the prince will choose her."

"I'll be sure to extend her my sympathies," Daemon scoffs.

Aunt Beatrix raises an eyebrow. "Pardon?"

"Thorne is an ass," Daemon grumbles darkly.

"Hush," Beatrix chides, looking over her shoulder as though someone might be listening through the wall of the moving carriage.

"He is." Daemon's eyes widen, and he gestures animatedly, punctuating his words with both hands. "Everyone knows it."

I reach out and knock Daemon's waving arm out of the way before he accidentally punches me in the nose. "It doesn't matter whether he is or not. Royalty gets to behave however they want."

"I've heard the court of Hydratta is just as bad," Daemon groans. "That's just what we need, another entitled fucking prick on a throne who—"

"Hush!" Beatrix chides again, louder. "I don't know what makes you think you can talk like that in front of me."

Daemon lets out a breath through his nose and tips his head back against the carriage seat, looking as if the world might come to an end at any moment. "All I'm saying is royal families seem to breed entitled assholes."

"Really? You don't say?" I grin.

He glares at me. "Shut up. I'd rather die than be king."

"We'll all die if you keep talking like that," Beatrix hisses. "Is that what you want? To get all of us executed? Or worse, banished to Dyaspora?"

Daemon and I both clamp our mouths shut, humbled into silence. Dyaspora prison is the worst threat I can think of, and my aunt is right; nobility or not, Fae have been banished there for far less than looking too much like their illegitimate father.

We fall into uneasy silence, and I let my head fall against the wall of the carriage. As long as I was talking, I'd managed to forget the queasy feeling in my stomach, but with nothing else to focus on, the bumpy road and the sloshing in my stomach is all too noticeable.

Gods, I've developed a weak stomach after living so long on land. I wonder if I'd get seasick if I ever returned to *The Adella*? Mercer and the others would undoubtedly die of laughter.

I close my eyes and try to think of anything to distract me from the rocking motion of the carriage.

I suppose a small part of me is excited to return to Hydratta after all this time. I prefer the warm climate there and the constant smell of the ocean. And if I'm honest with myself, there is one thing I'm truly excited about: finally knowing for sure if that boy Daemon and I met in the harbor was really Prince Kastian?

I've wondered about that boy often for the last eight years. At the time, I was certain it was the prince, but now I'm half-convinced that I was wrong and simply letting my childish imagination run away with me.

Once, when Aunt Beatrix brought me to court with her, I visited the castle library and searched for information about the Hydrattan royal family. A description, or better yet, a painting that might help put my curiosity to rest, but all I found was a single image of the king and queen and nothing about their children except their names and birth announcements.

King Sebastian and Queen Marbella of Hydratta have four children—an unusually high number for a Fae couple. The eldest is Princess Serena, followed closely by twins Dellanore and Avaline. The crown prince, Kastian, is decades younger than all three of his sisters, but he's the heir to his father's throne because, like Vernallis, the court of Hydratta practices male primogeniture; the custom that boys come before girls in the royal line, regardless of birth order.

The other two kingdoms of Ellender are different: In Thermia, the eldest becomes the heir, regardless of gender. In Solistine, there's no clear line of succession, and the heir is appointed by the previous ruler based on merit.

I wonder how the Hydrattan princesses feel about being overlooked in favor of their brother. I certainly wouldn't like it. Especially if there's any truth to the persistent rumors that the prince is just as arrogant and cruel as Thorne.

The boy in the harbor didn't seem so awful.

I shake my head. I'm being stupid and obsessing over nothing.

Surely that boy in the harbor all those years ago was just some street orphan, and even if he wasn't, what am I expecting to happen? That the crown prince will remember me? That he's wondered about me all these years and he'll pluck me out of obscurity to become a princess?

It's laughably unlikely—impossible, even—and childish even to consider.

I close my eyes, pressing my cheek more firmly against the wall of the rocking carriage. I listen to the wind outside and try to pretend I'm on a ship and the clip-clop of the horses hooves are really the footsteps of the sailors and the sound of the sails whipping against the masts.

I don't realize that I've fallen asleep until a hand shakes me awake.

"Dessa," Aunt Beatrix leans over me, shaking my shoulder. "Wake up. We've arrived." Her voice is exhausted, and though she doesn't say it, I can hear the implied *"finally."*

I sit up and rub my eyes, feeling the remnants of sleep slowly fade away, then lean over to look out the window of the carriage.

The scene outside is nothing like Vernallis. It's a vibrant tropical landscape bursting with color. Exotic flowers in shades of pink and blue dot the lush greenery, while towering palm trees sway gently in the warm breeze.

If I crane my neck just right, I can make out the side of a whitewashed stone wall that must belong to the palace, and a sliver of bright-blue sky. I take a deep breath, inhaling the salty sea air. In the distance, the rhythmic melody of ocean waves crashing against the shore whispers a beckoning chant.

"Open the door," Daemon demands impatiently.

I barely have time to process his words before he shoves me aside and grips the handle of the carriage door, yanking it open. The door swings wide, and Daemon leaps out, his boots hitting the ground with a solid thud. Truly excited for the first time in days, I gather my long heavy skirt and tumble out of the carriage after him.

Outside, the line of ornate carriages, each adorned with intricate crimson filigree, has come to a halt. Nobles dressed in wrinkled silks and crushed velvets begin to step down onto the cobblestone street, their faces relieved to be back in the fresh air. Many are holding jackets and shawls over their arms, as if they were unprepared for the much hotter climate.

I lift my gaze over the sea of noble heads, taking in the full splendor of the enormous white stone castle. Its towering turrets stretch skyward, each adorned with vibrant green flags.

"That must be them," Daemon says ruefully, pointing up at the castle.

I follow his gaze, and my eyes settle on the expansive, round balcony, which serves as a stage for five finely dressed figures. King Sebastian and Queen Marbella stand in the center, their crowns glinting in the sun. The king is tall, with midnight skin and curly black hair. The queen is fair-skinned but sun-tanned, and her long brunette hair is pulled up in an elaborate waterfall of braids.

Beside the king and queen are three beautiful women who must be the princesses. I know two of them are identical twins, but at this distance I can't tell which. All three are bronze-skinned and dark-haired, and dressed in stunning, colorful silk gowns.

I can't help but notice that there's no prince among them.

"Which one do you think is Princess Serena?" I ask.

Daemon looks unconcerned. "Could be any of them. I doubt Thorne will even know the difference."

I snort. He's probably right. Prince Thorne is certainly self-absorbed enough that I'd imagine all three princesses would be interchangeable to him.

I bite my lip. I'm dying to ask where the prince is, but Daemon will probably make fun of me for caring.

Fortunately, before I can make a fool of myself, my question is answered for me.

Behind the king and queen, two additional figures emerge onto the balcony. One is a tall, slender man with blonde hair and a pale complexion, different enough from the royal family that I can tell at a distance that he isn't one of them. He must be a high-ranking servant, or perhaps an advisor, as no one seems bothered by his presence, and he's engaged in what looks to be a tense exchange with the second newcomer.

I crane my neck, willing King Sebastian to step to the side so that I can see better.

To my excitement, he does. The king shifts, and finally the sixth member of the royal family falls into position beside his father.

The prince appears to be around eighteen years old, and entirely too handsome. His skin is a warm, sun-kissed tan, complimenting the striking contrast of his short, jet-black hair. Though it has been years since that unforgettable day in the harbor, the moment my eyes land on him, recognition strikes me instantly.

My heartbeat kicks up, racing against my chest. *I knew it.*

Like he can feel me looking, Prince Kastian turns his head and looks in my direction, and that single action sends me spiraling.

Before I can stop myself, my mind floods with every impossible daydream and childish fantasy I've suppressed for the last eight years. I can picture how we'll bump into each other at dinner, or perhaps outside in the garden. Prince Kastian will remember me instantly and admit that he's been looking for me for years. He still has the key I gave him, and on our wedding day he'll give it back to me as a token of affection and even though I'll have access to an endless supply of jewels, I'll wear the key as a necklace instead.

"What's wrong with you?" Daemon asks, nudging my shoulder.

"Nothing, I was just—*wait*, who is *that*?"

My voice cracks, and my jaw goes slack as an eighth figure appears on the balcony. An olive-skinned brunette in a pink gown steps outside and stands beside Prince Kastian. She leans over and says something in his ear, putting her hand lightly on his arm.

Daemon turns to look. "Dunno," he says, completely unaware of the turmoil now roiling in the back of my mind.

Aunt Beatrix finally climbs out of the carriage and comes to stand beside me. "That's Lady Lyra Von Bargen," she says, glancing curiously at me. "She's betrothed to the prince. The blonde man is her father, Magnus Von Bargen. He's an advisor to the king."

My stomach clenches with mingled disappointment and embarrassment.

I'm such an idiot, fantasizing about a prince who doesn't

know me and is already engaged to someone else. What was I thinking?

I look back at the balcony—at Prince Kastian and Lyra Von Bargen—and despite knowing how pointless and ridiculous it is, my stormy temper rises like a turbulent sea.

I'm not sure whom I'm angry with. Myself, I suppose, for being childish enough to feel envy over a Prince I've hardly even met. Still, the feeling is uncomfortably intense—possessive and disembodied, as if it's coming from a part of myself I didn't know existed.

And for the first time in my life, a little voice in the back of my mind whispers: *"Drown, drown, drown."*

ODESSA, PRESENT

It takes two days for the emissary to arrive from Hydratta

It's evening, and the garden buzzes with laughter and conversation. The weather is nice, so we opted for dinner in the garden. Almost the entire inner circle is gathered around the large dining on the patio, three quarters of the way through a delicious supper. The only person missing is Alix, who traveled back to the human realm this morning to visit her mother. Daemon sits at the head of the table, his posture rigid, and I can tell he won't relax until Alix returns home.

"That's nothing," Jett says loudly, grinning at Aurelia. "Did I ever tell you about how I robbed the richest merchant in Solistine?"

"Yes," Fox grumbles. "Many times."

"I wasn't talking to you, was I?" Jett quips.

Aurelia giggles. "What happened?"

Jett sits up straighter, spreading his arms wide like an actor performing one of the great tragedies. "It was a dark and stormy night."

"Shut up," Daemon grins and tosses a bread roll at Jett's head.

Jett catches the roll and takes an enormous bite out of it before fixing Daemon with an exaggerated glare. "It *was*. Have you ever experienced a rainy season in Solistine? Every night is dark and stormy."

Daemon rolls his eyes. "I'm sure."

Jett carries on as if there were no interruption. "The merchant was throwing an enormous party for all the wealthiest families in the city. He'd been talking for weeks about how this renowned sorcerer would be there to entertain the guests with tricks. I figured I'd have to find this sorcerer and convince him to make me disappear once I'd gotten in and robbed the place."

"And did you?" Aurelia prompts.

"Well, of course," Jett continues with a dramatic flourish. "But as it turned out, the man was a fraud. He didn't have any more magical ability than I do, and he certainly wasn't very strong."

"Why do you say that?" Kastian asks, frowning.

"Because he was so easy to capture. I tied him up, took his robes, and went to the party in his place. The merchant's house was just as grand as he'd bragged; art and gold everywhere, jewels on all the lamps and candlesticks. The robes were so large no one noticed all the things I shoved into the pockets."

Aurelia laughs. "Did you have to perform for the guests?"

"Only for a few minutes. Once the merchant realized I had no idea what I was doing, he kicked me out of the house himself. It was the easiest escape I ever made."

Everyone roars with laughter, and even Fox cracks a smile.

I stand halfway out of my chair and lean over Fox to reach for the platter of vegetables. Across the table, Kastian makes a disgruntled noise in the back of his throat. I glance at him, confused. "Can I help you, *Your Majesty?*"

His eyes flick up to mine, and he shakes his head once, his jaw tensing.

"Excuse me," a high-pitched voice breaks through the happy chatter around the table.

I retake my seat and twist around. In the doorway to the kitchen, a tiny pixie woman stands wringing her hands in her skirt. I smile widely. "Hello, Shar."

Shar smiles back at me, her rows of tiny sharp teeth glinting in the flickering candlelight. "Good evening, Lady Odessa."

I roll my eyes. Shar and I have known each other for years. She was once a servant at King Thorne's summer palace, where I was a lady-in-waiting to the king's various brides. Early in our acquaintance, I had to remind Shar often that I'm not *really* a lady. My father wasn't noble, and my aunt only became so after her marriage to the 11th Baron Ashwater, so no one had to address me by title. Eventually she'd grown used to using my name alone, but it seems that since Daemon took the throne any casual greetings have flown out the window.

"I know I can't convince you to sit with us," I say in a rueful tone, "so was there something you needed?"

Shar nods. "I'm sorry to interrupt your meal, but a visitor has arrived."

Around the table, everyone tenses.

"From where?" Daemon demands.

"Hydratta, Your Majesty."

"Fuck." Daemon gets to his feet. "I knew we should have stayed alert, but I thought we'd have at least another day before he arrived."

"This is better," Kastian says calmly. "Arriving while we're in the middle of a meal gives the impression that we didn't know the emissary would be coming."

"I wish Alix were here," Daemon mutters, running a hand through his hair. "Alright, fine. Fox and Jett come with me. Aurelia—"

"I'm already going," Aurelia says, her chair scraping against the floor as she stands. "I'll be up in the tower."

"Good," Daemon nods. "Dess—"

"I'm going with you," I say indignantly. "You can't keep me out. There's absolutely no reason I shouldn't be in a meeting that's *about* me, and since Alix isn't here, she'll want—"

"Calm down," Daemon puts a hand up to stop me. "I was going to say you should come with us, but fuck, if you're going to bite my head off..."

"Oh." The back of my neck heats. "Yes, well...I agree. I'm just going to change first."

Kastian glances at me, then turns to Daemon. "I'm coming too."

Immediately the table erupts in protests.

"I don't think that's a good idea, mate," Jett says.

"That's fucking stupid," Fox grumbles.

Aurelia glowers. "If I have to hide, then you certainly should—"

"Enough!" Kastian barks, his eyes still locked on Daemon. "I'm not asking your permission, Daemon. This isn't a request."

Rather than rising to challenge him back, Daemon just cocks his head in amusement. "Fine. After you then, *Your Majesty*."

"Don't call me that," Kastian snaps.

Daemon keeps grinning. "Well, if you're not asking permission, then what would you like to be called, *my liege*?"

Kastian says something venomous back, but I don't catch it as I'm already halfway out of the room.

Twenty minutes later, we gather in the sitting room off the entrance hall.

I'm slightly out of breath, having sprinted up three flights of stairs to my room. As a child, I deliberately chose the most secluded bedroom, farthest from my family and the servants. I regret that now because it's such a chore to climb all the way to my room and fight my way through my messy wardrobe all because I wished to look more presentable. I wish I hadn't bothered. I'm afraid I'm going to burst through the seams of my silk gown from all my heavy breathing.

The manor doesn't have anything resembling the grand throne room at the winter palace, but since Daemon and Alix don't keep every noble in the kingdom close by, they hardly need one.

Except in moments like this.

As I step into the cozy sitting room, I find myself wishing we were standing at the front of a long, imposing room where the emissary would have to walk toward us past hundreds of judgmental courtiers. If only for the spectacle.

Daemon settles into a high-backed blue and gold armchair. An identical chair stands empty beside him where Alix would usually sit. The rest of the furniture has been rearranged, so the rest of us are forced to stand gathered around the makeshift thrones.

I take my place behind Alix's empty chair, fighting the temptation to rest my elbows on its back.

Jett and Fox position themselves on either side of the two armchairs. Fox, as usual, is in his blue military jacket. Jett now wears a similar jacket that seems hastily borrowed and slightly tight around the shoulders. Finally, Kastian comes and stands beside me—for once, I don't say anything about it. Although I'd rather he kept his distance, I'm not an idiot. This little tableau is as much about projecting power and unity as anything else.

Outside in the hall, the front door opens, and we hear one of the servants greeting the visitor.

"Fox," Daemon mumbles under his breath.

Without a word, Fox crosses the room and exits into the hall to escort the emissary. We listen in tense silence as a male voice greets Fox. As usual, Fox makes no reply.

"You could have sent anyone else," I mutter.

"No, anyone else would have made the emissary think he's welcome here. He's not," Daemon hisses back.

Fox reenters the room, guiding a short, plump man in his wake. The man's balding head glistens under the light, accentuating his unattractive features. His skin carries a slightly grayish hue, and his overlarge ears are pointed and sharp.

I squint, attempting to figure out his species. Ellender is primarily inhabited by Fae, but other beings and hybrids are relatively common—I'm a perfect example of that. If I had to make a guess, I would say the emissary is part-Fae, but the other part is unclear. I'm tempted to guess "troll," though it seems impolite, even in my own head.

"Your Majesty," the troll-like man says, falling into a deep bow. "It's an honor to meet you."

Daemon gives a grunt of acknowledgement and shifts in his seat, obviously uncomfortable.

The emissary looks up and, seeming to decide that Daemon is not going to bid him to stand, straightens once more. "My name is Elio," he says in a nasally, overly accommodating tone. "I've come on behalf of King Magnus of Hydratta."

Beside me, Kastian stiffens. I resist the urge to reach out and grasp his fingers. *What the hell am I thinking?*

"We received the king's letters," Daemon says, "but I don't recall agreeing to a meeting."

"Forgive me, Your Majesty," Elio says. "Of course I can't speak to your private correspondence with my king, but I was under the impression that he wanted to ensure you received his message."

"I'll fucking bet he did," Kastian grumbles under his breath.

Elio's eyes dart upward and land on Kastian for the first time. I detect a tiny flinch of surprise from the emissary, but he doesn't say anything to acknowledge it.

"What does King Magnus want?" Daemon asks, his tone dripping with barely controlled contempt.

"The king is looking to forge an alliance...preferably an unbreakable one." Elio's eyes flick to me. "I assume, as Lady Odessa is attending this meeting, you're aware of the proposed union?"

I can't tell what the emissary thinks of the request—whether he's surprised to see me in the room or not, or even if he cares either way. Perhaps he's just a messenger, but I doubt it.

Emissaries are usually trusted friends or even family members of the ruler and are able to negotiate on the court's behalf. It's unlikely that Elio would be truly unaware of what his king is intending.

"We're aware," Daemon says flatly.

Elio's dark eyes widen. "And have you had the opportunity to consider the matter?"

"It's not fucking happening," Kastian growls.

Daemon smiles. "That about sums it up."

Elio clears his throat uncomfortably. "I understand this might seem like a sudden request, but if Your Majesty had been willing to meet with my king, I think you'd see that the alliance could be highly beneficial for all parties."

"How so?" I blurt out.

Elio looks up at me, but his reply seems more directed at Daemon. "Increased military support, expanded trade routes, assistance in rebuilding your capital and access to—"

Daemon cuts him off. "We don't need or want any of that."

My brow furrows. I realize that Daemon believes he's protecting me, but perhaps he spoke too soon. All of those things would be extremely beneficial to Vernallis, especially in the short term as we're rebuilding from the curse.

What we really need isn't a betrothal, it's an emissary of our own—someone who could negotiate for these things outright. Someone who could find out what Hydratta truly wants out of this alliance and why.

Seeming to be thinking the same thing, Elio speaks up again. "If Your Majesty would be willing to at least send Lady Odessa to meet with my king, perhaps a representative could accompany her and discuss all the benefits to both kingdoms in more detail."

"What part of it's not fucking happening didn't you understand?" Kastian barks.

Elio focuses only on Daemon. "Your Majesty, if you would just consider—"

"It's not my decision to consider," Daemon snaps. "But Odessa would never—"

"I'll do it," I blurt out, the words escaping my lips before I've fully processed the weight of the decision.

A charged silence echoes in the room. Beside me, Kastian goes rigid, as if struck by a sudden, electric jolt. I catch a glimpse of him whipping his head toward me, and the intensity of his shocked and furious gaze pierces into the side of my face like daggers, searing with an almost palpable heat.

"You'll what?" Daemon says, eyes narrowing on me.

I swallow thickly, my mind racing.

We need to find out what Hydratta wants and we can't just go crashing into their court demanding answers, but perhaps a diplomatic visit would be the perfect time to gather information.

Moreover, if something went terribly wrong, I wouldn't be on my own. Hydratta is mostly an island, and where there's water, assistance is never far away...

"I'll do it," I repeat, forcing my tone to remain even. "I'll at least go meet with King Magnus."

Elio's ugly face bursts into a wide smile that stretches his features to near breaking. He claps his hands together in delight. "Oh, that's wonderful. In that case we should discuss when you'll travel to Hydratta and perhaps who will be included in the entourage."

Daemon, completely ignoring Elio, swings around in his chair to look at me. "Dessa, are you sure? What—"

"I'm sure. Excuse me, I'm going to go upstairs and prepare."

Before anyone can stop me, I step out from behind Alix's empty chair and march across the room toward the door. The weight of every eye in the room pierces my back, but none more searing than Kastian's furious gaze, which feels like molten fire scorching into my very soul.

ODESSA, PRESENT

A sharp knock sounds on my bedroom door. "Dessa, are you in there?"

I look up at the door and freeze, my eyes widening.

I'm sitting on the floor of my bedroom, wearing nothing but a corset and panties, and surrounded by clutter. Next to me lies the crumpled silk gown I was wearing earlier, and in my hand is the exact green glass bottle with the little ship inside that I was admiring yesterday.

The bottle is the source of my confusion. I don't know where the hell it came from, and moreover, I'm not exactly sure how long I've been sitting here pondering it.

After leaving the meeting with the emissary, I practically ran all the way back up to my third-floor bedroom and shut myself inside. I leaned against the closed door, panting. *What the hell am I doing? Is this the best idea I've ever had? Or is it slow, drawn-out suicide?*

I reached behind me and tugged on the laces of my tight

gown, shucking it over my head and tossing it on the floor where it landed among dozens of other discarded gowns.

My room is—to put it kindly—a mess.

Everything from the floor to the furniture is covered in a mulch of clothes, old papers, and shiny trinkets. There are piles of books, packages from nearby shops that lie unopened, empty cosmetics bottles, and loose beads from broken jewelry covering nearly every surface. I've always had a weakness for collecting beautiful things...I've just never been good at keeping track of them all.

Because of the mess, I didn't immediately notice the ship in the bottle sitting innocently on the windowsill, reflecting gleaming green light all across the walls. Once I noticed it, however, any other thought flew from my mind. I have no idea how it got in here, and I'm not sure if I'm excited or disturbed to see it.

Now, the knock on the door sounds again, and Alix's muffled voice shouts from the other side. "It's me! Are you in there? I came bearing gifts!"

I jump to my feet, bottle still in hand. "One second!"

It takes more than a few seconds to wade back through the mess and reach the door. I kick a turned-over vase and a pair of trousers out of the way, and pry the door open. "Hi!"

Alix stands on the other side of the door looking bemused. Her hair is braided away from her face, and she's still wearing her human clothing—denim trousers and an oversized blue sweater. In her arms, she's carrying a large paper bag and at her feet an enormous gray cat is rubbing up against her leg.

Alix's gaze flicks over my lack of clothing and she cracks a smile. "I'm getting déjà vu."

I sigh and step aside to let her in, pausing to pet her cat— Sushi—under the chin. The cat allows a mere ten seconds of affection before nipping the tips of my fingers and bounding into the room after Alix.

"When did you get back?" I ask, shutting the door.

Alix tiptoes carefully over the mess to reach my bed. "A few hours ago."

I blow my tangled hair out of my face. "I didn't realize I'd been up here so long. I was just going to get dressed and..."

"You got distracted," she finishes for me with a grin as she sinks onto the corner of my bed and her cat leaps into her lap. "No worries."

I replace the ship on the windowsill, then bend to sift through the clothes on the floor until I find a robe. I pull it on over my underwear and pull the belt tight. "How was your visit with your mother?"

She rolls her eyes. "Same as usual. She's been trying to sell my Nana's house for over a year now and can't grasp that the town where Nana lived is condemned, so the house can't even technically be sold. The government will buy the property just to get rid of the headache, but they're not offering what my mom thinks it's worth, and she's going absolutely ape-shit over it."

"I thought this was Isabelle's house, not your mother's."

Alix laughs hollowly. "Oh, *it is.* My mom isn't even getting anything out of it, so this tantrum is 100% organic. I honestly think she's just bored now that Nana has been traveling a lot and I'm *'living in Europe.'*" She draws quotes in the air with her fingers. "She's really on the warpath now, too, because I accidentally let it slip that Nana is coming to visit me."

I perk up at that. "Belle is coming here?"

"Yeah, she'll be here for Christmas again this year. I don't know how much longer I'm going to be able to find excuses not to invite my mom. We might have to revisit the idea of telling her where I really am...but that's a problem for future-me." She sucks in a huge breath, having said all that without breathing. "*Anyway,* sorry. That's why I missed the meeting, but Daemon already filled me in on what happened."

"So I suppose you came up here to ask if I've lost my mind?"

Alix shrugs, petting Sushi absently. "I guess, but I also just wanted to show you my latest haul."

"Oooh!" My eyes widen, and I hasten to sit beside her and reach into the bag, pulling out handfuls of glittering plastic treasures.

"What are these?" I ask, holding a silver disk up to the light.

"I raided my mother's basement and found most of my old CDs. You put them in here—" she stops petting her cat long enough to pull a yellow plastic device out of the bag and hold it out to me "—and they play music."

My brow wrinkles. "How?"

She shrugs. "Something about the grooves, I think? I don't really know, but it's the only way I can think of to play music here until I can figure out how to get electricity."

I nod, pretending I know what she's talking about.

I love everything about the human world. I've always been fascinated by it, and now that Alix has been living here for a year, I've learned so much more about human culture than I ever dreamed. Still, much of what my friend says is slightly beyond my understanding.

"I wish I could figure out how to get internet here," Alix goes on, speaking more to herself than to me. "I thought maybe there would be a magic workaround, but until I can explain Wi-Fi to Daemon in a way that he understands, we're stuck with battery-operated devices."

I nod again. This time, I really do understand.

Well, almost.

I don't know what "Wifey" is, but I do know what she means about Daemon's magic.

All Fae are born with basically the same magical ability, albeit in varying degrees of power, but training from an early age dictates how they'll be able to use it. The four kingdoms of Ellender all specialize in training different skills.

In Hydratta, they teach creation magic; conjuring something out of nothing. In Vernallis, they tend to practice will-based magic. Daemon can compel nearly anything to happen—a door to unlock, the weather to change, a broken object to mend itself—but the limitation is that he needs to understand what he's trying to accomplish. If he doesn't understand this "Wifey" that Alix wants, then he can't create it for her. For that, she'd need someone from Hydratta...

"Have you asked Kastian to help you?" I blurt out.

Alix looks up at me. "No, I was thinking I'd ask Aurelia. Why?"

"Daemon and Aurelia both have will-based powers. I doubt either of them could conjure anything for you out of thin air, but in Hydratta they teach that kind of magic. You should ask Kastian about it."

Alix furrows her brow. "Would Kastian have enough power to do that?"

"Undoubtedly," I grumble. "He was trained really well as a child...I mean, I'm guessing he was."

"Huh. Okay, I'll ask him. Thanks."

I press my lips together into a flat line, wishing I had never brought it up. I don't want to think about Kastian right now—or ever, really—but it seems like my mind is inserting him into every possible conversation without my consent.

Sushi leaps off Alix's lap and begins trying to catch the dots of green light on the wall reflecting through the bottle on the windowsill. Alix takes advantage of his movement and my silence to shove a haphazard pile of clothing off the bed and lean back against my headboard. She crosses her bare feet over each other and fixes me with a shrewd look. "So, are you going to make me ask?"

I sigh and swivel to face her. "No, but I'm not going to let you talk me out of it either."

"Daemon thinks you're being impulsive by agreeing to this engagement."

I scoff. "He would know; he's not exactly the most cautious person I've ever met."

"We just want to make sure you're not trying to sacrifice yourself for our sake. We don't need Hydratta's help for Vernallis to thrive. We just need more time and—"

"This isn't about anyone else," I interrupt. "It's about me. I love living here, but I'm bored. I feel like I'm not doing enough."

"You're doing more than enough," she argues. "And technically you don't even have to do anything."

"What do you mean?"

"I love having you here, obviously, but I don't want you to think you have to work for us if you don't want to. You could do anything. Travel, or spend some time in the ocean. Whatever you want."

I ignore the ocean comment because that topic is far more than I feel like getting into now...or possibly ever. "I don't mind working. I like helping with the kingdom. I just don't know what I'm supposed to do. I don't have a real title or official responsibilities, and everyone else has managed to find a role here. Fox is running the army, Jett's the spymaster, Kastian is the advisor."

"You're an advisor too," she insists.

"You don't need a second advisor. You need an emissary. Isn't that what we've all been saying for months? Hydratta is a wildebeest."

"A wildcard?" Alix corrects, smiling.

"Yes, that. We don't know nearly enough about them to determine if they're a threat to us, and given the King's history with Kastian, I don't think we can rule out that they are."

Alix nods. "True."

"This is the perfect opportunity to gain more insight. They're our closest neighbor, and now that the curse is lifted and people are traveling to Vernallis again, don't you think we should know what kind of relationship Hydratta wants to have with us?"

"I agree," Alix says, surprising me.

"You do?"

"Yes, but you're talking about being *our* emissary, not *their* queen. There's no reason you need to marry the king for us to have a cordial diplomatic relationship."

"I know that. I'm not planning to. Just because I agree to visit doesn't mean we're really getting engaged."

She cracks a smile. "Are you sure? Because we don't have the best history with fake engagements."

I wave her off. "What happened to you was unusual, because of the timeline of the curse and because Thorne had already met Isabelle, but royal matches don't usually work like that. Usually there's an official meeting with one royal household hosting the other for several days, or maybe up to a week. There are dinners and balls and lots of opportunities to get to know each other without any obligation of commitment."

"You sound very sure."

"I am. When I was sixteen, Daemon and I both traveled with Prince Thorne's entourage to meet one of the princesses of Hydratta. That was when I..." I clear my throat. "I mean, that was when Daemon and Kastian first became friends."

She nods, seemingly unaware of my verbal misstep. "That's when you met King Magnus?"

I nod. I wish more than anything that I could elaborate on that meeting. I want to warn Alix about Magnus, but I can't. I can't talk about anything that went on back then, no matter how much I wish otherwise.

Alix's brow furrows. "If he only met you once as a teenager, isn't that strange that he wants to marry you? It's giving creepy age-gap romance."

"Not really. I can see why you'd think that, but age is sort of relative for us. It would be odd if he'd been a close acquaintance when I was a child, but if Fae spent time worrying about large age gaps, we'd never have survived as a species."

"I guess that makes sense," she says, still looking dubious.

"I'll admit that it's a little odd because King Magnus has a daughter my age."

She wrinkles her nose in disgust. "Do you know her?"

"Yes, unfortunately." I scowl, thinking of the last time I saw

Lyra. "But it doesn't really matter because I'm not actually planning to marry him."

I would rather die.

"Right," she says briskly. "So for this diplomatic engagement summit, would we all have to travel with you?"

I press my lips together, thinking. "Normally yes, but I don't think that can happen. You and Daemon can't go right now. Both because the court is still so new and because if Hydratta doesn't have friendship in mind it would be dangerous to have both of you there at once."

"That's what Daemon said too. He said he'd normally send Kastian with you."

"No!" I say too quickly. "Anyone but Kastian."

Alix looks startled. "Calm down, we know you don't get along. Anyway, Kastian can't very well waltz into the court of Hydratta as if nothing happened."

I swallow thickly. "Of course he can't."

"We thought perhaps Jett could go with you? He'd be helpful at gathering information, and he's a good fighter if something were to go wrong, but not in an obvious way. If we sent you with Fox, it would send the message to Hydratta that we're expecting you to be attacked."

I smile. "You're getting good at navigating court politics."

"I try. I've been going back and forth between reading business management books and watching *Game of Thrones* when I go home to visit my mom and Nana."

"What's that?"

She waves me off. "Never mind. So, are you alright with Jett tagging along?"

"Of course..." I bite my lip. "I'm surprised you're not telling me it would be safer to stay here."

She shrugs. "I mean, it would be safer...but even if I thought you'd listen to me, that's not what I'd say. I don't doubt you can take care of yourself."

"Thank you." I smile, a tiny bubble of excitement forming in my chest. I appreciate her faith in me, and although I'm nervous, I'm mostly excited at the prospect of doing something important.

"You have to be the one to tell Beatrix, though." Alix presses her lips together, holding back a laugh.

The excited bubble in my chest pops. "What? No..."

She grins. "Don't think you're going to pawn that pleasure off on me. She's your surrogate mother, you tell her."

My nose wrinkles with disgust—more at the word "mother" than anything else, but I've never told anyone why that word might bother me. I couldn't even if I wanted to.

"Will you come with me?" I ask.

Alix grins. "Not a chance. I already saw my mother today. I've sat through enough disappointed parental lectures. This one is all on you. At least Beatrix means well with her concern, I think my mother just likes being miserable."

"I'd happily trade," I grumble. "I hate being fussed over." It feels too similar to pity, which is a reaction I'd do almost anything to avoid.

"Think of it as your first official diplomatic negotiation."

I groan. "I'd honestly rather go to war."

Alix laughs. "Yeah, it seems like that's how everyone in *Game of Thrones* feels too."

It's nearly 10:00 p.m. when I head downstairs to look for Beatrix. A large part of me hopes she's already asleep...at least this way, I can say I tried to find her.

I make my way down the creaky wooden stairs, each step echoing softly in the empty house, and shoulder open the heavy door leading to the dining room.

The dining room is enveloped in darkness, with shadows growing more pronounced in the corners. The sole source of light is the full moon, which shines through the large windows and casts a glow on the polished oak dining table. My vision gradually adjusts, allowing the shapes of the furniture to emerge. Suddenly, something stirs in the shadows, causing my heart to jump into my throat.

"Gods fucking dammit!" I exclaim, jumping backwards. "You scared me."

"Sorry," Kastian replies, not sounding very sorry at all.

He's sitting alone at the far end of the long dining table, his broad-shouldered silhouette just visible by the light of the moon. He's holding a large goblet, gently swirling the liquid inside it. On the table in front of him sits an unlit candle, its wax dripped and hardened around the base as if it extinguished some time ago.

I storm across the room to the hutch where I know there are matches, grumbling under my breath. "I don't know why you'd want to sit in the damn dark. What are you even doing here?"

Kastian shifts in his seat. "I should be asking you that."

I stop short. "Excuse me? I'm not the one drinking alone in the dark."

He chuckles bitterly. "Do you really want to start trying to tell me what I can and can't do, Princess?"

"Fine, you're right." I turn my nose up, dismissing him. "I don't really care what you do, I was just looking for Beatrix."

The door to the kitchen is on the opposite side of the room, directly across from the door to the entrance hall. I square my shoulders and stomp past Kastian, refusing to look at him. I brush past him, but his large hand whips out and closes around my wrist, halting me in my tracks.

"Let go," I hiss.

"What are you doing?" he demands, making no move to drop my arm.

I narrow my eyes. "I just told you, I'm looking for Beatrix. I—"

I take an involuntary step back as Kastian gets abruptly to his feet, his chair clattering against the stone floor. Still holding my wrist tightly between us, he towers over me, close enough now that I can see every detail of his handsome face in the dark.

"I mean, what the fuck are you doing, Odessa? How can you even consider this?"

"I don't know what you're talking about." I try to yank my wrist from his grasp, but he won't let go.

His lip tips up in a contemptuous sneer. "Don't play dumb, it's not attractive."

"As if I care if you find me attractive. Let me go!"

Kastian makes an angry noise in the back of his throat. "I don't understand why you would ever agree to go to Hydratta. I know you're not this naïve."

I suck in a sharp breath, startled both by the anger in his voice and his sudden proximity. I haven't heard Kastian angry in years—not since before he went to Dyaspora—and a tiny, evil part of me likes it.

I like unravelling his careful self-control...I always have.

"Were you even listening to the emissary earlier?" I ask, jutting my chin out and meeting his gaze head-on. "They're offering us way too much with no explanation. Someone needs to go find out why. We need information about Hydratta, and this is the best—"

"It doesn't have to be you," he growls, cutting me off. "You're not a fighter. You're not even as strong as the average Fae."

"Why should that matter?" I demand hotly, finally yanking my arm from his grip to punctuate my point. "I'm more than capable of taking care of myself. And regardless, it's not really any of your business."

"Of course it's my business."

"Oh, please," I scoff. "You don't care about—"

"He killed my entire fucking family!" Kastian shouts in my face, all pretense of calm crumbling in a single instance.

Quick as a blink, my temper flares, matching his rage blow for blow. "I know!" I scream back. "That's the entire fucking point!"

I'm sure the entire house can already hear the echoes of us shouting at each other, but I can't bring myself to care as Kastian takes another aggressive step toward me. Instinctively, I back up, nearly tripping over the upturned chair. I stop when my spine is mere inches away from hitting the wall.

His lips pull back from his teeth in a snarl. "So you want to marry the male who destroyed my entire life? I don't know what I ever did to make you hate me so much."

The words are simple, but they hit me like a physical blow.

He really *doesn't* know—*and isn't that the entire point?*

"Your arrogance is staggering," I hiss. "Not everything is about you, *Your Majesty.*"

"Not everything is about me, but this sure as hell is. My mortal enemy, the man who organized the murder of my entire family and got me sent to Dyaspora, is going to marry my—"

I suck in a sharp breath at the same moment as he breaks off mid-sentence, looking suddenly confused. My heart thunders against my chest as I tilt my head back to meet his furious gaze.

"Your what?" I rasp.

His mortal enemy is marrying his...*what?*

What am I to him?

"My best friend's sister," he finishes, on a growl.

His best friend's sister. Of course.

I don't think that's what he was originally going to say, but I'll never know for sure. I don't think even Kastian knows what he meant to say.

Because until the day he dies he'll never remember me...and I can't ever tell him why.

I let out the breath I was holding on a growl and shove both hands against his chest. "Move. I can't deal with this, and I don't owe you any explanations."

Kastian doesn't move an inch, as if my shoving my entire body weight against him were no more than a light breeze. "Do you really think that Magnus will hesitate to hurt you too?"

"I think if you can't already understand why it's worth the risk to find out, then I'm not going to waste any more of my time explaining it to you!" I shove him again. "Now, move!"

"No," he snaps back, shaking his head as if to clear it. "This conversation isn't over."

"Yes, it is. Move, or I'll make you."

"And how are you going to do that?" He smirks bitterly. "What are you going to do, Princess? Cook my brain like that damn shopkeeper?"

"Maybe!" I snap.

"Try. It won't work."

"Of course it would," I hiss. "You're not that special, *Your Majesty*."

"Try," he repeats, taunting me.

I let out a growl of frustration. I cannot do this with him. This is all too much; too familiar. One hundred years of pent-up anger is at risk of exploding everywhere, leaving me shattered in the process.

Like she's rising to defend me before I break, the little voice in the back of my head that I always try to keep buried pushes to the forefront. The voice is all siren. She feeds on fury and desire and often can't tell the difference between the two. Now, she wants me to forget about hurt feelings and stupid mortal problems and take what she's always known belongs to her.

I lean forward until my mouth is barely a breath away from his. I hear myself speak in the same coaxing, seductive tone I used on the shopkeeper. The same tone I used on Kastian decades ago. "Move, Kastian."

For a fraction of a second I hold my breath, thinking maybe he's right—Maybe this time it won't work on him—but then I hear his strangled voice repeating the same surrender as every other man. "As you wish."

The siren inside me smiles with smug satisfaction, and I let out the breath I was holding. But before I can even think—before I'm sure if I'm glad or disappointed—Kastian follows my order and *moves*.

He leans in and captures my bottom lip between his.

For perhaps half a heartbeat I'm too stunned to react. Then, the shock sharpens into something molten, electric, and all too familiar.

I part my lips with a soft gasp, and that sound is like the opening note of a crescendo.

My back hits the wall, softened by his hand pressed against the stone, as he tilts his head to intensify the kiss. Kastian's tongue moves over mine, exploring with a slow, rough, and possessive fervor that sends shivers down my spine. He tastes of sweet dark wine and something else, something untamed and metallic.

My hands slam against his chest, fingers curling and clawing as they slide upward, seizing the fabric of his shirt in a fierce grip. He lets out a deep, guttural groan from the back of his throat, a primal sound that reverberates through both of us.

We've kissed before, but not like this. Before was innocent and new.

This is anything but innocent.

His hand abruptly detaches from the wall, and he seizes the back of my head, fingers tangling in my hair. My teeth catch his bottom lip, desperate and reckless. I let out a soft whimper, squirming as I push my hips firmly against his and feel the hard outline of his cock pressing into me.

I want his hands all over my body. I don't want to be slow or romantic. I don't need the foreplay—I'm already drenched in anticipation, and I just want to feel him inside me. I ache for it.

As if he read my mind, Kastian pulls back from my mouth, hunger flashing in his eyes. He seizes the delicate fabric of my dress at the neckline. The sound of ripping fabric fills the room as he yanks it down, exposing both of my breasts to the chill air. My already-hard nipples pebble into almost painful points.

He growls low in his throat. "Fuck."

I arch my spine as he traces kisses down my neck, moving lower, his lips searing my skin with fiery intensity as they enclose around one achingly taut nipple. A surge of electric pleasure makes my back curve even further.

I reach between us, fingers grazing over his belt. Reckless

passion and excitement flood me, and the siren rises to the forefront of my mind. She feeds on this—on desire and control.

She wants to devour him.

Like a cold wave over my head, panic hits me all too fast, completely washing away my arousal. I shove hard at Kastian's chest again. "Wait, stop!"

This time, he responds immediately to my shoving. He takes a step back, chest heaving with heavy breaths. "What's wrong?"

"I'm sorry!" I blurt out, scrambling to pull my dress back up. The thought of the siren sobered me all too fast, and now I'm reeling. "I didn't mean to do that."

"You didn't mean to do that?" he echoes slowly.

Oh no. He probably has no idea what I'm even saying right now, and it's all my fault.

Shame and disgust descend over me in waves as the horror of what I just did fully dawns on me. Accident or not, I can't believe I lost control.

I've never used the siren compulsion for its intended purpose. I've never—*never*—lured a man to my bed, and ultimately to his death. I'm revolted at the thought of purposefully doing that to anyone, even to Kastian. *Especially to Kastian.*

"It'll wear off if I leave," I mutter to myself, trying to push my way out from under his arm. "I'm so sorry, I—"

Kastian shifts, blocking me from leaving. "Where the fuck are you going?"

This cannot be happening.

I only ever use the siren song for small, inconsequential things, but that's not really what it's for. If I wanted to, I could demand anything.

Love me.

Give your life to protect me.

Drown yourself...

Walk away and never speak to me again...

"Move, Kastian," I demand, nearly crying now. "I'm serious. You need to get away from me, or it will only get worse."

"What are you talking about?" he demands, wiping roughly at his mouth with the back of his hand.

"I bewitched you," I wail hysterically. "But it's going to be okay. I'll leave, and it'll wear off in a few minutes."

Unless I somehow made him obsessed with me, in which case it won't ever wear off.

No, I can't worry about that right now. It will be fine; it has to be.

The sound of Kastian's laughter jolts me out of my spiral of shame.

"You didn't do anything to me," he scoffs. "At least, not the way you mean it."

"Of course I did. Why else would you kiss me like that? You *hate* me."

"I can think of a few reasons." He smirks. "And I don't hate you, Dessa, even if you are the most infuriating woman I've ever met."

I shake my head. "Of course *right now* you don't hate me, because I just sapped you of all your free will. Oh my gods, what is wrong with me? Why—"

"Odessa! Look at me!" he barks, his tone sharp and commanding. He grips the back of my head again, but this time instead of pulling me in for a kiss he yanks my head back so I'm forced to meet his eyes. "I'm *fine*. I mean, I'm clearly losing my mind, but not because of your magic."

I blink in surprise. His eyes are clear. "How is that possible?"

"I told you," Kastian says flatly. "Your power won't work on me."

I shake my head again, so confused and overwhelmed I can hardly think. "It works on all men."

His smirk returns. "I'm not all men."

Startled, I choke and almost laugh. "Arrogant prick."

His hand tightens in my hair. "Spoiled princess."

I shiver and for a long second we stand still and silent. Kastian lets his hand fall away from my hair, but he doesn't step back. My breathing turns ragged once more, and my mind reels.

If I didn't bewitch him, then this is just us, and somehow that's even worse.

Holding Kastian at arm's length, antagonizing each other, and convincing myself to hate him is the only way I've been able to survive the last year, but I can't do it again. Another year of this might kill me...something needs to give.

"Once," I blurt out.

Kastian's face twists in confusion. "Once what?"

"We do this once. Just to...get it out of our systems, and then we never have to think about it again."

His eyes darken, and his voice comes out hoarse and raspy. "You really think once will be enough?"

No.

"It will have to be because that's all I'm offering...if you want it, that is."

For a long moment, Kastian stays silent, conflict warring on his face.

My cheeks heat and my heart thunders against my chest so loud that I know he can hear it, just the same as I can hear the way his uneven breathing speeds up the longer he looks at me with indecision in his eyes. If I was wrong and he still doesn't want me, I might die of humiliation right here and now.

"Fuck it," Kastian growls.

He moves suddenly, gripping my thighs and hoisting me into the air before I've even had a moment to realize what's happening. He pins my body between the wall and his broad chest, and his hips press firmly into me, and I can feel the undeniable evidence of his desire, still hard and ready.

He doesn't kiss me this time, instead pressing his face into my neck as his hands glide over my sides, tracing the contours of my body, before settling around the curve of my ass, pulling me even closer.

I writhe against him, chasing the heat of several minutes ago.

My fingers tremble as I reach between us, feeling the cool leather of his belt beneath my touch. I fumble with the metal buckle, struggling to unfasten it.

He growls against my skin and shifts his hips, batting my hand away. "Stop,"

I whine in the back of my throat. I want to beg, but I force a teasing smile onto my face and keep my tone light. "Changed your mind already?"

In answer, he grinds his hips even harder into my core. "Not a fucking chance. But if I only get you once, then I'm going to make it count. I don't want to fuck you fast against this wall; I want all night to feel you come over and over on my fingers and my tongue so when I finally fuck you, you're begging me for it."

My eyes fly wide, and a tiny whimper escapes me. *Oh, fuck. I'm in so much trouble.*

Whatever happens now, I know once won't be nearly enough. I know that it won't matter whether I walk away or I drown in him all night long. In the morning, he'll still have ruined me.

KASTIAN, PRESENT

O*nce.*

Once is such a torturous trap.

On the one hand, it's perfect.

If I thought she wanted anything else from me than to "get this out of her system," I'd worry if it was fair to her to start something when I already know I'll never be able to form a soul-bond with her. But just once means I don't have to tell her.

On the other hand, *once* is like taking a single hit of opium and expecting not to want more. Like expecting a single drop of water to turn a desert into an ocean. I already know it won't be enough, but I'm past caring.

I feel like I'm cheerfully sprinting to my own execution as I carry Odessa up the stairs to my bedroom. I finally understand why the men who get lured in by the sirens die with smiles on their faces.

"Where are we going?" Odessa asks as we climb the stairs.

"My room," I say into her skin, unable to stop myself from

pressing my face into the curve of her neck, and breathing in her ocean and floral scent.

Dessa shivers but says nothing else until we reach my second-floor bedroom and I shoulder open the door. She twists in my arms, looking around.

The room is neat and clean with very little in the way of personal effects—just the way I prefer it. The furniture is whatever was here when I moved in, and the most I've done to change things around is put my clothes in the wardrobe.

"I like what you've done with the place," Dessa says sarcastically.

"Well, some of us like to see the floor," I tease her, thinking of her disastrous bedroom.

Looking affronted, she glances up at the ceiling, and her eyebrows pull low.

Fuck.

I see the wheels turning in her mind and I know she realizes that this room is directly below hers, and if I let her think about it too long, she'll also remember that the walls in the manor are relatively thin and the floors creak. I can always tell when she's gone to bed, when she's pacing in the middle of the night and when she trips over that mess on her floor.

Hoping to distract her before she has the chance to put two and two together, I kick the door closed behind me and cross the room in two strides where I put her down on my sharply made bed.

She scrambles onto her knees and looks up at me from beneath her eyelashes, not in a seductive way but more like she's nervous. For once, I think I understand why.

It's hard to pretend this is some rash, irresponsible mistake that we can blame on poor judgment in the heat of the moment. The walk between the dining room and my bedroom made it all too clear that whatever this is, it's a choice.

I reach out and run a hand through her hair, stopping when

my fingers graze her throat. I leave them there, not squeezing, just resting against her pounding pulse. "Don't look at me like that."

She blinks. "Like what?"

"Like you're about to bolt at any moment."

She flushes and bites her lip, her pulse fluttering beneath my fingers. I watch her violet eyes shift from my face, down my chest, and linger around my stomach. My blood heats and my entire body tightens, growing hot with anticipation.

"Is that better?" she asks, teasing.

A growl rumbles through my chest, and I flex my fingers against her throat. "Much, but I still want to hear you say it."

Siren or not, I need to hear her give over control to me or I won't be able to justify to myself all the depraved things I'm already planning to do to her.

She smiles wickedly, the heat in her eyes still simmering just below the surface. "I want it...just once."

Good enough.

My fingers tighten on her throat before I'm sure if I intended to pull her toward me to claim her mouth or shove her backwards against the bed. Somehow, I manage both at once, and our lips collide as she splays on her back, tugging at my shirt until I fall over her with one arm braced over her head.

All hesitance gone, Odessa opens her mouth, tangling her tongue with mine. Her fingers dig into my scalp, nails raking, pulling me impossibly closer until every inch of me aches to be inside her.

My hands roam, mapping the ridges of her ribs, the curve of her waist, memorizing the geography of her skin, knowing this might be the only time I'll ever be allowed to touch her. She arches under my touch, breath hitching as I slide my palm up, massaging her breast. She whimpers, and her hand joins mine, trying to tug down the neck of her already-torn gown.

I pull back from her, rocking back on my heels. "Turn around."

She cocks an eyebrow at me, but twists to show me her back. Her dress has hundreds of infuriatingly tiny buttons.

I groan. "Do you like this dress?"

"Not really," she says, out of breath. "You already tore it beyond repair."

"Perfect."

I grip the fabric in both hands and tear it down the center, tiny pearl-shaped buttons flying everywhere, pinging off the walls and floor. Underneath, she's wearing a corset that covers only her stomach to the top of her hipbones, leaving her breasts bare—probably to make them appear larger, despite the fact that she absolutely requires no help in that area.

She twists back around in the pooling fabric of her torn dress and smirks at me.

Unable to hold back, I gather the remnants of her dress and toss them onto the floor, then grip her thighs and tug her toward the end of the bed. She shrieks and falls flat on her back, and I slide back off the bed. Standing between her legs, I look down at her, taking in every inch of my prize.

Her long hair—which looks sometimes red and sometimes blonde depending on the lighting—fans out around her in waves. Her lips are swollen from kissing, and her skin is flushed all over. The lacy cream-colored corset pushes her tits up practically to her chin, and her blush-pink nipples are hard and just begging to be licked.

For the love of the fucking gods. She's so damn beautiful it's distracting. I want to blurt that out, just to expel the thought from my head, but I know Odessa already knows she's beautiful —she's likely been told that a dozen times a day since she was a teenager and I notice how she flinches when anyone brings it up.

So I bite the inside of my cheek to keep from speaking and focus on her soft skin beneath my fingers. I trail up her thighs until I reach the edges of her lace panties and dip my fingers beneath the lace to skim the divot where her leg meets her hips.

She gasps and wriggles her hips, sliding closer to me, clearly urging me to go faster. Half-obliging, I skim my fingers over the front of her panties, and she shivers. "Kastian..."

I bite the inside of my cheek harder, tasting blood.

I fucking love hearing her say my name, like she has a right to it. I want to hear her say it over and over. All night. Every day for the rest of my immortal life.

"Just once."

Suddenly frustrated, I fist the fabric of her panties in one hand and yank. The fabric tears, and I rip it away, tossing the scraps of ruined lace on the floor with the dress and all the tiny broken buttons. Odessa gasps in surprise and starts to sit up, but I splay my fingers across her lower stomach and push her back down. "Don't move."

Her eyes narrow. "Excuse me?"

I hold my hand firm against her stomach, not giving her an inch. "Didn't you hear me before? I want to feel you coming all over my fingers and my face, and then I'll consider letting you have my cock."

"You'll let me?" she hisses.

I ignore her. She'll figure out soon enough that I don't like to share control.

Odessa's expression is indignant, but I can see the lust and curiosity in the way she shudders when I run my fingers again over her bare cunt and dip between her folds. Finally, she whimpers, unable to maintain that haughty, annoyed expression as I slide one finger inside her and draw it back out slowly. "...So fucking wet for me."

I bring my fingers to my mouth and suck. Her eyes bug out of her head, focused on my mouth. She rolls her hips, and I chuckle, sliding my fingers back inside her. This time, I add a second and scissor them, stretching her tight cunt wide until she gasps.

My cock throbs, wanting desperately to be included, but I force myself to ignore it. I refuse to rush this and waste my only opportunity to own Odessa—claim her as mine, if only temporarily.

She bucks her hips and grumbles with impatience, and I give in—a little. "Play with your nipples."

She glares down at me over the swell of her tits. "You do it."

I laugh. "I could, but I think you'd rather I did this."

Still moving my fingers in and out of her, I run the thumb of my other hand over her clit, rubbing gently until she whimpers with approval. I add my pointer finger, rolling her clit back and forth between the two. She gasps, cursing under her breath.

I smile widely, recognizing the words instantly.

Language isn't often relevant in Ellender because the entire continent is enchanted with universal language, but every so often there's a word or phrase from one kingdom that cannot be translated into the language of another. I smile as Dessa curses fluently in Hydrattan. I like the reminder that we're originally from the same place, and in another life I would have been her king.

"Play with your tits," I tell her again. "Don't make me ask you again, or I won't let you come."

She growls, even as her hands come up to graze over her taught nipple. "You arrogant ass."

I grin and curl my fingers inside her, stroking over her inner walls. She mewls with desperation, her hips arching off the bed as I trace fervent circles around and over her clit, striving to mirror the rhythm of her fingers teasing her nipples. Her breaths come faster, turning into ragged gasps as a flush blooms across her chest and creeps up to her cheeks.

"Oh my gods," she hisses, her eyes clenching shut as her mouth falls open in a silent scream.

She tightens around me, and it's an agonizing struggle to restrain myself from yanking out my cock and thrusting into her.

As I watch her come, my heartbeat racing wildly, my shoulder blades begin to throb with a dull ache. My eyes widen in alarm.

That's not good.

Fae wings only appear in highly emotional situations, like when your life is threatened, or occasionally during sex.

I've never lost control with anyone to the point that my wings appeared during sex, not even when I was younger. I close my eyes and try to force my shoulder muscles to relax. *Deep breath in...*

I breathe in a lungful of Odessa's intoxicating scent at the same moment as she opens her eyes and looks up at me from the bed. It only makes things worse, and I swear I can feel the wings pressing against my skin as if trying to burst out.

Fuck me.

Mercifully, Odessa chooses that moment to distract me. "Not bad, *Your Majesty*."

My eyebrows pull low. "*Not bad*?"

"I'd certainly give you points for enthusiasm."

"You—"

I'm about to flip her over and spank her ass *with enthusiasm*, but my shoulders throb again, and I know I need to do something about it before things get out of hand.

Moving quickly, I undo my belt and drop it on the floor, then kick my boots off, not paying any attention to where they land. I hesitate for a moment with my hand on the top button of my shirt. If I take it off, she'll see the tattoo, which would require a lot of explanation I don't care to get into right now.

I glance at the dark windows and decide it's dim enough in the room to risk it—especially when soon Odessa will be far too distracted to notice.

I drop the shirt on the floor and climb onto the bed, then shift to lie flat on my back. I reach for Odessa, pulling her roughly on top of me. *Let the wings try to come out now.*

Completely unaware of the reason behind my sudden change in position, Dessa easily obliges. She adjusts, her knees falling to the bed, bracketing my hips. She grinds against my already painfully throbbing cock, and I dig my nails into her calves just to keep from losing control and impaling her.

I reach between us and run my fingers over her. "You're dripping all over me. Now tell me again how '*not bad*' that was."

Dessa looks dazedly down at me and manages to smirk. "I've had better."

My chest suddenly burns, and even though I know she's fucking with me, I can't stop myself from reacting. "That's bullshit. Who was it?"

She smiles smugly as she runs her palms up my chest and follows them with her mouth, trailing her lips up my neck. She stops when she reaches my ear, sucking on it and trailing her tongue over the pointed tip before whispering her reply in my ear. "Wouldn't you like to know?"

A growl of frustration rumbles through my chest. Yes, I would like to know. I want to know the names of everyone who's ever touched her so I can find them and kill them slowly and painfully.

The thought that she might have ever "had better" is unbearable. I want to destroy her for anyone else. I want to own her, want her undone and helpless. I want her to forget everything and everyone else but me.

I grip the outside of her thighs, tugging her forward, up over my chest. She rocks on her hips, and nearly topples over before her hands slam into the wall above my headboard.

I give her no warning before I dig my fingers into her ass and jerk her down, grinding her cunt onto my mouth so hard that her startled shriek is loud enough to wake the entire house.

She's still drenched from her first orgasm, so I don't start slow or ease her into it. I wrap both arms around her hips, hauling her forward, and flick my tongue greedily from her entrance all the way up to her clit.

I want to taste every inch of her, burn it so deeply into my mind that even when she's gone, I'll still be able to conjure it in the dark: the dizzying slickness of her, the way she gasps and swears in fragmented Hydrattan, the way her legs tremble uncontrollably as I flatten my tongue against her over and over in a relentless rhythm that makes her thighs shake and her knees buckle.

I wrap my lips around her clit and suck. There's a loud bang, like she slammed her palms against the wall, before she lets out a noise that sounds like both a sob and a laugh.

"Fuck, you're going to kill me," she pants, voice gone breathless and wild. "Don't you dare stop."

So I don't. I give her everything: swirling, licking, sucking, my nose buried so deep against her sweet, slick heat that I'm half certain I could literally drown in her. Drown with a smile on my face just like every other weak idiot who chased after a siren.

Odessa screams and convulses, thighs crushing my ears, nails scraping against the wall, and I ride out every wave, drinking her in, humming with satisfaction as she melts into me, boneless and barely coherent.

I let her slump forward as the aftershocks roll through her in fractured shudders. Then, when she finally catches her breath, I slide her off my face and onto my chest.

"Not bad?" I tease, licking her taste from my lips.

She glowers down at me, cheeks flushed, but the effect is ruined by the way her legs are still trembling. "You cocky son of a bitch."

"That's more like it."

I roll her gently onto her back and settle between her legs, licking a stripe up her inner thigh, slow and languid now. She writhes, hands slipping from the headboard to frame my face, fingernails raking lightly at my jaw.

"You're insatiable," she moans, voice half-resentful, half-awed.

I level her with a wicked smirk, then press a kiss to her hipbone, drawing it out until she's squirming again. "And you're delicious."

Her eyes flutter, pupils blown wide and dark. I can see her trying to gather herself, to summon up the energy to say something flippant or biting, but she's still undone, still shaking a little from the force of her orgasm. Good. I want her like this: spent, delirious, and at my mercy.

I slide up her body, planting hot, open-mouthed kisses on the swells over her breasts, along her sternum, the delicate line of her throat. She tilts her head to give me better access, and for a moment, I slow, savoring the way she tastes, the way her skin is still flushed and damp beneath my tongue.

But the self-control I've been so smugly congratulating myself for is rapidly going up in smoke.

My cock is so hard it hurts, a throbbing pulse that refuses to be ignored. All I can think about is how perfect she'd feel around me. How good it would be to lose myself in her.

She must sense it, because her hand snakes between us and she undoes the button of my trousers with a flick of her thumb. She reaches beneath the fabric and closes her fist around me, squeezing as if she wants to remind me who's really in control here. My hips jerk, and I rock involuntarily into her palm, biting back a groan.

Odessa shimmies higher on the bed and lets her knees fall wide. I brace my hand on the headboard above her, and lock eyes with her. There's a split second where the world thins to a pinpoint, every single muscle in my body wound tight. Her gaze is fire and challenge, her lips parted, her breath coming in shallow, eager pants.

I grip her by the hips, hard enough that I'll probably leave bruises for days, and line myself up against her center, fighting the primal urge to just slam into her, and instead let the moment crescendo—so that when I finally slide into her, almost painfully slow, there's no turning back.

She's impossibly tight and wet, the heat of her swallowing me whole. She wraps her legs tightly around my hips and reaches up to clasp her fingers around my neck. I thrust deeper, filling her again.

I hadn't intended to take her like this—facing each other—and it feels too intimate. I'm not sure how to feel about how I can see everything playing out on her face in real time—the startled lift of her brows as I bottom out, and then a beat later the shuddering release as her whole body accepts me in, clinging and pulsing with greedy need.

Her violet eyes flash indigo, and she holds my stare as her hips grind up, pulling me deeper, as if she wants to keep me right there at the edge of madness for as long as possible. I feel her everywhere: knotted around me, trembling against my chest, fingernails digging crescents into my biceps as she yanks me closer with every thrust.

I slam into her again, and again, only semi-aware of all the noise we're making and of the bed creaking and groaning as it slams into the wall. Buttons, torn clothing, bits of crumbled drywall litter the floor. The blankets and pillows on the bed are twisted, and feathers from the mattress float through the air.

The once clean, almost sterile, space looks like it was hit by a storm.

Hurricane Odessa.

Her mouth finds mine with a desperation so sharp it hurts; she bites my lower lip, hard enough to draw blood, and then lets it go with a gasp that's half-laugh, half-moan.

I slam into her one final time, and feel her tremble around me as I erupt with a shout inside her. And at the same moment, the muscles on my back ripple again, and there's nothing I can do to stop it before my wings burst from my shoulders.

KASTIAN, AGE 18

"Your home is beautiful!" Queen Regina of Vernallis gushes. "It's so impressive how you've been able to do so much with so few resources."

"Oh. Well, thank you," my mother replies, sounding startled.

"You will have to tell your kitchen to share the recipe for this fish with our chef. I'm always saying we should serve simpler meals from time to time."

I grind my teeth and stab my fork into my fish with unnecessary force.

The full dining room is loud and buzzing with activity, but almost none of the chatter is coming from the high table where I sit with my parents, the king and queen of Vernallis, their son Prince Thorne, and my oldest sister Serena. My other two sisters, Dellanore and Avaline, were excused from dinner, probably because my mother guessed—correctly—that they wouldn't be able to resist taunting the Vernalli prince.

I wish I'd been excused too. Dinner has been an uncomfortable affair, and we're barely halfway through the fish course.

Queen Regina exalts herself and seems to take her pleasure from tossing thinly veiled insults at my mother across the dining table. Mother is too polite to acknowledge it, so the Queen of Vernallis keeps blurting out more and more obvious slights in an effort to gain a reaction. On the opposite side of the table, my father is talking to King Florian. It doesn't seem to be going any better than Mother's attempts at diplomacy.

I glance over at where my sister is attempting to make conversation with Prince Thorne. I lean in to listen just in time to hear him make a rude comment about her appearance.

Fuck this.

I shove my chair back abruptly and stand. All eyes at the table turn to me, and my father raises a questioning eyebrow.

"Uh, I just need some air," I mutter, stepping back from the table.

Before anyone can stop me, I push my chair back in and stride toward the short steps that separate our raised table from the rest of the busy dining room.

"Excuse him," my father says behind me. "His betrothed just entered the hall. You know how young princes can be."

King Florian laughs, and the stilted conversation resumes.

I grind my teeth but don't turn around. I hadn't even noticed Lady Lyra enter the room, I simply had to leave before I did something stupid. Punching the prince of our neighboring kingdom would not be the best way to start this summit...even if he deserved it.

I avoid catching anyone's eye as I stride along the far side of the busy dining hall. Eight long tables, packed with food and finely dressed nobles of both courts, fill the cavernous room, their chatter echoing off the vaulted ceilings.

At least the courtiers all seem to be getting along.

In theory, we're here because Prince Thorne is interested in marrying my sister, but we all know that's not the real reason.

An event like this is intended to let the courtiers mingle with each other while the royals talk politics. Undoubtedly dozens of marriages and business agreements will come out of the next three days, but none of them will involve the royal families.

No one in my family has ever married outside our own court. My own uninspiring betrothal is the perfect example of that.

Despite my father's excuses to the Vernalli royals, I have no desire to stop and talk to Lyra, and I duck my head, pretending not to see her as I push open the heavy double doors and step out into the corridor.

Mercifully, no one else is out here. On one side of the long hall is the polished stone wall, which drowns out any sound from the dining room behind it. On the opposite side, the wall is open and lined with white stone pillars and a low railing, which overlooks the rocky cliffs and ocean beyond the castle.

I cross the hall and lean on the railing. In the distance, I can see the chimneys of the nearby city and the tall masts of the docked ships.

I've barely had a moment to catch my breath when the doors open again behind me, bringing the sounds of the dining room out into the quiet corridor.

"Your Highness?" a familiar voice asks as the creaking doors swing shut again.

"What is it, Magnus?" I growl.

Magnus Von Bargen, my father's favorite advisor, comes to stand beside me. I begrudgingly turn to acknowledge him.

Magnus is a thin, white man of above average height, with blonde hair, which hints that he's originally from Thermia— though I've never asked. Technically, he's my future father-in-law, but our relationship has never been anything other than prince and courtier.

"Your father wanted me to remind you that it leaves a bad impression on the court of Vernallis for you to disappear in the middle of dinner."

"He said that, did he?"

Magnus huffs a breath and throws me a placating smile. "Well, no, not precisely...but you know what I mean."

I sigh and roll my eyes—I understand exactly what he's getting at.

My father is incredibly predictable, and so set in his ways that Magnus can foresee his words before they're even spoken. Like earlier, when Magnus practically dragged me outside onto the balcony so the arriving Vernalli nobles would get the full effect of our entire family looking down on them. I don't like crowds or putting on political theater, but predictably, my father didn't care, and Magnus was sent to tell me so.

Father's predictability is why Magnus has become my father's chief advisor; essentially his sole advisor. Although Father doesn't typically take advice from anyone, if he ever chose to, Magnus's opinion would be the only one he'd consider.

"What do you think Father would do if I punched Prince Thorne in the middle of dinner?" I ask, conversationally.

To his credit, Magnus doesn't seem surprised by the question and considers it. "I think he'd tell you that if you must, save it for after dinner."

I let out a startled bark of laughter. He's absolutely right; Father wouldn't care about the violence, only that it was unplanned. Losing control is a far greater sin in my father's eyes than anything else. I could probably get away with murder as long as it was well thought out.

"I'll be back in a moment. Less than five minutes, I promise."

He gives me an almost affectionate clap on the shoulder. "Fine. But if you're not back by then, I'll send Lyra out here to get you."

I wrinkle my nose but just nod. I believe Magnus means well by sending his daughter, and I don't want to offend him by asking for someone else.

I've been betrothed to Lady Lyra Von Bargen since before I was able to speak in full sentences. I can only assume the arrangement has something to do with my father's affection for the man who just left, because it certainly has nothing to do with my affection—or lack thereof—for Lyra.

I don't precisely dislike her, but I've never been able to picture myself married to her either. Everyone says I'll feel differently about it when we eventually form a soul-bond, but I can't imagine that happening either. Bonds tend to form from intense emotional shared experiences, and I can't recall ever seeing Lyra show even a hint of emotion about anything. A full-scale riot could break out in front of her and she would nod and clap politely like she was attending the opera.

I turn back to the view of the open ocean, sucking in a deep, calming breath. The evening air tastes like the ocean and the sweet orchid blossoms blooming along the rocky coast.

The door behind me opens again, and I stiffen. *For fuck's sake.*

I spin on my heel, expecting to see Magnus. "I said five minutes, that wasn't—" I stop short mid-sentence.

It's not Magnus or even Lyra. Instead, there's a pretty girl with cascading red hair standing in the doorway, her blue eyes wide with surprise as my shout echoes down the hall.

I clear my throat and step back against the railing. "Sorry. I thought you were someone else."

The girl blinks up at me, letting the door swing shut behind her as the confusion clears from her face. I wait for her to bow her head and insist the uncomfortable moment was her fault—just like any other courtier would do—but she doesn't.

Instead, her eyes narrow and she scoffs. "Gods, I'm an idiot. I should have known," she mumbles to herself, before tossing her hair over her shoulder and flouncing away from me without so much as a curtsy.

I stare after her, dumbstruck.

"Excuse me," I blurt out, taking a lurching step after the girl.

Again, she ignores me. She walks down the hall, far enough that it's clear she's trying to put space between us, and leans on the railing overlooking the ocean just as I was doing a moment ago.

I sense my heartbeat quicken—it's not anger. It's indignation. Curiosity.

"Excuse me!" I repeat, striding toward her. "Did you hear me?"

The girl glances over her shoulder at me. "I don't know how it would be possible not to hear you. Do you always yell at strangers like that?"

I blink in surprise, and answer her out of sheer force of habit. "No."

"Good." She turns away to look at the ocean again. "I would hate to think all the rumors about you are true...although, evidently, most are. That's disappointing."

I stop a few yards away from her. "What rumors?"

She sighs as if I'm annoying her.

As if *I'm* annoying *her. Unbelievable.*

She waves a hand in the air, still refusing to face me. "Oh, you know."

My stomach lurches. "No...I don't know."

"You must know everyone says you're as arrogant and cruel as Thorne—" she clears her throat. "Sorry, *Prince* Thorne, I mean."

I blink several times. Who is saying that?

I'm not arrogant—at least, not in any way that I don't have every right to be. If I'm not especially personable, it's only because I detest large groups of people. I can't mingle with the court like everyone else. I have responsibilities, and—

I shake my head. Why am I even worrying about this? Who the hell is this girl who thinks she can insult me to my face?

"What's your name?" I demand, well aware that my tone is just as rude as she accused me of being.

"Why?" she asks without looking at me.

"Because I'd like to know the name of the person insulting me," I snap.

She looks over her shoulder again, and this time our eyes meet. For a second time, I feel the need to take a step back as my breath catches in my throat.

This girl is more than just pretty—she's stunning. Breathtakingly beautiful, in a way that's almost unsettling.

Her eyes, which I initially thought were blue, are actually a striking violet, like the orchids that grow around our castle. Her cheeks are flushed, and her cupid's bow lips look pink and swollen, as if she was just kissed. My eyes wander over her heart-shaped face, down her throat, and over her soft curves beneath a criminally tight dress.

My stomach does another strange flip. It's like I missed a step walking down stairs and for a fraction of a second I feel wildly out of control. I tear my eyes away and clear my throat, running one hand over the back of my neck.

"I'm Kastian," I blurt out, the words sounding foreign as if I've forgotten my own name.

The girl rolls her eyes. "I know."

I clear my throat again. "And you are?"

"Not any of your concern."

A growl of frustration bubbles up in my chest, and it takes a monumental effort to push it back down. I take a breath through my nose and let it out slowly, willing myself to stay in control.

"Clearly I offended you," I start again. "I apologize. I thought you were someone else, and—"

"Yes, so you said," she interrupts. "Apology accepted. Now, do you mind? I'm occupied at the moment."

I look from her out to the ocean beyond the castle and back, my brow furrowing. "Occupied by what?"

She lets out a sharp, annoyed breath, and answers without turning to look at me. "I wanted to see the ships."

I glance in the direction she's looking. There are at least two dozen tall masts on the horizon, but the harbor is too far away to make them out clearly. "I still don't understand."

"Do you have to?" she asks.

"I simply want to know."

She rounds on me again. "Right, but do you have to? You have every right to ask a question, but you don't have the right to hear the answer if I don't want to give it. Unless you believe you're so important that you can compel me to answer you. Do you think that? Do you believe that your curiosity is worth more than my privacy?"

I grind my teeth. I've been speaking to this girl for less than five minutes and already I have a thousand questions. I've never met anyone who seemed to dislike me from the moment I opened my mouth. I'm moving past annoyed and toward angry. This girl is infuriating...and oddly fascinating.

Before I can think of what to say, the door to the hall opens again. The red-headed girl doesn't move, but I look over my shoulder already knowing that it will be Lyra coming to find me just as Magnus promised.

Sure enough, Lyra walks toward us, back straight and holding her pink gown off the floor. She stops in front of me with her head bowed. "Your Highness."

I barely resist the urge to roll my eyes. This is why I don't feel any draw to my betrothed—she's never even used my first name. Lyra is always, always polite and controlled. Just like the rest of the court.

...and nothing like the rude, beautiful girl from Vernallis.

My gaze darts back to the red-haired girl, suddenly compelled to know what she thinks of this. She's looking at Lyra with a bitter expression in her violet eyes.

Maybe it's not specifically me she hates, just nobility?

But that makes no sense either.

She must be a Vernalli noblewoman, or why else would she be here? As the crown prince of Hydratta, only someone of equal rank would dare turn their back on me or call Prince Thorne by his first name. Yet she can't be a princess, as the king and queen of Vernallis have no daughters. Perhaps she's a duke's daughter with a high opinion of herself? I suppose any woman who looked like that would have reason to think highly of herself. Maybe—

"Your Highness?" Lyra asks again.

Shit.

I shake my head, realizing that I'm staring again—and not at my betrothed. I almost feel guilty. Almost.

"What is it?" I ask, my voice sounding slightly choked.

"My father sent me to find you. It's time to return to dinner."

I run a frustrated hand over the back of my neck. "Yes. Fine, let's go."

I automatically hold out an arm to her, but Lyra doesn't move. Instead, she looks curiously at the Vernalli girl. My heartbeat kicks up again, and I find myself turning to watch them with renewed interest.

I'm not sure I've ever seen two Fae women who looked less alike. Lyra is tall and willowy with fair skin like her father and straight black hair that she must have inherited from her mother. She's undoubtedly beautiful in her own right, but it's hardly her fault that the Vernalli girl looks like the paintings of sirens in my father's study.

"Forgive me. I don't believe we've been introduced," Lyra says, finally breaking the tense silence.

I hold my breath as I watch the girl's eyes dart around, like she's trying to find an exit. Finally, she turns to Lyra and curtseys, tilting her chin toward the floor. "Forgive me. It's my fault, my lady."

I choke.

That's the reaction I was expecting her to give me when she first walked into the hall...so why should Lyra get the respect I was denied?

I don't understand this at all, and I hate that I want nothing more than to figure it out. Figure *her* out.

"What's your name?" Lyra asks finally.

"Odessa," the girl says, with the tiniest hint of bitterness in her tone.

"It's a pleasure to meet you, Lady Odessa," Lyra says tonelessly.

"Not 'lady,'" the girl corrects.

"Duchess, then?" I guess, cocking my head.

"No," Odessa shakes her bouncing curls. "I have no title. Now, excuse me, I'll leave you two alone."

She bobs a half-hearted curtsy, which I swear feels sarcastic, and walks away without a single glance back at us.

I feel Lyra's searching eyes on me as I finally let out the breath I was holding.

I glance at my betrothed, and raise a probing eyebrow at her.

Honestly, I want her to say something about this. Not that I was doing anything inappropriate per se, but most girls would be jealous, right?

I'd take anything—a hint of a reaction. A glimmer of emotion. *Anything.*

"Well, shall we return to dinner?" Lyra asks flatly.

I nod, only slightly disappointed, and offer her my arm again even as my mind wanders back to Odessa.

I swear, she seemed slightly familiar.

ODESSA, PRESENT

I've made a huge mistake.

That's all I can think as I wait for Kastian to fall asleep so I can slink back upstairs to my room.

It's all I can think about when I climb into my bed, still half undressed, and it's all I can think about in the morning, when the sun rises and I'm still wide awake.

I ruminate on my overwhelming stupidity as I bathe and dress, choosing a high-necked gown to cover the obvious bruises on my throat where Kastian sucked on my pulse. Then, I berate myself some more for being so incredibly weak while I pack clothing into a trunk and drag it out into the hallway for the servants to help carry downstairs.

I knew sleeping together wouldn't break the tension between Kastian and me, and sure enough, I was right. The pulsing need that I've been stubbornly ignoring for months now has only magnified, and my self-loathing is at an all-time high.

I should have known better.

No, *I did know better.* So what's wrong with me? Was this just curiosity?

The last time I saw Kastian, we were practically kids. We've never gotten this far before, and I didn't know how good it would be. Now, a large part of me wishes I could go back to not knowing.

And then there are the wings...

Fuck, the wings.

I feel so incredibly stupid that I sink to the ground beside my trunk, practically collapsing amidst the mess of discarded clothing on the rug. I have to resist the urge to bang my head against the top of my trunk.

The Fae—both male and female—only show their wings when their life is in danger or around their bonded partners. Seeing any Fae's wings during intimacy always means the beginning of a bond is forming, but the sex alone shouldn't have triggered it—that's never happened with any other Fae male I've slept with, and it shouldn't have happened last night.

Kastian and I are not bonded.

We didn't form a soul-bond all those years ago, and there's no reason it should happen now. Not when this version of Kastian could never feel anything but lust for me. This version hardly knows anything about me—I've made absolutely sure of that. I've been nothing but unpleasant and aloof toward him, so how could this happen?

Maybe it's a residual reaction—some phantom feeling from years ago that he can't actually explain?

That must be it, but that only means I've made an even bigger mistake than I could have imagined.

If this goes any further, everything I did will be for nothing.

I'll be back exactly where I was a century ago, and this time there won't be anyone there to fix it.

I won't get a third chance.

Suddenly resolute in what I have to do, I jump to my feet. It's still close to dawn, and hardly anyone will be awake yet. I'll need to leave for Hydratta now, before anyone notices I'm gone. Maybe by the time I come back, this lapse in sanity between Kastian and me will have fizzled itself out.

It's a pathetic lie, even in my head, and I don't believe it...but I have to pretend, anyway. Otherwise, there's no hope for either of us.

Deciding not to wait for the servants to carry my trunk, I leave my room and grip one handle to drag it down the hall myself. I barely make it a few feet before I'm groaning with the effort. I packed far too much, and outside the water I'm not much stronger than the average human.

I hold my skirt with one hand and grit my teeth as I tug the trunk to the end of the hall. I practically whimper when I look down the long flight of stairs. If I drag this all the way down to the first floor, the bumping of the heavy trunk against the steps will wake the entire house before I've even reached the second landing.

"Do you need some help?"

I whirl around, my hand flying to my chest.

Aurelia is leaning against the wall behind me, sucking on what looks like a blue flower stem. She has tied her dark hair in two loose braids and is again wearing a combination of Fae and human clothing—wide-legged linen trousers, riding boots, and a white T-shirt that I assume Alix gave her. It says "A LOT GOING ON AT THE MOMENT" in big black and red lettering.

"You scared me," I grumble, sinking onto the top of my trunk to catch my breath.

"You startle easily lately," she observes, pulling the flower stem out of her mouth with a pop.

I frown. She's not wrong. I guess being constantly on high alert for the last year has made me jumpy. "I hope I didn't wake you," I mutter. "It's early."

"You didn't. I never went to sleep. I've been working on a new idea all night."

I nod in understanding. The door that connects her tower

room to the main house is also on the third floor, but seeing as she hardly leaves the tower anymore, I didn't expect to see her here.

Aurelia twirls the blue flower stem between her fingers, and my gaze catches on it. "What is that?"

"It's a ghostleaf orchid," she replies, frowning down at it. "I need it for a potion, but I can't stop sucking on them instead. They taste like marshmallows. Want one?"

"Um, no thanks."

"Suit yourself. So anyway, did you want help with that?"

I look from her to the trunk. Aurelia might look tiny, but she's full-blooded Fae and actually much stronger than me. She's also talented at magic and often makes things fly around the house without warning.

"Sure," I say, heaving a breath. "Thanks."

She puts the blue flower back in her mouth, then flicks her index finger at the trunk, making it rise into the air light as a feather. I trail along after her as she directs the trunk down the many flights of stairs.

"Why didn't you wait for someone to help with this?" she asks.

"Shhh," I hiss. "Keep your voice down."

She laughs, but lowers her voice when I shoot her another deathly glare.

"Are you trying to leave before any of us notice?" she whispers.

"Please don't say anything."

She shrugs. "It's not my business. I would avoid the kitchen though if I were you. Beatrix is already awake."

"Thank you." I sigh. "It's not that I don't want to say goodbye to anyone, it's—"

She waves me off, and her motion makes my trunk sway wildly through the air toward the wall before she stops it at the last second. "Oops. I need to work on talking with my hands. Anyway, I was just going to say I get it. I wouldn't want to see anyone after last night either."

My eyes bug out of my head. "Excuse me?"

She laughs again. "Oh, please. This is an entire house full of people with Fae ears, and frankly you were loud enough that I bet even Alix heard everything."

I take a deep breath through my nose and close my eyes. "Perfect."

We reach the bottom of the stairs, and Aurelia puts my trunk down near the front door. "Don't worry about it. It's not like the rest of us haven't snuck out of someone's room early in the morning."

I look sideways at her. Whose room is she sneaking out of? And who is "the rest of us" supposed to refer to? I desperately want to know, but I want to avoid getting caught more. *Priorities.*

"Right," I say with a deep breath. "Well, you'll have to fill me in on that when I get back."

"Of course." She smiles secretively and pops the flower back out of her mouth before holding it out to me. "You should take this."

I wrinkle my nose in disgust and lean back from the unpleasantly wet stem. "I'm alright, but thank you."

She shoves it at me. "Seriously, take it. There's a reason it's called a ghostleaf orchid. If you swallow it, you'll turn invisible. You never know when you might need to make a quick escape...or sneak out of the house unnoticed. Just make sure you chew really well. You have to break the fibers down for it to work. Otherwise, it just tastes good."

I frown at it, then take the wet stem gingerly with two fingers, already sure that I won't be putting it anywhere near my mouth. "Thanks."

She waves a dreamy hand in the air. "You're welcome. Safe travels."

I turn back, wondering if I should ask her to let Alix and Daemon know where I went, then change my mind at the last second. I'm sure they'll work it out on their own...but hopefully not before I've crossed the border out of Vernallis.

Elio, the emissary from Hydratta, spent the night in a private room in the barracks. I really don't want to creep into his bedroom so early, but I will if I have to. I'd do just about anything to get out of here unseen.

Fortunately, that's not necessary.

As I near the barracks, the tension in my shoulders eases, and I exhale deeply, relief washing over me. The short, balding man is already stepping out of the building. He halts mid-step, his eyes narrowing as they lock onto me, acknowledging my approach.

"Good morning, Lady Odessa," he says with a deep bow.

"Just Odessa," I correct, wringing my hands in my skirt. "Listen, by any chance are you ready to leave?"

His brow furrows in confusion. "Now? It's barely dawn."

"You're already awake, though."

He coughs. "Yes, well, I was just hoping to find some breakfast, and..." he trails off, looking startled as I step closer.

I've already decided what I'm going to do if he doesn't want to leave without saying a formal goodbye to the court, so I waste no time waiting for him to finish his sentence. "I want to leave right now," I say with a persuasive note in my voice. "We don't need to wait to say goodbye to anyone, and no one else is coming with us. You should go saddle the horses. Nothing would make you happier."

The emissary blinks at me, and I swear I can see him fighting the compulsion. Gods, it would be just my luck that the emissary turns out to have a stronger will than nearly every other man on the continent.

"Please?" I add, a little desperate.

Elio's eyes slide out of focus, and he blinks up at me with a vacant expression. "As you wish."

I let out a sigh of relief. "Go fetch the horses and my trunk. I'll wait for you here."

"As you wish," he mumbles again, already shuffling off toward the stables.

I heave another sigh and settle onto a coarse wooden bench by the barracks entrance to wait.

I should probably follow the emissary to ensure the compulsion doesn't wear off before we've left, but I don't want it to become too strong. I wasn't trying to hurt him. Hopefully, in an hour he'll be back to normal and won't remember why we left so abruptly.

Even so, I can't shake the nagging sense of guilt.

Over the past hundred years, I've scarcely resorted to compulsion more than a handful of times, yet here I am, having used it twice just this week.

Even if it's wrong to bewitch the Emissary into helping me, it's not nearly as wrong as the harm I could cause if I stay here. The harm I could inadvertently cause to Kastian, and to myself.

The rational part of me insists that the end justifies the means. After all, it's not like I'm causing any lasting damage...

At least, that's what I keep telling myself.

ODESSA, AGE 16

"I just wanted you to know that I was right."

Daemon turns to look at me, an expression of resignation already on his face. "Oh, here we go."

I glare up at him. "I was!"

It's the morning of the first full day of Vernallis's visit to the court of Hydratta, and Daemon and I are standing beneath the arched entrance of the Hydrattan royal race track. Nearly every moment of the next three days includes some sort of event or activity, all culminating in a masked ball on the last night of the summit. This morning's entertainment is horse racing. It's not exactly my idea of fun.

Daemon jerks his head in the direction the crowd is moving. "We should find a spot to watch before it all fills up."

"I don't care about watching the race."

"Well, I do. Come on, I'll buy you a lemonade before we sit down."

I roll my eyes, but trail behind Daemon down the small stone path that leads to the racetrack.

The track is an enormous oval, flanked on all sides by low fences, with spectators leaning against them, eagerly anticipating the race. Those avoiding the sun are seated on tall wooden bleachers. The highest seats, shaded by vibrant tents, are reserved for the most important guests. From here, I can see King Sebastian and Queen Marbella already settled in the most ornate box, positioned right behind the race's starting point. At the starting line, a dozen or so Fae men are preparing their horses to begin the race.

Daemon and I make our way to the back of an enormous line of people all waiting to buy food and drinks from the shouting vendors beneath rainbow-striped tent awnings.

It's clear who's from Vernallis and who's from Hydratta, because all the Hydrattan nobles are dressed perfectly for the humid weather in loose silks and thin, sleeveless garments. Both the men and the women seem to favor pants over skirts, and I even spot a few women in cropped shirts that clearly show they're not wearing any corsets underneath. I burn with envy.

I'd almost forgotten how warm it can get in Hydratta, and I'm already sweating beneath my light cotton gown. Around me, many of the other Vernalli nobles are worse off than I am, and I can see them peeling off layers the longer we stand beneath the scorching sun.

I turn my head in every direction, distracted and fascinated by all the colorful clothing and glittering jewelry.

"I can't stand the suspense," Daemon says, nudging me with his shoulder.

"What?" I ask, tearing my eyes away from the shiny gold beading on a nearby woman's skirt.

"Tell me what you were right about."

"Oh, yeah," I narrow my eyes, annoyed by the reminder of last night. "I met Prince Kastian last night."

"Did you?" Daemon asks, seeming uninterested.

"Yes, and I was right. He absolutely was the boy from the harbor all those years ago."

Daemon raises his eyebrows. "You sure?"

"Definitely."

"Huh. I owe him fifty gold, then. I wonder what he was doing that day without all his guards."

"Don't you dare bring it up," I hiss. "I don't want him to realize we've met before."

Daemon's furrowed brows pull even lower. "Why?"

"I just don't." I glance around to make sure no one is listening to us. "Please don't say anything."

"Fine, I won't," he says with exaggerated annoyance.

I let out a breath. "Thank you."

Daemon scrutinizes me closely. "Don't tell me you're still having fantasies of becoming a princess."

My cheeks heat. "I don't know what you're talking about."

"Please," he scoffs. "I thought you'd gotten over that, but you're just upset because your little fantasy was shattered. Don't tell me the prince wasn't everything you hoped he would be."

"You're horrible!" I hiss, my face flaming now. "I hate you."

He grins. "No, you don't."

I set my jaw in a scowl and refuse to look at Daemon again as we stand in the unmoving line.

Unfortunately, I'm only angry because Daemon is right.

After meeting the prince in the harbor, I spent years fixated on childish fantasies of becoming a princess. Eventually, I grew out of it, and I'd almost forgotten the entire thing until I was told we'd be visiting the court of Hydratta. Then perhaps I got my hopes up all over again.

Maybe I was a bit put out to realize that Prince Kastian was already engaged.

And then, *it's possible* that I was startled when I walked out of the dining hall and found him, not only right in front of me, but yelling at me.

And *alright*, perhaps I reacted badly to both those things and was a tiny bit rude to him. Very rude, actually. I'm probably lucky I wasn't thrown out of the castle.

But all of that is behind me now, and I am completely and

utterly fine. I'm unlikely to find myself alone with Prince Kastian again, and soon we'll return to Vernallis, and I can forget all about him.

We're just a few steps away from reaching the front of the line when a sudden roar erupts near the bleachers. Curiosity gets the better of me, and I stretch my neck to get a glimpse of the chaos. Instantly, a wave of regret washes over me.

Prince Kastian has just arrived with a group of guards, and he's waving politely to the crowd of nobles as he walks toward the stairs to the royal observation box. Suddenly, as if drawn by an invisible thread, he pauses mid-step, his gaze sweeping the crowd before settling firmly on me. Our eyes meet, and his expression flickers with recognition.

"Oh no," I yelp, ducking behind Daemon. "Hide me!"

Daemon leans out of my way. "What the hell are you doing? Stop being a freak."

"Shut up!" I hiss, bending my knees and trying to make myself as small as possible. "Don't draw more attention to us."

Daemon laughs. "I'm not the one drawing attention. What is wrong with you?"

Before I can answer, a stone drops into my stomach. Around Daemon's legs, I can see the crowd parting and the shadows of feet coming toward us. *Oh my gods, this is not happening.*

"Found it," I exclaim, pretending to reach for something on the ground then shoving my hand into my pocket as I stand straight again. "I dropped my hairpin."

Daemon rolls his eyes at me, but mercifully doesn't ask about it as he turns to focus on the approaching prince.

Prince Kastian stops in front of us. He's dressed far more casually than last night, in blue silk trousers and a loose-fitting white shirt. I raise my eyebrows when I see the edge of a black swirling tattoo on his forearm peeking out from beneath his sleeve. I've only ever seen sailors with ink on their skin. I never imagined that a prince might have tattoos.

"Good morning," Prince Kastian says after a slightly too-long pause.

"Morning," Daemon says brightly, as if he talks to royalty every day. He should probably bow to the prince, but of course he doesn't. Instead, he sticks out his hand for Kastian to shake. "Daemon Ashwater, twelfth Baron of Ashwater."

Prince Kastian looks a bit taken aback, but grips Daemon's hand anyway to shake. "Pleasure to meet you." He doesn't introduce himself, but instead glances over Daemon's shoulder toward me. "Nice to see you again, Lady Odessa."

Daemon looks over his shoulder and smirks at me before turning back to Kastian and feigning ignorance. "Oh, have you already met my sister?"

"Yes," Prince Kastian says at the same time as I say, "No, not really."

"I think I offended your sister last night," Prince Kastian says to Daemon. "I just wanted to apologize again."

Daemon steps out of the way, and both he and Kastian look at me expectantly. I know what I'm supposed to do—I should curtsey and insist that whatever awkwardness took place in the hall last night was entirely my fault. That's the polite way to handle a situation like this, but I can't bring myself to do it.

I find myself staring blankly at Prince Kastian, unable to speak even as a voice in the back of my head screams at me to say or do something. *Anything.*

"Right..." Daemon says, looking bemused. He turns back to Prince Kastian. "Well, Dessa and I were just going to get drinks and sit down. Care to join us?"

I shoot Daemon a deadly glare, which no one seems to notice.

Again, Prince Kastian looks a little startled. Probably he's too important to sit with lesser nobles. Probably he has to go sit with his fiancée and the other royals. Probably—

"Alright," Prince Kastian says.

I jerk my head up, suddenly finding my voice again. "No, you can't!"

"Why not?" the prince asks.

"Yeah, Dessa, why not?" Daemon asks, smirking.

My cheeks heat. "Don't you have to sit with your family?"

He shakes his head. "I could, but I don't have to. If you asked my father, it would probably be better for me to be seen mingling in the crowd."

I want to ask why he doesn't want to sit with his fiancée, but I know Daemon will never let me hear the end of it if I do. "Oh, never mind. Sit wherever you want, *Your Majesty*."

Prince Kastian smirks, the slightly arrogant look reappearing on his face. "Thank you for your permission. I'd hate to offend you again."

I turn stiffly back toward the line for lemonade, knowing that anything I say will only make an uncomfortable situation worse.

The line for the lemonade suddenly and miraculously opens up for us, and we collect drinks before the three of us find a spot in the stands, partially shaded by the royal boxes above us, and sit down to watch the race. I expect that the prince's guards will follow us, but they all seem to try to make themselves scarce. Perhaps that's how he was able to escape them so easily eight years ago.

Soon, all the seats fill in around us as nobles go out of their way to try to eavesdrop on our conversation with the prince. I can see a lot of them glaring at us, probably wondering why Daemon and I were singled out. I wish I knew.

To my absolute horror, Daemon and Prince Kastian get along immediately.

I don't know why I would expect anything less—Daemon gets along with everyone and doesn't seem at all concerned with my extreme discomfort as he chats animatedly to the prince. At least he doesn't seem likely to reveal our meeting years ago, or my secret girlhood fantasies.

"I'm expecting Seahammer to win," Daemon says, gesturing at a black horse near the end of the starting line.

"Not Triton?" Prince Kastian nods toward a chestnut stallion near the end. "He's favored to win."

Daemon shakes his head. "Absolutely not."

"You sound well-versed in racing."

Daemon shrugs. "I usually play cards, but I've been known to attend a race from time to time. I know that a horse is only as good as his rider, and I saw the jockey drinking his weight in wine at dinner last night. Anyway, Thorne will probably bet on that horse."

Kastian's eyes flash with interest. "So what?"

"So, I'd like nothing better than to see him lose," Daemon says irreverently. "I can't bet on the same horse; it would go against my principles."

Kastian laughs. "Fair enough, Thorne is an ass." He looks sideways at Daemon and me. "Sorry, I shouldn't have said that."

Daemon grins so widely you'd think he'd never been happier in his entire life. "No, not at all. Please do."

Kastian chuckles, then looks more closely at Daemon as if seeing him for the first time. "You don't care for your future king, then?"

My stomach jolts as I remember that Prince Kastian has met King Florian, and probably isn't blind or stupid enough not to realize that Daemon looks exactly like him.

Daemon opens his mouth, but before he can say something stupid—something that could get him killed—I stomp on his foot. "We don't have any opinions about the royal family. It's not really our place to comment."

Kastian's gaze immediately flicks to me. "Oh, is that so? You seemed to have a lot of opinions on royalty last night, Lady Odessa."

"I told you, I'm not a lady," I snap.

"But you're her brother, right?" he asks Daemon.

Daemon shrugs. "In every way that counts, but technically we're cousins. Dessa is from the non-noble side of the family."

"The better side," I blurt out before I can stop myself.

Daemon nods. "Can't really argue with that."

Prince Kastian looks vaguely intrigued, but doesn't comment on it further.

"Which horse is your favorite to win?" Kastian asks.

It takes me a moment of silence to realize that he's talking to me. I look up at him, and do my best to maintain a neutral expression. "I'm not betting."

Prince Kastian grins and if I didn't know better, I'd say he was pleased that I answered him. But I do know better, and I'm sure that can't be what he's thinking.

"Should I assume you prefer cards too, then?" he asks.

I shake my head. "I don't gamble. I don't have any money."

"Yes, you do," Daemon corrects, looking embarrassed.

"No, *you* have money, but I don't. If I bet on the race, you'll have to pay for it, so why don't you just keep the betting between yourselves and leave me out of it?"

"Which horse would you choose if you were to bet?" Kastian asks.

I look over at the riders. The race is about to start, and they're all maneuvering into place at the starting line. I wish I knew something about horses, but unfortunately, I don't. If this were a boat race, it would be a different matter. I survey all the horses, and eventually, my eyes settle on a gray one in the middle. Its coat appears nearly white as it shimmers in the sunlight.

"The white one," I say finally.

Kastian looks over at me. "Why did you pick that one?"

I shrug. "I've always liked beautiful things."

He nods, looking pensive. "You've beaten me to it then. That horse is named Sirensong, and it would have been my choice."

"Isn't that ironic?" Daemon mutters.

I elbow him in the ribs, and he wisely doesn't say anything else. Prince Kastian looks between us, but is evidently too polite to ask what we're talking about.

Kastian smiles at me. "I'll let you take Sirensong. I suppose I'll have to join Daemon in rooting for Seahammer."

I wave him off. "You can still have the white horse. I'm not playing, remember?"

"We could bet with something other than money," Prince Kastian says, looking sideways at me.

"Careful," Daemon glares at him. "I don't care if you're a prince, respect my sister."

Kastian's eyes widen, and he leans back looking alarmed. "You misunderstood, I didn't mean anything inappropriate."

Suddenly interested, I lean back to meet the prince's gaze behind Daemon's back. "Then what did you have in mind?"

Prince Kastian still looks wary of Daemon's scowl, but sucks in a deep breath before the casual smile reappears on his face. "How about a secret? If I win, you tell me why you wanted to see the ships."

My lip curls in a smile. That's hardly a secret—and if he'd been anyone else, I would have just told him when he asked last night, but I suppose knowing that it's bothering him is somewhat satisfying.

I hold out my hand for the prince to shake. "Deal."

Prince Kastian grips my fingers, but instead of shaking my hand he flips my palm over and brushes his lips over the back. I gasp, my breath catching in my throat.

Daemon clears his throat pointedly, and Prince Kastian drops my hand at the exact same moment as the sharp horn sounds over the crowd, signaling the start of the race.

The crowd jumps to its feet as the horses burst forward in a blur, hooves pounding and sending dirt flying into the air. Cheers and bets fill the air, competing with the speed of the horses. I jump up as well, propelled by the excitement around me.

Most Fae seem to be cheering for Triton—the favored horse— but there are a few shouts of encouragement for other names as well.

I spot my pick, the almost-white horse, near the front of the pack with the jockey determinedly hunched low over the saddle.

Kastian and Daemon's choice, Seahammer, is close behind, but it's so close it's hard to tell precisely who's winning.

"I thought you said you didn't care about racing?" Prince Kastian asks.

"I don't!" I shout over the noise. "I care about winning."

"You never told me what you want if you win."

I tear my eyes from the race and look over at him, startled to realize that he's right. Now, my mind draws a blank. What do I want?

Before I can think of anything, the cheering around us turns deafening.

The thunderous pounding of hooves finally ceases as the horse race comes to an end, a cloud of dust lingering in the air. My heart races as I whip my head around, eyes darting desperately toward the finish line.

The air around me buzzes with tension as voices rise in a chorus of frustration. I can see the faces of those who had placed their hopes—and money—on the wrong horses. Their brows are furrowed, and fists are clenched, some shaking betting slips in the air as if willing them to change.

"Who won?" I demand.

"You did," Daemon grumbles darkly.

With a smug smile already forming on my lips, I turn to Prince Kastian only to find him already watching me. He nods at me as if to say, "Your move."

My heart thumps wildly against my ribs. What does one do with an unspecified favor from a prince?

ODESSA, PRESENT

By the time Elio and I leave the village of Storia and ride halfway to the nearest train station, my compulsion has worn off. He's completely back to normal, just in time for me to realize that I don't particularly like him.

He talks over and at me as we ride, droning on and on about the various virtues of Hydratta and how much I'll like living there. I can't tell him I have no real intention of marrying the king, but neither do I care to listen to a report on everything from the weather to the recent tax yield. If he was talking about the military, I might find that useful information to bring back to Daemon and Alix, but I can't imagine they'll care that a recent cold front has killed off all the radish crops.

"I was born in Hydratta, you know," I tell the emissary, hoping that will make him realize that I'm not interested in a meticulous overview of the entire kingdom. "My father was a merchant who spent the majority of his time at sea, but our home port was in the capital of Hydratta."

Elio looks sideways at me. "And your mother?"

"She passed away shortly after I was born."

"Sorry," he says shortly.

I flatten my mouth into a thin line and tighten my hold on my reins. "It's fine. I don't remember her."

I'm sure the emissary realizes what my mother was—what I am—and perhaps it's the reminder that scares him into silence for the rest of the ride to the train station. Whatever the reason, I'm grateful for the reprieve. It's going to be a long few days traveling alone with Elio.

When we arrive at the station, I'm pleasantly surprised to see it busy and bustling. I'd wondered if last year's crash would deter the Vernalli citizens from traveling, but it seems not. The train platform is full of Fae, and even the occasional other creature—pixies, dwarfs, and trolls to name a few.

The enormous red steam engine still bears the colors and crest of the last King of Vernallis, but the guards patrolling the station are dressed in blue jackets to reflect their loyalty to the new regime. We leave our horses with a couple of Daemon's guards, instructing them to return the animals to Storia, then go searching for an open compartment.

"I don't care for traveling by train," Elio confides as we walk down the thin aisle, peering into full compartments along the way.

"I don't either," I admit. "I was on the train that crashed last year."

The emissary looks up at me in surprise. "Were you? How did you survive?"

"Oh...just lucky, I guess," I lie, my heart thudding as I remember the accident—remember Kastian grabbing me and flying us out of the speeding train.

I shake my head violently. I shouldn't be thinking about that —now, or ever. Mostly because of Kastian, but especially not when I'm about to ride the train again and my anxiety is already high.

We finally find an empty compartment near the back of the train. I sit on the red leather bench seat and I tap my fingers on the window, looking out onto the busy train platform. I wish I'd thought to bring something to do—anything, really.

"The last time I traveled from Vernallis to Hydratta was by carriage," I say, just to fill the silence.

Elio sniffs. "Did you travel through the swamps?"

"Yes, unfortunately."

He nods. "I'd never travel the swamps if I could avoid it. We'll be taking a ship to the island."

I nod in agreement—that's what I assumed we'd be doing.

While it is technically feasible to travel to Hydratta by land, it's not the easiest route. Although Hydratta is often called an island, it is actually linked to the continent of Ellender by a land bridge that stretches several miles. However, that area is swampy and dangerous, making ocean travel the preferred option.

Across the seas, there are two methods of getting to Hydratta: The traditional path takes around two days, while the quicker route can be navigated in just one night. However, the latter is fraught with danger due to the sea monsters and sirens that lurk in those waters.

At the thought of the sirens, an involuntary shudder travels through me.

I'm fine, I remind myself. *There's no need to go anywhere near the water.*

Now that Elio has exhausted his monologue about Hydratta, he seems to have little more to say to me. If anything, he seems anxious, and I have to wonder if his dislike of traveling by train is more of a phobia than he let on.

We sit in uncomfortable silence as we wait for the train to start moving. I almost wish I'd waited for Jett to come with me—I don't regret leaving, but it would have been nice to have someone to talk to.

The thought of Jett sends my mind spinning back to this morning, then to why I left so abruptly, and inevitably to last night.

I grit my teeth and close my eyes, as if I can physically force the memory of Kastian out of my mind. I can't think about that because I can already feel the floodgates beginning to crack. I'd been doing so well channeling my frustration into hatred this last year and convincing myself that this version of Kastian was not the same one I remembered...only now, I wonder if he hasn't really changed at all. The only thing he's missing is his memory of me.

I lean my head against the back of the seat and close my eyes, trying to ignore the lingering thoughts and emotions swirling in my head and focus instead on my mission. This is my first genuine opportunity to contribute to the kingdom, and I should be considering how best to gather information about Hydratta, while remaining diplomatic.

What feels like twenty minutes goes by, and finally I sit up. "Shouldn't we be on our way already?"

Elio wrings his hands in his lap. "I'm sure we'll be leaving shortly."

A shiver of discomfort creeps up my spine, though I can't pinpoint why. I dismiss it as leftover anxiety from the last time I sat on this train. *I'm fine. Everything is fine.*

Until, that is, I hear the screaming.

The shrill sound of a woman's shout rattles through the train, quickly followed by more voices. I jump to my feet, panic rising in my chest.

"Wait, Lady Odessa!" Elio exclaims, jumping up too. "Stay here."

"Not a fucking chance," I blurt out, forgetting to be polite. "I've heard that sound before. I'm not staying here another second."

I throw the compartment door open and dart out into the long hallway.

The only saving grace is that we're not yet moving, and all I need to do is reach an open door back onto the train platform. I look left and right, momentarily frozen with indecision about the best direction to run.

The pause costs me everything.

The emissary's small hand closes around my wrist and yanks me back into the compartment, slamming the door behind me. He grits his sharp yellow teeth at me. "Sit down."

"Don't touch me!"

He drops me, but moves to stand in front of the door, blocking my exit.

New dread sinks into my stomach. This isn't right. The emissary seems far too comfortable with whatever is going on—like he expected it. Like he's a part of it.

My eyes narrow, and anger surges in my chest, overtaking the fear.

I size up Elio—he's shorter than I am, but still Fae. I don't think I can physically overpower him, so my only chance is to use my persuasion again. I take a deep breath trying to calm myself— I've never had to do this while under threat, and I'm not entirely sure it will work. Or perhaps it might work too well.

Before I can gather myself, however, the compartment door opens again.

I don't recognize the man standing in the doorway. He's tall, with short dark hair and a slight beard. His skin is white, but sun-tanned, and he's wearing the sort of clothing that I associate with sailors...or *pirates*. He's wearing a weathered black jacket, fabric faded from the sun and salt, tall boots, and patched trousers. Completing the picture, he has a pearl earring dangling from one rounded ear.

I wouldn't have had to notice the ears to know he wasn't Fae —one look at the man's handsome face has my brain screaming "human!"

Humans tend to be afraid of me on first instinct because sirens look far more alien to them than the Fae do. This man must have been in Ellender for quite a while, because he doesn't even flinch as he leans around Elio and grins at me. "Hello, darling."

The pirate steps inside the train car, and Elio moves aside to let him enter, then puffs up his chest as if trying to make himself larger. "Mr. Connel, I presume?"

The pirate raises a brow at him, looking disgusted as if the emissary is no more than a bug creeping along the ground. "Who are you? I thought it was just the siren we were looking for."

"I'm Lord Elio, emissary to—"

The pirate cuts him off. "Yeah...sorry, mate, but I don't care."

"What—" Elio begins indignantly.

With a swift motion, the pirate draws a long, gleaming knife from his belt. In one brutal thrust, he plunges it into the emissary's stomach.

I let out a loud gasp as Elio's eyes widen in shock, his breath catching in a strangled cry. He clutches his abdomen, blood seeping through his fingers as he crumples forward, collapsing onto the hard bench seat.

My eyes widen with horror, and I scramble backwards along the bench seat until my back is firmly against the wall. I didn't like Elio—I found him pompous and untrustworthy—but I didn't want him dead.

The pirate steps back from Elio's limp body and wipes his bloody hands on his pants. He turns to me, and winks. "That's bloody better, don't you think?"

My ears are ringing. *I'm going to die.*

"Who—who are you?" I demand.

The pirate raises his eyebrows at me. "Sorry, darling. Can't hear you, and I'm shit at reading lips."

He tilts his head to show me his ears, which I'm surprised to see are stuffed with cotton—like sailors use to block out the wind and the sounds of the sirens singing beneath the ocean. My heart sinks. He must know exactly who I am to take that precaution, but how? *Why?*

Unbidden, my mind flies to Kastian's throwaway comment

the other day. *"You're the king's sister and the queen's best friend. If I were going to kidnap someone to hold for ransom, I know who I'd choose."*

Oh, shit.

"The name's Captain James Connell," the pirate says, holding out a blood-soaked hand as if I would ever want to shake it. "Captain of *The Sea Witch*. You might have heard of me?"

Captain James Connell—the name prickles at me. I remember it from somewhere, maybe a wanted poster, maybe a whispered warning in a smoky tavern. Even so, I shake my head vigorously, reacting to his question even as my brain spins.

Captain Connell looks slightly disappointed. "You haven't? That's too bad. I've certainly heard of you, Lady Odessa. You're a popular prize at the moment, did you know that?"

I clamp my lips shut, refusing to give him the satisfaction of a retort—even so, I latch onto every word. *A popular prize...*that must mean he doesn't want to kill me. At least, not yet. This is a ransom attempt, and I'd bet everything I own that Elio was in on it...though that doesn't seem to have worked out well for him.

Captain Connell squats down to my eye level. His eyes are dark blue, like the ocean, and look almost friendly—completely at odds with the blood on his hands. "Alright, darling, let me tell you how this is going to go. I'm sure you're planning to escape right now, but that's not bloody likely. Even if you got past me—which you won't—I have a dozen men out in the corridor waiting to grab you." He pauses for dramatic effect and the screaming and crashing from outside the compartment seems to grow even louder. I swallow thickly and Captain Connell grins. "See? So you're going to be a good girl and come with me quietly. We're going to be friends, you and I. But if you bite, I'll bite back. Got it?"

"Why would I believe that?" I ask, my voice coming out in a shaky whisper.

Whether he can hear me or not, I can't tell, but he must guess what I said because he leans closer. His voice is almost tender, coaxing, like I imagine I must sound using the siren voice. "Because, darling, if you don't come quietly I'll make our time together bloody unpleasant for you. I doubt you want that, right?"

I try to think, but my body is nearly numb—except for a cold spike of panic needling its way up my spine. I can't let him take me anywhere. I'd rather die here than be captured and subjected to the gods know what.

I force myself to focus. I can't bewitch him with cotton in his ears. He's human, but still a large man, so I can't out-muscle him. Even if I could, I heard what he said about the men in the corridor...I have to find a weapon.

I shift my gaze to the captain's belt. He has a pistol, holstered but not buckled. It's been over a hundred years since I last shot a pistol, and I'm not sure I remember how. Certainly not well enough to do it with shaking hands. Instead, my eyes flick back to the knife sticking out of Elio's abdomen at a crooked angle, the hilt smeared red.

"I'll cooperate," I blurt out.

Captain Connell grins at me, and gestures toward his ears. "What was that, darling?"

I struggle to my feet, trying to convey my compliance. "I'll go with you."

He laughs again—a deep, delighted bray. "Smart girl. After you."

He moves out of the way as if to gesture me forward in some sort of mockery of manners. I step tentatively toward the door, then lunge sideways toward the knife.

Captain Connell lets out a bark of laughter. "Not such a good girl after all, are you, darling?"

The knife handle is slick, but I grip it hard with both hands and pull. It doesn't come out. I yank again, twisting, and on the second try it slides free with a nauseating, wet sound. I gag, partly from the effort, partly from the spray of blood that spatters my arm.

In the span of a second, I whip around. Connell is reaching for me, and he moves at the exact moment I do. The knife plunges straight into his stomach, just below the ribcage. It's not graceful —my aim is off and the handle slams against his belt buckle, but the blade still finds flesh.

The pirate's eyes widen in surprise. He howls, a sound halfway between rage and agony, and staggers back, his entire body doubled over reflexively, arms clutching at his midsection.

For a split second I'm frozen, staring at what I've done. I cannot believe that worked. His blood splatters on the floor, and my breath punches in and out, sharp and irregular, as the reality of it lands: I've just killed a man.

Or tried to.

As I stare at the bleeding pirate, too shocked to move, his howls of pain change. My brain is slow to register that it isn't a moan. It's a laugh.

It starts low, like a cough gurgling through a throat full of gravel, but then it rises, deep and rolling. Mocking.

He struggles to stand straight again, his ocean eyes flashing with amusement as he looks up at me, his hand still clutching the wound in his stomach. He pulls his shirt up to reveal the full horror of the wound and grins with blood on his teeth as his fingers wrap around the knife handle. Then, without breaking eye contact, he yanks the blade out in one smooth motion. The sound it makes is grotesque—a wet, sucking pop, followed by a fresh rush of dark blood.

I watch in horror as the skin and muscles of his stomach knit back together, shifting and healing before my very eyes. He stands straight and holds the knife up, admiring it, then licks a stripe of his own blood from the blade.

My legs go rubbery, and I realize I've been holding my breath so fiercely I might faint. "What the fuck."

Connell flicks the knife as if bored, then tosses it aside. "That was a good try, darling" he says, voice full of mocking humor. "Next time, try going for the heart. Or, you know, run." He wipes his hands on his shirt, then gestures at the door. "Go on. I'll give you a five-second head start, no hard feelings."

I don't believe him for a second. But every instinct says: *move.*

That man is not human—I don't know what he is, but I'd rather run straight into his band of pirates than wait to find out.

I barrel past the still-grinning pirate, fling open the compartment door, and lurch into the corridor, half expecting to be cut down from behind.

Captain Connell holds true to his word and gives me a chance to run, but it's hardly a gift.

The hall outside is chaos incarnate, worse even than last year's train crash. Screaming passengers, overturned luggage, glass crunching underfoot. I duck low, sprinting toward the next car, slipping once in a pool of something—hopefully wine, not blood —and catch myself hard on the wall.

Behind me, the thump of Captain Connell's heavy boots follows me. He's not running, just... following. Stalking. Like he's got all the time in the world.

I reach the vestibule between cars and smash the release lever with unsteady hands. The door hisses open, and I stumble out onto the platform. The crowd is gone, and there's not a single guard in sight.

My heart pounding in my ears, I grab my skirts and sprint across the platform, not really seeing where I'm going. I round the side of the ticket booth and dart toward the road.

Then, suddenly, another pirate is in front of me, blocking my path. I scream and turn, trying to dart around him, but another man blocks that direction.

Suddenly, they're everywhere, swarming the platform and closing me in. There's nowhere to go. I'm caged, and every single man is grinning, like this is just some game to them.

From down the platform comes the slow, deliberate click of boots. He's whistling now, like he's in no hurry, and the tune sinks into me with bone-deep dread.

He's drawing it out; he enjoys the chase.

"We can do this the easy way, or the hard way," Captain Connell calls as he grows nearer.

I straighten my spine, and dig deep for a bravery I don't feel. "I dare you to take me back to your ship," I hiss, teeth bared. "I could drown you in seconds. You know that, right?"

The pirate finally stops in front of me, his bloodstained shirt still pulled up to show ridges of unblemished muscle. He bows, sweeping his arm in a grand gesture of mock chivalry, and when he straightens again, the smile that splits his face is all teeth and hunger. "That's the spirit, darling. I love a fighter."

KASTIAN, PRESENT

I made a huge fucking mistake.

That's all I can think when I wake up alone in my bed, my thoughts already on Odessa. I know she was here when I fell asleep, but her side of the bed is cold, and it looks as if she left hours ago. Knowing her, she probably waited for me to go to sleep and snuck out at the first opportunity.

Maybe she also realized what a terrible decision last night was.

It was a mistake, because it was far too good. Nothing that feels that incredible can ever be good for you.

Overnight, my fascination shifted into a full-blown obsession, and I know I won't be able to handle never having her again. But that's wrong.

Everything about this is wrong.

I shouldn't be able to want her so much. I should feel guilty about betraying my soul-bond, but I don't. Technically, I shouldn't have even been capable of touching her while bonded to someone else. So, what does this mean?

I sit up and squint around my destroyed bedroom. It

somehow looks even worse than last night—truly giving the impression that a storm tore through here leaving only wreckage behind.

There's probably a metaphor here somewhere, but I can't find it right now.

I swing my legs over the side of my bed and try to avoid stepping on the broken buttons and shards of a lamp I don't recall breaking as I make my way to the wardrobe. I'm oddly resolute—confident, even—as I dress quickly and climb the stairs up to the third floor.

I'm not entirely sure what I'm planning to do. I know this can't happen again, but I must be a masochist because I still want to talk to her.

I reach the top of the landing, my heart thudding in my chest as I stop in front of Odessa's door. Taking a deep breath, I knock softly and brace myself, waiting for the familiar clatter of her navigating her messy room, but there's nothing. Silence greets me instead. I knock louder. Again, there's no answer.

Cautiously, I test the doorknob.

It turns easily, but I need to lean heavily against the door to push it open. Clothes, shoes, books, and papers clutter the floor and obstruct the door. For someone like me who thrives on order, Odessa's room should be revolting. I know I must be really far gone because the chaos barely registers with me. "Dessa?"

I know before I've finished speaking that she's not here. My heart skips a beat as I scan the empty space, my gaze zeroing in on the green glass bottle sitting alone on the windowsill. A sense of unease settles over me.

Deep breath in...

Deep breath out...

If Odessa isn't in her room, there aren't many other places she might be. She could be by the lake or having breakfast with Alix. I shut the door and head downstairs.

When I enter the kitchen, I find it already full. Daemon sits hunched over a plate of fried eggs. Alix is beside him, animatedly discussing something with Jett across the table. Fox, silent as ever, leans against the counter, cradling a steaming mug of herbal tea in one large hand. Even Aurelia is here, sitting on the counter in Fox's shadow and kicking her feet as they dangle above the floor.

Everyone is here except the one person I care about finding.

Daemon glances up at me, his eyes narrowed. "Morning," he mutters darkly.

"Where's Odessa?" I ask without preamble.

Jett grins widely. "Shouldn't you know?"

"Shut up," Daemon and I snap at the same time.

Jett rolls his eyes and takes a large bite of his breakfast, his sarcastic reply coming out garbled around his food. "If you'd 'shut up' last night, then I wouldn't have anything to comment on, would I?"

I pointedly turn away from him and focus on Daemon. "Just tell me where she is."

My best friend's brow furrows, and he shifts uncomfortably in his seat, glancing away as if searching for an escape. "Don't fucking drag me into this. I don't care what you do with Dessa, but I don't want to know anything about it."

Alix turns in her chair to face me, blocking Daemon from view. "We haven't seen her. We thought she was with you...and maybe she changed her mind about leaving?" she raises a hopeful eyebrow.

I frown. Honestly, I hadn't thought about it. Somehow, the idea that Odessa might still leave after last night completely fled my mind. Like it was so inconceivable, it didn't even warrant thought.

I'm a fucking idiot.

"Where's the emissary?" I ask.

"They already left," Aurelia says lightly.

I look at her so fast that my neck cracks. "What?"

Aurelia hops down from the counter and crosses her arms over her chest. "She left this morning when it was barely light out. I helped her carry her things down."

"Why the hell would you do that?" Daemon barks.

Aurelia nonchalantly shrugs and inspects her nails, seemingly unaffected by his harsh tone. "Why wouldn't I? It's not my job to hold anyone hostage."

"Wait, so they're already gone?" Alix exclaims, jumping to her feet. "Why didn't you say anything?"

"You didn't ask," Aurelia says brightly. "And I told her I wouldn't tell...but I'm a romantic. Sue me."

I blink rapidly at her—I never have any idea what Aurelia is talking about, and I don't have the energy to sort it out now. Not when I can feel the beginnings of panic thundering through my chest.

"How did she convince the emissary to leave without saying a formal goodbye?" Alix demands of the room at large.

Daemon's eyes widen. "She could have just asked him."

"Compelled him, you mean?" Fox grumbles, entering the conversation for the first time.

"Right, but she rarely does that." Daemon glances at me with a slight accusation in his expression. "At least, she didn't before now. What the fuck did you—"

"Stop it," Alix cuts him off firmly. "Dessa wouldn't just leave without saying anything...right? There wouldn't be any point; she was leaving today anyway. Jett was going to go with her."

With anger and an unexplained panic rising in my chest, I turn on my heel and march out of the kitchen toward the front door.

"Where are you going?" Aurelia calls after me.

"To look for Dessa."

"There's no point! I told you, they left already."

I hear her, but I don't care. I need to check absolutely everywhere. I can't believe Odessa would actually leave like this.

Except, why can't I believe that?

She was perfectly clear last night about the fact that she intended to go—that she wanted to do something useful and that whatever happened with us was a one-time event. She told me exactly what she wanted. It just isn't what I want.

I ball my hands into fists as I step out into the courtyard in front of the manor, my thoughts already racing. Rationally, I know that this is a firm dismissal on her part and I need to accept it calmly.

Except that "rational" and "calm" are two things I can't even remember how to be at the moment.

It must be the siren magic.

That has to be why. Because there's no other rational explanation for why I feel so bizarrely possessive of Odessa, when she's gone out of her way to avoid and ignore me for over a year. There's no other reason why I suddenly can't stand the idea that she might be in danger. That has to be the reason my wings appeared last night. That must be the reason.

The door bursts open behind me, and Jett strides outside, Daemon right behind him. They're mid-conversation, and I only catch the end of what Jett is saying. "—just run back to the barracks and pack. I can leave in less than an hour and can probably still catch them."

I turn on my heel. "What are you talking about?"

Jett runs a hand through his messy black hair and turns to walk backwards toward the barracks. "If Odessa really left with the emissary, then they'll have to take the train. If I leave now, I can probably still catch them at the station."

"I'll go with you," I say, aggression leaking out of my tone.

Daemon claps a hand on my shoulder. "You can't, mate."

I throw his hand off and glare at him. "Don't fucking pull this with me, Daemon. I don't want to fight you, but I will."

Daemon raises both his eyebrows and puts his hands up. "Easy, Kas. I don't want to fight with you either—partly because I'd put you on your ass."

He's obviously joking, trying to lighten the mood, but I don't crack a smile. "You want to fucking test that?"

"Absolutely not," he says lightly. "Calm down and think

about this. We're talking about Hydratta, remember? You can't go there. If even a single guard spotted you, it would be an instant death sentence. Unless you think you can take on an entire army alone?"

I press my lips together in a flat line. I want to point out that *I* never told *him* to "calm down" when he was so obsessed with keeping Alix safe that he made Fox, Jett, and me watch her door around the clock.

But isn't that kind of the point?

Alix was Daemon's soul-bond, and Odessa isn't mine. This isn't like me. I don't act irrationally. I don't pick doomed fights I can't win, and I definitely don't challenge Daemon's leadership.

Deep breath in...

"I won't go to Hydratta," I say on an exhale. "Jett just said he's going to catch up with her on the train."

"And you're really going to turn around and come home after that, are you?" Daemon says skeptically.

No.

"Yes," I insist through gritted teeth. "I just want to make sure she's alright."

Daemon stares at me with obvious skepticism and exasperation on his face, and I suddenly know exactly how I must have looked last year when he was trying to convince me to lock him in a bathroom to keep him away from Alix.

I really don't like the comparison.

Less than an hour later, Jett and I set off on horseback in the direction of the train station.

I'm anxious as we ride side by side through the woods, even though we're already traveling as fast as is reasonable given the uneven ground. It's impossible to know how far ahead of us

Dessa is, and Aurelia's estimations of the time based on the shadows on the wall were enough to make me pull my hair out.

"Calm down, Kas," Jett says, looking sideways at me.

"Fuck you."

He laughs. "You really need to lighten up. You and Ashwater both are always wound so tight, it can't be healthy."

"I pray I live to see the day you find your soul-bond, and we'll see how loose you are then."

He startles, and his dark eyes widen so all the whites are visible. "Holy shit, is that what this is about? Is Dessa your bond?"

I stiffen. *Fuck.* I hadn't even realized what I'd said.

I run a hand through my hair, sighing. "No, she's not. That's not what I meant. I just meant that you'll be less calm when you find yours, that's all."

He raises a skeptical eyebrow at me. "Are you sure? Because, judging by whatever the fuck you're doing right now—" he waves a hand toward me "—I wouldn't be surprised."

"I'm sure."

"But—"

"I already found my bond," I say flatly, just to put an end to the questioning.

Jett's eyes widen. He doesn't bother to ask me who or where she is, because it's obvious. If I've already found my bond and she's not with me, then she's most likely dead. Or, at least, far out of reach.

"You never told me that." Jett gapes at me. "Does Ashwater know?"

I shake my head. "It's not something I like talking about—for obvious reasons."

He refuses to take the hint and asks, "When was it?"

Deep breath in...

"Decades ago. Before Dyaspora."

Deep breath out...

Jett rides in stunned silence for a minute, looking uncharacteristically somber. "Sorry, mate," he says finally. "That's awful."

"Yes," I say sharply. "It is."

As if awakened by my mention of it, the bond in my chest flares to life, throbbing painfully.

Absentmindedly, I reach up and rub my chest where my tattoo sits beneath my shirt over my heart. I only ever made one serious attempt to track down my bond mate after escaping Dyaspora, and the tattoo is the result—though not the result I expected.

Many of my memories from before Dyaspora have faded entirely or become fuzzy over the years, but I still vividly recall waking up on a rocky beach with only the vaguest memories of the night before and the unmistakable feeling of a new bond pulsing in my chest.

After over a hundred years, the feeling of the incomplete bond isn't something I often think about. I know it's there in an abstract way and if I focus, I can feel it—like how if I think about it, I can feel my own heartbeat. Now, it burns slightly, as if reminding me that it's there. I wince and try to ignore it.

"So I'm just saying Odessa is not my bond, if anything, whatever this is—" I wave my hand around like he did "—is because she's a siren."

Jett's expression is skeptical. "I suppose."

"Do you notice the siren magic?"

"From Dessa?"

"No, from all the other sirens we know," I snap. "Yeah, obviously from Dessa."

He thinks about it for a moment, and my pulse beats erratically as I hold my breath waiting for his response. I already regret asking, and know that no matter what he says I'm not going to like it.

"Not really," he says finally. "Maybe when we first met I noticed, but not anymore."

I grunt in something like agreement. I suppose that's the best answer I could have hoped for.

"Granted, she's never tried to use it on me," Jett continues, seemingly thinking out loud. "I wouldn't say no if she tried, but—"

"Alright, I get it," I cut him off irritably.

That answer wasn't helpful at all, and I'm annoyed with myself for asking.

We continue on horseback, the rhythmic clopping of hooves echoing through the quiet woods. It's a long trek—more than an hour to reach the nearest train station—but at last, a faint glow appears on the horizon, and I know we're nearing the village.

I can't get the idea out of my head that something is wrong. Probably, the train has already left and is halfway to the port by now.

It would be far faster to fly...

I roll my shoulders and shove that insane thought from my mind.

"Hang on!" Jett says abruptly.

I startle and pull back hard on my reins. "What is it?"

He doesn't answer, just slows his own horse and leaps off, hitting the mossy forest ground before the beast has come to a complete stop.

"What the fuck are you doing?" I demand.

Jett darts off into the trees, returning a moment later leading a chestnut mare by the blue and gold braided bridle.

I glance down at my own blue reins and my heart sinks. "Is that one of our horses?"

Jett nods. "Looks like it. If Dessa and the emissary rode to the train, I assume they'd leave their horses with some of the guards to bring back to the estate. If this one is wandering around alone not far from the station..."

He doesn't finish his thought, but I fill it in on my own. If the horse is wandering around alone, then either they never made it to the train station or something happened to the guards.

With my heart pounding out of control, I dig my heels in and gallop toward the village.

Though one loose horse isn't exactly proof of a catastrophe, I can't get it out of my head that something happened to Odessa. I feel it—a bone-deep ache that I'm sure means something is wrong.

That feeling is made all the worse when we reach the station and I leap from my horse, breath coming out in quick pants.

The enormous red steam engine is still here, its doors open wide and faint smoke still coming from its exhaust pipes. The station building itself looks abandoned; no ticket master at his window, no shouting porters, not even a stray dog skulking in the corner.

Jett and I exchange a meaningful glance, and he puts his hand on the knife in his belt as we sprint toward the train.

I don't even bother reaching for my own weapon. My blood is pounding, and at the moment I'm sure I could tear someone's head off with my bare hands.

Inside the train is chaos.

I run down the thin aisle, cataloging everything without really processing what I'm seeing. Broken glass, carts and luggage overturned, doors to compartments hanging open.

"Kas!" Jett shouts behind me.

My heart jumps into my throat, and I spin, finding him bent down in the entrance to one of the compartments. Beside him is the dead body of a dark-haired man—a conductor, by the look of his uniform—sprawled face-down in a pool of black-red blood soaking into the carpet. His cap lies several feet away as though knocked off during a struggle.

Rage roils in my gut—not for this man's death specifically, but that this happened at all. "I'm going to look for Odessa."

"Wait," Jett says, "slow down."

"Don't fucking start—"

"I care about Dessa too, but just look at this for a second." He gestures toward the man's pockets, which are turned out. "Whoever did this was obviously after money or valuables."

"What makes you say that?" I ask through gritted teeth, anger and impatience making my stomach churn.

He stands up and pokes his head into another open compartment. "The compartments all show obvious signs of hasty looting: drawers yanked out, brass fixtures missing."

"Why the fuck would anyone take the fixtures?"

Jett laughs hollowly. "When you say shit like that you're advertising that you've never been poor."

I bare my teeth. "I was in Dyaspora just like you."

"Yeah, but before I mean. It's obvious you never had to steal to eat, because if you did, you'd know that brass can be melted down and sold."

I shake my head. This is a fucking waste of time. "Fine. So it was bandits; that doesn't make me feel better. I need to look for Dessa."

He nods. "Of course, but I don't think she's going to be here."

"Why?" I demand, pulse pounding.

"If whoever did this was just trying to make quick money, they won't have gone out of their way to kill anyone."

"Tell that to him," I growl, gesturing to the dead conductor with my foot.

"He worked for the train, so he probably tried to stop them," Jett says calmly. "The guards would have tried to stop them too, so I'm guessing they're dead. That's why we found the horse wandering around alone."

"Get to the point," I growl.

"My point is thieves wouldn't have killed random bystanders. Too messy. Odessa isn't the type to pick a fight, and she's not stupid. If she was here when this happened she probably ran away."

My pulse slows the smallest fraction, but I still feel like I'm struggling to breathe. "I'm going to look anyway."

"Of course. You search this side of the train and I'll go the other way."

I nod curtly and walk away from him, peering into compartments as I pass.

I'm relieved that Jett's assessment seems to be right. Most of the compartments have been ransacked for anything valuable, but I don't see many bodies.

I'm starting to calm down—thinking it might be better to search the woods around the station—when I stop short. My heart leaps into my throat, and my vision seems to tunnel in on itself.

At one end of the carriage, a door hangs off its hinges, and a pool of blood seeps out into the corridor. Lying in the pool is a short, balding man dressed in the bright green colors of the Hydrattan court.

"Jett!" I yell over my shoulder, then rush over to the body. I flip him over just to be sure.

The blank eyes of the Hydrattan emissary stare up at me, unseeing.

Heart pounding and panic surging through my veins, I fling the emissary aside and propel myself into the compartment behind him. I frantically scan the space—Odessa is nowhere to be found—but that does nothing to calm me down. Where the fuck is she?

"Fuck," Jett says behind me, letting out a low whistle. "Someone stabbed him."

I turn back around and find Jett pressing a palm to the emissary's forehead. "He's not completely cold yet. This only happened a few hours ago, I think."

"He didn't seem like the type to fight bandits," I say, unable to keep the anger out of my voice.

Jett nods in agreement. "And their compartment isn't ransacked, look."

I don't have to look—I already noticed that the compartment where Elio and Odessa must have sat still has all its brass fixtures.

"I'm going to search the woods," I announce, stepping irreverently over Elio's dead body and marching toward the nearest door.

"I'll go with you," Jett says firmly. He seems far more worried now than he did before finding the emissary, and I don't dare ask what he's thinking. My head is already fucked enough as it is, thinking of all the possible things that could have happened to Odessa.

We burst out of the train car and onto the platform.

Jett and I don't speak as we look over the rows of abandoned benches and forlorn luggage. Instinctively, we split up, covering more ground; he veers left toward the baggage carts while I sprint toward the edge of the platform where a line of wilted hedges marks the border between civilization and forest.

I'm moving through a fever dream, but my body won't let me slow down. My mind races as fast as I run. Where's Dessa? Was she taken? Did she run? Is she hurt?

At the far end of the platform, beyond a toppled cart piled with crates and barrels, something shifts. For half a second I think it's an animal—a dog or maybe a bird—but then it moves again.

A man in blue lurches upright from behind a set of dusty lockers near the ticket booth. He staggers forward two steps before collapsing against a post, leaving behind a dark smear on the painted wood. The blue uniform is instantly familiar—I have one like it myself back at the Ashwater estate.

Jett spots him too, calling out in alarm. I'm closer, so I shout first and tear across the platform at full speed.

The guard lifts his head at my voice. He looks barely conscious; his face is pale beneath streaks of dirt and blood, one side contorted in pain or confusion. He blinks once, twice, as if he can't quite process what he's seeing. His hand shakes as he fumbles for something at his belt—a weapon, maybe—but it drops limply to his side when he recognizes me.

"Lord Kastian," he pants.

I don't recognize this particular soldier, but I'm not surprised he knows my name if he's spent any time at the barracks in Storia. I skid to a halt beside him just as his knees buckle again and he slides down onto the flagstones. There's a brutal gash running from his cheekbone to jaw, and blood seeps through his fingers as he presses them hard against his face.

"Kas," Jett pants as he catches up from behind me, "is he—?"

"He's alive," I say grimly. "Barely."

My hands are already moving without thinking—I press a hand to the soldier's cheek, feeling the warmth of magic glow beneath my fingers.

I've always been good at healing magic—it's one of the things that Hydratta is known for, along with conjuring things out of thin air. I really need more time to heal effectively though, and I'm too impatient to wait long.

"There," I mutter after a minute. "That should stop the bleeding at least."

"Thanks," the soldier coughs. "I appreciate it."

"What happened here?" I demand.

"Pirates," he rasps.

"Pirates?" Jett asks, sounding skeptical. "You mean bandits?"

The soldier shakes his head and winces at the movement. "No, I mean pirates. Don't know what they were doing here."

"How do you know it was pirates?" I ask.

"Just looked like it, plus they called their leader 'Captain,' and I heard one of them say something about 'going back to the ship.'"

"Where were they from? Hydratta?"

His brow wrinkles. "I'm not sure...Solistine, I think."

"Why do you say it like that?"

"It was strange. They were wearing Solistinian colors—lots of yellow and orange—but they had the wrong accents."

"What did they look like?" Jett asks.

The soldier shrugs. "I don't know—mostly men? I think I saw one woman with them."

"No," Jett corrects. "I mean skin and hair colors. Did they look like me?" He gestures at his own dark hair and golden skin. "Or darker like Kastian?"

The soldier shakes his head. "Mostly white with brown or

blonde hair. Without the Solistinian clothing, I would have assumed they were from Vernallis."

"Not from Thermia?" I clarify. "Their population is mostly fair-haired and pale too."

He shakes his head. "No, Thermians are usually tall. These men were average."

Jett and I exchange glances. He shakes his head, clearly not understanding this any more than I do.

At the moment, I don't really care who these pirates were, just where they are and if they have Odessa.

Obviously thinking along the same lines, Jett bends down to the soldier's eye level. "Did you see Lady Odessa?"

He nods. "She gave me her horse. The emissary from Hydratta was with her."

"He's dead," I grunt.

The soldier looks alarmed. "I didn't see her after that. I think I got knocked out."

I let out a breath. He clearly lost consciousness and probably only survived because whoever hit him thought he was dead.

Jett stands straight again and catches my gaze, jerking his head to the side like he wants to talk privately. We walk a few feet from the man and drop our voices so he can't hear.

"I think he's confused," I growl.

"Me too," Jett agrees, "I think it's odd that he would think they were from Solistine based on their clothes, unless it was really obvious. It's not like the entire kingdom dresses exclusively in yellow and orange. That sounds almost intentional."

I nod and have to swallow a growl of frustration. I agree with him, but that brings us no closer to finding Odessa.

"Let's assume for a minute that they took her," Jett muses.

The growl I've been holding back bubbles up from my throat, and Jett looks at me with alarm. "Easy. I'm just saying, let's assume for a minute that this was all about kidnapping Odessa, and that's why the emissary was dead but her compartment wasn't ransacked."

Deep breath in...
Deep breath out...

I force myself to remain calm enough to speak. "I just said the other day that she's at risk of abduction. If I were going to try to get Daemon to pay a ransom, I'd choose Odessa."

"Not Alix?" he asks.

I shake my head. "No, because then he'd fucking murder whoever did it and anyone else in a ten-mile radius. If they kidnapped Odessa, then he'd still do everything possible to get her back, but there's a slight chance the kidnappers would survive."

A very, *very* slight chance.

Practically none at all, because I would fucking kill them myself.

"Agreed," Jett says thoughtfully. "I think we should go to the harbor. It's the only lead that makes sense, and if that soldier heard them talking about getting back on a ship."

I nod tightly. I don't feel good about the plan, but I don't think I'll feel good about anything until I know exactly where Odessa is. At least this plan feels like doing something. If I don't do something soon, I'm going to explode.

"Our horses are over there," I say, walking back over to the soldier. "Can you ride?"

The man looks up at me and tries to sit up straighter. "Give me a minute, but yeah, probably."

"Take the horses and go back to the estate. Tell Daemon what happened."

"Kas, we need the horses if we're going to get to the harbor," Jett says.

I shake my head. "It'll take too long."

"Well then, what—"

He stops mid-sentence, his eyes widening as my wings slowly stretch and unfurl from my back. I stretch them wide, feeling the tension release from each joint, and give them a gentle shake.

I have to go find Odessa—wherever she went. Hydratta, anywhere in Ellender, or the bottom of the fucking ocean...

KASTIAN, AGE 18

"We missed you at the race today," Mother says over dinner.

I take a sip of my wine, feeling all eyes on me. "I went to mingle with the crowd. Isn't that the point of these events —to get to know one another?"

Father nods, looking pleased with my response, but his is the only smile I see. Prince Thorne exchanges a dark glance with his father, King Florian, then turns to me. "I didn't realize you were friendly with any members of our court."

I take another sip of my wine to give myself a moment to think. "I wasn't until today."

Thorne and King Florian exchange another glance. It looks to me like one of those silent conversations my father and I sometimes have. The king clearly wants Thorne to do something, and Thorne is making a silent effort to resist. He evidently loses, because he looks back at me a second time and smiles.

"I can introduce you to some of my friends tomorrow if you

like. You might have more in common with them than with the, uh, *lesser* nobility."

I frown, but my father catches my eye and nods almost imperceptibly. I resist the urge to sigh. "Sure," I say to Thorne. "I'd like that."

Prince Thorne and King Florian look satisfied and go back to eating their dinner. I watch King Florian out of the corner of my eye. When he glances up, I notice that his eyes are a familiar emerald green.

A sense of satisfaction washes over me. I knew I wasn't imagining things.

"I think I've inadvertently caused a problem," I say, marching into Magnus's study later that evening.

My father's adviser is standing by his large arched window, holding a bit of parchment up to the light. At the sound of my entrance, he lowers the paper and spins to face me. "Your Highness, good evening." He smiles. "What was that you said?"

"I think I've caused a problem," I repeat, stopping in the middle of the room and crossing my arms.

Magnus steps away from the window and crosses to stand behind his heavy oak desk. "What kind of problem?"

"Did you know that King Florian has a bastard son at court?"

Magnus's eyebrows raise. "No...well, I should say, not officially. Why?"

I bite the inside of my cheek, trying to think of the right words to describe the problem.

Normally I would go to my father with something like this, but he's currently far too busy with the summit for such a trivial issue, and I'm sure he would somehow make this out to be my fault. Magnus isn't my first, or even tenth choice of confidant, but he's the only person I can think of who would be able to help me.

"I spoke at length with the son today," I explain. "I didn't know who he was at first, but upon a second glance, it was impossible not to see the resemblance to the king."

"If you noticed a resemblance, then I'm sure it's no secret. What's the problem?"

"I think the Vernalli royals must have noticed us speaking. I'm concerned they'll think I was making some kind of political maneuver."

"I wouldn't worry about that," Magnus says bracingly. "They're not likely to say anything to you about it."

"It's not me I'm concerned about."

"Then who? Don't worry about the summit, Your Highness. Nothing will derail our negotiations with Vernallis."

I grind my teeth. He doesn't get it.

Because of course, like my father, Magnus would only ever think about politics. He doesn't care about individual people.

"I'm worried about the son and his family," I explain slowly. "It occurs to me that my accidental intervention could look like favoritism, and in that case, Florian might want to get rid of the embarrassment. Perhaps a trip out of their own kingdom might be a good opportunity for there to be an 'unfortunate accident' that mysteriously removes the threat to their line of succession."

Magnus raises his eyebrows. "You care what happens to Florian's bastard?"

I fight to keep my tone even. "Only so much as I care about what happens to any friend. He was a good guy. I don't want him killed because I didn't research the parentage of who I randomly chose to sit with."

I hold my breath as Magnus looks down his nose at me. I wish I hadn't come to him with this—I should have just swallowed my discomfort and asked my father about it. Or, better yet, I should have handled it myself.

"Fine," Magnus says finally. "If you're concerned that your friend will be harmed within the borders of Hydratta, I can take care of that for you. I'll ask extra guards to watch him and his family…but I can't control what happens when they return to Vernallis."

I nod. "That's good enough. Thank you."

"Kastian," Magnus calls after me as I turn to leave.

I stop short, startled. Magnus hardly ever uses my first name —not at least without a "Prince" ahead of it. I turn back around. "Yes?"

"While we're discussing it, I should mention that this isn't the first I've heard today of your new acquaintances."

My stomach sinks. "I really didn't know who Daemon was. I—"

"It's not the bastard prince I'm talking about. Who was the girl?"

My stomach sinks lower. "His sister, I think. Or, maybe a cousin?" I say, trying to make it sound as if I'm not sure. "She's untitled. I'm not entirely sure how she ended up at this summit."

He looks at me shrewdly, leaning over his desk. "But you spent a lot of time with her?"

My stomach churns. I suddenly feel as if I'm being scolded by one of my childhood tutors. "I think you must have been misinformed. There wasn't anything going on that you should be worried about."

He raises an eyebrow at me. "Do you know what that girl is?"

Beautiful.

Interesting.

Entirely too tempting.

"No, what do you mean?"

"Several courtiers reported to me today that you were spending time with a siren. That's not a good idea. Not for you or for the future of this court. The sirens have abilities that would make any man behave against his usual nature."

My eyebrows raise, not least because this is the first I'm hearing that Magnus has courtiers who report to him—about *me*.

Does my father know that's happening? Did he perhaps put Magnus up to it, or is the advisor acting alone?

And all that aside, what does he mean Odessa is a siren?

"You have to be mistaken," I say sharply. "I told you, she's the Baron of Ashwater's cousin. Her family is all Fae."

"And how do you think sirens came to be?" he says, a note of condescension in his tone.

"I don't know. I never thought about it," I growl, unable to keep the annoyance out of my voice.

Magnus sinks into the chair behind his desk and gestures for me to sit in an armchair across from him. I decline, choosing to stay standing.

He narrows his eyes at me, but continues his explanation. "The sirens are only ever born female, so in order to keep breeding they crawl out of the oceans and entice Fae males to father their children. Technically, all sirens are half Fae—though that half doesn't often materialize."

"Usually, the sirens return to the sea before their daughters are born and the spawn never know what life is like to live on land. Rarely, however, a siren is coerced or imprisoned on land long enough for the baby to be born and raised among the Fae. Then, they become something altogether more dangerous."

"More dangerous in what way?"

"In the sea, sirens are predatory pack animals. They live and hunt in large groups, and communicate telepathically. Their thoughts are constantly connected to one another in a hive mind, where the only decision maker is the leader—usually called the queen. All sirens have higher intelligence and the capacity for independent thought, but they don't use it. The queen is the only one who thinks and behaves similarly to the Fae."

The hair on the back of my neck stands up, but I shake it off. "I don't know what this has to do with Odessa."

"All sirens have the ability to compel Fae to do anything they want, but they rarely use it for reasons other than breeding. A siren who was raised on land, however, would become a sort of queen in her own right because she wouldn't be connected to the hive mind of other sirens. She could use her powers of compulsion for anything she wished."

"You must be mistaken."

He puts both palms flat on his desk. "I wish I were. All but the oldest of our kind have forgotten that for generations Fae tried to breed landlocked sirens intentionally to take advantage of their unique powers. Every kingdom in Ellender wanted one because a queen with the power to bewitch her subjects would be unstoppable."

A shiver travels over my spine. A ruler with complete and total control over their kingdom. I can actually see exactly how that would be appealing, but more importantly, I can see how it would be a crime against nature. Rulers shouldn't have total control or else they become dictators.

My mind is reeling, but I force my face and voice to remain stoic. "You're not old enough to remember that."

He laughs. "No, but I'm well educated and I've read about how the attempts to breed sirens was abandoned and even outlawed in some places."

"Why?" I ask, in spite of myself.

"Because they're nearly impossible to control, and their persuasive abilities made them dangerous to the very rulers who sought to use them. Your friend is exceedingly rare, and also quite young. I doubt she or her lesser noble family know exactly what she's capable of."

A sudden, sharp burn sears through my chest, like a bolt of lightning striking from within. My heart races, pounding against my ribcage, and an overpowering protective instinct surges through me.

"This is all very interesting," I say, forcing my tone to remain neutral, "but I really think you must be imagining things. I don't think that girl is a siren queen, or whatever you want to call her. Even if she was, I barely spoke to her. I doubt I'll see her again."

He raises his eyebrows at me, then sighs, looking resigned.

"Fine. I hope you're right, because it wouldn't be good for a prince of Hydratta to be bewitched by a siren. Your future is too important for that."

I turn on my heel and walk out of the office. "Don't worry, Magnus, I'm well aware of what my future holds."

ODESSA, PRESENT

I wake up to the familiar feeling of the ground rocking beneath my feet and immediately know I'm on a ship.

I slowly push myself upright, wincing as I press a trembling hand to my pounding head. The world around me is a blur of shadow, the kind of darkness that swallows everything whole. I squint, but the inky blackness offers no hint of where I am. A chilling dread crashes over me, sending my rational mind into a frenzied spiral.

For years I've longed to return to the ocean, I just never envisioned it quite like this.

"Stop it," I command myself. "There's no point being afraid. Do something."

The words sound brave, but in reality do very little to calm my racing heart or drown out the throbbing in my head.

I take a few deep breaths, then force myself to stand up.

I know I'm in a cell, made from iron bars so old that I can smell the rust even over every other putrid stench; piss, mold, and something acrid that might have once been food or perhaps a dead rat left too long to rot.

I crawl across the disgusting ground, feeling along the walls with my hands. It's laughably tiny: a cube barely big enough for me to lie down—not that I would ever want to lie down on the slick floorboards.

I find the door to the cell and feel along it until I reach the lock. I'm unsurprised to discover that no amount of shaking will open the door, and I can't even think about picking the lock in this darkness. My shoulders slump in defeat.

I'll have to wait for someone to come down here to check on me. They'll have to, unless they're planning to starve me, which isn't a possibility that I want to dwell on. If Captain Connell wanted to kill me, he could have done it on the train...right?

I fumble in the dark for the edge of my long skirt and tear it off at the knees, laying the fabric down on the ground to put a barrier between me and the filthy floor, and sit down to wait.

This is undoubtedly and by far the worst thing that has ever happened to me. Yet, none of it feels real, which I think must be a sign that I'm in shock—or that the blow to my head rattled my brain.

I try to force my sluggish mind to focus despite my splitting headache.

Captain James Connell...I know I've heard that name before, but where? I might think it was years ago aboard *The Adella*, but that was far longer ago than any human lifespan.

Then again, the captain might look human but undoubtedly is not.

I know I stabbed him. I might have stabbed him in the stomach instead of the heart, but he still should have died—or, at least, the wound should have slowed him down. What kind of creature looks human but heals instantly? Not even the Fae heal so fast, as if by magic.

Most magical creatures are hard to kill, but there are ways. A wound to the heart will kill almost anything, as will fire, beheading, and drowning. The Fae can live for hundreds—if not thousands—of years, but they still need beating hearts and air in their lungs.

I lean my head back against the iron bars and let out a soft moan of mingled pain and frustration.

It was so incredibly stupid of me to go off on my own for no better reason than to avoid looking Kastian in the eye. Now, I would trade practically anything to go back and do that moment over.

But of course, as I've often thought lately, there are only so many second chances, and I've already used mine up.

After what I think must be hours, my stomach starts to growl.

An hour after that, the growling turns to shooting pain.

Just when I'm growing so hungry that I'm contemplating gnawing on my leather shoes, I hear a loud creak of hinges and a shaft of light streams down the stairs. Seconds later, the glow of a lantern and a pair of feet come into view. I hear the jingle of keys with every step, and my already racing heart beats double time.

This is my chance.

I jump to my feet and rush to the bars of my cell, eagerly waiting for whichever pirate has come to bring me my supper. I'm sure he'll have cotton in his ears like Captain Connell, but perhaps if I shout I can still bewitch him. It's my only chance.

An enormous wave of disappointment crashes over me when the figure reaches the bottom of the stairs and raises their lantern to illuminate their face.

It's a girl—or, a woman, I suppose. I can't tell in the dim light how old she is or whether she's Fae or human.

Regardless, her presence makes my life harder.

The siren song isn't a danger to women. It only affects men because its purpose is finding fathers for our children. Apparently,

Captain Connell knows more about sirens than the average man, which doesn't bode well for me.

As the girl walks closer, I see that she's probably Fae, though it's still hard to tell with her dishwater-blonde hair covering her ears and a layer of dirt and grime coating her unsmiling face. She's tall for a woman and bone thin. Her maroon striped dress is torn in some places and mended in others, and there's soot and dirt on her apron. She holds a full plate of food and a lantern in one hand, and in the other she brandishes a pistol that looks slightly too large for her to hold comfortably.

"Where are we going?" I ask, without bothering to say hello.

"Don't talk to me," the girl hisses, her voice quavering slightly.

"I can't influence you if that's what you're worried about."

The girl says nothing as she steps up to the door to my cell. She puts the lantern down and shuffles the plate in her hands to reach for the keys on her belt without lowering her pistol.

My gaze locks on the keyring, and I lick my dry lips.

"Step back," the girl says, her voice shaking slightly. "I'm going to open the door and put the plate down. Don't even think about trying to get past me or I'll shoot you."

I appraise her carefully.

From the way she's dressed, I think she must be a servant—and likely not a very well-paid one. There aren't many women on ships, so either she was incredibly desperate for a job or her husband or lover is among the crew. Either way, I doubt she's familiar with how to shoot a pistol. Guns are human inventions and uncommon in Ellender—most Fae wouldn't have ever even seen one.

"You don't know how to shoot that, do you?" I ask.

"I do," she says, the lie clear in her voice.

I roll my eyes. "Put that down. You're more likely to blow your own hand off than successfully shoot me."

The girl looks warily at the pistol, then back to me. "But then you'll run at me the moment I open the door."

"I promise that I won't, just tell me where we're going."

She gives the pistol another suspicious glance before placing it on the floor. "Solistine."

I raise my eyebrows. Why on earth would we be going there?

The desert kingdom is on the other side of the continent, and we'd have to sail all the way around Hydratta to reach it. "That's likely to take over a week."

The girl shakes her head. "Not the way Captain Connell sails."

I scoff. "He could be the best captain in the world and still not be able to affect the weather."

"Shows what you know," she says snidely. "Captain Connell is the only man in Ellender able to sail through the Strait of Scylla."

My eyebrows raise and my mouth falls open. "You cannot be serious. That's a death sentence."

"Shut up!" She hisses, looking alarmed.

I scowl. Sailors are superstitious by nature, but I'm not jinxing them by speaking the obvious truth. Years ago, I recall hearing my father and Mercer talking about the Strait of Scylla. The passage is faster than any other route between Hydratta and the mainland, but no one dares to sail there since it's full of carnivorous sea monsters.

"How much longer until we reach the strait?" I demand. "How long have we been sailing? How—"

I break off as a sudden loud bang rattles the deck above us. Both the girl and I look up in unison, startled, as the muffled shouting grows louder.

My stomach does an anxious flip. What if we're already in the middle of the Strait of Scylla and the ship is being attacked?

The captain might not be able to die, but he's going to get the rest of us killed.

Well, I won't die.

Even if this ship sank, the moment I touched the ocean I would transform into my other form.

If that happens, I might prefer to die.

"You jinxed us," the girl hisses angrily at me. She drops the plate of food on the ground outside the cell and turns on her heel to run back up the stairs.

Before she can make it ten steps, the door at the top of the stairs opens again with another loud creak, bringing with it the unmistakable sounds of chaos from above.

Footsteps thunder down the stairs, and my breath catches, before I hear the unmistakable sound of a familiar voice. "Dessa?"

"Over here!" I shout, confusion and relief washing over me.

Jett reaches the bottom of the stairs and runs toward me, boots slipping slightly on the filthy floor.

The servant girl's face flushes with panic; her eyes dart between us and the stairs like she's weighing how fast she could make it past Jett and whether she'd survive.

Clearly deciding to risk it, she darts forward and shoves Jett hard in the shoulder and bolts for the stairs.

"Stop her!" I yell. "She has the key!"

He changes direction mid-motion and lunges for the girl. She shrieks as he knocks her to the ground and grapples for the keys at her belt.

"Just take them!" the girl yells. "Let me go!"

Jett snatches the keys from her and jumps up, not sparing a single backward glance as he charges toward me. "Alright in there, Dessa?"

"What are you doing here? How did you find me?" I nearly wail, my grip on the bars the only thing keeping me upright.

"Long story," he gasps, breathless, his eyes scanning me for signs of injury. "I'll tell you once we're safe. Are you okay?"

"More or less."

"Thank the fucking gods," he breathes, relief obvious on his face.

With trembling hands, he fumbles through several keys, each failed attempt heightening the tension until finally, the right one clicks. The lock releases, and I stagger out of the cell, tears streaming down my face as I fling myself into his arms. "I can't believe you're here."

Jett holds me tight, his hand firm on my back. "Don't celebrate yet," he warns, his voice steely. "We still have to get off this godsdamn ship."

As if on cue, another crash sounds up above, and I look toward the stairs, suddenly realizing that it's odd none of the pirates have rushed down here to stop Jett from reaching me. Whatever is happening above deck must be taking all their focus. "What's happening up there?"

"Kastian," Jett says, as if that's the only explanation necessary.

My eyes widen, and my heart skips a beat. I struggle to find words, and my voice comes out hoarse and breathless. "Oh...he's here too?"

Jett rolls his eyes, clearly not fooled by my attempt at nonchalance. "Just come on. I can't stay down here a second longer; it smells like shit."

I laugh slightly hysterically, and out of instinct, I reach for my long skirt to lift it as we dash toward the stairs. Only then do I remember that my dress is torn, leaving my knees exposed.

I suppose that's the least of my concerns right now.

Jett ushers me up the slick, wet stairs, and we emerge onto the top deck.

I blink rapidly, the low evening light feeling surprisingly bright after the darkness below. I inhale a huge gulp of fresh air, but there's no time to savor it.

All around us is chaos; sailors run this way and that, men scream, and barrels and crates slide across the deck as the ship rocks back and forth as if in a storm.

"Watch out!" Jett shouts, pulling me back into the stairwell just as a massive wave crashes over the deck. Salty droplets spray my face and drench my front, but I'm lucky to have escaped the worst of it.

The crew is not so lucky.

Pirates scream as many sweep overboard into the churning sea. Others cling to the masts and walls to avoid falling.

I whirl around, bewildered by the wild, frothy waves crashing against the ship despite the clear evening sky above.

Then, all at once, I understand.

On the other end of the ship, Kastian stands firmly at the center of the deck, surrounded by the remaining pirates as they close in around him. Blood coats his tattooed arms and one side of his face, but he doesn't seem to notice as he cuts into each pirate almost methodically, sending them crumpling to the ground one by one.

Then, like he can feel me looking, he turns and our eyes meet across the deck. My heart races, constricting my chest as if it's caught in a vice. My breathing turns shallow, and in that moment two things become absolutely clear:

This is the Kastian I remember—the one I fell in love with a hundred years ago.

And it's too late to save us. We're already doomed.

17

THE PRESENT

KASTIAN, PRESENT

Three deckhands charge toward me, their blades drawn. I hold my own sword steady and plant my feet as the pirates close in.

Deep breath in...

They close in around me, and I pivot, my blade a sharp blur as it slices through the air. The first pirate lunges, and I strike left, my blade meeting his with a clang before slipping past to find flesh. Another strike swings wide, and I duck right, feeling the rush of air as his weapon narrowly misses. With a swift upward slice, my blade catches the third pirate in the stomach, and his eyes widen in shock as he crumples.

Deep breath out...

I don't let myself think about it as the last pirate falls at my feet, his blood mixing with the salty water covering the deck. I can't stop to process what I'm doing or why because it's far from over.

The commotion was enough to rouse every pirate on the ship,

and within moments, they emerge from below deck and surge toward me, brandishing their mismatched sabers and axes. I turn to face the oncoming wave, and my arms move before my mind catches up: block left with the hilt, deflect right with the flat of my sword, duck low and slice at exposed thigh.

Blood spatters across my face, and a body slumps to the deck before me. Another pirate grabs at my shoulders; I twist and smash his nose with my elbow. He drops his knife—I catch it midair and fling it end-over-end into the belly of a man lunging for my legs.

I lose track of time—seconds stretch into an eternity as more pirates pour onto the deck, trampling their dead and dying comrades in their desperation to reach me.

The weight of the crowd presses in on every side until there's no room to swing my sword without hitting flesh. Not that it matters much—the blade is already slick with blood, my hands slipping on the hilt.

I take three more blows—one to the temple, a shallow cut on my calf, and a slash across my upper chest. I barely feel it, instead feeling an absurd desire to laugh.

I'm outnumbered ten to one, probably about to die for a woman who barely knows I exist.

That damned siren curse.

Out of the corner of my eye, I catch a glint of steel hurtling toward me. My heart races as I realize I had let my guard down for just a split second. Time seems to stretch as the knife arcs through the air, its sharp edge gleaming in the setting sun. I can almost feel the cold metal as it zeroes in on my cheek, and my mind screams at me to move, but my body refuses to respond.

Without really thinking about it, I reach for the ocean.

Magic sizzles across my skin, and the ship lurches, knocking the knife off course. A fraction of a second later, a wall of water rises beside the ship and erupts over its side—impossibly high, impossibly fast—drowning portholes and severing rigging lines as it falls onto us all.

Men scream and clutch at ropes, while others are swept into the rolling dark below. Even those who keep their grip are battered senseless by gallons upon gallons of icy seawater slamming down onto their backs.

In under ten seconds, half the pirates are gone, and as the wave recedes the world settles back into clarity again. I'm left standing alone, gasping for air.

Fuck me.

I could have just died ten times over, but still all I can think about is finding Odessa.

Without knowing why, I lift my gaze and my breath constricts.

As if I summoned her, Odessa stands poised at the far end of the ship, just inside the doorway to the lower deck. Her eyes lock onto mine across the ruined deck, and that instant sends an electric current through my entire body.

She's alive and looks unharmed, and now finally I can breathe again.

I take one lurching step toward her, but that's as far as I get before I hear a strange rhythmic cracking, and turn instinctively toward the sound.

A lone figure is walking toward me down the center of the soaking wet deck.

I shake my head, dazed, and it takes a long moment for me to connect the clapping sound to the man in front of me, and even longer to realize that he's *applauding.*

As soon as our eyes meet, the man's face lights up in a wide grin, and he claps more enthusiastically. "Bloody well done, sir," he calls. "I always appreciate an impressive battle, even if it is at the expense of my crew."

My brow furrows. *What the fuck is going on?*

"Who are you?" I demand, hand flying to the hilt of my sword.

The man stops several yards from me and makes a sweeping bow, his electric blue eyes flashing with genuine humor. "Captain

James Connell at your service. I won't ask if you've heard of me. I don't think I could stomach the rejection if you haven't."

"I haven't," I growl.

He brings his hands to his chest as if stabbed in the heart. "Gut wrenching. Nevertheless, one must carry on, right?"

I shake my head, still feeling dazed.

The strange man—Captain James Connell—is clearly deranged. He's dressed slightly better than the crew I just slaughtered, but still looks like a pirate with salt-stained trousers and an oversized jacket over a scarred, bare chest. Beyond that, the man is *pretty*, which isn't an adjective I can recall ever using to describe another man. He's obviously human, and has the same strange allure that Alix does—the beauty that comes with being slightly unusual.

The man is smiling widely and seems entirely unbothered by this bizarre exchange. If he's really the captain of this ship, then I've just killed most of his crew. Yet, he doesn't seem to care. He must be out of his mind, but that won't stop me from killing him.

I reach for my sword again and he mirrors me. "I assume you've come in search of the Lady Odessa. That, I can understand. I wondered when we got the contract, you know? Why would anyone go to so much sodding trouble over one woman? But then, 'course I saw her and it all made sense."

I bite back a growl. "Are you fucking done?"

Still smiling, Captain Connell draws a curved saber from his belt and points it at my chest. "Right, sorry, got carried away. Shall we fight for her, then? You strike me as someone who only fights when you mean it."

"Funny, you strike me as someone who's about to die."

He rolls his wrist as if testing the balance of the blade, then levels it again between us. "I hope you're right."

Before I can process what he said, he lunges forward with a lazy, half-hearted swing of his sword, and I raise my own blade to clash with his in a metallic clang. Our swords meet in midair, and I step back to brace myself, feeling the force of his strike reverberate through my arm. Quickly, I regain my footing and drive my sword forward, catching him off balance and sending him stumbling backward. Connell recovers and drives me backwards toward the center of the ship.

We trade blows like that for several long minutes, almost as if sparring for fun.

Connell is an odd fighter—it doesn't feel as if he's really trying to kill me, but neither is he letting me find a moment to land a fatal strike. More importantly, he forces me to keep both hands on my sword to keep up with his quick motions, preventing me from drawing another wave from the ocean to wash him overboard.

"So," Connell says conversationally between swings, "where did you learn to fight?"

"Prison," I grunt, slashing at his shoulder.

He laughs, ducking just in time to avoid losing an ear. "Fascinating. I might say the same of myself—in a manner of speaking."

He whirls, and I only just lean out of the way in time to avoid catching his blade in the throat. I duck low and sweep my blade toward his shins.

"You're human?" I ask—though it's more of a comment than a question.

"Originally," he replies, spinning just in time to stop me from planting a blade in his flank. "Ooh, nice one. That was close."

"Is this a game to you?" I growl.

"Isn't everything?" He grins. "It's not bloody often I get to practice with a real fighter, and undoubtedly you were well trained."

"Don't expect me to thank you."

"Oh, I don't." He feints left. I block high, but he pivots low, taking my feet out from under me. "Because I do believe I was trained better."

I hit the deck hard, the sword tumbling from my grip. Connell steps on my hand to prevent me from reaching it and stands over me, saber tip at my throat.

"Good show, mate. Truly." He says, breathing hard. "But this is where you beg."

My face hardens. "I've never begged for anything for my entire life and I'm not about to start with you."

I knock his boot away from my hand and raise my fingers just in time to conjure a jet of water from midair. It's imprecise and weak, but the motion surprises Connell long enough for me to roll out of the way—barely.

I scramble for my sword, fingers closing around the wet hilt just as Connell brings his down in an arc.

Our blades lock, crossguards grinding, and I shove him back.

He's stronger than I expected a human would be and doesn't move easily. I let out a grunt of effort and shove harder, finally forcing him back a step at the same moment as another wave of ocean water crashes into him. Connell staggers, and I slam the flat of my sword against his temple, and he goes down hard.

I kick the saber away, then kneel on his chest. "This is where you beg."

He grins up at me, eyes bright with mirth, as if this is all a grand joke staged for his amusement. "Isn't that what I've been doing?"

"Beg," I repeat.

His eyes flash. "Please, let this be the end."

A disconcerting shiver of discomfort passes over me, but I shove the feeling aside as I draw the blade across his neck, fast and sure.

His blood wells up and he keeps grinning up at me as he draws a last ragged breath. I kneel there a long second, breathing hard, feeling nothing but the ache in my limbs and the way the deck tilts beneath me.

When I finally stand, the world is quiet.

I gradually become aware of the throbbing in my right arm and upper chest. I don't remember being hit there, but the blood coating my shirt proves otherwise. I lift the hem of my shirt to wipe sweat from my face, and it too comes back bloody.

Fuck, this is going to hurt tomorrow unless I can find a healer or muster up the energy to heal myself.

I'm not even sure how many men I just killed. Twenty? Thirty? Captain Connell could have been ten men on his own—he was one of the best fighters I've ever seen.

But I suppose I wanted it more—I had more to fight for.

And now I need to go find her.

I blink blood out of my eyes and my breath heaves as I stumble across the deck toward where I saw Odessa watching me. She's not on deck anymore, but she and Jett can't have gone far. I'll find her and—

Without warning, something smashes into the side of the boat. We rock to the side, and I falter, catching myself just before I fall onto the deck.

I whip around just in time to see a towering column of water erupt over the port side, turning the world into a blinding spray of white mist.

For a fraction of a second, I think it was my doing—that I somehow conjured another wave without meaning to—but then reality takes over.

Emerging from the depths is a gigantic black tentacle, as thick as the mainmast and lined with suckers that could easily rip a man's head clean off. With terrifying speed, it slams down onto the deck, shattering the railing into splinters.

Before I can react, dozens of tentacles burst from the frothing sea in a frenzy—some thick as tree trunks, others sinuous and searching—slamming down with bone-rattling force. One lands so near I taste its briny spray. It wraps around the starboard cannon, ripping the heavy iron free with a sound like thunder.

I duck, roll, and slash at the thing with my sword, but the blade only carves a shallow groove in its slimy hide.

It wraps around my leg, yanking me off my feet and into the air. I slice at it, over and over, but the grip tightens, winding up my legs until it wraps around my chest and squeezes. I gasp for air, but can't find it. My vision grays at the edges.

Then, from below, a saber flashes—a thin, precise cut, severing the tentacle at the base. Blood and seawater pour from the wounded monster, and the tentacle writhes for a second before it's yanked overboard by the unseen creature.

I crash to the deck, gasping, struggling to regain my breath.

Out of nowhere, a scarred hand reaches toward me, and I look up into the face of its owner. Standing over me, wild-eyed and very much alive, is Captain Connell, hand outstretched to help me up.

What the fuck?

His throat should be open. His chest should be empty. But he stands, blood-drenched but grinning. "Alright, mate?"

Shock reverberates through me, and I scramble to my feet. "I killed you."

He laughs, spitting blood onto the deck. "You wouldn't be the first."

I gape at him, a thousand questions flooding my mind, but I don't get a chance to ask any of them. Whatever monster is beneath the ship recovers, and returns with a vengeance.

Its flailing tentacles emerge from below in a shower of ocean spray, and for one disorienting moment I think the whole ship is about to roll over. The deck tilts beneath my feet—a slick plane canted forty-five degrees toward oblivion.

Somewhere behind me, I hear a chilling scream—a raw note of terror that vibrates through my spine like a struck bell.

I spin just in time to see Odessa and Jett charging up from below deck. Her face is wild, dress torn, and her hair plastered to her cheeks. She screams again as a tentacle, swift as a whip, flies toward her.

"Dessa—down!" I shout, helpless to do anything from so far away.

Jett grabs her arm and yanks her aside just as the appendage crushes the deck where she'd been standing, boards splintering under its weight.

The impact is so strong it splinters the mainmast; above us, rigging and canvas come crashing down in a billow of torn cloth. The mast groans like something dying slowly, its shadow looming as it tilts at an impossible angle.

Another tentacle wraps itself around the broken mast and heaves, snapping it off at the base with a thunderous crack that reverberates through my bones. The deck lurches; splinters rain down like daggers. The upper rigging, still tangled with black sails and snapped lines, falls straight at us.

Odessa and Jett are right underneath it.

I don't think—I react.

Something primal surges inside me: hot and electric at the core of my chest. In one motion I reach out—not with my hands but with something deeper—the magic answers instantly: ocean water boils up in a heaving wave that collides midair with sailcloth and wood debris, knocking both clear before they can crush her.

But even as relief floods me, another tentacle sweeps toward them from the port side—this one studded along its length with jagged barnacles that could strip flesh from bone.

Jett shoves Odessa back again, hard enough that she stumbles onto one knee. The tentacle catches him hard in the chest and swings him wide over the ruined deck.

Another scream has me tearing my eyes from Jett. My vision tunnels down to Odessa's terrified eyes as she crouches on the deck, her arms over her head.

My own wings spring from my back as I run toward her, lifting off the ground without even thinking about it.

I reach Dessa in seconds. She screams again as I scoop her into my arms, rising into the air just as another tentacle smashes into where she stood seconds prior.

"Are you alright?" I shout. It's such a basic question and not nearly enough to describe the terror and adrenaline that flooded me the moment I saw her, but it's all I can get out.

"I think so?" Odessa screams back over the wind. "Are you?"

"Barely."

I look around frantically for a place to put her down out of harm's way while I go back and help Jett, but there's nowhere. We're in the middle of the godsdamn fucking ocean and—*wait.*

"I'm going to put you in the water," I tell her. "I need to go get Jett."

"No!" she screams, a stronger note of panic than I've ever heard before rising in her voice.

"You'll be fine. I'll come right back."

"Please, no!" she screams again. She reaches out with both hands and grabs my face, forcing my eyes to hers. "Do not put me in the water, Kastian. *Please!*"

I stare into her wide violet eyes and for half a second I can't think, I just nod. I don't know what she's so scared of—a siren shouldn't be afraid of a sea monster—but I can't deny her anything when she's looking at me like that. "Okay, I won't."

Odessa lets go of my face and releases a breath. "Good. I swear to the gods, if you do, you'll never see me again."

My mouth twists with annoyance—no, *anger.*

Even now, hovering in the air over the wreck of the ship I just rescued her from, she's so determined to hate me she'd threaten to disappear. "You don't have to threaten, Princess. You could just ask."

She stiffens in my arms but doesn't say anything else, twisting to look down at the nearly ruined ship below us. I fly lower, searching for Jett, all the while trying to figure out how I'm going to reach for my sword without putting Odessa down.

Mercifully, in a flash of indigo blue feathers, I spot Jett flying low over the ship below. I let out a relieved breath and feel Odessa do the same.

I have no fucking idea how he escaped the monster's grasp, but he seems fine. He's whooping through a mouthful of blood, face split open in a wild grin as if fighting monsters was his true calling in life.

"Jett!" I shout to get his attention.

He turns midair to look at me and I swear he seems disappointed to be leaving the fight behind as he flies toward us.

Jett and I rise into the air and I squint into the distance, searching for the nearest land.

"Head south," I tell Jett, jerking my head toward my homeland.

He gives me a long look, but doesn't comment on it as we turn to fly toward the land on the horizon.

Just before we leave, I risk a glance back at the ship just as another tentacle punches clean through the keel, snapping centuries-old beams like dry reeds. At the prow, silhouetted against the setting sun, stands Captain Connell—somehow alive, absolutely refusing to die.

He's caked with blood but still upright, sword flashing as he hacks at anything that moves. oncoming limb and laughs—actually laughs—as if he'd been waiting all day for a disaster to validate his existence.

Then a tentacle as thick as a chimney wraps around Connell's waist and hauls him straight up off the deck.

He catches my eye at that moment and grins like a lunatic even as his ribs are nearly crushed by suckers the size of soup plates. "Let's pray this time it sticks!"

My stomach lurches uncomfortably.

I already hate myself for what I'm about to do.

"Jett!" I yell over the din. "Grab him!"

"Are you fucking kidding?"

"I wish."

With a shrug, he tucks wings tight and dives straight for Connell, slicing through mist and smoke. At first, it looks like they're both going to get crushed together by the monster's grip —but Jett skims low over the ruined deck, slashing through barnacle-studded flesh with a knife I didn't even realize he was holding.

The tentacle spasms; Connell slips free and drops screaming toward certain death. Jett swoops underneath at exactly the right instant, and snags Connell under both armpits. They spin wildly together before Jett recovers control, beating upward with everything he has left.

And below us, the last fragments of the ship vanish into the sea.

18

THE PAST

KASTIAN, AGE 18

"I'm going to go stand near Lord Ren until he asks me to go sailing," Dellanore states confidently.

"That's not fair!" Avaline hisses, rounding on her. "I'd intended to sail with Ren."

"Then you should have said so." Dellanore smiles smugly. "I saw him first so naturally I should be the one he asks."

"I'm not sure why this matters, seeing as he hasn't even looked at either of you," I say mildly.

The twins fix me with identical scowls. "Shut up, Kastian!" they snap at nearly exactly the same time.

I roll my eyes. My sisters are all older than me, but you would never know it from the way they talk to each other. The twins, Dellanore and Avaline, can't avoid arguing for more than ten minutes at any given time. One would think they hated each other, except that they always take each other's side against anyone else—usually that person is me.

"Why are you interested in Lord Ren?" I ask, already regretting involving myself in their argument. "He's a third son with barely a title and no money."

Dellanore raises her eyebrows at me. "It's not as if either of us needs the money."

"Yeah, but he's fuc—I mean, he's *entertained* nearly every woman at court."

Avaline rolls her eyes. "Then he's probably quite good at it."

"Ugh, never mind." I wrinkle my nose in disgust and step away from them, leaving them to their pointless squabbling.

It's late morning on the second day of Vernallis's visit to our court, and dozens of nobles stand around the wide grassy lawn between the castle and the enormous freshwater lake that takes up a third of the castle grounds. Normally, the lake is home to a gaggle of swans, but today it's dotted with dozens of small rowboats, and I frown as I watch couples climb into the boats and set off paddling around the lake.

On my left, a cluster of noblewomen are eagerly attempting to capture my attention, evidently wishing for an invitation to join me on a sail. I lower my head to avoid making eye contact.

I hate whoever's idea this was.

I've already made it a priority to keep track of where Lyra is, so I can steer clear of her and avoid the awkwardness of having to join her on a sail out of courtesy. Right now she's safely on the opposite side of the lawn talking to her father.

I don't find the idea of rowing around the lake nearly as romantic as the rest of the court seems to, and I have no desire to share a boat ride with anyone. The thought of engaging in forced small talk with a stranger, with no means of escape short of leaping overboard, makes me shudder.

Unless, I suppose, I was trapped in a boat with someone worth talking to.

At that thought, I find myself scanning the crowd, both knowing and refusing to acknowledge who I'm looking for.

I spot Daemon by the lake, looking relaxed and confident while surrounded by a crowd of giggling girls. I wonder if I could send my own group of admirers his way? He seems to enjoy the attention.

Regardless, if Daemon is here, then Odessa must be around here somewhere. I let out a sigh and roll my neck, trying to release some of the tension building at the base of my skull.

Despite knowing I shouldn't, I can't stop thinking about Odessa Ashwater.

Rather than deter me, Magnus's warnings last night have only made me more interested. I'm not entirely sure I believe Odessa is a siren. It would certainly explain her beauty, but I've only ever thought of sirens as monstrous and deadly. I've never heard of one living on land for any great length of time.

If only I'd won our bet yesterday, I could have asked her about it and demanded she be truthful in payment. Instead, I'm waiting for her to demand her favor of me. I'm oddly looking forward to it.

I raise my gaze to scan the lawn again, not even bothering to try to convince myself that I'm not looking for Odessa.

Finally, I spot her distinctive hair, flaming red in the sunlight, and my heartbeat kicks up, pounding against my ribs.

Dressed in a blue gown and a wide-brimmed hat, she's standing at the end of the small dock and talking animatedly with a man clad in a red jacket. I shift to the left, attempting to see past the crowd separating us. My heart sinks when I realize who she's speaking with—Lord Ren, the same degenerate bastard my sisters were fighting over.

As I watch, Lord Ren points toward one of the boats, prompting Odessa to smile and nod in agreement. Suddenly, a wave of intense anger wells up inside me. My stomach burns and turns hard, my breath coming faster. Before I know it, I'm moving.

Hundreds of eyes follow me as I sprint across the lawn. I vaguely wonder how many of them will report to Magnus about this and what my father will say later when he hears that I've shoved Lord Ren into the lake and held him under until he stopped breathing.

I come to a screeching stop at the dock's edge and walk briskly toward Odessa and the lord, struggling to suppress my violent fantasies.

Lord Ren holds Odessa's hand, helping her to lower herself into the boat. She settles her wide skirt around her and fixes her hat before finally lifting her gaze.

I witness the precise instant when she sees me.

Recognition flickers across her face. Her violet eyes widen, and for the briefest heartbeat, her lips curve into a soft, involuntary smile. But then, as if catching herself, her expression shifts, and her brows knit together in a disapproving frown.

Lord Ren, still standing on the dock, pivots to see what has caught Odessa's attention, and his eyes grow large upon spotting me, breathless from running. His eyes widen even more as he glances beyond me, undoubtedly noticing the hundreds of nobles gathered on the lawn, all focused on us. "Your Highness, what—"

I don't stop walking, knocking my shoulder hard into Ren's. "Sorry, this boat is taken."

"What—" Lord Ren teeters, but doesn't fall into the water— an immaculate show of restraint on my part.

I elbow him out of the way and step into the boat.

Odessa grips the edges of the boat, and her mouth falls open as if words have momentarily escaped her. She finally regains her composure, crossing her arms tightly over her chest. "What the hell do you think you're doing?"

"Rowing," I reply, grabbing the oars.

"Get out!" She hisses, looking anxiously around at the crowd on the lawn. "Everyone is staring."

"They'll stare more if I get out now." I raise the oars and push us off from the dock, leaving Lord Ren gaping after us.

Odessa shifts in her seat, looking out over the water as if seriously considering jumping overboard. Evidently, she decides it's not worth it, because she stays put but crosses her arms more tightly over her chest and refuses to look at me as I row away from the dock.

"Lovely day, don't you think?" I ask her.

She sniffs, but doesn't say anything and I'm tempted to laugh. I think I might like teasing her, if only because she looks cute with that stubbornly miserable expression on her face.

"Are you really going to ignore me?" I ask after a silent moment. "This will be a very boring ride if you refuse to talk."

"Why would I want to talk to you? You kidnapped me and stole my boat!"

I try to repress a smile. "I'd hardly call this kidnapping."

"Then what would you call it? Piracy? Villainy?"

I can't hold back my grin. "I'd call it heroism. Believe me, you did not want to be stuck in the middle of the lake with Lord Ren. I was saving you."

"Oh, please," she scoffs.

"Ren is an arrogant, penniless gambling addict with a reputation for ruining virgins. You can do better."

"Better like you, you mean?" She scowls and holds up her fingers as if counting off a list. "Arrogant." She puts down a finger. "Has gambled literally every time we've met."

She puts down another finger, even as I interject: "I don't see how one bet on a horse race could be considered an addiction. We weren't even using money."

She ignores me, still counting down my supposed shortcomings. "—has undoubtedly ruined dozens of virgins."

I choke. "Dozens is a bit extreme."

She raises her middle finger pointedly before putting it down. "Guilty of kidnapping and thievery."

"I thought we'd covered that already."

"And—" she says, making a fist with her remaining raised fingers and fixing me with a vicious scowl, "—unfaithful."

"In what possible way am I unfaithful?" I demand.

"You have a fiancée, whom I have yet to hear you mention even once." A ringing silence follows this statement, and Odessa's eyes flash with triumph. "Tell me again how you are better than the man whom you just shoved out of the way to steal his boat?"

My eye twitches. My discomfort is made no better by the fact that I can see other rowboats floating suspiciously closer to us as their occupants try to eavesdrop on our conversation.

I let out a huff of breath. "I don't have a fiancée."

"Liar," she snaps. "You're betrothed to that woman I met the other night."

"Betrothed, yes, but not engaged."

She looks at me like I'm insane. "Do you need a language lesson, *Your Majesty*? I would have thought you'd have the best tutors possible, but evidently they've neglected to teach you the meaning of the word 'betrothed.'"

The corners of my mouth tip up and I row faster, trying to escape the other boats and find a shred of privacy. "I know what the word means, thank you, but a betrothal and an engagement are not the same thing."

"Excuse you, but—"

I cut her off before she can gather steam and run me over with her argument. "Betrothals happen between children and they're broken all the time. Lyra's father is my father's favorite advisor. The betrothal agreement is really more about them than it is about us. It's a public boon my father bestowed on Magnus."

"But you're still promised to marry her."

"Eventually, maybe, in twenty years the betrothal could turn into an actual engagement...but I doubt it ever will."

"Why not?" she asks begrudgingly.

"Because we're not well suited. I doubt either of us would be particularly bothered if the other found their soul-bond and the agreement was dissolved."

She looks up at me, eyes assessing. "I didn't think royals cared about finding their soul-bonds."

"We don't," I answer shortly. "It's certainly not a requirement for a marriage, but obviously it would be preferable."

She nods tightly. "I still doubt you're supposed to be seen showing obvious favoritism for another woman."

"Is that what I'm doing?" I challenge her.

Her cheeks flush, and goes back to staring off into the distance, refusing to meet my eyes. "Oh, never mind."

I smile, pleased that I've managed to get under her skin.

She's not entirely wrong, though. I probably shouldn't be so obvious—especially as I'm not exactly known to show public affection for anyone. That's probably where the impression that I'm arrogant comes from. I don't really enjoy talking to anyone, but it's not because I think I'm above them. I just don't like people.

Except, for some reason, I like Odessa—and maybe Daemon too, though in an entirely different way.

With that in mind, I direct our boat beneath the branches of a weeping willow dipping into the water and stop, letting the branches serve as a curtain between us and the rest of the lake.

Odessa looks up, startled. "Why did you stop?"

"I'm not much of a fan of rowing."

"Of course you're not," she hisses, rolling her eyes. "We can't stay in here, though."

"I thought you didn't want people staring at us."

She widens her eyes in incredulous disbelief. "You cannot seriously be this naïve. If we stay here, people will think we need *privacy*."

"I don't really care what anyone thinks."

"Of course you don't, you're a prince. But what do you think they'll say about me?"

"What do people expect is going to happen?" I blurt out before I can stop myself. "Am I supposed to have my way with you in this boat? That would be an impressive feat of acrobatics."

The tiniest hint of a smile appears on Odessa's lips, but she refuses to relent. "Please, just row out from under the tree."

"Fine." I sigh, and pick up the oars again, moving us just

beyond the cover of the willow. Odessa looks marginally pacified, though still unhappy.

"Did I do something to offend you?" I ask, as we float along the bank in plain sight of the rest of the lake.

She lets out a bark of laughter. "Was I not clear about that already?"

"Not now," I clarify, waving her off. "I meant before. I've never met anyone so intent on disliking me before I even opened my mouth."

"You certainly opened your mouth when you shouted at me in the hall."

"I am truly sorry for that, but I can't imagine that's the problem. You don't seem like the type to be scandalized so easily. I must have done something else."

Her cheeks flush pink. "I don't know what you're talking about, *Your Majesty*."

"Bullshit," I blurt out without thinking.

Odessa laughs, for real this time, her entire face lighting up. She relaxes slightly, and I let out a breath. I suddenly find myself vowing to use as much foul language as I can think of in her presence if it makes her laugh.

"I don't know why you keep seeking me out," she says.

It's not really an answer to my question, but she's at least looking at me now, so I'll take it. "I don't like leaving debts unpaid, and I owe you a favor."

"Oh, right, that." She bites her lip. "Perhaps we should just call it forgiven."

My stomach does an uncomfortable flip. If she forgives my debt, then there's no rational excuse I can come up with to seek her out again...and that's unacceptable. "No, I can't accept that. You must think of something I can give you."

"Why do you even care?" she asks, a note of accusation in her voice.

"Maybe I just like you," I reply honestly.

Her face flames scarlet this time. "Impossible. You just met me the other day."

"How long do you need to know someone to know if you like them?"

She thinks about it for a moment, face still flushed. "Three days. Minimum."

"Why three?" I ask, genuinely curious to understand how her mind works.

"Well, this summit is three days—" she gestures around the lake "—that must be long enough for Prince Thorne and Princess Serena to get to know each other."

I scowl, unable to help myself. "There's no chance my sister will marry your prince, but I take your point. So, in three days, will you accept it if I say I like you?"

She shakes her head and looks down, once again refusing to meet my eyes. "No."

"Why?"

"You know nothing about me, and I haven't been exactly nice to you."

I laugh, and row our boat a few feet to the left to avoid a pair of swans swimming past. "So you admit you're being intentionally difficult. I must have offended you. What did I do?"

"Nothing," she hisses, glancing around again as if searching for an escape. "But you cannot expect me to believe you truly like me, Prince Kastian. You don't know me. Whatever you think you feel isn't real."

I ponder that, pushing myself far beyond the usual amount of effort I'd exert on anything, and really trying to see this from her point of view.

I suppose that anyone who looks like Odessa would have already encountered dozens—maybe hundreds—of men who are only interested in her because of her beauty. She's probably already jaded and distrustful of anyone claiming an interest in her.

"Fine, I take your point," I say.

She relaxes slightly. "Thank you."

"So the only solution is for you to let me get to know you better."

She stiffens again. "Excuse me?"

"Tell me what you want in payment for the horse race. Surely you can learn a lot about a person from what they'd ask for if they could have anything in the world."

Her eyes narrow. "So you'll be judging me? Will I get more points if I ask for something altruistic instead of gold or jewels?"

"There's no point system. I just want to know what's important to you."

She looks conflicted, then sighs, her shoulders slumping. "Fine," she breathes. "I want to see the ships."

"The ships?" I repeat, uncomprehending. "The ones you were looking at the other night, you mean?"

She nods. "I want to go to the harbor and see them."

"The masked ball on the last night of this summit is being held on a ship. You'll get to see them then."

She shakes her head. "That's not what I mean. I want to go see them alone, but I can't get out of the castle and go wandering around during the day. I'll be missed, and I'm not stupid enough to go alone at night."

I nod. I'm glad to hear that, at least. I can't imagine what would happen to a girl as beautiful as Odessa if she went down to the harbor alone after dark.

Actually, I can imagine it, and the idea sends a jolt of combined panic and anger through me, so strong that my knuckles turn white on the oar handles.

"I'll take you," I blurt out.

She looks down her nose at me. "You can't take me to the harbor. People would recognize you. I was thinking you could send some of your guards with me."

"I think you'd be surprised how few people would recognize me out of context. I used to escape my guards all the time as a child, I'm very familiar with the city."

She smiles, a slightly knowing expression I can't quite understand appearing on her face.

I jump on that smile like a starving animal on a shred of meat. "And if I don't take you myself, how will I get to know you better?"

She presses her lips firmly together, looking as if she knows this is a bad idea.

I know it's a bad idea too, but I think for entirely different reasons than whatever she's worried about.

"Fine," she says finally. "You can take me to see the ships."

"Good," I say, even as a warm elated glow washes over me.

"But that's all," she adds, "and I make no promises about being nicer."

I grin. "I wouldn't expect you to."

I get the impression that Odessa is like the swans swimming around the lake—thorny and slow to trust, but infinitely loyal thereafter.

I'm looking forward to winning her over, because when I do it will feel like I've won something priceless.

Something *inevitable.*

ODESSA, PRESENT

I squint into the darkness, trying to make out the land on the horizon.

The sun has finally set, and it's dark as midnight as Kastian, Jett, Captain Connell, and I fly over the ocean toward the land in the distance. My neck aches and my legs hurt where Kastian's fingers dig into them, but I don't dare to complain.

I'm all too aware of all the places our skin touches. Of the feel of his muscled arms around me and powerful chest mere inches from my cheek. All I can smell is his wood and citrus scent.

A full-body shiver travels through me, and Kastian's arms tighten. "Are you cold?"

I shake my head. "No."

Godsdammit, why does my reaction to him have to be so obvious?

Looking for something to take the focus off me, I reach up to touch a gash just below Kastian's collarbone. "Does this hurt?"

He flinches as if my touch burned him. "A bit."

"I can look at it when we land," I offer.

"Can you heal wounds?"

"Not really, but I'm good at dressing them."

He nods and offers me what I think is a smile—though it's hard to tell in the dark. "I can heal it myself with magic. I just need to sleep first. I'm too tired right now."

"Sorry," I mutter, feeling slightly guilty.

He's tired because of me—because he came to rescue me and because I couldn't let him put me down in the water. My chest tightens, and there's a pain at the back of my throat.

"Don't be sorry," he says quickly. "I could heal myself now if I were better at it, but I've never been that talented at healing."

"Please, I've seen you use magic, and you're excellent at it. You created a tsunami today."

"That's different, but I'll take it. I think that's the nicest thing you've ever said to me."

My heartbeat kicks up a tiny bit and I try to ignore it as I put on a flippant tone. "I guess I can be pleasant to you. *Once*. In exchange for saving me."

"How benevolent of you," he says dryly. "You really seem to like that word."

"What word?"

"*Once*."

I suck in a startled breath and feel my cheeks heat. I'm suddenly glad of the darkness hiding my blush.

I clear my throat. "I assume Daemon sent you to find me?"

He pauses. "No, actually. He sent Jett."

I swallow thickly. The question is on the tip of my tongue— *why would you come after me? Why do you care?*

I know if I ask, he'll give me the true answer, but I don't want to know. Because once that gets voiced out loud, it can't be taken back and we're already in such a precarious position as it is.

"Bloody hell!" Captain Connell says loudly, exasperation in his voice. "Are you trying to rip my arms from the sockets?"

"Shut the fuck up," Jett grumbles, sounding far more serious than his usually cheerful tone. "You're lucky I haven't dropped you yet."

"I might sodding prefer that to losing both arms."

"What are you two shouting about?" Kastian growls.

"I think I see a spot to land." Connell says. "Thank the gods. Do you know how uncomfortable it is to dangle like this for hours on end? Some might call that cruel and unusual."

"We could have let you drown." Jett grumbles, adjusting his grip under Connell's arms. "I still might. You're godsdamned heavy."

I immediately stiffen, suddenly worried that I'm heavy too.

"You're not," Kastian mutters, as if he can read my mind.

My cheeks flush deeper, and I'm once again desperately glad for the darkness surrounding us.

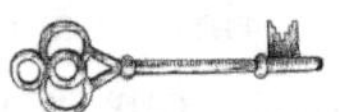

We land on the edge of a cliff overlooking the ocean. Even by the light of the moon, it's too dark to see much of anything, but the air is thick, laden with the aroma of brackish water and decaying plant matter, overpowering even the scent of the ocean behind us. As soon as Kastian puts me down, my feet sink into the muddy ground.

"Finally!" Captain Connell's voice cuts through the silence, and there's a smacking sound and a grunt, as if he clapped Jett hard on the back. "Thanks for the ride, mate. Excuse me a moment, I've had to take a piss for the last hour."

"Charming," Kastian says dryly as we hear the sounds of Connell crashing away through the underbrush.

"What did you expect?" I ask. "He's a pirate."

"I wasn't talking about him. I meant this cliff." He punctuates his point with a squelching sound as he tries to pull his boot out of the muck.

"Again, what did you expect? This is Hydratta."

"Not a part of Hydratta I've ever been to," he says grimly.

"Should we let the pirate wander off on his own?" Jett asks, coming to stand beside Kastian and me. The three of us step closer to make out each other's faces by the light of the moon. I turn and squint through the darkness in the direction of the rustling bushes.

I shrug. "I doubt he'll try to run. There's nowhere for him to go."

Kastian looks at me. "Why do you say that?"

"I think this is the edge of The Weeping Quagmire." I shudder. "It's the stretch of swamp that connects Hydratta to the mainland. I'd recognize the smell anywhere."

"Why? Have you been here before?"

I nod. "Prince Thorne made the entire court of Vernallis travel by land to Hydratta during his potential engagement summit with your sister. We rode by carriage through here for days."

As soon as the words leave my mouth, I wish I could take them back. I must be exhausted, because I completely forgot to watch what I say when it comes to Kastian's past and my part in it.

As far as I know, he doesn't remember that I was even there when the court of Vernallis visited Hydratta, but unfortunately he's not stupid, and I know he caught my slip from the way I can feel his eyes burning into the side of my face.

"We should move," I suggest, trying to cover the mistake. "Find an inn or something. I don't want to spend too much time out here at night. The swamp is full of creatures just as horrifying as that sea monster."

"Agreed," Jett says. "But what do you want me to do with the pirate?"

"I don't care what we do. Did either of you have a plan for him?"

"Not really," Kastian says, stifling a yawn. "I just figured we'd want to question him about why he took you."

"And a reason he was pretending to be from Solistine," Jett adds. "That wasn't a Solistinian ship. It had the yellow flags, but it was built in the style of Vernallis."

"How did you two find me, anyway?" I ask.

"A guard at the station recognized that you were taken by Solistinian pirates," Kastian explains. "We went to the harbor, but there were no ships from Solistine, so we flew over the ocean until we saw the flags."

My brow furrows. They flew? I understand how they could fly leaving the ship—at that point our lives were in danger—but before? How can that be?

"We'll have to ask the pirate for more information," Jett says flatly. "There has to be a reason for the disguise, and also for why he killed the Hydrattan emissary but left you mostly unharmed."

I frown, remembering how quickly and remorselessly Connell killed Elio on the train—almost like he'd planned it before coming inside. "That's a good idea. I should have thought of that myself. I'm just so damn tired and I haven't eaten since yesterday. I can't think straight."

"That's two nice things you've said to me in under an hour," Kastian comments, a smile in his tone. "Are you feeling alright, Princess?"

"*Focus*," Jett says, turning to look toward the rustling bushes. "Honestly, we might be better off questioning him right here, then killing him."

"Maybe," I hedge, "but there's only one problem with that. He can't die."

"What does that mean?" Jett turns quickly back to me. "Anything can die if you try hard enough to kill it."

Kastian looks at me, a searching question in his gaze. "Did you kill him too?"

I nod, not bothering to ask what he means by "too"—I wouldn't doubt that if I was able to stab Captain Connell in the stomach, Kastian probably could and did carve him to ribbons.

"On the train," I clarify. "If he were a normal man, I would have escaped, but he just healed in front of me."

Kastian smiles, looking vaguely proud of me, and I tear my gaze away before I let it go to my head. I'm not a trained fighter, but I'm not useless, and I had a powerful motivation not to be captured.

"I don't understand what you guys are talking about," Jett complains.

"Perhaps I can help with that," Connell says, his voice growing louder as he moves back toward us through the darkness. "And in the future, I might suggest that if you don't want someone to overhear your conversation, perhaps try keeping your voices down. Just a thought."

"We don't care what you heard," Kastian growls. "You're not going anywhere."

Connell moves to stand at Jett's shoulder and rolls his eyes. "Again, threats only work if you have something to back them up with. You're a talented fighter, mate, but as you've so expertly observed, I cannot die."

Jett gapes at the pirate, and I swear there's a hint of excitement in his black eyes. "Truly? You can't die?"

Connell shakes his head and sits down on a nearby log to unlace his boot. "No, I can't," he says, pulling the boot off and tipping it over to pour a flood of seawater onto the swampy ground.

"How?" Kastian demands. "No one is truly immortal."

"Well, obviously that's not true," Connell says flippantly. "You're immortal, aren't you?"

"No, we're not," I cut in. "We age far slower than you...or, slower than humans, I mean. But we do eventually age, and we can be killed."

"I suspect that might be true for me as well," Connell says, looking pensive. "I bloody hope something might kill me one day, I just haven't found it yet."

Kastian shakes his head, looking extremely frustrated. "Stop talking in riddles. You look human, but clearly you're not, so what are you? A doppler?"

"I don't have any ever-loving idea what that is so I don't think so," Connell says sardonically. "I was human once, a very long time ago. Still am, actually, now I come to think about it. I don't believe anything about my actual body has changed much."

"But—" Kastian begins, a real note of anger creeping into his voice.

"Calm down, mate," Connell says. "I'm explaining it. I am immortal because I'm the captain of *The Sea Witch*."

A ringing silence follows that statement, which is broken finally by Jett. "The ship that just sank, you mean?"

"Yes, although she hasn't really sunk. *The Sea Witch* never truly dies—I'm sure the next time we come across a port she'll be there waiting for me, just like she always has before."

Kastian and Jett exchange glances which clearly say they think Connell is insane, but I'm not so sure. "I've heard of ships like that," I say slowly.

"You have?" Kastian asks.

I nod. "When I lived on *The Adella*, the sailors would tell stories about immortal ships captained by spirits who were trapped on board until they'd fulfilled some prophecy."

"See?" Connell says, winking at me. "Thank you for your faith in me, darling."

"Don't talk to her," Kastian growls, taking half a step in front of me.

I roll my eyes, but make no move to step away from him.

"So what's your prophecy?" Jett asks Captain Connell.

The captain shrugs. "I don't have one—at least, not that I'm aware of. *The Sea Witch* just needs a captain, and I am it."

"What about your crew?" I ask.

For the first time, Connell scowls. "You'd have to ask your man about that one, darling. If not for him, they'd be alive and well."

"They shouldn't have helped you kidnap her," Kastian says without a shred of remorse.

"Why did you take me?" I ask.

Connell's eyes flash with interest. "Ooh, that's an interesting story. I tell you what? I swear I'll tell you all who sent me after the beautiful Lady Odessa as long as you don't leave me here in the swamp."

"Why do you need us?" Jett asks. "I thought you couldn't die."

"I can't," Connell says, turning to Jett. "But I don't fancy being eaten by some monster either. I've never tried that before, but I'd imagine it would be unpleasant."

I snort. "'Unpleasant' sounds like an understatement."

"Exactly, darling." Connell winks again. "Let me stay with you all as far as the nearest town, and I'll tell you who hired me to kidnap you. I promise it's a story you're going to want to hear."

"How do we know you won't stab us while we're sleeping?" Kastian asks.

Connell gasps in mock indignation. "I would never, it's against the seaman's code."

I roll my eyes. "There's no such thing as the seaman's code."

"Fine, you're right, but then I'd have to refer you to my earlier point. I'd rather not get swallowed by a swamp rat, and I figure I've got a better chance with you three watching my back."

"Stay right there and don't move," Jett says slowly, jerking his head for Kastian and me to follow him.

"Aye aye, Captain," Connell says sarcastically, sinking back onto the log to wait.

We walk across the cliff until we're out of earshot—out of earshot for a human at least. We'd probably have to go further if he turned out to be anything else, but the wind helps some.

"What do you think?" Kastian asks in a low voice.

"I think we should question him right here," Jett says, a more serious note in his voice than I've ever heard. Jett is always the one smiling and cracking jokes even in the most dire of circumstances, but since we escaped the ship, he's seemed subdued. Perhaps this is just his reaction to being tired and hungry.

At the thought of food my stomach growls loudly and I press my hands to it. "I think we should do whatever is fastest. I want to find an inn."

"Is that safe for you?" Jett asks Kastian. "Since we're in Hydratta."

Kastian gnaws on his lip. "Probably. This is so far on the outskirts of Hydratta I doubt any of Magnus's soldiers are posted in the villages, or that they'd immediately recognize me if they were. I'm more worried about whoever wanted to take Dessa and why."

"Connell said he won't tell us anything until we reach a town," I remind him.

Jett's black eyes flash in the darkness. "He'd tell us. There are lots of ways to convince someone to talk."

My eyebrows raise so high they reach my hairline. "Torture him, you mean?"

Jett's silence is answer enough, and a shiver travels down my spine. Part of me wants to ask if he knew how to torture someone before Dyaspora, or if that's a more recent skill. Is that what he's been doing as the official spymaster for Alix and Daemon?

I don't want to know.

"It's dark as fuck out here," Kastian says, cutting into my thoughts. "I can barely see either of you and you're right in front of me. I imagine it would be hard to torture someone if you couldn't see what you're doing. I think we should let him stay with us until we reach a town at least, but then we're not splitting up. We keep him with us and bring him back to Vernallis."

"Fine with me," Jett says after a long moment. "Dessa?"

"I agree," I say quickly. "Whatever we do, I'd like to do it quickly. I need a bath, a change of clothes and a bed before I can even think about making a real plan."

· · ·

W e leave the cliff and walk for over an hour. The swamp is disgusting and full of buzzing insects, which sting my face and bare legs. Every so often we hear something slithering along the ground, or a creature howling in the trees above. Every time something moves out of the corner of my eye, I'm certain it's going to be some sort of jungle beast leaping at me, ready to bite my jugular.

No one says anything about it, but I know I'm not the only one who's afraid because both Kastian and Jett's wings are out. I keep feeling Kastian's feathers brush against my arm, and after a while I stop bothering to flinch away on principle.

Connell stumbles over a root on the ground and swears loudly. "You know, when I said I wanted to stay with you, this isn't quite what I had in mind."

Jett tugs hard on the belt binding the pirate's wrists. "You should feel lucky this is all we've done. I'm sure I could do a lot of interesting things to a man who can't die."

"Really?" Connell asks, sounding interested. "Please, do share."

"Don't," Kastian grumbles. "This walk is hellish enough without listening to graphic descriptions of torture."

"Suddenly squeamish?" Connell asks, with a smirk in his voice. "I'd have thought you'd be desensitized to violence after murdering my entire crew."

"There will be a hell of a lot more violence if you don't shut up," Kastian grumbles.

I ball my hands into fists and try to tune out their bickering; I'm already barely hanging on to sanity as it is. I'm not used to walking this much and my legs and hips ache. I'm starving, my skin feels dirty and sticky, both from the cell and the humid air.

If I could just fix one of those things—food, a bath, a bed—I think I could pull myself together.

I screw my eyes up and try to think of positive things.

At least I'm alive—at least we're all alive. At least I'm not stuck in the brig anymore.

As Alix says, it could always get worse...

ODESSA, AGE 16

I jitter with excitement and anxiety all afternoon, then practically run down the halls to dinner. There's some sort of dance performance during dinner meant to entertain the courts, but I'm so wound up I can barely eat, let alone pay attention.

"Did you have a pleasant time at the garden party, Dessa?" Aunt Beatrix asks, when she finishes applauding for the dancers and finally picks up her glass of wine.

"Yes," I nod as I push my food around my plate, making little piles rather than eating.

"Did you meet any of the Hydrattan courtiers?"

"No one important," I lie.

Daemon and Aunt Beatrix exchange dubious glances, which makes me think they already heard about this afternoon's chaos with the boats. I meet Daemon's eye, trying to communicate that I do not want to talk about this—*please*.

"You might not have met anyone interesting, but I did," Daemon says loudly.

Aunt Beatrix rolls her eyes. "Girls, you mean."

"Exactly." He grins, launching into an overly detailed story about some noblewoman and a dog, and completely taking the attention away from me. I can't tell whether he did it on purpose or not, but either way I'm grateful because his monopoly on the conversation means I can sit quietly and think.

Part of me wonders if I should cancel this evening.

I don't go on dates. I don't have many friends aside from Daemon, and I certainly don't allow myself to become too interested in anyone.

Everyone I've ever cared about has been taken from me against my will, and I dread the day I lose anyone else. Even with Daemon and my Aunt Beatrix, I'm constantly waiting for the other shoe to drop—for the moment we say goodbye and never see each other again.

Prince Kastian thinks he likes me, but I have no idea how that could be possible when I've been nothing but rude to him. Not that I regret it—how else am I supposed to act when, in all likelihood, I'll never see him again after tomorrow?

I've been trying so hard not to let my imagination run away from me, knowing if I get my hopes up I'll be crushed when nothing comes of it. He's a prince. He's betrothed—though not engaged, which seemed to be an important distinction that I hadn't understood—and I'm just me.

This is likely going to end in disaster, and I'll be the only one who gets hurt.

But what if it doesn't? A tiny voice in the back of my mind whispers.

I waver back and forth about meeting Kastian as I bathe after dinner and pick out my favorite dress—the ocean blue one with pearl buttons. I'm still unsure as I brush out my hair and wait for Aunt Beatrix to go to sleep so I can sneak out unimpeded.

Finally, the clock strikes 9:00 and I jump to my feet. *I'm going.*

It's a terrible idea, but I'm putting on my dress and tying my hair into a long braid.

I must be insane, but I'm poking my head out of my room to make sure Aunt Beatrix isn't waiting for me.

I'm going.

I'm lucky, and Aunt Beatrix isn't anywhere in sight as I creep out of my room and down the long white stone corridor.

The castle is mostly quiet, and while I pass the occasional guard or servant, no one pays me any attention. That's good, because I don't know what I would say if anyone asked where I'm going. Prince Kastian didn't say it was a secret that we were leaving the castle together, but he did mention having to escape his guards as a child.

My memory conjures up the image of the green-jacketed guards pushing through the crowd at the harbor and Kastian jumping off the wall to escape them. That makes me think that what we're doing is a secret—which only makes it more fun...and more dangerous.

Kastian told me to meet him in the hallway outside the dining room where we first met the other night—or, where he thinks we first met. I'm dying to ask him if he still has the key I gave him eight years ago. He probably doesn't...but what if he does?

What if every stupid, impossible daydream I've ever had is about to come true?

I reach the hallway, which is open on one side like a balcony, and lean against the railing to wait. From here, I can just barely make out the masts of all the tall ships in the harbor, and my heartbeat speeds up in excitement.

"I feel like I've seen this exact scene before," Kastian's voice interrupts my thoughts.

I turn around and can't help but smile when I see him walking toward me.

He's wearing a green cloak which looks achingly familiar. It can't possibly be the same one from 8 years ago, as Kastian is nearly two feet taller than he was then, but the overall look is the same. He has another cloak—blue, this time—thrown over one arm.

"I wasn't sure you'd come," Kastian says, coming to a stop a few feet away from me.

"Likewise. I'm sure you're much busier than I am, *Your Majesty.*"

He smiles. "Why is it that when you say that it sounds like you're calling me an asshole?"

I grin. "I don't know, maybe you should consider why you're hearing it that way—internalized self-loathing isn't healthy."

He rolls his eyes but keeps smiling as if he's caught somewhere between amusement and exasperation. "I brought you this." He thrusts the cloak at me. "I'd rather not be recognized if we can avoid it."

"Ooh, so this *is* a secret. I wasn't sure." I take the cloak and fall into step with him as he leads us down the hall.

"Not a secret exactly, I'm allowed to leave the palace, but it's still a good idea not to draw attention to ourselves."

"My Aunt Beatrix is always saying the same thing to Daemon and I—mostly to him, I guess."

He nods. "Because he's Florian's son."

I look sideways at him. "How did you know?"

He laughs. "I have eyes."

"Yeah...so does everyone else. It's becoming more of a problem lately. It's making my Aunt Beatrix nervous."

"Why?"

I bite my lip. I probably shouldn't tell him this. Then again, as he just said, it's not much of a secret. "Because Daemon and Thorne are close in age. They go to school together. Or, at least, they did until Thorne finished his schooling last year."

"I take it Thorne doesn't enjoy being forced to spend time with his half-brother?"

I shake my head. "No, he doesn't. It wasn't always as much of a problem, but now that Daemon is older and looks so much like the king, there's a lot of tension at court. My aunt is afraid that the king will kill Daemon, or at least have him sent away."

"Are you worried about that?" Kastian asks, his eyes searching my face.

"Yes," I admit. "I think he should leave the country as soon as he finishes school. He could move here to Hydratta, or maybe to Solistine."

He looks at me sharply. "If Daemon moved to Hydratta would you go too?"

I shrug. "Probably. It's not like I have that many other friends to leave behind."

Kastian seems to think about it. "As much as I'd like you both to come here, I'm not sure that's a good idea."

"Why?"

"I don't know King Florian that well, but if my father had another son, the most dangerous thing he could do would be to disappear. Then there would be rumors which could turn into legends and either I or my father would have to hunt him down to remove the threat."

The blood drains from my face. I hadn't thought about it like that, but he's absolutely right. Daemon is already attracting followers without even trying. If he were exiled, the legend would only grow.

"What would you suggest he do?" I ask.

Again, Kastian seems to consider it. "I think he should join the army as soon as possible, even if that means leaving school early. He needs to make himself useful, and more importantly, he needs to appear loyal to both Florian and Thorne. That's his best possible chance."

I nod. "I'll pass that on."

We reach the end of the hall, and Kastian holds open a door to a winding, white stone staircase. I pick up my skirt to keep from tripping and walk ahead of him down the stairs. We reach the bottom of the stairs and pass through another door, finding ourselves in a garden.

Kastian smiles. "I promise nothing will happen to any of you while you're in Hydratta," he says firmly. "But that would be an easier promise to keep if you let me convince you to go literally anywhere else tonight."

It's a warm evening, but I still pause and throw on the blue cloak. When I've finished fastening it around my neck, I furrow my brow up at Kastian. "You don't want to go to the docks?"

He shakes his head. "I will, of course, if that's what you want. It's only a short walk from here, but it's not the safest place in the kingdom."

"Oh, I'm well aware." I laugh. "I've spent a lot of time there."

It's his turn to look skeptical. "Are you going to explain why or leave me to try to imagine?"

I bite the inside of my cheek, thinking, as we walk through the garden and out onto the road that leads up to the castle. We don't pass any guards at the gate and I wonder briefly if that's normal or if Kastian did something to make sure we weren't stopped from leaving the castle grounds.

"You're not done talking to me, are you?" Kastian asks with a teasing smile.

"No, I was just thinking."

"Good, I thought maybe I offended you again."

He's clearly joking, but my face falls. He's right, I have been so standoffish he probably thinks I'm offended by everything in sight. That's not really it at all. It's just that I'd rather keep anyone away from me than allow them to get close ,only to inevitably lose them.

I don't know how to be open with anyone.

"I grew up on a ship," I blurt out. "That's why I want to go see them."

I internally cringe. As far as an attempt at transparency, that was a bit stilted.

Kastian raises his eyebrows. "Really? I thought you grew up in Vernallis."

"I did. I mean, both are true. I went to live with my aunt and cousin when I was eight."

"Is your ship docked in the harbor?"

"It's not my ship—not anymore, anyway—and I don't know, but I'd like to just check. I'd hate myself if I was in Hydratta for the first time in years and I didn't at least check."

Kastian looks at me appraisingly, before his face breaks into a smile. "Alright, let's go look, then."

He holds out an arm for me to take, looking very princely despite his cloaked disguise. I take his arm and try to ignore the fluttering in my stomach. I fail miserably, and by the time we walk into the harbor I swear it feels like my heart is going to explode. At least Kastian was right, and it wasn't a very long walk—any further, and I know I'd say something stupid. Like, how this is everything I've imagined since I was a little girl.

"Do you see your ship?" Kastian asks when we reach the dock.

I raise a hand to shield my eyes. and squint into the setting sun over the water. "I don't know. Can we get closer?"

"Of course," he says, but there's a slight wariness in his tone.

I know what he's worried about—the harbor is dangerous. The docks are disgustingly dirty and full of all sorts of vicious and desperate men; pirates and murderers and thieves, but I love them anyway.

I grip his arm more tightly and pull him along the dock, my head turning every which way, hoping to catch a glimpse of *The Adella*.

"If we find your father's ship do you want to go aboard and see him?" Kastian asks.

My stomach lurches unpleasantly. "He's dead. So no, I don't think that would be possible."

"Oh, I'm sorry." He clears his throat, obviously horrified. "I thought—"

"It's alright," I interrupt. "He's been gone for a long time."

"Do you see the ship though?" he asks stiffly, as if he's afraid I'm going to burst into tears. "Maybe we could still go aboard..."

I shake my head, disappointment washing over me, then tilt my face up to meet his eyes. "It's not here. That's alright. I knew it was a long shot. Thank you for taking me, anyway."

"We could still go on one of the ships if you want. That one's mine," he points toward an enormous gleaming ship docked near the very end of the pier.

I stare at it, swallowing the overwhelming desire to laugh. "HMS Kastian Stormbreaker," I read aloud. "Does having a ship named after you make it yours?"

He smirks. "I would think so, but I meant literally. My father named that ship after me when I was born, but it became mine when I turned sixteen."

I raise an eyebrow. "Do you ever use it?"

"No. It's a war ship, so it doesn't get used much—which is a good thing I suppose. We'll be using it for the first time tomorrow to hold the ball. There's already a crew aboard getting ready, so we could go up there now...if you want, of course."

My pulse speeds up with excitement. "If it's not too much trouble..."

Kastian's slightly nervous expression breaks into a wide grin and he grips my hand tightly, pulling me toward the other end of the dock. "It's no trouble at all. I'd be an idiot not to agree to anything that makes you smile like that."

I flush and look down, biting my lip as my heartbeat speeds up.

I can't believe this is happening.

The prince *likes* me and it feels like every stupid, impossible, little girl's fantasy I've ever had is coming true.

And maybe it won't end in tragedy...maybe, just once, someone won't leave.

ODESSA, PRESENT

We find a river and stick as close to the bank as possible, theorizing that when there is a town, it will be near the water. It's a good theory, except it doesn't work. We never reach an inn.

I suppose I should have realized this was a possibility. I don't remember passing through many towns on the way from Vernallis to Hydratta, but that was so long ago I'd convinced myself I'd merely forgotten. Now, I recall that there were many nights we slept in the carriages since there was nowhere to stop and rest.

"Alright, I can't walk anymore," Jett says finally.

We come to a halt behind him. Internally, I'm screaming with excitement. I can't walk anymore either, and I've been seriously debating asking Kastian to carry me for the last hour.

"I agree," Kastian says. "But I don't think we should camp here."

As if to punctuate his point, a loud cackling laugh—somewhere between the cry of a monkey and a dog—echoes out of the forest to our right. I wrap my arms around myself and shiver.

"If you want my opinion—" Captain Connell begins.

Kastian cuts him off. "We don't."

"Whoa, calm down, mate. You don't even know what I was going to say. In my opinion, we could stop here and take shifts sleeping."

"I think I see a clearing between the trees over there," Jett says, seeming to take it for granted that we've all agreed to stop. "We'll camp there. I'll make a fire,"

I sigh and look toward the river only a few yards away. "While you do that, I'm going to rinse off. I don't think I've ever been this disgusting in my entire life."

"Wait!" Kastian barks, jogging over to me as I move away from Jett who is already working on a fire. "Where do you think you're going?"

"Didn't you hear me?" I ask, trying to keep my voice neutral.

He reaches out and wraps his fingers around my wrist, pulling me back. "You can't go in that water."

My lip curls. "I truly appreciate you saving my life, Kastian, but that gratitude will dry up fast if you start thinking it gives you the right to order me around."

He makes a frustrated sound in the back of his throat. "I'm going to have to save you again if you go in that water."

I raise my eyebrows at him, before remembering he probably can't see me. "If anything, I'd be safer in the water."

"It's freshwater. You won't transform."

"So?" I grind out.

"So, I'm sure that water is full of all sorts of evil, poisonous shit."

"I'll risk it," I snap, tugging my wrist out of his grasp. "I'm not afraid of anything in the water, I'm afraid of what's up in the trees." I point up, where I swear to the gods I can see the glinting eyes of some animal watching us. I shiver, hoping it's nothing more dangerous than a bird.

"But—" Kastian begins again.

"I wasn't really asking your permission," I hiss. "I'm going to rinse off whether you like it or not."

"Fine," he growls. "Fuck me for expecting the princess to go a single night without bathing. It's obviously far better to risk being swallowed by a swamp snake than to be slightly uncomfortable."

"You don't understand. It's water. I'm not afraid of anything in the water."

"Good, because I doubt whatever is in there is afraid of you either."

"Ugh," I huff out a sharp breath. "I'm not wasting my time explaining this to you." I turn on my heel and resume walking toward the water, only to realize he's following right behind me. I stop and whirl on him again. "What the hell are you doing?"

"Bathing, apparently," he grumbles. "Even though that's categorically fucking insane, you weren't asking permission, right? So we're going. Lead the way, Princess."

I gasp, surprised both by the annoyance in his tone and how we could have misunderstood each other so extremely. "I'm bathing. You are staying by the fire."

"That's not going to happen. If you're going to swim with snakes and eels and whatever other fucking horrid thing is in that water, then I am too."

"But—" I splutter. "But I'm bathing."

It's dark so I can't really make out his face, but somehow I already know he's smirking at me. "It's not as if I haven't seen it before."

My cheeks flame, and I cross my arms over my chest. "Let's just get this really clear right now. That is not going to happen again. Ever."

"I remember," he says, striding past me toward the river. "You said 'once.'"

I jog after him, my face still burning. "Exactly. Once. So, we never really need to talk about this again, and it's not appropriate for you to bathe alongside me."

"Appropriate or not, it's happening. Or, you could do the

smart thing and deal with being dirty for one more night. Up to you, Princess."

I grind my teeth. As usual, he backed me into a corner without even trying. I'm stubborn, but so is Kastian, and I know he'll never give up and walk away.

There's probably a greater meaning in there somewhere, but I refuse to acknowledge it.

"Fine," I growl. "Whatever, just don't look at me and stay over there." I point vaguely down the river.

I realize how absurd I'm being—it's so dark I doubt he can see where I'm pointing, so there's hardly any point in telling him not to look at me, but I can't seem to make myself think rationally at the moment.

"Whatever you want," he grumbles, and I hear his footsteps moving several feet away from me. "But don't expect me to go too far. I'm not leaving you alone again."

My heart skips a beat, but I force myself to ignore it.

That is, until I hear the unmistakable sound of Kastian unbuckling his belt and shucking off his clothing. My cheeks burn.

I shake my head trying to clear it, and walk a few yards further away before peeling off my own ruined clothes.

My dress hangs in grimy tatters, stained with mud and grime, and I doubt it can be salvaged. Underneath, my stockings are torn, the fabric frayed and clinging to my legs like cobwebs. My bloomers are no better, marked with dirt and dampness, and my corset feels stiff with sweat and debris.

I hesitate, fingers hovering over the laces of the corset, knowing that once I unlatch it, it might be impossible to put back on without help. My chest is too heavy to comfortably go without it, and the unpleasant thought of walking around without support until we reach a town flits across my mind. Even so, the lure of feeling clean is stronger. I pull off the corset and drop it on top of all my other clothes, leaving me completely naked aside from the darkness.

Even though I can't see him, I can feel Kastian's burning gaze on me as I finally step into the water. The bottom of the river feels slimy under my feet, and the water isn't as deep or as cold as I would like. Still, anything is a relief after the disgusting brig and the humid walk through the swamp.

I wade deeper, but even at its deepest point, the river only comes up to my waist. I blush realizing that Kastian is so much taller than me it might not even cover his hips.

I sink low, dunking my shoulders, and quickly scrub the dirt from my skin and hair. I move automatically, unable to focus on what I'm doing when I can hear Kastian's breathing and the sound of the water moving around him.

We don't speak, but the silence and the sounds of the swamp only heighten my awareness of him. The tension is so thick it feels palpable, like I could reach out and touch whatever is crackling in the air between us. Every inch of my skin tingles, and my muscles feel too tight, too alert.

"So, you've been in this swamp before?" Kastian asks. His question cuts into the tension, but provides no real relief. His tone is casual, and he sounds like he's a respectable distance away, but I still stiffen.

"Mmmm?" I hum a noncommittal sound that doesn't really mean yes or no.

"You said you traveled this way with Daemon and Beatrix when Thorne was courting my sister."

Fuck.

Fuck, fuck, fuck!

I knew I messed up by mentioning that earlier, and that Kastian isn't oblivious enough to have missed it. Now what the hell am I supposed to say? I can't exactly tell him I lied before. That sounds crazy, and he wouldn't believe me, anyway.

"Yes," I say stiffly. "I did."

"I don't remember that," he says, his voice sounding slightly closer now.

Of course he doesn't. That's the entire point.

"Oh, well, I'm sure you were busy. I don't know why you'd remember me when we never met."

"I feel like I would remember you. I can't imagine not noticing you."

I stiffen. He sounds closer than I'd thought he was, and I'm not sure which of us drifted nearer to each other. I have a sinking suspicion that it was me, and I plant my feet firmly, refusing to give in to whatever my traitorous body has in mind when my head is screaming that this is all far too dangerous.

"See?" I blurt out, desperate to change the subject. "You were wrong. There's nothing dangerous in the water."

He snorts. "I wouldn't say that, but you're right that I haven't spotted any crocodiles."

"I wouldn't need your help even if there was a crocodile," I mutter.

"Sure you wouldn't."

"No, really," I snap. "I'm much stronger in the water than on land."

"Does it matter if it's fresh or saltwater?" he asks, sounding suddenly curious.

I dunk my head in the water and flip my hair back before answering. "I don't know. I haven't had many opportunities to test my strength in the ocean."

"Why?" he asks, voice sounding even closer now. This time I'm sure it wasn't me who moved, but for some reason I don't back up.

"Because I lived in Vernallis," I lie. That's part of the reason, but nowhere near the entire truth of why I've hardly ever spent much time in my other form; why I've only ever swum in the ocean once in my entire long life.

I bite the inside of my cheek, worried that I've said too much and Kastian will ask more questions that I won't—that I physically can't—answer. But he doesn't.

"Show me," he says, voice far too loud in my ear.

I jump, realizing he's right behind me, and whip around. He's close enough that I can make out his outline now and a hint of his expression as he looks down at me.

"What the hell are you doing?" I demand, voice shaking slightly as I cross my arms over my chest. "You were supposed to stay over there."

"Then how would you save me if there was a crocodile?" he asks, clearly trying not to laugh.

"Oh, now I'm doing the saving?"

"Maybe. Show me how much stronger you are, and then I'll decide."

"I'm not showing you anything; you're already hurt."

"I'm fine, it's just a couple of flesh wounds. They'll heal by tomorrow even without magic, and you owe me one for saving you."

I bristle. "In exchange for saving me you want to know how strong I am?"

"I can think of a lot of things I want, but I'll start with this. Let's call it academic curiosity."

"Fine," I hiss, already knowing I'm playing with fire. "Give me your hand."

Kastian holds out his hand, and I feel for it in the dark, my fingers brushing accidentally against the hard ridges of his muscled stomach. A shiver travels through me as I finally grip his hand and squeeze. "This is as hard as I can squeeze your hand above water."

"That's barely anything."

My brows furrow. "Yeah, well, here's half as hard as I can squeeze it under the water."

I give him no further warning than that before I plunge both our hands beneath the surface of the river and squeeze. I feel the bones shifting in his hand beneath my fingers, and some dark, long-dormant part of me enjoys knowing that I could crush his fingers if I wanted to. I could pull him down with me beneath the undertow and never let go.

"Fuck!" Kastian yells, pulling his hand back from me in a shower of river water.

"I told you," I reply, smugly stretching out my fingers like a cat might unfurl its claws. "You're the one who asked."

He shakes out his hand. "Fuck, Princess. I think you broke it."

"I didn't. I could have, though. Maybe think about that the next time you decide to corner me in the dark."

He laughs darkly. "I'll definitely be thinking about that the next time, but only because now I know I don't have to hold back for fear of breaking you. You can take it."

I inhale sharply. He was holding back before?

Oh gods.

I wish he hadn't said that because now I can't think about anything else.

My entire body tingles with awareness, and suddenly the illusion of our conversation fades, bringing back the reality that we're standing here, naked, and far too close in the dark water. The tension between us sizzles in the air.

Kastian notices the shift too because his breathing turns shallow. His burning gaze lands on me, and even in the dark I can feel the path of his eyes traveling over my face, down my neck and across my collarbones, then lower.

My breathing turns ragged. Heat blooms on my skin, and I feel my breasts tighten, nipples pebbling. I'm caught between the stubborn desire to cross my arms over my chest and sink low in the water so he can't see anything, and the desire to...not do that.

He moves nearer, the water separating as he approaches, and I feel the heat emanating from his body. Every nerve in me tingles with anticipation.

I watch, barely daring to blink, as Kastian's hand reaches out, almost hesitant, brushing against my cheek with a gentleness that surprises me.

My heart thunders in my chest as his fingers trace my jawline slowly, memorizing the curve of my face as if afraid this might be the last time he'll ever get to. There's something almost reverent about his movements, a stark contrast to the raw intensity simmering beneath his composed facade.

Then his hands find their way to cup my cheeks fully, anchoring me in place. "Gods, I thought I fucking lost you earlier."

"You can't lose what you never had to begin with."

His thumb brushes over my lips. "That's true."

My breath catches, but before I have time to consider the implication of what he just said, his mouth crashes against mine in a searing kiss, all-consuming and demanding.

I kiss him back without thinking, opening my mouth to whimper against his lips.

He swallows the sound, sinking lower in the water until we're practically at eye level and pulling me tighter into his bare chest.

I feel dizzy, and my knees go weak. I dig my fingernails into his biceps, trying to stay on my feet, until he slips a leg between my thighs to hold me up.

My breasts brush his chest, my pulse pounds in my core, and my skin catches fire. It's madness and clarity all at once, like running headlong into a storm knowing full well you may never come out the other side unchanged.

"Wait," I mutter against his lips when I finally find my voice amidst the chaos unraveling inside me. "This is a terrible idea."

I'm not really talking to him—I'm mostly talking to myself—but of course Kastian answers anyway: "Why? I don't think you hate me nearly as much as you pretend to."

I don't hate him at all, actually.

I've tried to. I've tried so, so hard not only to hate him, but to make him hate me in return. I've been horrible to him at nearly every opportunity, but either I'm not very good at it or Kastian is a glutton for punishment.

Or, maybe, it's that even if he doesn't know it, some part of him still remembers me.

I whimper as his fingers trace my ribs and lower, digging into the flesh at my sides. I can feel him hard against me, and it would be so, *so* easy to rock my hips forward and join together once more.

My pulse throbs at the very thought of it, and I can feel the heat building between my legs.

Kastian leans forward to kiss me again, but I lean my head back. One of us has to think rationally, and it has to be me. After all, I'm the one cursed to know the truth.

"This has been a terrible day," I breathe, even as I pull away from him. "You just saved my life, and now we're stuck in a swamp."

"So?" he rasps.

"So, this is what I would call 'a traumatic event.'"

I mean it as a joke. Sort of. Okay, not really at all, but I mean for Kastian to think I'm joking.

Kastian doesn't laugh. Instead, he stiffens, and I'm sure he knows what I'm getting at.

No one knows exactly how soul-bonds work, but most Fae think they're triggered by shared emotional events. I expect Kastian will know what I mean and will back off. He clearly wants to fuck me, maybe even thinks he has feelings for me, but I doubt he wants to form an accidental soul-bond. Even the past version of him—the version with all his memories intact—never talked about bonding.

"That's not going to happen," he says tonelessly.

"It could," I comment, moving backwards away from him. "So unless you want to end up stuck with me forever, we need to stay away from each other for a while."

I grit my teeth, and I'm grateful for the darkness because I'm sure if he saw my face he'd know how much those words cost me to say. He'd know how painful it is to pretend I don't want this more than anything.

"No, it couldn't happen." Kastian breathes a long sigh. "I already found my bond and lost her, so it definitely couldn't happen again now."

I freeze, and for what feels like several long seconds my heart forgets how to beat.

He already found his soul-bond? *When? Who?*

Some long-repressed roar, like crashing waves, rises in my chest. My vision tunnels in on itself, and for a moment all I can think is *drown, drown, drown...*

"I'm sorry," Kastian says.

His comment snaps me back to reality, and I blink quickly to clear my darkening vision. I force myself to laugh. "Sorry? Why are you sorry?"

"I should have told you that before...everything."

I laugh again, and it sounds slightly hysterical to my own ears, but I hope that's only because I know how my mind is reeling. "You didn't have to tell me anything, and you don't need to be sorry. This is good, actually. This means there's no risk of accidentally triggering anything that neither of us wants."

"Fine," he says, tone unreadable. "If that's how you feel, then come back over here."

"No," I say shortly, the forced calm in my voice growing more and more shrill by the second. "No, this was a bad idea to begin with, and I'm just glad we came to our senses."

"Is that what happened?" he asks, the water shifting as he trails after me toward the dry bank.

"That's exactly what happened," I snap. "I said only once, remember? And I meant it, so this was a perfect reminder. I'm going to get dressed and go back to the campsite. Hopefully Jett has that fire going by now."

I march toward my pile of clothes and tug my ruined dress firmly over my head, ignoring any of the underclothes in favor of speed.

He has a soul-bond already.

A soul-bond he lost years ago.

A soul-bond who isn't me.

Kastian is conspicuously silent, and I get the impression he's building up to say something. My heartbeat quickens, and I lace my boots up at top speed, terrified to hear whatever he wants to say.

I grab the rest of my things and speed-walk toward the camp, not even bothering to be afraid of the swamp animals in my haste to get away from Kastian.

"You know, I never said 'once,'" he says finally.

I glance over my shoulder, heart pounding with anxiety. "What is that supposed to mean?"

He stops a few feet behind me, and I can practically hear the smirk in his voice when he answers. "It means that once was your rule, so you're the one who will have to break it."

"Why the hell would I do that?" I hiss, voice coming out a little breathless.

"I don't know, Princess, maybe because you want to?"

"You're delusional," I bite out. "And you have a bond."

"I *had* one," he corrects. "Not anymore."

I bark a humorless laugh. "That's not how it works, and you know it. Bonds are forever."

"Maybe you're right," he says, definitely smiling now. "But I'll bet it'll be less than three days before you're begging me to touch you again, and when you do, I'll be more than happy to test it."

KASTIAN, PRESENT

My hand still throbs as I follow Odessa back through the dark swamp. My breathing is ragged, but I'm actually grateful for the pain because it's the only thing distracting me from my agonizingly hard cock.

Good fucking gods.

Realizing how strong Dessa is in the water was possibly the hottest damn thing I'd ever seen, even if she did nearly break my hand.

I've only ever been with Fae women, and I didn't realize until that moment that I'd been holding back. Now, I'm picturing all the ways I could have her without having to worry about being careful. Bathtubs, the lake behind the manor, the middle of the godsdamn ocean.

Maybe I should be glad she stopped us before I let her drown me, but I'm not glad—not at all.

I'm not sorry that I told her about my soul-bond either, even if it was painful. I wish I could have seen her face better to know what she really thought about it.

The bond in my chest throbs, reminding me it's there. It feels like the bond itself knows I'm teetering on the edge of rejecting it altogether and is holding on stronger, trying to maintain a connection to a woman I can't even remember.

I flex my throbbing fingers, trying to ignore the equal throbbing in my chest.

For years, I thought I might go search for my bond at some point. It was a vague idea, dependent on my escaping Dyaspora, which wasn't something I really believed would ever happen. I tried not to think about the bond, and it mostly stayed quiet... that is, until I escaped and it suddenly became more active—stronger—than it ever was before.

Absently, I reach up and rub my chest where my tattoo is.

Eventually—hopefully—Odessa will see it and that will take a fair bit of explaining. I can't even imagine what she'll say—but like the reality of the bond it doesn't matter because I've already made up my mind.

Odessa is going to be mine. She's already mine, and no fated bond or siren curse is going to stop me from claiming her.

It's a feeling that has been coming on slowly for a while, and only became more intense the other night in the dining room, and even more so when I saw her on the boat. I saw her face, and her expression wasn't hatred or dismissal or any of the other haughty masks she wears when she's trying to act like I don't matter to her. She wanted me just as much as I wanted her. She showed her hand, and now I'm going to take her for everything she has.

The entire flight across the ocean, all I could think about was how to tell her.

I need to tell her she's lying to herself if she thinks there isn't something here.

Tell her that whatever I did to make her hate me can't be so bad that I can't fix it.

That "once" will never be enough. I'm fairly sure I could wake up with her beside me every day for the rest of my life, and it would still never be enough.

That she can pretend to hate me, but it won't change the fact that whatever this thing between us is, it's inevitable.

I'm already certain of all of that; I just need to make her believe it too...and I need to do it before she gets any more ideas about going back to Hydratta.

I don't care if she's gathering information for Vernallis. Even if it's just a political maneuver, the idea of her even pretending to consider another man's proposal makes me want to murder something; find the nearest swamp creature and rip its head from its body, if only to relieve some of the pressure building inside me.

Add on the fact that Magnus is my lifelong enemy...it's inconceivable.

If Odessa tries to go back to Hydratta once we've made it out of this swamp I don't know what I'll do. Lock her up, maybe, or follow her to Hydratta myself even if I am walking into certain death.

At this point, the thought of death might be a relief.

At least then I could have a rest from all this need. Need for retribution. Need to protect her. Need to be near her. Need for her...

"Kastian?" Dessa asks, pulling me from my thoughts.

I look up quickly, thinking wildly that she's changed her mind and wants to go back to the river. Or, that she somehow heard my thoughts and knows how hopelessly obsessed with her I am.

I clear my throat and try to keep my tone even. "Yeah?"

"Where are we?"

I squint at her silhouette between the trees. She's not that far ahead of me, but admittedly it's still so fucking dark I can barely see my hand in front of my face and I haven't been paying much attention to where we're going. "What do you mean? Weren't you walking back to Jett and the pirate?"

She backtracks a few steps and comes to stand in front of me, her face almost visible in the low light. "I was, but where are they? I can't find them."

An uneasy feeling creeps down the back of my neck, and I

turn in a circle. All I can see are the outlines of trees and rustling leaves. "They were camped near the river, right? We didn't walk that far to get away from where Jett was making that fire."

"I know." Odessa worries her lip. "It couldn't have been much more than a quarter of a mile, probably less, but we've been walking longer than that and we should be able to see their fire. The trees aren't that thick."

A sharp, electric jolt of anxiety surges through my chest, pushing aside every other feeling. Maybe I shouldn't have left Jett alone with that pirate, but Jett can more than take care of himself, and the pirate is immortal. So what the fuck happened to them?

"Jett!" I shout, feeling somewhat stupid as my voice echoes back at me. Odessa and I pause, holding our breath, waiting for a response, but we're only met with silence.

"If something attacked them, we would have heard it, right?" Dessa mutters. "Jett! Jett?"

"What! Fuck—ahh!" Jett's voice rings out through the woods, first sounding startled, then rising with panic in the space of a second.

My heart races as I instinctively sprint toward the noise. I tear through the dense, swampy underbrush, creating much more noise than I should, all the while following the direction of Jett's yells. Odessa jogs after me, her labored breathing nearly as loud in my ears as Jett's voice.

"Kas?" Jett yells. "Where are you? Help me!"

I skid to a stop, turning in a circle. I can hear him close by, but I can't see him anywhere.

Dessa catches up, stopping behind me. "Where is he?" she pants.

"I'm here!" Jett's voice yells from somewhere close by on the right. "Look down. I'm stuck in the fucking mud."

I turn, scanning the ground, struggling to see anything in the dark. Then, I catch a glint of eyes and I jump a foot in the air, startled.

Jett is sprawled on the ground, his position unchanged from

when we last saw him, but now half of his body is swallowed by the thick, sticky mud. His head and most of his chest are still above the surface while his legs seem to have disappeared into the murky depths of the sand, creating the impression that the earth itself is trying to pull him under.

I jog over to him and bend down to see better, sure that the dark is making me hallucinate. Immediately I feel my boots sinking into the ground as well. I swear loudly, and leap back, a wet squelching sound filling the air as I pull my feet free. "What the fuck happened?"

"I don't know." Jett grunts as he shifts his shoulders trying to pull himself free. "I was so damn tired I fell asleep. I didn't even realize this was happening until I woke up and heard you yelling." He gasps for breath. "Can we talk about this later? Pull me out!"

Dessa falls to her knees on the ground beside Jett and starts trying to push the sand out of the way. She lasts about three seconds before she shrieks and tries to scramble back. "My knees are sinking!"

I grab her by the shoulders and pull her back, both of us tumbling into the swampy underbrush, panting.

"I wish I could fucking see," I grumble, struggling to my feet and pulling Dessa with me. "It's so dark that if we try to help and step in the wrong place, we'll get stuck too."

"Can you conjure a light?" Dessa asks.

I shake my head, then remember she can't see me. "No. I mean, I could usually, but I'm spent, and fire isn't really my strong suit."

"You're better with water," she says, like she's thinking out loud. "Can you try anyway? I can't think of how we're going to get him out if we can't see what we're doing."

I close my eyes, drawing in a breath. It's not as simple as just *trying.*

Magic, like everything else, comes with a price—and usually that price is your energy. I've already used an enormous amount of magic today, more than I've used at one time since before Dyaspora. I haven't slept or eaten anything since yesterday, and I lost a lot of blood fighting those pirates.

Still, Jett is practically my brother, and with Odessa asking me with that hopeful note in her voice, I can't say I won't even try.

I take another deep breath and sit down on the ground.

"What are you doing?" Jett asks sharply.

"Sitting so if I pass out I won't fall that far," I say dryly.

"You're not serious?" Dessa asks, bending down beside me. "Is that likely?"

I shake my head. "Likely? No. Possible? Yes. Just give me a minute.

"No offense, Kas, but I'm not sure I have a minute," Jett says, a slightly hysterical note in his voice.

"Stop moving," Odessa instructs him. "And don't panic; you're only going to sink faster."

"How do you know that?" he demands, no less panicked than before.

"Just trust me," she says, that soothing siren note creeping into her voice. "Try to stay calm."

I tune out both Dessa and Jett as I try to focus. I take another deep breath in and, incredibly, I can still smell Dessa's floral scent, even over every other swampy odor. I try my best to ignore it.

I inhale deeply, feeling the cool air fill my lungs as I concentrate with all my might. Usually magic comes easily to me, but right now it feels as if I'm trying to drag a boulder through water. My muscles protest with a dull throb, and my eyes sting from the strain.

After a few minutes, stars appear on the edges of my vision, and gradually warmth gathers in my palm. Another deep shuddering breath and a flickering flame dances into existence.

I clutch the flame between my fingers, feeling the heat build against my skin. Just as the searing pain scorches my palm, I fumble around for something to hold it with. My fingers close around a jagged piece of wood, and I light the end before quickly shaking my hand to extinguish the small inferno.

"That didn't look so hard," Odessa says casually.

I look up at her, and now that I can see her face better, I can tell she's lying—or at least, trying to deflect from her worry.

"It wasn't," I lie back, handing her the small torch before pushing to my feet. I step back a few paces, afraid of standing in the rapidly sinking sand myself, and look around for anything I can throw to Jett. "Dessa, hold the light up. I can't see."

She does, and my eyes land on a long vine, slightly thicker than the average rope. I pull it down and toss one end to Jett.

"I hate this damn swamp," Jett growls, reaching for the vine.

"Likewise." I grunt, pulling with all my remaining strength as Jett, panting heavily, moves back and forth, trying to help me free him.

It's slow work pulling Jett out. The light makes things marginally easier, but it also means I can now see where we are, and part of me wishes I couldn't.

The swamp is a murky maze of tangled vines and tall, gnarled trees that reach towards the moonlit sky. The path is littered with slimy mud and puddles of dark water, and in the shadows, I can see the flashes of eyes and the outlines of enormous creatures moving and slithering between the trees. The spot where Jett is stuck—which we'd chosen as a campsite because it seemed to be a clearing between the trees—is clearly open for a reason. He's lying in the middle of a pool of quicksand.

"When we get you out, we should get the fuck out of here." I pant. "I can't believe nothing has attacked us yet, or walked into some poisonous plant, or fallen into—"

"Alright, we get it," Dessa interrupts sharply. "I agree. I'd rather walk until I physically collapse from exhaustion than try to sleep in here. Good thing we didn't lie down to sleep too, or we'd all be stuck by now."

"Wait, where's the pirate?" I ask.

"Shit, I nearly forgot," Odessa yelps, the torch light flickering as she turns in a circle scanning the ground. "Oh my gods!"

"What?" I gasp, still entirely focused on pulling Jett from the sand.

"I can see just his hand moving over there," Odessa screeches. "He must still be alive."

"Fuck," Jett breathes. "Better him than me I suppose. He can't die under there."

"That sounds worse," Dessa whimpers. "We literally buried him alive."

"We didn't do anything," I snap. "Don't think about it. I'm more concerned about getting Jett out than the prick who wanted to kill you."

She mumbles something under her breath and steps away from the waving fingers, but makes no more comments about it as I yank and twist the vine, struggling to pull Jett free.

It takes nearly five whole minutes to extract Jett from the sand, at which point he crawls across the muddy ground, coughing hard. "Fuck me. I never thought I'd say this, but I think I'd go back to Dyaspora before trying that again."

"To hell with this swamp," I agree. "Let's go. I suddenly feel like I could run ten miles if the alternative is this shit."

"What about Captain Connell?" Odessa asks, looking down at the hand still poking out of the sand. "We can't leave him here buried alive."

I close my eyes and stifle a groan. Honestly, if we didn't need the pirate for questioning, I wouldn't lose a wink of sleep over leaving him here. Being buried alive for eternity feels like a reasonable punishment for capturing Odessa.

I look at Jett, silently communicating our shared indifference. He rolls his eyes and leans over to plunge his hand into the sand near Connell's waving fingers. "I can feel the belt around his wrists. Bet he's glad we tied him up, now. Otherwise, I don't know how we'd ever get him out."

"Funnily enough, I still doubt he'll thank us." I sigh. "Alright, throw me the vine."

It takes even longer to pull the pirate out of the sand. Partly because he'd sunk far further below the ground than Jett did, and partly because the urgency I felt to free Jett isn't nearly as consuming when it comes to Connell. Now I just feel exhausted and bitter to be wasting my remaining physical energy on our murderous prisoner.

Still, we finally get him out and the three of us collapse on the ground.

"Bloody hell," the pirate swears, crawling across the muddy ground, coughing and spitting as he tries to clear the sand from his lungs. "Of all the ways I've died, that might have been the worst."

"You're welcome," Jett says darkly.

In answer, Connell spits out another mouthful of mud and flops down on his back, panting.

"Don't lie down," Odessa says, slightly hysterically. "Sorry, I just know I'm not nearly strong enough to pull you out if this happens again."

She's right, but my entire body still screams in protest as I get to my feet again. "We have to fly out of here," I say to Jett. "Do you think you can?"

He nods, his ragged breathing still coming out in loud gasps. "Yeah, I'm feeling pretty familiar with my own mortality at the moment."

He stands up and closes his eyes for the briefest second before his wings burst into existence.

"Oi, careful!" Connell yells as the feathers smack him in the face. "Giant bloody pigeon, trying to take my eye out."

Jett turns and smacks Connell with his wing, before grabbing the man under the arms. "I swear to the fucking gods if you complain once that I'm not holding you nicely enough, I'll make it really nice for you when I drop you back into the swamp."

I smother a smile and turn to Dessa, my own wings spreading behind me. She's still holding the torch in front of her face, and a feeling of satisfaction washes over me as her eyes widen at the sight of the wings.

"Something wrong?" I ask.

She shakes her head. "No, I just swear I've seen more wings in the last year than I ever did in the century before that."

"I assume you've been in a lot more trouble this year than you were in the last century."

"Lucky me," she breathes. "Well, shall we?"

I reach for her and she drops the torch. It hits the ground and extinguishes, leaving us in total darkness as I slip one arm gently under her knees and the other around her back, feeling the warmth of her body against mine. She loops her arms tightly around my neck, her fingers brushing my hair. My heart races, not from the weight of holding her, but from the closeness, the scent of her hair, and the soft rise and fall of her breath.

As I push off the ground, the bond in my chest throbs painfully—as if reminding me once again that it's there.

THE PAST

KASTIAN, AGE 18

Relief washes over me the moment that Odessa and I board my ship.

As a boy, I used to come down to the harbor to watch the fights. Partly, it was out of defiance, partly boredom, and in a large part it was a desire to see something different from my comfortable life within the walls of my gilded palace.

I certainly saw something different.

I've seen enough to know exactly how dangerous the harbor can be, and that's how I know I don't want Odessa anywhere near here.

Unfortunately, I'm realizing in real time that I'm entirely weak to giving her whatever she wants. She probably could have asked for the Hydrattan crown jewels, and I would have found a way to get them for her.

I'm fucked, but I can't bring myself to care.

Standing on the deck, I lean against the cool metal railing near the ship's bow. The vessel remains docked, yet Odessa beams with delight.

Everything about her has changed since we boarded the ship. She seems relaxed and happy. Her hood has fallen back, revealing her bright eyes and flushed cheeks, as the brisk, salty sea breeze whips little curls out of her braid and away from her face.

"What does Stormbreaker mean?" she asks cheerfully.

I furrow my brow, frowning at her. "My name?"

She turns to smile at me. "Yes, of course I know it's your name, but what does it mean?"

I'm not sure I've ever told anyone the origin of my name before, but suddenly the words are tumbling from my lips and I can't stop. "It's my mother's surname from before she married my father. Her family are known for their magical talent. For centuries, they would help hold the tide back from the city during large storms. We have walls for that now, but the name stuck."

She nods. "I've always wished I could use magic like that."

"Can't you?" I ask.

"Not really. Maybe I could if I was trained as a child, but I never knew anyone who used magic until I went to Vernallis."

I bite my lip. "Do sirens have magic?"

She looks sideways at me, and to my surprise, she snorts a laugh. "How long have you been waiting to bring that up?"

I let out a sigh. I wonder how it would have gone if I'd asked her the same question before we were on the ship and she was clearly in her element. Probably not nearly as well. That's good to know. It seems my plan worked and I am getting to know her after all.

"Sorry," I say, smiling back at her. "One of my father's advisors said something about it, but if you don't want to talk about it..."

"It's fine." She waves me off. "It's not as if it's a secret I can hide."

She flushes lightly, and my eyes trace over her almost unnaturally beautiful face. No, of course she wouldn't be able to hide what she is. Even before Magnus told me, it was all too obvious that there was something unusual about her, I just didn't know what it was.

"I didn't know until someone told me," I admit. "I've never seen a siren before. There are a lot of them in the waters around the palace, but I was always kept well away from them."

"That's probably a good thing. From what I've heard most aren't very friendly."

"You're friendly."

She snorts. "I wouldn't go that far, but I know what you mean. For example, I'm not likely to make you jump off this boat to your death."

I raise a curious eyebrow. "Could you do that?"

She frowns, looking uncomfortable for the first time. "I'm not sure, maybe." She bites her lip, looking as if she's not sure if she should elaborate, so when she does I feel as if I passed some nebulous test. "For a few years now I've been able to sway people my way when it comes to small things, but for obvious reasons I've never tried anything as serious as drowning. Even if I wanted to do that, it's not as if I had anyone to teach me how it works."

I find myself leaning closer to her, hanging on her every word.

I've always thought sirens were monsters—far closer to wraiths or vampires than they were to Fae, but Odessa is quickly changing every preconceived idea I've ever had.

"Have you met other sirens?" I ask.

She shakes her head. "My mother, I suppose, when I was very young, but she left and I don't remember her."

"Left...not died?" I hedge, fairly sure that this has taken too serious a turn and I should try to steer it back toward something light.

"She went back to the ocean," Odessa clarifies. "That's... normal for sirens, I think. They—we—don't usually stay on land for very long."

"What about you?" I can't help asking, thinking of Magnus's comments about the landlocked sirens in the ancient courts of Ellender.

She shrugs. "I've never been in the ocean before."

I raise my eyebrows. "Never? How is that possible?"

"Even though we lived on a ship, my father was very careful not to let me go in the water. I think he believed I might not come back...and maybe he was right, who knows? After he died, I went to Vernallis where we lived hundreds of miles from the nearest sea."

"How did your father die?"

"Drowned himself," she says bluntly. "That's how the legend goes, isn't it? Men who love sirens always go mad and drown in the end."

Her eyes narrow on me like she's searching for something in my reaction. I get the feeling I'm being tested, but I'm not sure how.

"I'm sorry that happened to you," I say quickly. "I shouldn't have asked."

She presses her lips together in a flat line, and I can't tell if she's disappointed in my diplomatic response, or simply saddened by the memory of her father. "It's alright, it was all a very long time ago." She shakes her head and gives me a brittle smile. "That's enough about me, though."

"I'm not sure it could ever be enough," I blurt out. "I enjoy listening to you talk about yourself."

The side of her face turns pink, and she ducks her head, letting her hair fall in a curtain between us. "You're very blunt, you know. I've never met anyone who just said how they feel so clearly." She frowns, like she's thinking. "Maybe it's because you're a prince. You've never really had to hide your feelings or opinions from anyone."

I bark a startled laugh. "That's not true at all."

"It isn't?" She sounds skeptical. "So you're telling me that the average courtier would correct you if you said something rude?"

"Well, no," I admit. "But you're giving me way too much credit. I absolutely can't just go around saying whatever I want. I rarely talk to courtiers at all."

She turns sideways, leaning against the side of the ship to look at me. "Really? Why?"

"Because I'm an arrogant asshole, obviously."

She smiles. "Maybe a little, but not nearly as bad as I expected."

I snort. "That's a ringing endorsement coming from you. I might faint from so much praise."

Her smile widens. "I have very discerning taste. But really, why don't you talk to anyone?"

"Because I have nothing to say. I've never been good at polite small talk, and it's not as if I can be completely open with any of them about real topics."

Her eyes flash with interest. "Tell me, then. What's something you can't talk about with courtiers?"

My stomach churns. "I can't say that I'm here tonight instead of safely in the palace."

She frowns. "That's not what I meant, and you know it. Tell me something real."

My gaze meets hers, and this time I know for certain that she's testing me, I just don't know how to pass. She wants to hear something real—something unrestrained—but I've been trained my entire life never to lose control like that. I'm not even sure I know how.

"I don't want to be king," I blurt out before I can stop myself.

She rolls her eyes. "Yeah, sure. Who would want to rule an entire kingdom? That sounds awful."

"No, really." I widen my eyes, hoping to make her understand. "I don't. I never have."

Her eyes narrow. "I didn't think that was the kind of thing you had much of a choice about."

"I don't. My parents spent years trying for a son because Hydratta probably wouldn't accept any of my sisters on the throne."

"That's stupid," she says bitterly. "There are other kingdoms that are ruled by queens. The throne of Thermia has passed from mother to daughter for generations."

"I know, believe me. If Serena wanted to be queen, and the kingdom would accept her, I'd be more than happy to step aside, but that's just not how things work here."

"Why don't you want to be king?" she asks, seemingly taking me more seriously.

I suck in a breath, falling silent as I think.

This isn't the kind of thing I've ever told anyone. My family doesn't talk about our feelings, I've never had a tutor or advisor that I was especially close to, and all my friendships have always felt slightly hollow. Like, if I weren't a prince, I'm not sure they would look twice at me.

Subsequently, there's never been anyone I could tell that I've felt this way for a long time, and I'm not sure how to explain it now.

"I don't think I would be good at it," I say finally.

"Most royals aren't very good at ruling," Odessa says. "No offense."

"Yeah, but most of the time they don't realize it. Like, I doubt Thorne will have any idea of what a bad king he'll be when he eventually takes the throne. He'll probably think he's an amazing ruler and everyone loves him, even if your entire country goes up in flames."

She snorts. "Probably, but let's not jinx it."

"Sorry." I smile. "Thorne is a bad example because he's genuinely an asshole. I only meant that I would *know* I wasn't a good ruler, which would make everything so much worse."

"What makes you think you'd be a bad ruler?"

So many things.

I hate diplomacy and playing politics, and I've never been able to pretend to get along with someone I didn't like.

I like being alone, or spending time with a few close friends, rather than mingling in crowds or throwing parties.

And most of all, I can't stand watching someone do something stupid and not fixing it for them. I can't delegate. If there was a problem in the kingdom, I wouldn't be able to just watch it happen or hand it off to someone else to fix it; I'd need to fix it myself. I'd need to control the entire situation, regardless of what anyone else thought.

I don't know how to explain all that to her though, so I ask: "Do you know what kings do during wars?"

She shakes her head. "No."

"They watch." I sigh, and lean against the railing. "Kings send other people to fight, but they don't go into battle themselves. They ride onto the battlefield and stay at the very back of the army, watching all the foot soldiers get slaughtered."

"You'd want to get slaughtered instead?" she asks, and again I have that inexplicable feeling I'm being tested.

"No, but I wouldn't want to watch either. I would never want to send someone to do a job I could do better myself."

"And yet you claim you're not arrogant," she says with a teasing smile.

"I'm not, I'm just cursed with needing to control everything. Actually, it would be better if I was arrogant. Even good kings need to be a little arrogant because that's the only way anyone can be in charge of thousands of people without having a nervous breakdown."

I look sideways at her, trying to read her reaction to all this. She doesn't seem like she's about to run screaming off this boat, which I suppose is a good sign.

"I don't know anything about being a king," Odessa says matter-of-factly. "But on ships, the captain is always the best at everything—best sailor, best navigator, the strongest fighter. I once saw my father cook an entire week's worth of meals for the crew himself because our chef had fallen ill—the captain knows how to do every job because if you're in the middle of the ocean and you lose your crew no one is going to save you."

"That I can understand," I say, smiling.

"So what would you do if you weren't going to be a king?"

"Based on what you just said, maybe I should be a ship's captain. This ship, for example."

She looks around the deck of my ship and smiles. "All the other ship captains would make fun of you for sailing around on a boat named after yourself."

"I could rename it. It could be *The Odessa*."

Her cheeks flush, and her smile widens into a grin that somehow makes her look more beautiful and more tangible at once. "But really, what would you do?"

I shake my head, tearing my gaze away from her smiling face before I make an idiot out of myself. "I don't know, actually. Maybe I'd be a soldier, or I could do what my mother's family did and help keep storms from reaching the city."

"I could see you doing that."

"What about you?"

"What do you mean?"

"If you could be anything, what would you want to be?"

She shrugs, and opens her mouth to answer, but before she can say anything we're both distracted by shouting coming from the docks below.

Odessa leans over the railing, her fingers curling around the wooden beam as she squints at the scene below. My heart skips a beat, and I swallow the impulse to grab her waist and tug her back to safety. My mind races—surely she won't fall. The thought is completely irrational, and yet a vivid image of her slipping over-board flashes through my mind.

I give my head a brisk shake to clear it and narrow my eyes, focusing on the commotion below. A cluster of men at the docks flail and shout, fists flying as they jostle and grapple in a chaotic brawl.

"Who do you suppose started it?" Odessa asks, shooting me a smile that feels as if she's sharing a private joke with herself.

"They're boxing. When I was a kid, I used to sneak down here to watch. It was far more interesting than anything my tutors had to say."

She looks over her shoulder at me, biting her lip. "I know."

My brow furrows. "What do you mean you know?"

She laughs lightly, and points back toward the fight. "I bet you 50 gold that the human will win."

"I thought you didn't gamble."

"It's not gambling when it's a sure thing. I've seen him fight before."

Her eyes widen, as if she's trying to tell me something with her look alone. I don't understand what she's getting at, and I look from her to the fight below, confusion swirling in the back of my mind.

My eyes land on the human-looking man in the ring—the one I know is really a doppler who has been scamming unwitting Fae for decades—and all at once a memory comes to the forefront of my mind and the answer hits me with more force than any of the punches being thrown down below.

It's her. The girl from the pier...

The memory is hazy. It must have been ten—no, eight—years ago now, but I remember meeting a boy my age and his sister...a sister who is the entire reason I started lying about my name every time I left the castle grounds. The sister who gave me an old brass key that I still have back in my room at the palace.

I knew Odessa seemed familiar.

Words fail me and all I can say is: "You!"

She smirks. "Glad you're finally catching on, Your Majesty."

"I've met you before," I clarify, just to ensure I'm not going insane. She nods once, and an overwhelming feeling of disbelief washes over me. "How is that possible?"

She shrugs. "How is it possible that anyone has met before? Coincidence, maybe? Or luck? Or perhaps it wasn't that unusual if you spent a lot of time around those docks as a child."

I hear her, but I'm not exactly listening. My head spins. This girl, whom I've only known for a matter of days but already holds all my attention, has actually been in the background of my life for years.

How many times in the last eight years did I take out that old key and look at it, wondering where it fits? How many times did I make up a fake name and think of the bold red-headed girl who made fun of me for not hiding my identity better?

This doesn't feel like a coincidence to me. It feels bigger than that.

"You gave me your key," I say, more of a statement than a question.

She nods. "I'm sure you've long since thrown it out."

"No, actually, I didn't...I still have it, but why?"

She smiles, looking pleased even as a pink flush stains her cheeks. "I don't know. At the time it just felt right. Objects can be promises, you know."

I nod, even though I don't really know what she means. Whatever sailors' superstition that is, I'm not familiar with it, but in some small way I feel like I understand. "What's the key for?"

She smiles. "Treasure, supposedly. Or, who knows? Maybe it was just old junk."

I shake my head wordlessly.

If there's any treasure to be had, it's her. It's finding her again, and the inexplicable feeling I have that this was always meant to happen.

Like maybe there's a version of history where she never went to live in Vernallis with her aunt and I met her on some random day in Hydratta.

Like maybe if I'd never tried to talk to her in the hall—if I'd never stolen her boat and wasn't standing here now—that we'd run into each other again sometime in the future.

Like, that key isn't a promise; it's the anchor of some invisible string, drawing us back together.

I extend my hand, fingertips grazing the side of her face. Her soft gasp is carried away by the ocean breeze, and for the briefest second, the air between us crackles with a raw intensity.

Then, I grip her chin and bring her mouth to mine.

And in that moment, everything changes.

ODESSA, PRESENT

The first town we come across is barely more than a few ramshackle huts along the side of the road, but compared with the bank of the swampy river, it might as well be paradise.

"Eat first or sleep first?" Jett mumbles to himself, a smile spreading across his face as we land in front of the largest shack. "I can't decide. Do you think somehow I could do both at once?"

"I think if anyone could, it would be you," I reply.

He grins. "Stop, you're making me blush."

I smile back at him, glad to see that his mood has improved since leaving the swamp. Seeing a serious look on Jett's face kind of creeps me out.

We find the tiniest, most dilapidated inn I've ever seen and traipse inside.

It's a small, square room, with a few small tables on one side and a short bar on the other. There's a door at the far end that looks like it leads upstairs. The room is empty except for a weathered-looking bartender, who startles as we walk in as if he was about to fall asleep on the bar.

I make a beeline for the bar and slump against it, exhausted. "Four rooms, please. Oh, and something to eat...and if you could have bathtubs brought up to the room, that would be excellent." I suck in a breath. "*Please.* Sorry, did I say that already? Thank you so much."

The man looks a bit dazed by my rapid questions, and doesn't have time to answer before Jett comes up behind me and leans on the bar to my left. "Actually, make it three rooms. I don't think we should let Connell out of our sight for too long. I'll tie him to the end of my bed or something."

Captain Connell shuffles up behind Jett, his wrists still bound. "Would you compromise my virtue like that?" he asks sarcastically. "Scandalous."

Kastian elbows Connell out of the way and stands on my other side. He puts a hand on my lower back. "Two rooms. I'm not letting you out of my sight either."

"Are you going to tie me to the bed too?" I ask acidly, not really thinking about what I'm saying.

His eyes flash. "I think we can work something out."

I choke, and Jett thumps me on the back, all the while holding back laughter.

"We've only got one room," the innkeeper says, interjecting for the first time. "And I can make you something to eat, but you won't find an inn for miles that will offer bathtubs."

My face falls. "One room? But there's no one else here."

The innkeeper squints at me. "It's the middle of the night, girl. All the rooms are taken. You can have the one or go somewhere else, but I'll warn you, it's a long trek to the next town, and no one is going to lend you a wagon at this hour."

My heart sinks. "Is there at least more than one bed?"

The innkeeper doesn't answer, just bends to pull an old-fashioned key out from under the bar. "That will be thirty gold."

I cough. "You're not serious. That's outrageous, I—"

"Take fifty," Kastian says, reaching over my shoulder and passing a handful of coins to the innkeeper. "And bring the food up to the room as soon as it's ready. Thank you."

Kastian takes the key and ushers me toward the stairs, Jett and the pirate following behind us.

"You didn't have to overpay him," I grumble.

"I did. We're traveling without any luggage, the pirate is bound with a belt, and all of us look like we've been in a fight. I doubt we'll run into any of Magnus's guards, but the last thing we need is for that innkeeper to get suspicious and send a message to the nearest outpost."

I bite the inside of my cheek. "Fine, you're right. One room though…"

"It's better than being swallowed up by quicksand."

I laugh hollowly. "Things could always be worse, right?"

We reach the top of the stairs and find our room. It's not quite as revolting as I'd imagined, but that isn't saying a lot. There are two rickety beds with mismatched linens and a small wash table in the center. No lamps except for a candelabra, and the only bathing room is down the hall. I use it quickly, and console myself with the thought that even if there were a bathtub available I probably wouldn't want to use it in a room with three men.

I snort at the thought; how very un-siren-like of me.

When I return from the bathing room, I find Jett tying Connell's restraints to the end of the nearest bed while the pirate complains loudly. Kastian is sitting on the other bed unlacing his boots. I stop in the doorway, not entirely sure where I'm supposed to go.

Kastian catches my eye and pats the bed next to him. My eyes widen and I shake my head once.

He grins. "Don't worry about it, Princess. I'm going to eat my supper and then fall asleep in seconds. I'm so tired I doubt even you could tempt me to stay awake."

My cheeks heat, and I look down to hide my smile even as I scold myself.

Stop being stupid. You know better than this.

I do know better, but I'm too tired to care. I kick off my own boots and climb onto the bed next to Kastian, just as a knock sounds at the door and the innkeeper arrives with our dinner. It's not especially exciting—cold soup, bread and cheese—but my heart leaps, anyway.

"How do you expect me to eat soup without the use of my hands?" Connell complains from the floor. He looks over at me and winks. "Unless you want to feed me, darling. Then I'd gladly stay bound."

Kastian goes stiff as a board beside me and sucks in a couple of deep breaths before his shoulders relax again. When he speaks, his voice is firmly even. "Can you die of starvation?"

"No," Connell grumbles, "but it's not a pleasant experience, and I won't tell you shit about who wanted to kidnap your darling until you feed me."

"How about we won't feed you shit until you tell us?" Jett asks around an enormous mouthful of bread. "This can go both ways, you know."

The pirate narrows his eyes. "Out of curiosity, are you planning to let me go at any point?"

"No," Jett and Kastian say at the same time.

"Then what's the point of my helping you at all? We're nearly out of the swamp and you can't keep me tied up forever. I'll escape eventually."

"You can try," Jett says, a menacing edge creeping into his tone.

Connell also notes Jett's tone and cocks his head curiously. "Have you got two different personalities, mate? No judgment, I'd just like to know who's sleeping next to me."

"Alright," I say, standing up before Jett can respond. "Enough of this."

My legs ache with exhaustion as I cross the small room in two steps. I'd far rather eat and go to sleep, but I get the strong feeling that until we've resolved things with the pirate, no one will get any rest.

I bend down until Connell and I are at eye level—which isn't exactly hard given that even seated, he's more than half my height. I grab a large piece of cheese from the tray and shove it into the pirate's mouth. "Here, chew on that for a minute while you listen to me."

His bright-blue eyes widen with something like interest, but he nods and remains silent, his mouth full of cheese.

"Right, so let's review." I hold up my fingers, counting them down as I talk. "I heard you talking to Elio on the train, and I can already guess that he had something to do with why you were there." I put a finger down. "I know you were sailing under Solistinian colors but your ship was obviously built in Vernallis." Another finger. "And I know, just from having spent any time with you at all, that whoever hired you would have had to pay a hell of a lot." I make a fist with my remaining fingers. "That's a lot of information right there, and I'm sure I'll figure out the rest just as soon as I get to Hydratta, at which point all your bargaining power will be gone."

Connell swallows his cheese and grins at me. "You're bloody sexy when you're angry. God, I fucking love redheads."

Kastian stands up, looking murderous. "I'm going to put my fist through your skull and pull out your fucking spinal cord. How's that for sexy?"

Connell licks his lips. "I've never tried that one before. Alright, have at it. Give it to me slow and deep."

Jett snorts something between a laugh and a sound of derision, and Kastian takes another menacing step toward Connell.

"Wait!" I put up a hand to stop him. "I've got this. I don't need your help."

To my surprise, Kastian stops, but doesn't sit back down on the bed. I can feel him looming over me like a shadow, and oddly I don't hate it. I grab a piece of bread from the tray and shove that in Connell's mouth too. This time, he opens wide, ready for it. "You're much more tolerable when you don't talk."

He shrugs, and winks at me as he chews his bread. He already looks more relaxed, which is exactly what I intended.

Thus far, Kastian and Jett just keep threatening him, but I can already tell that won't work with Connell. There are two ways to persuade someone to help you—the carrot and the stick. It's time to try a little carrot.

"Let's try this again," I say. "You are probably never going to get away from us. If you could be killed, I'm sure these two would have done it already, and you're not going to get any better treatment back in Vernallis. I doubt my brother would bat an eye at keeping you in our wine cellar and letting Jett here try his hand at defeating true immortality."

Connell's eyes narrow, and he tries to say something around the bread in his mouth. The tone of his muffled words is harsh and angry.

I put up a hand to quiet him. "You didn't let me finish. See, I'm not personally a fan of torture which would make me a very good friend for you to have." The corner of my mouth tips up in a sneer. "Understand what I'm saying, *darling*?"

Connell swallows and grins. "Why don't you give me more of that cheese before I think of something to say about our new friendship that will set off your attack dog." He winks at Kastian. "How are you doing over there, mate? What's it like to have your woman taking—"

I grab another piece of cheese and shove it in his mouth. I don't know what he was going to say, but I think we're all better off never finding out.

"To quote you," I say slowly, "'we can do this the easy way or the hard way.' You tell us what we want to know now and I'll make sure you're not tortured when we get to Vernallis. Or, you can try to keep your secrets, but I'll warn you that's not going to last long."

"You really think I'm afraid of pain?" he asks, swallowing the rest of his cheese. "I've died so many times I could fill a burial ground ten times over. Give me your worst, darling. I'll enjoy it. You can do whatever you can think of, and I'll just keep begging you for more."

Something dark flashes in his eyes that makes me think he's not bluffing. Threats of pain will not work on this man. But what about threats of another kind?

"Have you ever met a siren?" I ask.

"Sadly not. I'm pleased to meet you though. Feel free to show me whatever it is that makes men lose their minds."

"Oh, I will," I say, a syrupy sweetness in my voice.

His eyes widen in surprise, and I feel Kastian shift behind me but no one says anything.

I lean closer to the pirate until I can see my own reflection in his ocean-colored eyes. "Imagine this. I could ask you to tell us the truth and you would. I could tell you not to leave this room, and you wouldn't be able to. Then I could ask you to do more. You could spend the rest of your immortal life as my puppet—no control, no escape—aware of what's going on but completely unable to control your own body."

"Maybe I'll make you test all the ways you can't die...being swallowed by an animal was an interesting idea. Or we could visit the quicksand again, or maybe I just tell you to drown. Drown indefinitely, never ending, never dying, just stuck at the bottom of the ocean until—"

"Alright!" Connell says testily. "Fine, you win, darling. Fuck, I thought you weren't interested in torture."

I stand up, brushing dirt from my dress and smile at him. "I'm not, but it is in my nature."

I walk back over to the bed and sit down. Kastian is staring at me, wide-eyed, but I can't quite read his expression. He doesn't seem alarmed or surprised, exactly...more like intrigued.

I reach for my own portion of dinner, finally sitting down to fill my aching stomach as Jett takes over questioning the pirate. "Alright, now that's settled. Who tried to kidnap Dessa?"

"And why?" Kastian adds.

Still looking a bit shaken, Connell sits up straighter. "The King of Hydratta."

"That doesn't make sense," Jett says instantly. "She was headed to Hydratta already, and if they were the ones to plan this, then why would you kill their emissary?"

"King Magnus hired us to kidnap the darling Odessa and make it look like Solistine did it."

"Why?" I demand, my mind spinning. "What did Solistine do?"

"No idea," Connell says. "Give me another bit of bread and I might think of something."

Looking wary, Jett reaches over and puts another bit of bread into the pirate's mouth. Connell smirks and takes an unusually long time to chew and swallow before he finally answers. "So far as I know, Solistine didn't do anything."

"If you lie our agreement is off," I snap.

"I'm not lying, darling. I can't say I know the King of Hydratta that well—royals don't usually spend much time socializing with their hired killers, you know—but I didn't get the feeling this was about Solistine. It was about you."

"Me?" I ask incredulously. "He doesn't even know me...not really, anyway."

"Not *you*, darling. *You*, like your court. It was about Vernallis."

My head spinning with questions, I turn to Kastian, who hasn't said anything. "What do you think?"

He blinks at me, as if coming out of a stupor. "I believe him."

"Really? Why?"

"This is exactly the kind of thing Magnus would do. The bastard is incredibly opportunistic and cunning, but he's also patient. He waited years to find the moment to usurp my father."

And he made multiple plans when his original ideas got foiled. I think, wishing desperately I could say it out loud.

"He did?" I ask, as it's the only thing I can physically force from my throat.

Unaware of the war I'm waging inside my head, Kastian nods. "He's been lying low for a while because conquering Hydratta was destabilizing."

"And he won," Jett adds. "No offense, Kas, but it's not as if you've been much of a threat to him. He's likely thought he was untouchable until now."

"Hang on," Connell says, glancing from Kastian to me to Jett and back. "Just to be sure I have this straight, you're *Kastian*. Like *Prince Kastian*? The one who was supposed to have died years ago?"

Looking resigned, Kastian just nods.

Connell's eyes widen in apparent delight as he nods from Kastian to me. "And you're with her?"

"No," I say flatly at the same time as Kastian says: "Yes."

Connell grins. "...and she was going to marry the king who killed your family and stole your throne?"

"Yes, sort of." I answer at the same time as Kastian says: "Absolutely fucking not."

Connell cackles with laughter. "Oh, that is absolutely poetic. I wonder if King Magnus knows or if it's a coincidence. Gods, I wish I could be there when he finds out. I'd pay real money for that."

"Alright, shut the fuck up," Jett snaps.

Connell turns his attention to Jett. "Wait, who are you then? What's your role in this deliciously tragic little drama?"

"I'm the guy who you're really fucking lucky you didn't meet on that train. If I'd been there like I was supposed to be, then we wouldn't be sitting here now having this conversation."

Connell cocks his head. "You know, I actually believe that. Unlucky for me then that you weren't. I could have avoided so much unnecessary suffering."

"Can we get back to the actual point?" I grumble. "All I want is for this conversation to end so we can go to sleep."

Kastian nods tightly, his brow furrowing with exhaustion. "If Magnus wanted your kidnapping and death blamed on Solistine, he must have had a reason. I'm guessing that the reason is Daemon."

"What do you mean?"

"Magnus knows Alix and Daemon are new rulers, but they're building an army. They're only a few years away from being extremely dangerous if they wanted to be. My guess is he wants them as allies in case they wake up in ten years and decide to conquer the entire continent."

"They won't," I say confidently.

"Yeah, but Magnus doesn't know that," Jett chimes in. "I think Kas is right. Magnus is covering his own ass, and he's willing to sacrifice Solistine to do it. Ashwater would go to war with Solistine if he thought they ordered your death. He and Alix already said as much in our meeting the other day."

"Was that really only a few days ago?" I sigh. "I feel like I've lived years since then."

"Hang on," Connell says. "I never said anything about death. He didn't want us to kill her, just kidnap her."

"What was the endgame of that?" I ask.

Connell shrugs, but Kastian interjects. "That makes sense too, actually."

Jett nods. "I agree. So, let's say you're Magnus, you propose a betrothal to Dessa as an alliance between Hydratta and Vernallis, but you know that's not likely to work out because Dessa is hundreds of years younger than you and looks like that," Jett gestures toward me.

I blush, but don't interrupt. Neither does anyone else as Jett stands up from the bed and begins pacing, still thinking out loud.

"So you know the betrothal is a long shot, but you have a backup plan of organizing Dessa's kidnapping. As soon as the kidnapping becomes public knowledge, you contact Daemon and get him to agree to go to war against Solistine together. Then, maybe, you rescue Dessa and she's so grateful that the marriage works out anyway. But even if not, you've just gotten yourself the alliance with Vernallis which was the entire goal to begin with."

He stops to take a breath. "You have to admit, it's kind of a brilliant plan. Any way you look at that, it works out for Magnus—there's no scenario in which he doesn't get the alliance."

"Except for this one," Kastian growls. "Now that we know what Magnus had planned, Dessa won't go to Hydratta and we'll go back to Vernallis and tell Daemon before Magnus can get to him."

"How long do we have, though?" I ask the room at large. "King Magnus will be expecting Connell's crew to kidnap me, so when was he going to contact Daemon about the potential war?"

"I can answer that," Connell says. "If—"

Anticipating his request, Jett shoves a piece of cheese in Connell's mouth. The pirate swallows, then grins at Jett. "I see you're learning. Good boy."

"Just get to the point," Jett says grumpily.

"We were told to sail through the Stait of Scylla and around Hydratta until we reached Solistinian waters. Once there, I was supposed to wait for Hydratta or Vernallis to come after us. It would have been a suicide mission for anyone else, but for me..." he trails off, smirking.

"How long would it take to reach Solistine?" I cut in. "It would usually take over a week, but you were going by the Strait of Scylla...so five days?"

"Six," Connell corrects.

I heave a deep breath. "Alright. We've already lost two days as far as I can tell, by the time we've slept we'll only have four days left to reach Vernallis before Magnus contacts Daemon and Alix and tries to start a war. That's not a lot of time—without flying or taking the train, I'm not even sure it can be done."

"It'll have to be possible," Kastian says flatly. "Magnus already destroyed one kingdom, I'm not going to let him do it again or manipulate our friends into helping him do it. Someone needs to stop him, and I've been waiting nearly a century to do it."

ODESSA, AGE 16

I practically float back to my room, my heart racing wildly and my lips still tingling.

I'm so full of excitement I can barely keep my thoughts in order and my skin feels warm everywhere Prince Kastian touched me, as if his fingers have left an indelible mark. That was my first kiss—and what an overwhelmingly perfect kiss it was.

Every doubt I had before this evening has fled.

He remembers me.

He still has my key.

Everything is falling into place.

Maybe my childhood fantasy of being a princess isn't so crazy after all. Maybe this was always meant to be.

My thoughts come to a crashing halt when I turn the corner and see a slim woman in a purple dress standing—no, leaning—against my door. For a moment, I waver in confusion, stopping just as the figure turns toward me and my blood runs cold.

"Ah, you're back," Lady Lyra Von Bargen says, pushing off the wall. "Finally."

My excited heartbeat falters, and suddenly my pulse is racing for an entirely different reason. "Lady Lyra," I greet her stiffly. "It's a pleasure to see you again."

"Is it?" Lyra asks, with a note of condescension in her voice. "How odd. I'm not pleased to see you at all."

I reel back. "Then what are you doing outside my room?"

She sneers. "I think you know."

My heartbeat pounds with mingled anxiety and agitation, like I can't quite decide if I should turn and run in the other direction or stand here and confront her.

The other day, Lyra seemed meek and timid, but clearly that was just an act because she's anything but meek now. She glares at me, green eyes flashing, and everything from her posture to her severely styled black hair says that she came here seeking an argument.

But, how did she even know where I was? Did she see Kastian and I leave together or was someone on the pier spying on us?

I raise my fingers to my lips, which still feel swollen, then drop my hand and square my shoulders. "I don't know what you're talking about," I say finally, deciding to claim ignorance.

"Today on the lake," she clarifies. "Everyone saw you together."

A small amount of relief washes over me. So, she doesn't know where I was just now—but that's not necessarily better. "Are you concerned about my speaking to Prince Kastian? You might have to ask him about it, after all, he stole my boat. I never tried to seek him out."

"I suppose a siren wouldn't have to make an attempt," she says with a sniff.

"Again, I'm not entirely sure what you mean. It's very late. Could we discuss this tomorrow?"

"You're meddling in matters above your station," she snaps. "The prince and I have an agreement."

"I thought you weren't engaged," I begin, suddenly

wondering if I'm the problem here. Maybe I've made a terrible mistake.

"We're not," she says flatly.

Relief washes over me for the briefest moment before my irritation sparks again. If they're not engaged, then what is she doing here? We don't know each other, and clearly she's trying to intimidate me. She's making it impossible for me to defuse this situation, and I can feel my stormy temper rising like a tempest on the sea.

"Forgive me, but I don't understand what you were thinking coming here to confront me like this," I say coldly. "Excuse me, but I'm going to bed."

She doesn't move, refusing to let me step past her to enter my room. "Prince Kastian and I are not engaged, that's true, but there's an agreement between our families. I'm sure you already know that."

"I truly don't know what you're talking about, but if I did, I'd know that whatever agreement you have is flimsy at best and he fully intends to break it."

Her nostrils flare, but she doesn't look surprised. She doesn't look the slightest bit hurt either, which tells me this isn't a heartbroken girl in front of me; it's a calculating woman who is worried about her position in society.

"Look," I start again, making another attempt to push past her. "Whatever you're doing here is entirely unnecessary. I hardly know the prince any more than I know you. He stole my boat, that's all."

Her nostrils flare again. "If you knew anything about Kastian, you'd realize how wildly out of character that is. He doesn't engage with anyone, and now suddenly he's making a spectacle of himself over you? I know what's going on here."

Again, my pulse speeds up, and for the first time I look at her with interest. What does she think is going on here? Because I'd desperately like to know. I feel completely out of my depth already, and I'd die for an outside perspective, even if it is from the most unlikely and unpleasant source.

I press my lips together. "Enlighten me."

She sneers. "You've bewitched him."

I blink at her, startled. Whatever I was expecting her to say, it wasn't that. "Pardon?"

"You heard me. You used your siren magic to raise your social status, but it won't work. The Hydrattan royal family would never allow their reputation to be damaged by rumors of being influenced by a siren."

I roll my eyes. "I didn't do anything to him. You're wrong."

"I should hope so," she snaps. "Because if I'm right we both know how this ends. He'll die and you'll be put to death for murdering a prince."

My back goes completely rigid. "Excuse me? What do you mean he'll die?"

She narrows her eyes at me. "Don't play dumb."

For once, I'm not. I actually don't know what she means.

I know there are rumors and legends that sirens turn men insane, but that's an exaggeration. I've seen it happen with my father, but that was only after Mother left...and it didn't happen immediately.

I've never thought that I might kill someone.

"You're wrong," I say icily. "That's just a rumor. Not even a rumor—it's a legend. A fairytale."

She looks at me and her angry gaze turns almost pitying. "I'm not sure if you're just very naïve or very stupid, but be careful because ignorance won't save you. You'd better stay away from Kastian and any other Fae man because when they die it will be your fault."

And with that, she turns on her heel and wafts down the hall, leaving me standing alone feeling numb and cold.

ODESSA, PRESENT

I wake to the warm feeling of bare skin on mine.

For a long moment, I just lie there with my eyes closed, breathing deeply and enjoying the feeling of closeness. Of safety.

I can't remember the last time I shared a bed with someone—usually, I can't stand to stick around after a night of fun, both because I've rarely found a man I liked enough to want to actually get to know, and because I'm always aware that the longer I linger the more likely it is that I could doom some innocent man to an early death.

So where am I now? Whose heavy arm is wrapped around my hip, and why am I so warm?

All of a sudden, reality hits me and my eyes pop open.

Shit.

I'm lying on my side in the small rickety bed in the inn.

When I went to sleep, I'd done my best to put space between Kastian and me, inching to the very edge of the mattress, but at some point in the night we gravitated back together because now I can feel every part of my back pressed against his chest, and his arm is trapping me close to him, pulling my ass against his hips.

Shit, shit, shit!

A tight knot of anxiety twists in my stomach as I lie there, feeling the warmth of his body too close for comfort.

Part of me is tempted to jump up and yell at him for touching me, but Kastian is asleep. And even if he weren't, he isn't really doing anything wrong or unusual.

Fae males are notoriously intense and possessive, and I should have expected his reaction after we slept together. As far as he's concerned, I probably already belong to him—an idea that sends a traitorous little spark of excitement shooting down my spine.

Except, he already has a soul-bonded mate out there somewhere. And even if he didn't, we can never be together. He has no idea what could happen if we go down this path again, and just because I can't tell him doesn't mean it's any less of my responsibility to keep my distance.

How many times do I need to remind myself that I know better than this? That exhaustion and gratitude at being alive is not an excuse to ruin the only truly selfless act I've made in the last one hundred years.

Slowly, I inch out from under the covers, making sure not to ruffle the sheets or rustle the mattress. Holding my breath, I rise to my feet, the floorboards creaking softly beneath me. My eyes adjust to the dimness, and I scan the shadowy room.

The room is still dark, but I can see the first light of dawn peeking in through the curtains drawn over the window. Jett is sprawled out on his stomach in the other bed, the sheets tangled around his legs, his face buried in the pillow. Across the room, Connell is slumped on the floor, his back propped against the wall. His head tilts slightly to the side, eyes closed, a soft snore occasionally escaping his lips.

Thank the gods they're all still asleep, because I need to go outside and think.

I reach for my muddy boots on the floor beside the bed and

carry them with me as I creep as quietly as possible across the room. Reaching the door, I say a little prayer to myself that it won't creak, before easing it open and slipping out into the hall.

As soon as I'm standing in the dim, empty hallway, I let out an enormous sigh of relief.

It's not lost on me that this is the second time in less than a week that I've escaped a bed with a sleeping Kastian in it, and that fact makes my stomach churn with shame and remorse—and, unfortunately, just the tiniest hint of arousal.

Oh my gods, what the hell am I doing?

I slide down the wall and sit on the floor to pull my boots on, all the while my heart pounds as if I just ran for my life rather than sneaking out of bed. Standing again, I walk swiftly down the hall to the small bathing room.

It's empty—thank gods—and I lock myself inside before leaning on the sink and sucking in several deep breaths.

My eyes dart up toward my own reflection in the age-spotted mirror and I wince.

I'm a mess, emotionally and physically.

I can't remember ever looking this bad in my life—the circles under my eyes are a dark purplish blue, my hair is tangled and dull, and there's still dirt on my skin despite my attempts to wash off in the river.

At the thought of the river my stomach does a stupid little flip that sends tingles all over my skin and makes my pulse throb low in my belly.

"Stop it!" I tell myself firmly. "Pull yourself together."

Teeth gritted with determination, I splash some soap and water on my face and use my torn dress to try to really scrub at what's left of the dirt. Then, I take off the dress and I perform the same treatment on the rest of my body and rinse my tangled hair in the sink before knotting it into a tight braid. Finally, I rinse my dress in the sink.

The dress is barely more than scraps at this point. In addition to the torn, short skirt, there's a large hole in one sleeve and a rip along the neckline. The once-lavender fabric has stretched due to my not wearing a corset, and is stained so the color is more of a mauve, even after I've finished washing it.

I will never turn my nose up at a dress ever again. From now on, if it's clean, I'm wearing it, no matter what it looks like.

I finish washing the dress and pull it back on. The damp fabric sticks to my skin and drips on the floor, but I'd much rather be wet than dirty.

When I'm finally done, I smile slightly at my reflection. It's far from perfect, but I feel a little better. More like myself.

With another deep breath, I unlock the door to the bathing room and step out into the hall, thinking vaguely that I'll go find us some breakfast, then wake the others to get ready to leave.

As I pass the room where the men are sleeping, I glance at the door, wondering what Kastian will think if he wakes up and finds me gone.

"Stop it," I tell myself again. "You know better."

Those words are starting to lose meaning, but I can't stop myself from thinking them.

I have to know better. I have to be fine.

There's only forty-eight hours more of this, and surely the next inn we stay at will have more than one room. Then we'll be back in Vernallis, and I can go back to avoiding Kastian like the plague.

It feels like a lie even in my head, but I desperately cling to it anyway as I walk down the short hallway and reach the stairs.

I'm hardly paying attention to anything around me until an angry voice from downstairs bursts through my thoughts. "It doesn't seem like you've got any trouble here. Why would you waste our time?"

I come to an abrupt halt on the stairs, my intuition screaming at me to stop and listen.

"I sent the message last night," the innkeeper's wavering voice replies. "I didn't realize how long it would take you to get here, and I thought—"

"We were stationed over an hour away," the angry voice replies. "The king has every damn guard in the kingdom on high alert and we haven't slept in two days. We finally got a few hours to sleep, but then I had to drag my men out of bed and through that fucking swamp because your messenger said your village was in trouble. So imagine my surprise when we get here and everyone is still asleep."

"They looked dangerous, Sir. There were four of them in all. Two tall males with tattoos—"

"Are tattoos illegal now?" the angry voice interrupts.

My heartbeat kicks up with anxiety. One of those voices is definitely the innkeeper, and while I can't place the other one, they're absolutely talking about us.

My pulse pounds in my ears as, quietly as I can, I edge down the remaining two stairs to the landing, and poke my head a few inches around the wall to see what's going on.

Sure enough, the innkeeper is standing in the middle of the empty tavern. There are four men in front of him, all dressed in green military jackets—Hydrattan royal guards. The largest guard, the leader, is the angry voice arguing with the innkeeper.

I stifle a gasp and pull my head back before they can see me, just as the innkeeper tries again to explain himself to the guard. "You should have seen them. One had to be six and a half feet tall and he had a couple of fresh wounds, like they'd been in a fight. The other one was covered in mud and dragging a third man around with a belt tied around his wrists."

"A belt?" the guard asks, sounding interested for the first time.

"There was a woman too. She wasn't bound up, but her dress was torn. I thought she might be a prisoner as well."

A cold dread washes over me and I inch my way back up the stairs, holding my breath.

It seems like Kastian's gold did absolutely nothing to deter the innkeeper from calling the local guards, and the only reason we've been left to sleep so long is because it took them awhile to get here. Sooner or later, they're going to come up here to check on us and we absolutely cannot be here when they do.

I'm not that worried about Jett and me. If not for the kidnapping plot, we'd be in Hydratta anyway and we were technically invited to be here. I'm worried about Kastian. He should never have set foot in Hydratta because the second someone recognizes him he's going to get dragged in front of King Magnus...or worse.

"Wake up!" I hiss, as I step back into the small room where the men are still sleeping.

Surprisingly, Jett sits up immediately, taking no time to blink sleep from his eyes as if he was already semi-alert. "What's wrong?"

"We have to leave right now."

I lock the door behind me and test the knob, making sure it doesn't budge. Then, I cross the room quickly and throw open the curtains, letting the faint morning light stream inside. The light hits Kastian in the face and he shields his eyes as he too sits up to look at me. "What's going on?"

"There are Hydrattan guards downstairs looking for us," I whisper, nervous that somehow they'll be able to hear us moving around from downstairs. "Someone kick Captain Connell awake, we need to go now!"

Kastian throws his legs over the edge of the bed and starts pulling on his boots as Jett walks over to the pirate and shakes him awake. "Hey. Get up!"

"Bugger off, mate," Connell mumbles. "I just finally got to sleep. Do you know how uncomfortable this floor is?"

"I'll make it more uncomfortable if you don't get up now." Kastian says over his shoulder.

"What's happening?" The pirate asks through a yawn.

"There are guards downstairs looking for us," I repeat. "That innkeeper called them in after all, he thinks the captain and I were kidnapped."

"Well, he's not wrong, darling," Connell says. "But don't

worry. It may surprise you to know that a man of my profession isn't much of a fan of royal guards. I won't sell you out."

My stomach lurches. It hadn't even occurred to me that Connell might sell us out until he brought it up, which only goes to show how ill-suited I am to sneaking around or doing anything illegal.

Fortunately, Jett jumps in, clearly not struggling at all with suddenly being on the wrong side of the law. "I don't believe him. He was working with Magnus. His best bet is to walk right up to those guards and tell them he needs to deliver Dessa to the king and Kas and I have captured them both.."

"Ye of little faith," Connell says with mock horror. "Do you really think I'd stoop so low?"

Jett scowls. "I think you'd lick the soles of those guards' boots if it meant you'd go free."

"It doesn't matter what Connell does," Kastian says, getting to his feet. "We can't even walk past those guards. If any of them recognize me, we're fucked."

My already racing heart skips a nervous beat. "How are we going to get out of here without walking through the front door? I didn't see any other exits."

Kastian comes up behind me and leans over my shoulder to look out the small window. He tries to shove it open, but it doesn't budge. "I could break this," he says slowly. "But I don't think any of us could fit through anyway, and especially not with wings."

I turn to Jett. "You're the one who's always telling those stories about how you escaped from one heist or another. What do you think?"

His dark eyes dart from left to right as if he's cataloging the room in his mind. "If we can't get out, we need to hide until they think we've already left and go look somewhere else."

"But where?" I moan, gesturing around at the sparsely furnished room.

Before anyone can answer, we hear movement downstairs, and

the muffled voices grow louder. Jett swears harshly, and I feel sweat bead on my brow and along the back of my neck beneath my braid.

I wish desperately that the floor might open and swallow us whole. That a larger window might appear. That we could turn invisible.

Wait a minute.

That thought sparks something in the back of my mind, and an idea hits me just as the sounds of boots on the stairs reach us.

"Which room?" the guard's angry voice demands, loud enough that it feels as if he's already in the room with us.

"Top of the stairs on the far left," the innkeeper says. "I put them all in one room to make things easier."

Asshole! I knew every room couldn't be taken.

Indignation shoots through me, even though that's not really the point right now and we have far more important things to worry about.

Focusing on the issue at hand and the idea swirling around in the back of my mind, I shove both hands into my pockets, feeling around into the corners. *Please, please still be there. Please, please!*

My fingers close around a tiny wilted flower stem, so shriveled and droopy that it had fallen into the very deepest corner of my dress pocket. I pull it out and hold it up in triumph. "I've got it!"

"Got what?" Kastian whispers, his eyes on the closed door.

I don't bother to explain, just break the stem into smaller pieces and shove a bit at him. "Eat this."

He looks at it in disgust. "What is it?"

"Just trust me."

He meets my eyes, and without question pops the stem into his mouth. "That's sweet like candy. Now really, what is it?"

My heart skips a beat, but I don't need to answer as in that exact moment Kastian disappears. One moment, he was standing next to me, and the next I'm looking at the unmade beds.

Jett gasps loudly. "What the hell is that?"

"Aurelia gave this to me. She said if you eat it, you'll turn invisible."

Connell raises his eyebrows in disbelief, but Jett grins with excitement. We've been living with Aurelia long enough to know that she's a little odd, but her magic is more advanced than anyone I've ever met, and it nearly always works.

"Fuck yes," Jett gasps excitedly. "Give me some."

I break the rest of the blue stem into more pieces and try to hand him one, just as a heavy knock sounds on the door.

"Open up by order of the Kingdom of Hydratta."

My stomach lurches with panic.

Jett looks at the door and shoves my hand away. "Never mind. You take it."

"What—" Kastian's disembodied voice begins.

"You two take it," Jett cuts him off. "You're the ones in danger of being recognized. I'll distract them for you."

"Excuse me," Connell says dryly. "What are you expecting me to do?"

Another loud knock sounds on the door, harder this time as if the guard is pounding with his fist. A second later, the doorknob rattles as the guard tries to shove his way inside.

"Dessa, eat it," Kastian's voice hisses.

I feel Kastian's large hand reaching for me, tugging me sideways as I pop the stem into my mouth and chew.

My first thought is that Aurelia was right—the flower tastes like marshmallow—then, a cold sensation washes over me, like ice water crawling slowly over my skin. I freeze, looking down at my body only for a split second later to find myself staring at the empty floor. I gasp.

"Stay quiet," Jett demands, striding over to the door, then raises his voice, shouting to the guards outside. "Be right there!"

An invisible hand that can only be Kastian's reaches for me, feeling along my arm to my ribs. His fingers close around my waist, and he tugs me sharply down to the floor between the wall and the edge of the bed. I'm not expecting it, and I fall sideways, a tiny yelp escaping my lips.

"Why are you all wet?" Kastian's bemused voice tickles my ear, his warm breath fanning over my invisible skin.

"Uh—" I begin.

"Shhh!" Jett hisses.

I freeze.

It's the strangest sensation of my entire life. I'm lying half on the floor, half on Kastian. I can feel the wood beneath my hip and his chest rising and falling against my back. His arms wrap around me from behind in something like a hug. I can feel his breathing in my ear, but when I look down, I can't see anything except the dirty wood floor, as if I'm peering through my own legs.

Jett walks over to the door, raising both hands to his hair and messing it up, making it look even more as if he just rolled out of bed, then in one movement he pulls his shirt over his head and tosses it on the floor, revealing a heavily muscled chest.

He stops just in front of the door and looks back at Connell. "I'm going to send him away. You stay quiet or I swear to whatever God you believe in that I'll make you regret it."

Then, Jett swings the door open and leans against the doorframe, using his body to block the rest of the room. "Morning, officer," he says cheerfully.

"Why didn't you answer the door?" the guard demands, looking Jett up and down.

"I was asleep," he says with an exaggerated yawn. "Can I help you with something?"

The guard seems to falter, perhaps surprised by Jett's casual tone. He peers around Jett's bare shoulder and into the room beyond. I hold my breath, all my muscles tensing as Kastian's arms tighten around me.

"We were told there was a disturbance up here," the guard says slowly.

"Disturbance?" Jett asks innocently. "I didn't hear anything."

The guard frowns. "We were told there were four of you and two might be hostages."

Jett laughs. "I think there must have been a misunderstanding. No one here is being held against their will."

Before Jett can do anything to stop him, the guard shoves him out of the way and pushes into the room. I gasp, and Kastian clamps a large invisible hand over my mouth, squeezing me even tighter around the middle with his other arm.

The guard stomps into the small room and stops, his eyes widening in surprise when they land upon Captain Connell, whose wrists are bound securely to the end of the wooden bedframe with Jett's leather belt. Connell raises his eyebrows in mock innocence, lifting his fingers in as much of a genial wave as his constraints allow, and offers the guard a lopsided grin. "Morning, mate."

The guard's expression darkens, and his hand instinctively moves towards the hilt of his sword. "What the fuck is going on in here?"

Behind the guard, Jett shifts uneasily on his feet. His eyes dart from side to side, like he's trying hard to think of a plausible explanation and coming up with nothing.

"Er..." Jett begins tentatively, clearly stalling for time.

My heartbeat pounds with nervous anxiety, and I can feel Kastian's heart doing the same against my back even as his fingers press against my mouth.

"Ah, don't look so shocked," Connell says, winking at the guard. "Just indulging in a little... recreational restraint. You know how it is—some folks pay good money for this kind of treatment."

Leaping on Connell's excuse, Jett grins and strides across the room to stand beside the pirate. He gives Connell a light, open-palmed slap on the cheek. "Did I say you could talk?"

Connell's eyes sparkle with mischief. "Forgive me, Master," he utters with mock solemnity, his voice dripping with an irony that I'm not sure the guard will be able to detect.

The guard's brow furrows deeper, and I swear I see a flush rise up the back of his neck. "Er...right. Fine then. As long as no one is getting hurt."

"That's half the point, mate," Connell says. "It's no fun without a little—"

He breaks off as Jett slaps a hand over his mouth and gives the guard an innocent smile. "Sorry. I can gag him if you want. I'm sure he wouldn't mind."

"Er, no, that won't be necessary," the guard clears his throat, looking definitely embarrassed now.

The guard takes a step toward the door, but Kastian and I still don't move, and he doesn't take his hand off my mouth.

"Hang on," the guard says, stopping at the door. "I thought there were four of you in here."

"There were," Jett says flatly. "I don't know where they got to. They're newly bonded, and you know how that goes. Must have snuck out while we were sleeping." He chuckles as if he and the guard are sharing a private joke at mine and Kastian's expense.

The guard's shoulders relax. "Fine. Sorry to disturb you. If I were you I'd be on your way, though. Find another inn for whatever this is."

"Excellent suggestion," Jett says cheerfully, following the guard to the door. "We'll do that. Thanks a lot."

He shuts the door behind the guard and immediately his easy smile slides off his face. He presses his ear to the door for a moment, listening. "He's going back downstairs."

Kastian sighs and finally lets go of my mouth. "Fuck me," he breathes in relief.

I scramble up, still uncomfortable with how I can't see my own body as I move. I slump onto the bed. "Well, that was insane."

"You can say that again, darling," Connell says. "As if I'd ever submit to this sort of treatment. I'd rather tie the knots than be the prisoner if you catch my drift."

I ignore him and turn to Jett before remembering that he

can't see me trying to catch his eye. "Jett, do you think those guards will linger?"

"Not sure," Jett says, walking back over to where he threw his shirt and bending to pick it up. "But I think we should leave separately just in case. If that plant wears off and they see four of us leaving, it will cause all sorts of new questions, and the last thing we need is any of them looking at you or Kas too closely."

"How long does the invisibility last?" Kastian asks from somewhere near the window.

"No idea. Aurelia didn't give instructions."

"Let's assume it could wear off at any moment, then," Jett says. "You two should leave now, and we'll leave in half an hour."

"You sure you want to be alone with the pirate?" Kastian asks, sounding dubious.

"I resent that, sir," Connell snaps. "Perhaps I'm the one in danger, you ever think of that?"

"You're definitely the one in danger," Jett snaps, then turns toward the wall where he seems to think Kastian is standing. "It'll be fine, I've been stuck with worse people for far longer than a few days."

"Where will we meet you?" I ask.

"It will probably take two days to reach the border of Vernallis without horses or flying," Kastian says, his voice coming from the complete opposite side of the room from where Jett is looking. "Let's meet there two nights from now."

Jett agrees, and they speak in fast whispers, working out the details of where and how we'll meet back up.

Hardly listening, I instead turn to look in the direction of Kastian's voice, suddenly very glad we can't see each other.

Two days alone with Kastian traveling through the swamp with no one else to play buffer. I think I'd rather be stuck with the pirate.

27

THE PAST

ODESSA, AGE 16

I lie awake for hours staring at the ceiling of my luxurious guest room. Lyra left quite some time ago, but I can't seem to get her words or her vicious scowl out of my head.

Lady Lyra Von Bargen is clearly much more calculating than I would have thought from our first meeting, but it's not even her I'm worried about. She didn't really threaten me, she just stated what she believes to be a fact; as far as Lyra knows, sirens are cursed to kill any man who loves them.

I wish I could dispute it. I wish I knew for certain that she was wrong, but I'm not sure. Of course I've heard the legends about sirens, but I assumed they were just that—legends. I've never felt any desire to turn any man into my slave. I've never wanted to drown anyone.

Except, that's not true.

I thought about drowning just the other day, the moment I realized that Prince Kastian was engaged to someone else. But, was I thinking about drowning him or her? I'm not sure, and I'm equally unsure if the difference matters.

And what about Papa? I can't ignore the brutal way my father died. What if he hadn't wanted to drown that day eight years ago? What if he was somehow compelled, and what if my mere existence is enough to doom Prince Kastian to the same fate?

I don't know what to believe, and it's the uncertainty that's killing me.

I grit my teeth and kick the covers away from my body, throwing them to the floor in a heap. I can't keep lying here doing nothing. I'm going to lose my mind.

I stand and cross to the window, pressing my forehead to the cold glass. The palace grounds fan out in front of me—sprawling gardens, the ocean in the distance, and the occasional flare of torchlight as a patrolling guard passes beneath the window.

My gaze catches on the horizon, on the ocean in the distance, and suddenly I can't be here anymore. I feel like I'm suffocating. I need to go outside. I need to move, to breathe.

With trembling hands, I snatch my quilt back off the floor and wrap it around my shoulders. Then, moving with a purpose I don't quite understand, I open the door and slip out into the corridor.

The hallway is dark, the sconces guttering low. I creep past the other guest suites, careful not to make too much noise.

The entire castle is asleep, and the corridors are even quieter than they were when I met Kastian mere hours ago. I pass no one as I hurry toward the hallway outside the dining room, then past the open balcony and toward the stairs.

I let my fingers trail along the banister as I descend the staircase, steadying myself against the swirl of vertigo. Reaching the bottom, I let myself out a side door into the gardens.

The sky is still dark, but the moon is full, and the silvery light is enough to see by as I wander through the palace garden. Eventually, my feet carry me to an ornate metal fence on the very edge of the palace grounds.

I walk along the fence, and it doesn't take long before I come across a gate beyond which a rocky trail disappears into waving dunes. Far off, the vast expanse of the ocean stretches out, its waves crashing rhythmically against the jagged shoreline.

As I stand frozen, one hand on the gate, a ghostly wail rings through the night louder even than the sound of the distant crashing waves.

Suddenly I know exactly where I'm going.

I grip the cool metal of the gate, swinging it open with a creak, and step onto the path, feeling the salty breeze brush against my skin as I make my way toward the inviting sound of the sea.

I've never done anything like this before. I've never even wanted to, but I could swear the idea has gripped me like a compulsion, and now I know I won't be able to think of anything else until I've at least tried.

I pick my way over the rocks and dunes to the patch of sand below. When I reach the small beach and pull my slippers off and drop them on the ground along with my blanket, letting my feet dig into the sand and the ocean air nip at my skin.

Heart pounding with anticipation, I walk toward the shoreline.

The moonlight on the water combined with the rolling waves is hypnotic. Inviting.

Pausing for just a heartbeat, I watch the gentle waves roll in, their white frothy edges curling and retreating. Then, with a deep breath, I step forward, allowing the chilly tide to sweep over my toes.

The reaction is immediate.

The moment my feet break the surface, something electric jolts through me—an uncoiling, a *remembering*.

I don't feel pain, exactly, but there's a sensation—a prickling that starts at my toes and races up my calves, as though a thousand invisible needles are stitching something new into my bones. For a breathless instant, the world blurs: stars above, black water below, and my body caught between.

I stare, transfixed, as my toes elongate and press together, the nails thinning and fusing into a single, glistening membrane. Tiny silver scales bloom up from my ankles, intricate as embroidery, catching the pale glow with each movement. It's beautiful and horrifying all at once.

I flex my new webbed toes, and the sensation is so strange, so fundamentally not-me, that I'm seized with vertigo. I sway as the transformation crawls higher, up the line of my shin, scales rippling, as if they have a consciousness of their own and are eager to claim more territory.

"Enough," I gasp, jerking backward.

Like a fog has lifted from my mind, reality slams into me. I wrench my foot from the water with a violence that's almost comical, only I misjudge my balance and land hard on my ass in the sand, limbs tangled and heart hammering.

For several minutes, I sit and stare at my feet, watching the imprints of scales fade away. My heartbeat pounds against my ribs, beating an anxious chant.

Oh my gods.

There's such a stark difference between knowing what I am and knowing with absolute certainty that there's something intrinsically different about me than anyone I've ever known. The knowledge that I could walk into the water right now and never come back is too huge a concept to even consider.

I sit in silence for a long time watching the rolling waves. Minutes pass—hours maybe—until finally I hear a distant ghostly sound.

I've heard the sirens before, during long voyages on *The Adella* when our ship had to pass through dangerous waters. I remember my father and his crew stuffing their ears with cotton or locking themselves below deck to resist the hypnotic cries.

Perhaps it's simply because I'm one of them, but the song doesn't sound compelling to me. Neither does it sound frightening. It's a distant chorus of unearthly voices, rising and falling in complicated harmony, swelling with longing so sharp it makes my teeth ache.

I listen as the ethereal song grows steadily nearer until the air around me shudders, and I'm not surprised when the first dark shapes begin to appear in the water, illuminated by the shaft of moonlight.

One by one, a dozen ghostly heads rise out of the water, their faces turned toward the shore. The moon casts their silhouettes in shades of gunmetal and pearl, their eyes reflective as mirrors.

They're watching me. All of them, like they're one single mind spread across a dozen bodies. Their eyes are searching, but they hold no curiosity. There's hunger there, and wariness, and something else: recognition.

I consider running. Turning and bolting up the dunes, maybe locking myself in my room and pretending this never happened. But the song holds me in place, the melody threading through my veins, pulsing alongside my heart. Fear and fascination wage war inside my ribcage.

I don't move.

From the farthest cluster of silent, staring faces, a single figure breaks away from the others. She swims with impossible speed, her arms slicing the water in smooth, deliberate strokes, her body undulating almost like a squid.

The other sirens scatter, giving her a wide berth, as if she's the only one with the right to break away from the herd.

The siren swims until she's no more than twenty feet away, visible only by her moon-pale skin reflecting against the blackness of the water. As she nears the shore, her head breaks the surface and her features sharpen. I stare, open mouthed.

The siren's hair is long and matted with seaweed and salt. Her black, glassy eyes are too large for her face and her lips are thin blue ribbons outlining viciously sharp teeth. Her skin looks thin and seems to be stretched over the bones of her face, making her look emaciated and deadly.

Fear grips me, and once again I feel the urge to flee. This time, I scramble backwards, nearly rising to my feet.

Without warning, the siren stands, water cascading off her naked skin in rivulets. Before my eyes, her pearlescent scaled skin recedes. The sharp bones of her face disappear beneath supple flesh, and her seaweed-like hair shifts into long, flowing blonde waves. On her head, she wears a crown of coral and pearls, like an oceanic queen.

She walks toward me and there's something wild, almost catlike in the way she moves. It's frightening and yet familiar; I see echoes of myself in her. Her eyes are violet like mine, her face is heart-shaped and symmetrical, and her figure is full and curvy. At a distance, she could *be* me.

She takes a step onto the sand, then hesitates. Then, she crosses the beach between us and silently kneels on the sand in front of me. Close, but still just out of reach, her arms resting lightly on her knees.

The silence between us stretches taut as a bowstring.

I want to speak, but my mouth is dry and the words die in my throat.

Would the siren even understand me if I spoke?

I've never worried about being understood before, as the continent of Ellender is enchanted with universal language, but suddenly I'm uncertain if that enchantment would extend to creatures of the sea.

I open my mouth, unsure what to say. What comes out is a breathless, garbled question: "How did you know I was here?"

The siren flexes her jaw and clears her throat, as if she's not used to speaking. She clears her throat. "We always know when one of us enters the water. We can feel every part of the sea...can't you feel it?"

"No." I shake my head automatically, but even as I do, I realize that perhaps she's right. I can feel...something, I think. I can't see all the sirens in the distance, but I know they're there, watching us.

The siren frowns at me, and again, it takes a moment for her to form the words, but when she does speak it's clearer than before. "You'll feel it once you've returned to the water."

My eyes narrow. "What do you mean?"

"We've come to welcome you back," the siren says.

I shake my head. "No. I don't want to go into the sea. I was just...curious."

She looks troubled. "But dear, the water is where you belong."

I recoil slightly. "Dear" is a far too familiar thing to be called from this strange, beautiful monster.

"No, it isn't. I'm sorry, I shouldn't have come here." The words come out brittle, hollow in my chest. I stagger to my feet, brushing sand off my legs with hands that can't decide whether they want to tremble or clench into fists.

With a grace I'll never possess, the siren gets to her feet and stands directly in front of me.

She's taller than I am by a head, and even in the uncertain moonlight, I can see the faint lines around her mouth, the pale webbing of scars at her wrists and throat. She's impossibly beautiful, but I'm sure that she's far older than she looks. Certainly older than me—maybe by decades or maybe by centuries.

"We don't belong on land, Odessa," she says almost kindly.

I stiffen. "How do you know my name?"

She ignores my question, continuing as if I didn't speak. "You don't belong here and you never did. You can pretend, but the sea will take you back. Sooner or later, it always does."

"It can't take me back if I never lived there to begin with."

She cocks her head. "I don't understand. You *belong* in the sea."

"No."

"Why?" she asks, seeming earnest.

"I'm not like you, I have a life here. Family... and people who matter to me."

She tilts her head, her expression unreadable. "Your family is in the water. You have people here who matter to you now, but they won't last forever."

"What does that mean?" I demand.

"No one here will ever truly understand you. Sooner or later you'll find a way to destroy anyone you care for on land. Some of us do it with teeth," she adds, flexing her webbed fingers, "and some with songs so beautiful they rot the heart from inside."

It's the closest thing to a warning I've ever been given, and it cuts deep.

I press my hands to my chest, like I might hold the words inside and keep them from spreading. "But what if I don't want to be like you? What if I want to stay here?"

She regards me with something like pity, glancing down at my legs, and my still-fading scales. "If you stay on land, you'll never be whole. Not really. You'll be—" She searches for the word. "Lonely. Always. It's that loneliness that will drive you to destroy anyone who might try to compete with your love for your true home and family. Or, you can join us. You'll never be alone again...but you'll have to let everything else go."

The wind picks up, salt and sharp and full of secrets. I shiver, blanket clutched around my shoulders, and realize the other sirens have vanished from the sea, only this one left, as if the rest of them have already written me off as a lost cause.

Still, I feel the need to make myself clear. "I'm not going with you."

She tilts her head at me and she almost looks sad. "That's your choice, but if you want to stay on land, then you must never return to the water."

"Why?"

"In the water, we are as one. One mind, one...intention. There's no room in the ocean for a siren who will not join the pack, except as the queen...and there's already a queen. So, if you ever return, you must join the pack, or I'll have to kill you myself."

The siren turns and walks back toward the water and I almost turn away too, but then the words spill out of me, raw and childish. "Wait."

She hovers on the edge of the rising tide. For a second she looks almost hopeful. "Yes?"

"You said we destroy anyone we love...is that from experience? Did you ever love anyone?"

For a long time, she doesn't answer. The waves crash, the moon drifts, and I wait. When the silence finally breaks, her voice is tiny.

"Yes. And I broke him in the end. It's what we do." Her gaze hardens. "You can try to outrun it, but it's already inside you. The only thing left is to decide who you're willing to hurt."

KASTIAN, PRESENT

It takes less than fifteen minutes for the invisibility to wear off, but thankfully by then Dessa and I have already left the village.

She reappears next to me, and I blink

I'm holding her hand—mostly so we wouldn't lose each other while we couldn't see, but it's strange. The moment she pops back into existence and I see her, fresh-faced with her hair braided, I get the strangest sense of déjà vu.

"You're staring at me," she says tightly, tugging her hand out of mine.

I shake my head and run my fingers over the stubble coating my chin. "Sorry. The invisibility wearing off surprised me."

She nods once, and turns away from me, her gaze fixed firmly on the riverbank in front of us.

We've already discussed how we're going to reach the border of Vernallis, and there simply aren't a lot of perfect options.

We can't fly right now while I'm not under direct threat, and even if we could I wouldn't want to. While it's still light out and we're within the borders of Hydratta, the last thing I want is to be spotted swooping around the sky. For the same reason, we've decided to avoid the main road, which means walking through the swamp once more. Neither of us wanted to spend any time somewhere so dangerous, so we made our way to the river.

Now, we walk along the edge, our feet occasionally slipping into the murky, shallow water. I suppose it's better than quicksand.

"You can't conjure a boat, can you?" Odessa complains as we walk.

I frown. "Probably."

She stops and looks at me. "I was joking. Can you really? I'd kill to sit right now. My legs are still tired from yesterday and I'm going to burn these shoes when we get back to Storia. I'm never picking beauty over comfort again."

I smile, unable to look at her without immediately thinking of what a contradiction she is.

Only the other day I was thinking I didn't really know Odessa that well, but these last few days have been enlightening. Odessa is bold and seemingly fearless, but she's also delicate. She doesn't like to be uncomfortable, and won't bother to contain her displeasure if everything isn't exactly to her liking.

"You would have made a good princess," I comment.

She reels back, her eyebrows rising into her hairline. "What on earth would make you say that?"

I'm not really sure why I said it, actually, except that it feels true. Maybe that's why I keep calling her Princess?

"Nothing," I say shortly. "Never mind. I think I can conjure that boat for you though, now I'm feeling better. Hang on."

She stops walking, still looking perturbed, and leans against a nearby tree to watch me as I walk around the edge of the swamp collecting tree branches and making them into a pile on the edge of the river.

I'm not surprised that she doesn't offer to help, but I'm not bothered either—in fact, I prefer it this way. If she had offered I would have felt obligated to accept her help, when I'd really rather just do the job myself. Odessa is clearly content to let me handle the boat, but I know that she'll be genuinely grateful when I'm done—even if it is the only nice thing she says to me today.

After gathering a substantial pile of twigs and branches, I lower myself to the swampy ground, crossing my legs. I close my eyes and take a deep breath, centering my thoughts. The air around me tingles with energy, a subtle hum that quickens my pulse. A surge of warmth spreads from the pit of my stomach, radiating outward

Slowly, the pieces of wood lift from the ground, rising like marionettes. They twist and turn in midair, aligning and snapping together with an audible click, gradually transforming into the sleek outline of a rowboat.

Dessa gasps. "Oh my gods, that's incredible."

A smug satisfaction washes over me. "Glad you're pleased."

Dessa offers me a small smile. "When we get back, you should definitely help Alix with her wife."

I stand again, dusting dirt from my hands before frowning. "Her wife?"

Odessa frowns back, looking as confused as I feel. "I think that was what it was called. Wifey? She wants to use machines to play music and talk to her mother."

"What kind of machines?"

"I don't know, you'll have to ask her." She shrugs, and clambers into the front of the boat. "Throw me an oar, I'd like to get going."

I climb into the boat behind her. "It's fine, I'll row."

She's not facing me, but her shoulders stiffen and I can tell she's scowling. "I can help, you know. I'm not useless just because I'm not as strong as you."

"I definitely didn't say that. I would never call you useless."

"Then give me an oar."

I push our little boat off the edge of the bank and into the center of the river. "No really, I've got it."

She makes an indignant sound in the back of her throat. "Excuse me, Your Majesty. I worked in the palace for years. What makes you think I'm too fragile to help row the boat?"

She's completely misunderstanding what I'm trying to get at, but for whatever reason I can't resist needling her. "You worked as a ladies maid, that was hardly physically taxing."

She sniffs. "It's not as if you did any real labor either, *Your Majesty*."

I decide not to remind her that I spent decades mining for ice in Dyaspora, because I know that's not what she meant and I'm sure the thought will sour her mood even more. "Look, I want to row. I like having something to do, but you obviously don't. You're only offering because you feel guilty for not helping build the boat, but you really don't have to." She looks over her shoulder and glares at me, but I don't let her get a word in. "It's not a bad thing to just relax, Princess."

"Because I'm not capable of manual labor, you mean?" she asks dangerously.

"No, I didn't mean it like that. I meant, you're...soft. I like that about you, and I don't want help anyway."

She scowls and her cheeks heat as she turns around again, facing the front of the boat. "You're too blunt."

I grin. "Yeah, but you like that, too."

She doesn't say anything, but the red flush doesn't leave the back of her neck for nearly an hour as I row us down the swampy river.

F or several hours we don't talk.

I focus on the repetitive hypnotic motion of rowing, and Odessa looks all around us, her attention darting from passing birds, to plants, to the occasional animal. If I'm honest, I kind of like the silence. It's comfortable. Like, I could easily pretend we're getting along and out on a boat ride for fun rather than because my former kingdom wants to murder both of us.

"How much longer do you think until we reach the border?" Odessa asks, when the afternoon sun has moved beyond the middle of the sky and is creeping toward the western tree line.

I clear my throat. "I don't know, geography was never really my thing. I thought we'd get there by tonight."

"What if we don't?"

"I don't know. Soon we'll have to stop at least to eat something."

She nods, eyeing the little bundle of leftover bread and cheese that she split between us and Jett and wrapped in a stolen pillowcase from the inn. "I'm never going to take Beatrix's cooking for granted again."

I chuckle. "Me too. Hopefully, we'll be back to being force-fed third helpings by tomorrow."

"True," Odessa sighs. "I'm guessing Jett and the pirate took the main road, so they'll probably reach the border before us even though they left later. I'm worried we won't get back to Vernallis in time to warn Daemon and Alix."

I make a sound of agreement, but I don't really know what to say. I'm worried about that too, but evidently not worried enough to fly because even when I concentrate I don't think I could make my wings appear. Not like they did when Odessa was in danger...

"We'll stop at a town near the border and buy some more food and a couple of horses," I say. "It'll be fine."

She lets out a long sigh. "I guess it'll have to be. Part of me hopes that if we don't make it back in time, Daemon and Alix will wait before launching a sudden attack on Solistine."

"What does the rest of you think?"

She laughs darkly. "That I would be offended if they waited even ten minutes to react after finding out I was kidnapped. Does that make me selfish?"

I laugh too. "No, I think that makes you normal. And you don't have to worry about it, everyone was really fucking quick to react once we realized you'd snuck off."

An awkward silence falls over us for a moment, and I know

we're both remembering the reason why she left. I want to ask her about it, but I doubt I'll like her answer. I know she's not as unaffected by me as she wants to pretend, but I also know that for whatever reason she's determined not to just give in to what both of us want.

Maybe it's because of the soul-bond? Maybe she's worried about starting something when I'll never be able to bond with her. Except, no...that can't be it. Not all of it, anyway, because she's been standoffish for months with no clear reason. I used to think she simply didn't like me, but now I'm completely at a loss.

Perhaps there's someone else she's interested in?

Just the idea sends a spark of jealousy shooting through me, but the feeling isn't as intense as it would be if I really believed she wanted another man. I've never seen her give much attention to anyone else, and it's not as if she doesn't have the opportunity. Every time our friends visit the local pub, there's always a line of men watching Odessa or waiting to ask her to dance, but I've never seen her indulge any of them.

Come to think of it, I've never seen her pay half as much attention to anyone as she does to purposefully ignoring me. Almost like, in a strange way, I already have all her attention.

The bond in my chest pulses, and I bite back my frustration.

It's not fucking fair it should be there when I'll never know who triggered it or why, and it's especially painful that it reacts every time I think about Odessa. Like the bond is somehow aware that she's a threat.

"I'll have to think of an excuse to get back into Hydratta," Odessa muses, pulling me abruptly from my thoughts.

I blink dazedly. "What?"

"Sorry," she says absently. "I was just thinking that after we get back to Vernallis and warn everyone what's going on, we're all going to have to think of a safe way for me to go back to Magnus's castle—I mean, your old castle. Sorry."

"Hang on, I think I must have heard you wrong," I bite out,

staring a hole into the back of her head. "Why the fuck would you want to go back there?"

She looks over her shoulder at me, violet eyes reflecting gold in the setting sun. "Why wouldn't I?"

An involuntary growl rumbles out of me and I swallow, trying to shove the feeling down. It doesn't work and I stop bothering, deciding I don't care. "He kidnapped you. Even if he didn't intend to kill you, you still could have died."

"Yes, but I didn't," she says reasonably. "I doubt he'll try again so soon. Didn't you say he was a pragmatist?"

I stop rowing in the middle of the stream and stare at her. "I feel like I must be misunderstanding you, because this sounds like you're thinking something fucking crazy."

Her eyes narrow. "Just because Magnus is evil doesn't mean we can ignore him. It actually means we should go out of our way *not* to ignore him so he doesn't do something stupid."

"Like try to kill you and blame it on another kingdom, you mean?"

"Like trying to get another kingdom to help him attack Vernallis," she says flatly. "I decided to be the emissary to avoid problems like this. I'm not going to go hide at the Ashwater estate because something went wrong this time."

"Oh, I see." I sneer. "So I'll just be on standby, shall I? To come rescue you from the next disaster."

I swear I see sparks flash in her eyes, but when she answers her voice is coolly detached. "If you are, it won't be because I asked you to. And stop snarling at me. I don't belong to you, you don't get to have an opinion on where I go or what I do to help our court just because we slept together *once*."

"Yeah, *once*," I grumble, starting to row again.

I'm really starting to hate that word.

My mind fogs over, thoughts scattering as molten anger sears through my veins. She wants to put herself in danger again and just the thought of it sends a violent tremor rattling through me.

And on top of that, she felt the need to remind me that I have no right to feel like this.

My fists clench involuntarily, nails digging into my palms around the handle of my oar.

"Calm down," Odessa says. "Gods, Fae men can be so dramatic."

"Excuse me?" I grit out.

"You're all so painfully predictable. Possessive, aggressive, and irrational. It's not really your fault, I guess. Give it a week and I'm sure you'll go back to normal."

My eyes practically bug out of my head. She thinks this is normal? No, whatever the reaction I'm having is not fucking normal.

She's right that Fae as a whole—both men and women—can be domineering, but that's a hell of an understatement compared with how I feel at the moment.

I'm going to fucking lose it.

I've never really lost control of myself before—unless you count yesterday on the pirate ship, but even that was relatively contained given the circumstances. Now, I don't know what's wrong with me. I'm shaking. Sweating. About to burst out of my own skin.

The only time I've ever seen anyone react even close to how I feel was that time when Daemon ripped another man's arm off for touching Alix, then forced me to lock him in a bathroom to keep him away from her.

Immediately banishing that thought from my mind before I can dwell too long on it, I steer the little boat toward the bank of the river before I break my paddle in half by mistake.

"Why are we stopping?" Odessa asks sharply.

"I need a break."

I need to splash some water on my face and maybe walk away from Odessa for a few minutes because at the moment I'm not entirely sure if I'd rather strangle her for wanting to do something so insanely stupid as risk her life again, or throw her down on the nearest river bank, rip her dress off, and prove that she's mine and I have every right to react however I want to her suggesting otherwise.

I stab my paddle into the muddy riverbank and scramble out of the boat, not even caring that I'm standing in water higher than the tops of my boots. Then, I bend to drag the rowboat up onto the bank, so it's half on land, half in the reeds along the side of the water.

Odessa glares at me from the boat, her arms crossed and for the second time today, I have the strangest feeling like I've been here before...or done this before? Something is nagging at the back of my mind, and I can't quite figure out what it is.

I let out an angry sigh, and tear my eyes away from her. "I'm going to dunk my head in the water. Just give me a minute."

She rolls her eyes. "I'm not bathing with you again if that's what you're trying to do."

"I wouldn't fucking dream of it, Princess. I don't expect you to do anything that wasn't mostly your idea."

She lets out a short breath, clearly offended, as I kick my wet boots off and roll my trousers up over my knees before pulling my shirt off and tossing it into the boat.

Suddenly, Odessa gasps. "What the fuck is that?"

I freeze, thinking she's seen an animal, and turn in a circle before catching sight of her face. She's staring at me—or more specifically at the tattoo on my chest.

Shit.

In an instant, all the righteous rage that was coursing through my body evaporates and is replaced by panic. I put both my hands up, as if calming a wild horse. "Listen, I can explain."

Her eyes widen and her mouth twists into an almost comical snarl of horror. When she answers her voice is clipped, gravelly, like she's having a hard time forming the words. "I'd hope so, *Your Majesty*. I'd love to hear you explain why you have a tattoo of my face on your chest."

ODESSA, AGE 16

The sky is turning pink with the first light of dawn when I finally leave the beach.

I run up the dunes and across the rocky cliff and along the path toward the garden wall. Salt crusts my lips, my calves ache, and the siren's ethereal voice echoes over and over again through my mind.

Never be whole. Always lonely. I broke him; it's what we do.

I shove my way through the iron gate and stumble into a jog, tugging the heavy wool blanket tight around my shoulders, blinking away tears that are half wind, half panic, and make for the palace up ahead.

I can already hear the castle kitchen stirring in the distance, the clatter of pans and the bark of orders, and further off, the rhythmic thud of horses' hooves on packed dirt. I keep to the trees surrounding the lush garden, moving as fast as I dare, heart hammering my ribs like it's trying to punch through and escape.

I'm so intent on avoiding the gardeners that I almost miss the sound—a familiar shout, sharp and surprised. "Odessa!"

I freeze, heels digging into the mulch, the blanket bunched in my fists. Horror washes over me.

He cannot be here right now. This can't be happening.

But it is.

I turn slowly and see Kastian riding toward me down the path astride a sleek dappled mare, his hair mussed, his coat half-buttoned.

Our eyes meet, and he grins. Before I can react, he's already vaulting off the horse and closing the distance between us in five long strides. He stops so close I can smell the wood and citrus scent clinging to his skin. "Good morning," he says, still grinning widely.

I don't return his smile. "What are you doing out here?"

He blinks in surprise. His eyes lock on mine, and in an instant, his easy smile flickers, replaced by something wary and sharp.

He gestures toward the horse, like the answer is self-evident. "I always go riding early in the morning." His gaze drops to the tangle of my hair, the nightgown plastered damp to my legs, and finally to the blanket, where my knuckles are bone-white and shaking. "But maybe I should be asking what you're doing here."

There's a brief, horrible pause in which I try to invent a plausible lie and come up with nothing. I consider telling him the truth—about the siren, about Lyra, and about every horrible thought racing through my head. But I can't.

"I couldn't sleep," I say finally—at least it's the truth, if not the whole truth.

He raises an eyebrow. "I don't tend to sleep well either, but usually I get dressed before wandering around the castle."

I feel my face flush. "Right...I wasn't thinking."

He studies me, and I realize how ridiculous I must look: bare-legged, hair wild, salt drying in streaks on my cheeks.

Kastian shrugs off his black coat and drapes it over my shoulders, right on top of the blanket. "There," he murmurs.

I try to protest, but the words catch in my throat. Instead, I clutch the coat tighter, half grateful, half furious at how easily he sees through me. "Thanks."

His smile reappears. "Go back inside and change. I'll wait for you here."

"Why?" I blurt out, not even trying to soften the sharpness of it.

He looks slightly confused. "I thought we might go to breakfast together. Did you have other plans this morning?"

I want to say yes; I want to say I will go with you anywhere, even if it is only to breakfast, but I can't forget the siren's warning. Can't forget the icy certainty that nothing good can come of this.

I shake my head and force a bitter laugh. "I don't think that's a good idea."

Kastian's brows draw together, and he looks at me with such raw confusion that it almost hurts. "Did—did I say something wrong?"

I force a smile. "Not at all."

He steps closer, hand rising as if to steady me, but I sidestep his reach, hugging myself with both arms. My skin prickles with awareness of him, and the distance I'm putting between us is both a relief and a punishment.

He lets his arm fall, fingers curling in a frustrated half-fist. "Odessa," he says, and this time there's steel under the concern. "Seriously. What happened?"

"Nothing."

"I thought you had fun last night."

"I did, but that's all it was, right? Fun. Tomorrow I'll be going back to Vernallis."

His dark eyes trace over me intently, and I can see on his face that he's thinking hard. Steeling himself for something.

"But what if you didn't have to leave?" he says finally, more of a statement than a question. "I thought perhaps you could stay longer. Your family can stay too, of course, as guests of the palace."

My pulse pounds in my ears, and my vision blurs, darkening on the edges. "Why?"

"Because I want you to."

"You hardly know me."

Anyone else would flush with embarrassment, but Kastian is far too direct for that. He looks entirely unabashed. "I've known you for three days. Isn't that how long you said? Anyway, I'm not suggesting we get engaged today."

"No." I shake my head again, panic rising in my voice. "This isn't going to work."

Prince Kastian grabs my hand, whirling me around so I'm forced to look him in the eye. "Why? Is it about becoming royal? You don't have to worry about that. You'll make a good princess. You're already better suited to being royal than I am, and I have three sisters who can help you."

My lungs seize. This can't be happening. He's thinking about a future. With me. And I can't stop picturing all the ways it might end. All the ways I'm destined to ruin him.

"I can't—"

He still doesn't understand, because his hand tightens on mine. "I'm not asking you for forever. Not now. Not unless you want it. You're right that we don't know each other well, but there's something here. I like you. I just...don't want you to go."

My throat is on fire. "This is dangerous," I croak. "Us. It's not—"

He takes a slow step closer, and his hand is warm and trustworthy where it meets my skin. "What's dangerous about liking someone?"

I nearly choke. "You don't understand."

He steps even closer. "Then explain it to me."

He's so close now I can feel the heat of him through my blanket and his coat thrown over my shoulders, and for a second the world tips. I want to lean in. I want to pull him to me and never let go, but the warning is pounding in my skull:

When a siren loves, she loves down to the bone. All that's left to decide is who you're willing to hurt.

If I'm going to hurt someone, I don't want it to be him.

I gather the blanket tighter and force myself to meet his eyes.

I've hardly ever done this before—only a few times, mostly by accident, when I really wanted to get out of lessons for the day or to have some trinket from the local shops. I suddenly wish I'd thought to ask the siren how it works while I had the chance, but there's no use in regretting it now.

I push the siren song into my voice and use that coaxing note. "You shouldn't trust me. You shouldn't want me."

Kastian's eyes narrow in confusion. "What are you talking about?"

A tiny spark of panic lights in my chest. Maybe I'm not doing this right. It isn't working.

I suck in a breath and try harder, stepping closer so I can more easily stare into his eyes. "Stay away from me."

Again, I'm not sure it's working. He's staring at me, but it's not with that vacant look I've seen a handful of times before. Or is it? His face has gone blank. Slack. Unreadable.

"Is that what you really want?" he asks finally.

I breathe out a sigh of relief. "Yes, that's what I want. I want you to never speak to me again. Stay far away from me. Nothing would make you happier."

He blinks a few times, and when he answers his voice is flat and emotionless. "As you wish."

ODESSA, PRESENT

"It's a long story," Kastian says, his eyes wide and pleading. "Just listen."

Listen? How can I listen when all I can hear is the pounding of my heart in my ears.

A moment ago, I was all too aware that Kastian was furious with me. Everything from his livid expression to his growling tone made it entirely too clear that I'd accidentally pushed him too far.

I probably should have expected it.

I've seen this happen dozens of times before with Fae couples. At first, the jealousy and intensity is hard to watch, but after a while, the couple either forms a soul bond or the feeling wears off and they go their separate ways.

I'd assumed—convinced myself, perhaps—that the same would happen with us. Obviously we're not forming a soul bond, and as I'm determined not to destroy his life for a second time, whatever possessiveness he's biologically wired to feel for me will wear off, eventually.

At least, that's what I thought up until five seconds ago.

Now, I'm staring at Kastian, standing up to his knees in the swampy river. His shirt is off, and his chest, broad and sculpted like a statue, gleams with a sun-kissed tan, the lines of muscle defined and hard. Black swirling tattoos cover both his arms and the right side of his chest. Right over his heart, a shockingly realistic portrait of my own face stares back at me.

I feel like the ground has fallen out from under me.

"That's me!" I hiss, pointing an accusatory finger at the tattoo.

"It wasn't intentional, I swear."

"How the fuck would you get a tattoo of my face without meaning to?"

He closes his eyes, squeezing the bridge of his nose as if warding off a headache. Then, he wades back out of the water and stands in front of me on the riverbank. "This is a long story."

"We've got all the time in the world, so you better start talking," I hiss, my hands shaking with...something. I don't know. Shock? Horror? Excitement? I'm not even sure what I'm feeling at the moment.

"Remember, I told you about my soul-bond?" Kastian begins.

My eyes widen and I hear my own voice coming out of my mouth, sort of disembodied as if I'm having a dissociative experience. "You're not saying—"

"Just listen," he insists. "I told you I found my soul bond, but lost her. The truth is, I don't even remember her."

All at once, my feelings about the tattoo take second fiddle to a crashing wave of guilt. This is my fault, then. I don't know how it's possible, but there's only one reason he wouldn't remember his bond. It's the same reason he won't remember anything else until the day he dies—because I let the sirens take his memories.

"I'm sorry," I say in a small voice.

"It's not your fault," he says quickly. "I noticed the bond shortly before getting sent to Dyaspora. I don't fully remember what happened. One morning I woke up and it was just...there."

A shooting pain throbs in my chest as if I've been stabbed in the heart. I grit my teeth. "Explain to me why that would inspire you to get a tattoo of my face."

He winces, raising an arm to drag his hand over the back of his head. The motion makes his muscles contract, only bringing the tattoos into sharper relief.

"For the last century, I've never stopped thinking about the bond. I'd always thought if I ever escaped Dyaspora I'd go looking for her—whoever she is. I should have gotten out of prison and immediately felt the urge to go back to Hydratta to find her."

I cock my head, hating myself for being curious about this story. "That didn't happen?"

"No. Once I was free I never felt any strong urge to go back to Hydratta. After Daemon and Alix bonded and I saw how they were together I started to wonder if I'd been wrong all along about the bond. Except that I can still feel it," he reaches up and rubs his chest, "right here."

My head spins and I feel a bit faint. If we weren't standing on the muddy, swampy riverbank I'd sit down and put my head between my knees.

I'm sure Kastian has no idea how he could form a bond and not remember it, but I know. I know exactly how it could have happened...except that it makes no sense, because there was no one there he might have formed a bond with. Except, well, *me*... but if that were the case wouldn't I know?

One of the few certain things that everyone knows about bonds is that once formed they can't be broken. The bond is a biological shift that can only happen once. Males tend to feel it first, and once bonded, they will never leave their partners—ever. That's why there's nearly no such thing as infidelity among the Fae.

I can't believe I hadn't really thought about that until now. I was so focused on my horror at realizing he's bonded and my obsession with trying to keep us both alive, that I never realized that if Kastian really bonded with someone else who isn't me, he shouldn't—wouldn't—be able to be here with me now. The other night could never have happened.

But that doesn't feel like it makes perfect sense either. If we'd bonded decades ago, surely I wouldn't have been able to carry on living my life ever since. I know that women tend to feel the bond second, but I've never heard of something like this where a bond started and was left incomplete for decades.

"How the hell could this happen?" I wonder out loud, meaning the question more to myself than to Kastian.

Kastian shakes his head, looking frustrated. "I've been asking myself the same fucking thing for years. So, about six months ago I decided to do something about it. I decided to find her—whoever she is—at least to know if she's still alive."

My throat feels dry, and I run my tongue nervously over my lips. "So what did you do?"

"I went looking for an oracle."

My eyebrows raise even higher, as if they might disappear into my hairline. "I don't remember you ever taking a long trip away from the estate."

"I didn't." He runs a nervous hand over his neck again, his agitation obviously building. "As I'm sure you know, premonition isn't an ability that naturally occurs among Fae. Human sorceresses sometimes have psychic abilities, and there are other monsters that claim to have it, but it wasn't as if I could just walk into the local tavern and find someone to help. Aurelia told me about another sorceress she knew who might have a strong enough psychic talent to help."

"You told Aurelia about this?" I ask, momentarily distracted. "I didn't realize you were so *close*."

There must be something bitter in my voice because his eyes flash, and for a moment he looks almost pleased before his contrite expression returns. "We're not, but she asked me about it directly. I don't know how she knew; I assumed it was part of her magic."

"Hmm," I hum, my lips tight. "Alright, so what happened?"

"The other sorceress lives near the border of Vernallis and Thermia and was willing to talk to me. She has psychic abilities, but they're very specific. She only practices premonitions through art."

My brow furrows. "I don't understand."

"She goes into a trance and inks her visions on a person's skin, then wakes up and doesn't remember exactly what she saw. I agreed to do it. At this point, what would one more tattoo matter?" he raises his arms, both entirely covered in ink from wrist to shoulder, and shrugs.

"But I don't understand," I say again, my frustration rising. "This doesn't explain anything. I'm not your soul bond. I can't be —this is insane."

"I know you're not," he says, shaking his head. "But the day before I saw the ink oracle we'd had an argument."

"We what?" I demand, incredulous.

"We'd had an argument," he repeats. "I poured half the lake on you, remember?"

I blink, startled. I remember exactly what he's talking about, which is saying something since Kastian and I seem to find ourselves sniping at each other at least twice a week.

Except, that day was different.

I remember him coming to my room to apologize—something he'd never done before. It made me uneasy, as I was all too aware that I could never simply exist peacefully with him. I could never call a truce and be friends with Kastian, because if I let my guard down for even a second something catastrophic could happen.

Something like *this*, for example.

Something like standing alone with him on a darkening riverbank, terrified that this conversation is careening toward the edge of something neither of us can walk back from.

"How did that fight change your tattoo?" I ask, my throat dry and my voice wavering.

Kastian's gaze flicks down at the river. He picks up a pebble off the ground and flips it from thumb to forefinger before tossing it into the water. For a moment we both watch the ripples before they disappear into the flowing stream.

His jaw flexes, and he sucks in a deep breath before continuing. "Part of the process was that I was supposed to think about the bond while she worked, but instead I kept thinking about the argument we'd had. It was the last thing on my mind before the trance, and the whole thing spiraled from there. By the time she was done and I realized what happened… it was too late to fix it."

I gape at him, horrified. "You're telling me that you went through an arcane tattoo ritual designed to reveal the love of your life, and now you're stuck with… that?" I gesture at the portrait. "Because you were mad at me?"

He huffs a bleak laugh. "In my defense, you're extremely distracting when you're angry."

I don't laugh. I'm too overwhelmed to pretend.

I'm not sure what I'm supposed to do with this information. The urge to run courses through me, yet I'm rooted to the spot, unable to move. I stare at the portrait again, tracing the lines of it with my eyes. It isn't just my face—it's a memory. A whole scene, in astonishing detail: my eyes narrowed, jaw set, and lips curved into a slightly mocking smile. At first glance, I almost look angry, but the longer I look, the more details emerge. I look…sad. There's so much longing in my eyes it's almost painful.

"Why didn't you just get it removed?" I ask, finally.

Kastian gives me a tight smile. "You can't remove an oracle tattoo. Believe me, I asked. It's like a prophecy. It's supposed to be permanent."

"That's the dumbest damn thing I've ever heard. You could have at least gotten it somewhere less… obvious."

He shrugs. "She said the heart is where prophecy sits best. Besides, I wasn't thinking straight."

For a while, neither of us speaks.

I want to ask how he feels about all this; not merely the facts of what happened, but what he really thinks of me.

But I'm not brave enough.

Evidently, Kastian is far braver than I am because he finally turns to me. "What are you thinking?"

I cross my arms over my chest as if to shield myself from his searching eyes. "What do you want me to say, Kastian?"

"I don't know, just tell me what you're feeling."

I bark out a strangled laugh. "As if that's so easy. You first."

"I don't mind the tattoo," he says firmly. "I know I should, but I don't. I don't want to get it removed."

My heart skips a beat, and I look at him, really look, and for one terrifying second I think I believe him. My chest aches, and I feel stupidly close to tears. "What is your soul-bond going to say when she sees it?"

He shakes his head. "I don't know. I'm not even sure I care anymore."

My heart doesn't just skip—it stutters—and panic grips me. "What the hell do you mean?"

Kastian's eyes lock on mine. "I mean, maybe I don't care about finding my bonded mate anymore."

I laugh, a pitiful half-choke that's more air than humor. "That's not possible. Soul-bonds are forever. You should never want anyone else more than your bond."

"Then why do I want you instead?" he demands almost angrily.

The words hit me like a slap; for a breathless moment, all I can do is gape at him. My heart pounds so loudly it drowns out the sound of the river. "You're not serious."

"I'm not?" He raises an eyebrow and steps closer, looming over me. "What about me has ever made you think I'm not 100 percent serious about everything?"

"Oh, I don't know," I hiss sarcastically. "Maybe I'm a little confused because a second ago we were talking about how you'd been pining for your missing soul-bond for decades."

"Yeah, until I met you."

"Don't say things like that."

"Why not?" He asks, incredulous. "It's true. I want you more than I've ever wanted anything. If a soul-bond is stronger than that, then I don't want it. I'd go insane."

The word "insane" hits something deep inside me and I flinch, the memory of my father's fate slamming into me like a rogue wave. Then, even more painfully, I remember what nearly happened to Kastian all those years ago. My heart pounds so loudly it drowns out the sound of the river.

"You're confused," I say, shaking my head. I hate the way my voice trembles, so I dig my nails deeper into my palms, grounding myself in pain. "You want me because I'm a siren. Anything you feel—anything you *think* you feel—for me, it's just an illusion. None of it is real."

He jerks back as if I've hit him, but I press on, needing him to understand—needing to believe it myself.

"I've seen this happen before," I say, my words tumbling over each other in my haste. "It doesn't matter how strong-minded you are, or how much you want to fight it. Siren magic always wins."

"That's not it," he says angrily. "I thought it might be at first, but it's not. Your power doesn't work on me."

I bite back a grown. He doesn't know that it's already worked on him at least once. He's not immune just because he resisted it the other night in the dining room. "I can't have this conversation again. Siren magic works on all men."

"It doesn't work on Daemon," he says, seemingly grasping at straws. "He told me."

"That's different." I close my eyes, feeling immeasurably tired. "It doesn't work on Daemon because we're related. It has nothing to do with his willpower. You resisted it the other night, so you probably have a stronger will than most men, but the compulsion still works on you...just, slower, I guess."

"I don't believe that." Kastian steps closer, and there's a fire burning in his eyes as he grabs my chin and forces me to hold his gaze. "Odessa, listen to me. I know I should care about the bond, but I don't. I should have been obsessed with finding her, but I'm not. I tried for months to ignore it, but the only person I can think about is you."

My legs threaten to collapse, so I dig my heels into the mud and cross my arms tight over my chest, as if I can keep all my insides from spilling out in front of him. "None of that matters. You don't get to rewrite the laws of nature just because you feel like it, Kastian. Ultimately, you have a soul-bond out there somewhere. I'm just a complication you're going to regret the second your real bond walks back into your life. And that's assuming I don't accidentally kill you in the meantime."

He steps in close, eyes boring into mine, daring me to run. "Go ahead and keep talking, Princess. You won't convince me to give up on you. Do you really think I would be wasting my time on the most stubborn woman on the damn continent if I wasn't just as persistent?"

"There's persistence and then there's idiocy," I retort. "You're not hearing me. We're not meant to be together."

"Who the hell believes anyone is meant to be?" he barks. "Soul bonds aren't fated, they're formed over time."

"So you say, but no one really knows that. It could be fate."

"You're honestly saying that you believe it's *fate* that I had one traumatic experience a hundred years ago which I can't even remember, and because of that I'm doomed to never love anyone? I don't believe that, and I don't give a fuck about fate. I don't want it, I only want you."

His chest heaves with deep breaths, and the words hang in the air between us, heavy and all too final.

My throat and eyes burn, and I stare at the river, at the shifting current, trying to find some kind of answer in the movement of the water.

What is there to say? That he's right? That I feel the same? That I've always felt the same, even on the days I'd rather die than admit it?

Kastian is looking at me like I'm the center of his universe and I want to give in.

I want to think his bond was never real, or maybe it got broken, or maybe—terrifyingly—maybe it was me all along. But I can't. It's not safe. Not for me, and definitely not for him.

"Here's what I find interesting," Kastian says, his tone softening slightly. "You keep saying that I'm confused. I'm the one with the problem—"

"Because you are," I interrupt angrily.

He presses on, refusing to let me derail the point. "You keep insisting I can't possibly care about you, but you've never said you don't feel the same about me."

My mouth opens, ready to shoot back a dozen half-baked defenses, but I have nothing. For once, I can't find a single clever thing to say that wouldn't sound like a lie.

"What do you want me to say?" I ask again, almost pleading this time.

"Say you don't want this." Kastian demands, voice low and tight, a single bead of sweat carving its way down his jaw. "Say you don't want me, and I swear I'll leave you alone."

I stare at him, at the inked memory of myself splayed across his chest, and I can't do it. I see every jagged line of his longing written across his face. There's no more mask, no measured calm; he's laid himself out in front of me, raw and reckless.

I suck in a shaky breath, but it hurts—like inhaling broken glass. "I can't," I whisper, the words barely audible. "I can't say that."

For a moment, there's silence. Then, slow as sunrise, a triumphant smile blooms across Kastian's face. It's not the cocky half-grin he wears for the world, but something softer and infinitely more dangerous.

He moves in, so close I can see the wildfire in his eyes and feel the heat radiating off his skin. I'm paralyzed, frozen by the realization that all my careful plans have come to nothing because I can't find a way to lie and say I don't care about him.

He reaches out, hand trembling, and cups my jaw, his thumb tracing the line of my cheek He leans in and my vision tunnels, my body humming with the inevitability of what's about to happen. He's waiting, giving me a final chance to push him away, to lie to him, to run.

But I don't. I won't. I'm so tired of running.

Kastian closes the last few inches between us, his lips crashing against mine in a kiss that's all desperation and defiance, and somehow I'm kissing him back, fierce and hungry. He tastes like salt and summer storms—like every reckless thing I've ever craved and never thought I'd have.

The river's roar fades to nothing, the whole world narrowing down to the press of his mouth, the harsh hitch of his breath, the sound of my own pulse pounding like war drums in my ears.

I'm drowning, and I don't even care.

ODESSA, PRESENT

Kastian breaks our kiss, panting hard. "What are you thinking right now?"

I let out a wild gasp. "I don't know."

Eyes darting over my face, as if searching for my reaction, he grips my waist, pulling me flush against him. Then, he slides his palms down the curve of my waist to my hips. The tips of his fingers graze the short, ragged hem of what's left of my dress, then slip beneath the fabric, brushing over the skin of my thighs. "What about now?"

I shiver, struggling to focus on anything but his fingers inching higher on my thigh. "I'm—I'm thinking I should stop this before it's too late."

He laughs darkly as his fingers reach the edge of my panties, skimming over the lace at the point that my thigh meets my hip.

"What's funny?" I ask breathlessly.

"You."

My eyes narrow, but my retort gets lost in a gasp when he hooks his fingers around the lace of my panties and tugs them down over my hips, letting the fabric fall around my knees, locking my legs together. The cool air meets my sensitive skin, and I swear I'm going to catch fire.

Kastian bends his head, pressing his face into my shoulder. He lets out a breath, and I can feel it warm against my ear. "It's hilarious that you believe you can still run away from this. It's already way too late, Princess. You're already mine."

I suck in a sharp breath; shock or arousal or fear, I'm not really sure. I try to step away, but his fingers tighten on my bare hips holding me close. At the same time, his lips trail down my jaw, nipping at the edge of my chin and then my throat, tongue hot and wet against my pulse. I shudder, every inch of me alive and raw.

He makes a low possessive sound in my ear. "I love how even when you're lying to yourself, you're still so fucking wet for me."

I make a small, pathetic sound of half-hearted protest. "You can't know that, I'm not—"

Without warning, he reaches between my legs and cups me, his large hand covering my entire mound as if it belongs to him. He curls his fingers, drawing them through my center, and a whimper escapes my lips.

"Sorry, what were you going to say?" he asks in my ear as, with the heel of his hand pressed hard against my clit, he shoves two fingers inside me.

"*Fuck*—" My whimper turns into a strangled scream.

My back arches, and my hands land on his shoulders. I dig my nails in, desperate for something to keep me grounded in reality. My pulse pounds in my core, throbbing around his fingers. He's not even fucking me with them, just holding me there, captive and entirely under his control.

Kastian pulls back just enough to meet my eyes. Fingers still buried inside me, he holds my gaze, and our heavy breathing falls into sync. His dark eyes are hypnotic, refusing to let me look away. Refusing to let me forget for even a second who's touching me. Who's making every nerve in my body light on fire.

As the seconds drag by, my skin heats and frustration takes over. I roll my hips, desperate for friction.

Kastian laughs again, and grips me tighter, nearly lifting my feet off the ground with one hand. "You can't have it both ways, Dessa. You can't be dripping wet and begging me to fuck you and keep insisting that there's nothing between us."

His fingers curl inside me, punctuating his point, and I let out a moan. It's overwhelming—more than pleasure, almost pain, the kind that makes my brain shut off and my body take over.

"Fine," I gasp.

"Fine what?"

"Fine, I give up. I want you, but—"

He doesn't seem to care about what I was going to say next. At my admission, suddenly he's moving again, sliding his fingers out of me and pulling me to the ground. In seconds, my panties are gone from around my ankles and I'm straddling his lap, my knees digging into the dirt.

He cups my ass and pulls me flush against his hard cock straining against his trousers. I move against him, rolling my hips and creating a satisfying friction. The coarse fabric of his trousers brushes against my clit, making it throb, and I feel the initial stirrings of an orgasm growing deep in my belly.

He tugs the sleeves and neckline of my dress down until my breasts spill free. His mouth is on me in the next instant, hot and hungry, lips parting around my nipple. He bites and sucks as if marking territory, and the shock of pleasure is immediate and electric, snapping straight from his tongue to the base of my spine, making my toes curl and my legs nearly give out.

All my breath shudders out in a ragged moan, my body arching into him, desperate and greedy for more. I rock my hips over the hard length of him, faster until I'm whimpering, writhing, nearly incoherent. The roughness of his trousers is torturous and perfect, and I dig my nails into the back of his neck, silently begging for more.

He looks up at me, lips swollen and wet, a deep flush creeping up his throat. I can't get enough of him, and he knows it. He crushes me to his chest, hands everywhere at once; squeezing my ass, palming my breast, sliding up my bare thigh to stroke between my legs.

I'm gasping, wordless, and he presses his lips to my ear. "That's it. Let go for me."

My entire world narrows down to the heat of his touch and the dizzying rush of blood in my ears. My hips rock against him, frantic, and his fingers find my slickness again, circling and teasing until my knees buckle and I'm sobbing with need.

"Louder," Kastian demands.

I obey instantly, crying out, not caring how loud I am or who might be listening. Let the whole damn continent hear; let them know I tried to resist and failed, gloriously. Spectacularly.

Looking pleased, Kastian kisses me again, slower this time, as if memorizing the taste and shape of my mouth. His hands never leave my skin, mapping out every inch of me.

He gently shifts me backward off his lap, guiding me down toward the ground. As he leans over me, our eyes meet for a moment before I slide back further. Suddenly, I feel the cool, damp sensation of the muddy riverbank against my back, the squelch of wet earth clinging to my clothes.

I stop moving, and Kastian must sense the shift in me, because he slows, eyes searching my face. "What's wrong?"

I shake, still out of breath. "We're getting—" I gesture at my bare legs, the mud, at the both of us, "—absolutely filthy."

He laughs and cups my face, kissing me hard and fast before pulling back. "You really would have made a perfect princess. Far too dignified to fuck in the mud."

A flush crawls up my neck. "I wouldn't say that's a particularly high bar."

"Maybe not, but I hadn't even noticed. I can't think about anything but how fucking good you're going to feel wrapped around my cock."

Good gods.

Another wave of heat coats my skin as Kastian stands to his full height, taking me with him. My legs wrap instinctively around his hips, and I cling to the back of his neck, helplessly aware of how good it feels to be in his arms, of how I never want to be anywhere else.

He carries me away from the river's edge. I cling tighter, and the movement presses his cock harder against me through the rough fabric of his pants. I can feel his heartbeat thrumming where my thighs grip his waist, and the urge to writhe against him is almost overwhelming.

"Where are we going?" I manage, voice unsteady.

He nods at our battered little rowboat, pulled up half-heartedly on the shore.

"You're going to have your way with me in this boat?" I ask, smiling. "That's quite a feat of acrobatics."

Of course, Kastian doesn't understand my reference, but he smiles anyway and steps into the boat, taking me with him. The boat rocks alarmingly, and for a second I'm convinced we're going to capsize. But he moves with surprising grace, lowering me onto a seat and then dropping to his knees in front of me, half-kneeling in the hull.

I just stare at him kneeling in front of me, my head spinning.

He's devastatingly, heart-stoppingly handsome. His features could be sculpted from stone, and his dark eyes exude an aura of power and intensity that could shatter worlds. His gaze locks onto mine with such ferocity and possessiveness that it feels like I am the very center of his universe.

I want him so badly it aches.

I reach down and grip the hem of my ruined dress, dragging it over my head, leaving me bare before him.

Kastian's tongue darts over his lips as his eyes drag down my body. "My gods, you're so fucking beautiful."

The corners of my mouth tip up in a smug smile. I usually hate being told how beautiful I am, but suddenly I love it.

He runs his palms up my thighs, slow and reverent, as if he's trying to memorize every inch of me. He bends and follows his hands with his lips, dragging his mouth up my inner thigh and leaving a trail of hot, open-mouthed kisses. When he reaches the spot between my legs, he pauses, like he's savoring it—savoring me—like I'm the last thing he'll ever taste.

He slides his hands under my ass and pulls me to the very edge of the seat, pressing my knees up and out until I'm shamefully, helplessly open. The air is cold on my slick skin, but his breath is hot, and he doesn't waste any more time.

His mouth descends on me—hungry, greedy, relentless. His tongue works magic, curling and flicking, and I arch back, hands fisted in the edge of the boat, knuckles white. I think I might actually black out from the intensity, from the way he devours me.

He pulls away just long enough to look up at me, lips glistening, eyes wild. "You taste so fucking good," he says, and before I can think of anything to say, he ducks back down, tongue plunging into me again, and all I can do is writhe and take it.

He devours me, and when I start to shake, when I feel that second warning pulse at the base of my spine, he grins against me and doubles down.

The orgasm hits hard and fast, an electric bolt that leaves me gasping, crying out, shuddering so violently I almost slip off the seat. Kastian holds me steady, licking me through it, not stopping even as I beg him to.

I want to say his name. I want to curse him, but all I can do is whimper.

He finally pulls away, wiping his mouth with the back of his hand, and then he kisses me, deep and filthy, sharing the taste of myself on his tongue.

I should be horrified, but gods, I love it; I love *him*.

It's not really a surprise, but it feels like it. I haven't let myself think that in so long that now the thought makes me want to cry.

I lean forward quickly, wanting to lose myself again before that traitorous thought has time to take root.

I reach out, my hands scrabbling at Kastian's waistband, fumbling with his belt. I want to feel him, all of him, inside and against and around me until I can't tell where my body ends and his begins.

He grabs my wrists in one hand and pulls me back, raising my arms over my head. "Lie down."

I glance behind me at the small boat, trying to figure out how this is going to work. Keeping my arms over my head, I lean backward, my head and shoulders rest on the bottom of the boat and my hips remain raised on the bench seat.

Kastian smiles down at me, looking satisfied. This time there's no hesitation, no slow build. He rips open his trousers, freeing himself with one hand.

My eyes widen and I can't help but gasp. He's *huge*.

It was too dark the last time we slept together to know exactly what I was getting myself into, and while I remember feeling how big he was, how I was stretched to practically my limit, seeing it is something else entirely.

He slides a hand beneath my thigh, hiking my leg up around his waist. Holding his cock in one hand, he presses himself against my entrance, rubbing the head through my wetness until I'm whimpering shamelessly.

He leans down, his breath hot against my ear. "Tell me you want this."

"I want you," I gasp, and I mean it with every fiber of my being—with every desperate, ruined thought in my head.

He pushes inside me, slow and deliberate, and the sensation of him stretching me open is so perfect, so overwhelming, that for a moment I can only hang suspended in pure white heat. Every muscle in my body clenches around him, and I arch up to meet him, my back bowing off the wooden slats of the boat.

"Fuck," he gasps, pausing to let both of us adjust. "I knew once would never be enough with you."

"I knew that too," I admit on a gasp.

His eyes flash with hunger. "Yeah?"

I nod, trying to tell him with my eyes what I can't say out loud.

He moves inside me, slow at first, savoring every inch, the head of his cock grazing places inside me I didn't know existed. My breath comes ragged and desperate, each thrust deeper, harder, until he finds a punishing rhythm, hitting that perfect spot inside me with every stroke. I wrap my legs around his waist, locking him inside me, and the urgency ratchets higher and higher.

Kastian sucks his thumb into his mouth, before reaching down and finding my clit, rubbing small circles as he thrusts harder, deeper. I whimper and raise my hips, meeting him stroke for stroke, daring him to break me.

The boat rocks beneath us, water slapping against the hull, the thud of flesh on wood keeping time with the frantic pulse in my veins. I've never felt more alive, more real, more desperate to hold onto this exact moment and never let it go.

Spluttering a steady stream of curses, Kastian braces a hand on the seat behind my head, the other wrapping around my thigh and hoisting it higher, angling me open, until I swear I can feel every inch of him all the way up my spine. The new angle is obscene—too much, and at the same time, not enough—and it rips a cry out of me and I see stars.

I bite the inside of my cheek and taste iron, but Kastian doesn't slow down. Not when my body is shaking around him, not when my nails dig long red lines down his thighs. "Oh my gods."

Kastian looks down at me, eyes gone molten and wild. "Look at me, Princess."

I do. Our gazes meet and he thrusts into me again. He falters for a single shattering moment, grinding himself so deep inside me I almost scream. My breath catches high in my chest, and I gasp out his name. "Kastian."

Kastian's wings explode from his back: massive and gleaming, so dark the green tips appear black. The force of them unfurling shakes the boat, the air around him seems to tremble, and for a moment, I'm terrified by the raw, impossible beauty of him. But more than that, I am consumed by the way he looks at me: He holds my gaze, hard and unbreakable, as if daring me to say something. To voice what I'm sure we both know is true.

"Des," he rasps, "I—" but he doesn't finish.

Because his next thrust is deliberate. Slow, raw and desperate and I clamp around him in a sudden, violent spasm, everything inside me coiling, tightening, then detonating.

My vision goes white at the edges, and I scream as I'm split open and remade, piece by piece.

Kastian groans, low and guttural, and I feel his own climax hit as he thrusts one final, brutal time. He shudders, wings flaring wide, and for a heartbeat we are a single, fused entity.

And at that moment, the impossible truth hits me all at once, and settles in my chest.

Bonded.

It's impossible, and yet I know it's true. I feel an ineffable... something blooming in my chest, strange and electric and terrifying, but before I even have a chance to examine it; before I can say something, the universe intervenes with cruel efficiency.

A shout cracks through the night, echoing over the water— followed by another, louder this time. The sound slices through the happy, blissful bubble around me, popping it and making me crash back to reality.

My body locks up and I sit bolt upright, a cold wave of terror rushing through my veins. I peer into the darkness and for a moment I'm not sure what I'm looking at. I can't see anything clearly, just a smear of torchlight and movement at the edge of the swamp.

"Shit," I whisper, because that's about the level of eloquence I'm capable of at the moment.

Kastian is instantly alert, his wings snapping tight against his back. He's off me in a split second, and yanking his trousers back on and jumping out of the boat.

"Who the fuck is that?" he asks, speaking more to himself than me.

The lights are closer now, bobbing and weaving through the trees. Shouts echo across the water, the voices multiplying—at least half a dozen, maybe more. I can't pick out any words, but I know a search party when I hear one.

"Someone is looking for us," I hiss, fumbling along the bottom of the boat looking for my dress. "Or they're looking for someone else and are about to find us instead. Either way, I doubt we want to be found."

"I don't understand how, though," Kastian hisses. "Unless, someone recognized me on the way to the inn. Or, you, I suppose."

"We didn't see anyone."

"That doesn't mean they didn't see us," he says grimly.

My mind is racing, but I can't think through what he's saying because I'm still completely naked. "I can't find my dress!"

Kastian turns in a circle, then grabs my shredded, muddy dress from where it must have fallen among the reeds along the water. He thrusts it at me, and I snatch it, fumbling to pull the fabric over my head. My whole body is slick with sweat, and the dress sticks, halfway tangled over my chest and shoulders.

Dear gods, this is how it ends. I'm going to die in this boat with my tits out. It's both tragic, and somehow, deeply, darkly funny.

"*Help me,*" I hiss through gritted teeth.

Kastian doesn't hesitate, grabbing the fabric at the shoulders, yanking it hard enough to pop a seam. The dress falls into place, and I try to smooth my hair back.

There's no time for anything else.

The lights are almost on us, and now I can make out the silhouettes—figures in dark armor moving with purpose toward us. One of them shouts again, something guttural and harsh.

Kastian stands rigid. His sword is somewhere on the ground near the boat, but he doesn't seem to need it. Instead, his right arm is raised half in the air, and I can practically see the sparks of magic growing in the air near his fingertips.

"Don't do anything stupid that will get you killed," I whisper. "If they're bounty hunters, they'll want us alive."

Kastian gives me a look. "Sure, for now."

Before I can respond, a sharp, tinny whistling flies through the air over my head. There's a sickening thump of impact, and Kastian lets out a bark of pain, then stumbles.

I scream, equal parts surprised and terrified, and bend to try and help him. I don't know what that sound was, but Kastian is doubled over, still standing, but with a hand pressed to his shoulder.

"You should listen to the siren," a condescending female voice shouts out of the trees. "Don't do anything stupid."

I look up just as a figure steps out of the trees, half a dozen more melting out of the darkness behind them. They're wearing familiar green jackets beneath pitch black armor, and moving toward us slowly in an organized formation. At the front of the pack, the leader is carrying something in front of them. I squint, and realize they're pointing a crossbow at Kastian's chest. A horrified gasp escapes me, just as Kastian reaches for the arrow I now see protruding from his chest and yanks it out of his flesh with a sound that makes my stomach roll and bile rise in my throat.

"Don't move," the soldier with the crossbow says, as if we didn't get the message from her *shooting at us*. "The arrows are poisoned. Just one shouldn't kill you, but if you try to fly, I'll shoot you out of the air and who knows what a few more doses of poison will do."

I gasp, and squint toward the soldier with the crossbow. She's definitely female, but taller than average and packed with muscle. She's wearing a well-tailored Hydrattan military uniform and her dark hair is braided tightly into a crown on the top of her head.

That confirms it. They're not bounty hunters, they're soldiers. *The king's* soldiers.

My gaze darts to the other soldiers—also women. Apparently, King Magnus didn't want the slightest risk that I might compel his troops to let us go. But how could he have known to send these women after us if he didn't know where we were?

Something isn't making sense, but I suppose it doesn't matter while there are weapons pointed at us.

The crossbowman studies us, torchlight shining off her face. "Both of you, walk toward me with your hands up. Now."

Kastian glances back at me, then toward the soldiers. Clearly, he's thinking fast, and I don't think I like whatever he's planning. "Let her go, and I'll come with you," he says, his face twisted with pain.

"No!" I hiss.

The soldier scoffs. "Not going to happen. The king wants both of you."

"*The king* isn't stupid," Kastian snaps back. His hand is pressed to the wound in his shoulder and he looks to be swaying slightly, but his voice never falters. "Capturing us like this won't get him the alliance he wants. Take me back to the capital. I'll go without a fight, but if you touch her—"

The soldier's laugh is a single sharp note. "You're hardly in a position to bargain, prince. In a minute you won't even be conscious." She shifts her aim, pointing her crossbow directly at Kastian's other shoulder. "But don't worry, we won't touch the siren. The king doesn't want her damaged. You, on the other hand, are fair game so I'm not going to say it again; hands up, or I keep shooting and we'll leave you here to die while we take the siren back to our king."

Kastian doesn't move, doesn't blink, doesn't even flinch, his jaw set in a line so rigid it might snap. I can tell he's thinking about fighting anyway, and I can't let him. There's too many soldiers, and Kastian already looks like he's about to pass out from the poison on the first arrow. What if he doesn't survive the second one?

Adrenaline floods my system and self-preservation wins out over pride. I raise both hands into the air and stumble forward toward the nearest soldier.

ODESSA, AGE 16

I run blindly toward the castle, head down, not caring who sees me in my nightgown. My only thought is to get as far away from the garden as possible before the burning at the backs of my eyes spills over.

I clench my hands into fists, willing myself not to cry.

I've always been good at hiding my tears in public, but this time I can't. Despite my best effort, the tears come. My vision blurs and by the time I reach the castle corridor I'm snuffling audibly, so lost that I nearly plow over a servant carrying a stack of linens.

"Sorry—" I gasp, but the girl's already scuttling away, her face carefully blank.

A fresh wave of embarrassment crashes over me. I know I need to pull myself together before I'm spotted by someone who knows me, but the palace is a maze and I'm suddenly, desperately lost. On a whim, I yank open the first door I see and slip inside, letting it thump shut behind me.

The hush is immediate and heavy. I press my back to the door and slide down, the coat and blanket pooling in a heap around me.

My brain replays Kastian's face over and over: the confusion in his eyes, the way his smile collapsed inward, as if I'd punched him in the gut.

I can't hold it in any longer, and the tears spill over. I sob uncontrollably. Each sob racks my body, making my shoulders quiver with the intensity of it all.

I let the emotions flood out, feeling the hot trails of tears mingle with the snot trickling down my face. My chest heaves with each ragged breath, and I cry until there's nothing left but the sound of my uneven breathing echoing in the quiet room.

When my tears dry up and I can't cry anymore, I slowly raise my head.

I've stumbled into someone's office. At least, that's what I think it is.

The room is oval-shaped with tall bookshelves and flickering sconces lining the walls. In the center of the room is a heavy oak desk with a large armchair behind it and several books and papers scattered across the surface.

I push to my feet and cross to the large arched window. Outside, I can see the edge of the lake behind the castle, where Kastian stole my boat.

I frown deeply and tear my eyes from the water. Instead, my gaze lands on the large desk. Curious, I cross the room and pick up the nearest book from the desk. The title, "Beasts of Southern Ellender" jumps out at me and my brow furrows. Sticking out of the top of the book is a torn bit of parchment, obviously being used as a bookmark. I let the book fall open in my hand to the place the owner of this office must have marked.

For some reason—perhaps because it's the only thing on my mind at the moment—I expected the book to be marked at a chapter about sirens. I'm wrong. The title of the chapter, written in large curling letters, is: "Dopplers, tricksters and shapeshifters."

I'm about to start reading when I hear the sound of footsteps in the hall. I freeze, listening hard. It's probably just one of the servants and—

The doorknob rattles.

My heart leaps into my throat, and I drop the book and dive beneath the desk just as the door swings open.

"—I don't really care. If your betrothal falls through now, then all the work I've done has been for nothing," a male voice says, shutting the door behind him.

"I tried," a girl whines back. "But I don't know what else I'm supposed to do."

I clap my hand over my mouth to stifle a gasp. I know that voice—it's Lyra Von Bargen. But who's the man? And worse, what will happen if they see me under here, hiding in an office barefoot, tear-streaked, and wearing a nightgown?

I can't even imagine the humiliation—and that's assuming I'm not in trouble for snooping.

I pull my legs in tighter and hold my breath as a pair of feet walk across the room and stop at the window just out of my line of sight

"For one thing, you could put an ounce of effort into making him like you," the male voice says, sounding weary.

Lyra's feet follow the man, and she stops directly in front of the desk. If I wanted I could reach out and grab her ankle.

She pops a hip out and sighs loudly. "You've been telling me for years that royal marriages have nothing to do with affection. What happened to your orders to be as bland as possible so the king and queen would think I was a safe, unthreatening choice of bride?"

"Evidently I've misjudged things," the man says bitterly. "The king wasn't nearly as concerned as I thought he'd be about his son spending time with a siren."

My eyes widen, and I bite the inside of my cheek until I taste blood.

"You talked to King Sebastian about it?" Lyra asks.

"I did...and he didn't seem to mind. Fucking idiot, this is why he has no right to sit on that throne. He's completely blind to every possible threat."

"Obviously," Lyra says pointedly.

There's a long pause, the scrape of a chair across the floor, and shuffling out of sight. "What did the siren say?" the man asks.

Lyra sighs again, more frustrated this time. "Nothing of substance. She doesn't seem very bright to me."

My eyes bug out of my head. *Are they talking about me?*

What am I thinking? Of course they are. There aren't any other sirens at court.

But why?

"She could still be dangerous," the man says.

"I doubt it," Lyra scoffs.

"What do you mean?"

"I mean that she's a self-absorbed child too wrapped up in melodramatic fantasies to be either dangerous or useful. I thought for sure she'd gone out of her way to bewitch the prince, but when I brought it up to her, she just stared at me with those big glassy eyes, almost like a fish. I'm almost certain she had no idea what I was talking about."

A pang of discomfort hits my chest. I don't care what Lyra thinks about me, but it's still not pleasant to realize you're being insulted behind your back.

I need to know who that man is, and why Lyra is talking to him about me. My heart is pounding so hard against my ribs I'm terrified they'll hear it as I lean forward slightly, the top of my head skimming the underside of the desk. I peer past Lyra's legs and finally spot the man now sitting in an armchair by the bookshelves.

My eyes narrow in confusion. I'm not positive, but I think it's her father—the man I saw on the balcony with the royal family the day we arrived. He's tall and blonde and dressed in expensive, fashionable clothing.

He's an advisor to the king, I think. I'm sure I heard someone mention his name since we've been here. Marcus...no, *Magnus*.

Magnus happens to glance in my direction, and I lean back quickly before he can see me, my pulse thundering out of control.

"Hmm," Magnus mumbles. "Interesting. I suppose the siren is quite young. It's possible she doesn't know what she's capable of."

"I truly don't believe she does," Lyra says flippantly. "I almost felt sorry for her."

Magnus snorts. "Don't. She may not be much now, but given some time she could be quite dangerous. For now, though, I think you may be right, but in many ways that's worse."

"Why?" Lyra asks.

"If the siren isn't intentionally meddling, then perhaps Prince Kastian is genuinely infatuated with her. If that's the case, then the compulsion won't wear off if we dispose of the siren. It won't matter what we do to her. He still won't want to marry you, which derails the entire plan."

Sweat begins to bead on the back of my neck and my hairline as I bite the inside of my cheek hard to keep myself from making a sound.

"I don't want to marry him either," Lyra says flatly.

"That's irrelevant," Magnus snaps. "You'll marry whomever I tell you to, especially if it means elevating this family. Your job was to secure our position in the royal family, but obviously you've failed."

"I told you, I—"

Magnus cuts her off, standing from his chair and pacing across the room. "If Kastian won't see reason, perhaps he can be useful in another way."

"What do you mean?"

Magnus reaches the window and stares out at the grounds, his back to Lyra. "We kill Kastian and blame it on the girl. Or her family, perhaps. Either would work as I have it on good authority that her cousin is the bastard son of King Florian."

"What?" Lyra asks, incredulous.

Her shocked tone echoes the wave of horror washing over me. *Kill Kastian. Blame my family...*

Magnus carries on as if Lyra didn't speak. "Yes...this could work. With the right evidence, we can have Vernallis declared an enemy of the state. The people will demand retribution and it will push Hydratta into an expensive and unwinnable war—King Sebastian will be destabilized by the war and the loss of his heir, and eventually it will create enough unrest that we'll be able to stage a coup."

Lyra's breath hitches. "You'd start a *war* over this? You never said—"

"I'd do whatever is necessary to secure the line of succession. Our line," Magnus says, and there's something almost tender in that last word.

"Wait!" Lyra snaps, sounding afraid now. "I didn't agree to this. Marriage is one thing, but I never wanted to kill anyone. A war is going too far."

Magnus turns to her, and it's only luck and his focus on Lyra—that keeps him from seeing me under the desk. My skin has gone clammy and cold. If they see me now it's not going to be merely a humiliation. They'll kill me.

"I'm doing this for you," Magnus says almost kindly. "Don't you understand? This is the only way to get what we're owed."

Lyra makes a noise of derision in the back of her throat. "You don't care about me. You never have. You only want the throne."

"Of course I care about you, who else could I trust to help me with this?"

"No," she says. "I'm not doing it."

Magnus's face twists with anger. "You are. I'm sure I don't need to remind you what will happen if you disobey me."

There's a long silence where I desperately wish I could see Lyra's face because after a moment, Magnus smiles. "Good. We'll have to move quickly to make the plan work. It will have to happen tonight."

"Tonight?" Lyra asks, her voice trembling slightly.

"Yes, we'll kill Kastian tonight at the ball, and by tomorrow the plan will be set in motion. Mark my words, a century from now our family will sit on the throne and no one will even remember King Sebastian or Prince Kastian."

ODESSA, PRESENT

My ass hurts, my wrists burn and my head pounds. At the same time my thoughts are racing, my heart aches, and I'm shaking so much my teeth chatter.

Every single part of me feels like it's going to break, both emotionally and physically.

I'm seated on the back of a horse with my wrists bound in front of me, a blindfold over my eyes and another strip of fabric shoved in my mouth. My horse is being led by one of the Hydrattan soldiers, and I have no way of knowing where we are or how much longer it will take to reach Magnus's castle.

If I focus, I can hear Kastian breathing somewhere to my left.

Before they put my blindfold on, I got a glimpse of the arrow wound on Kastian's shoulder. I hadn't realized he'd been magically healing himself while the soldiers closed in on us, but he must have, because the wound looks nearly cured. Unfortunately, it doesn't seem like he was able to purify the sedative poison because he's still out cold.

None of that matters though, as long as he's alive.

I keep reminding myself that Kastian isn't dead and neither am I. As long we're alive, everything will be fine.

I repeat that in my head over and over, trying to believe it, but the longer we ride, the harder it is to remain optimistic. My thoughts become more frantic and question after question occurs to me.

How did the soldiers find us?

Why were they sent in the first place?

When Kastian and I don't turn up at the border, will Jett realize what's happened, or did they find him too?

And most of all, why would Magnus want to kidnap me, *again.* I was willing to go to his castle anyway as the emissary, but now he's destroyed any hope of peace. When Daemon finds out about this—that the Hydrattan soldiers shot and poisoned Kastian, and took both of us against our will—I know he'll crush Hydratta, even without his growing army.

I can't think of a single answer, and the uncertainty makes my mind race, drowning out anything else. Drowning out the thoughts of what was happening just before the soldiers arrived— what I thought I felt...what it might mean...

Something inside me seems to leap at that thought, and even though I'm blindfolded, I turn my face toward the sound of Kastian's breathing.

The feeling in my chest is almost like a heartbeat, but different somehow. Warmer. I'm almost certain I know what it is, even if I don't understand exactly how it got there.

Somehow, Kastian and I are bonded.

That can only mean we always were—or at least, he knew we were even if he didn't remember why.

I don't understand how this happened, but I swear I'm going to find out. We're going to get out of this and talk about the bond. I'm going to find a way to undo the vow I made a hundred years ago.

I'll fix everything—first, we just need to survive.

We ride for what feels like hours—long enough for my legs to go numb and my anxiety to transition to despair.

The soldiers don't talk much, communicating only in grunts and the occasional sharp order. The silence becomes its own sort of torture—every hoofbeat a reminder that we are utterly at their mercy, and there's nothing to do but wait and pray I can still hear Kastian breathing when the ride ends.

Eventually, the sounds of the swamp disappear, and the air gets easier to breathe. Brightness shines beyond the fabric covering my eyes, and the rhythm and sound of the horses' hooves make me think we've finally reached a main road. Soon after that, the horses slow. There's a brief, jarring stop and some clattering as one of the soldiers dismounts.

I jump at the sound of a sharp voice somewhere to my right. "Bend down so I can reach your blindfold. I'm going to take it off so you can see while you get down from the horse."

I bend as much as possible despite the restraints, and a hand grasps the fabric over my eyes and tugs it away. The sudden light burns, and I have to squint until my eyes adjust.

We've stopped in front of an achingly familiar white stone castle. I glance up and see the wide, round balcony on its face. It's empty, which is something of a relief. I was expecting to see King Magnus standing there, watching us arrive, just as Kastian's family did a hundred years ago.

I turn my head, searching for Kastian, desperate to see if he's alright and to gauge his reaction to being back here after so long. My eyes land on the soldiers standing by their horses, looking exhausted after the long journey. Kastian isn't among them. Cold dread washes over me. Oh gods, what if I've been listening to one of the soldiers breathing all this time? What if they left him in the swamp? What if—

"Mmmm," I try to speak, the gag muffling any actual words.

The Fae soldier who took off my blindfold snorts, unimpressed. She's dressed identically to the soldier who shot Kastian, but she's slightly thinner and her braided hair is a dull blonde

She grips my calf and hauls me down from the horse. I lose my balance and nearly collapse, but she holds my shoulder until I can balance. The world seems to tip and roll around me, but I steady myself and glare up at her with every ounce of fury I can muster.

"Mmmm!" I try again, more insistently.

She rolls her eyes. "Don't scream."

She yanks the sodden gag out of my mouth, and I gasp, tasting blood and cloth and the sour reek of my own breath. "Where's Kastian? What did you do to him?"

The guard's grip tightens on my arm. "He's alive," she says, like it's an inconvenience.

"If Magnus hurts him—" My voice cracks.

"*King* Magnus," she corrects me with a scowl.

"Fuck your king."

She scowls harder and shoves me forward a few paces. "From what I heard, you will be."

My eyes widen and I draw back. That thought is not only revolting, it fills me with a deep aversion and disgust that feels so much stronger than any reaction I was capable of yesterday. Could that be a side effect of the potential soul-bond? Or perhaps I simply never thought of it in such vivid terms before

"Move!" The soldier barks, nudging me to walk. "I can't carry you, so your only other choice is to be dragged, and we're going up lots of stairs. Personally, I'd just walk."

I glower at her, refusing to move. "Tell me where Kastian is!"

The soldier sighs in exasperation. She ignores my demand and, evidently giving up on the idea that I'm going to cooperate, uses every ounce of her Fae strength to wrench me up the path toward the castle. She yanks so hard that I hear my shoulder pop. A jolt shoots through me from clavicle to fingertip, and I bite the inside of my cheek to hold back tears that have nothing to do with the pain.

To distract myself from the throbbing in my arm and the desire to cry with frustration, I focus on analyzing the courtyard as I'm dragged up to the castle.

Magnus must have selected all the female soldiers to go find me, because every other guard we pass is male. I sneer at the dozens of men stationed around the front of the castle, all dressed in identical bright green jackets.

When Alix and Daemon took over Vernallis, they changed all the guards' uniforms from red to blue. To many, it had seemed like an unnecessary move, but this is precisely why they did it. Magnus's court looks exactly like the court of King Sebastian and Queen Marbella, and if I didn't know better, I would think nothing had changed from a century ago. It makes the new regime feel like pretenders to the throne—which in this case, is exactly what Magnus is.

As we pass through the white stone archway into the castle courtyard, few of the guards swivel to look at us. Every single one has thick wads of cotton jammed into his ears.

"Looks like you're all afraid of me," I mutter as we cross the courtyard and enter the palace, passing by two more guards with cotton in their ears.

"The king doesn't like to take any chances," my guard answers, her tone reverent and her eyes turning wide and earnest.

I glare at her, disgusted. She seems like the type to worship power. "You must be young to think your king is a god. I remember Magnus when he was just a social-climbing advisor. He wasn't impressive then, and he's still nothing now."

She spins abruptly to face me, and I see the anger snap in her eyes before I feel it in my jaw—her palm cracks across my face, hard enough to split my lip. The taste of blood explodes in my mouth.

My face burns, and for a second I'm too stunned to react. The guard smiles, looking satisfied, and starts to turn away.

My surprise clears and without thinking, I lunge, knocking into her hard enough that both of us go tumbling backward into the stone wall of the entrance hall.

She grunts as her head bounces off the white marble. My hands and wrists are still bound, but that doesn't stop me from driving my elbow straight down onto her nose. There's a sickening crunch, and she howls, vivid red blood spattering onto the bright white floor.

I jump to my feet, and for a glorious second I think I've won. I turn to run, but before I've gone a single step, a heavy weight slams into me from behind. Another guard materializes from nowhere to wrap his arms around my waist and pin me. He's massive, all thick slabs of muscle, and he lifts me off the ground, my feet kicking uselessly in the air.

The female soldier is already back on her feet, her nose bleeding rivers down her face. She wipes it with the back of her hand and glares at me like she's deciding which part of me to break next. She pulls off a glove, exposing her pale, sharp-nailed fingers, then slaps me again—this time on the other cheek.

"You bitch!" she snarls, voice muffled by her own blood. "I'd kill you if the king didn't want you alive."

"Lucky me," I spit back, not even aware of the pain in my face.

She presses a hand to her bleeding nose, and her eyes dart to the other soldier. "Take her inside. I'll follow you."

"What?" the guard holding me nearly yells. "I can't hear you."

"Take her inside!" the soldier screams.

Either he can hear her now, or he just assumes what to do, because the guard doesn't hesitate. He carries me across the entrance hall and through the arched doorway. The female soldier follows, pinching her nose and grumbling furiously under her breath.

My lips curve into a smile. At least no one can say I went quietly.

The interior of the castle is almost exactly as I remember it: high domed ceilings, archways carved with flowers and stars, sunlight streaming in through colored glass and splattering rainbows over the white marble floors.

The soldiers don't take me to the throne room. Instead, we veer left, down a corridor lined with ancient tapestries. At the end of the hall is a winding marble staircase, which ascends at least eight levels before finally ending with a heavy wooden door.

The guard holding me stops on the top landing, and steps aside so the female guard can unlock the door. She looks slightly out of breath as she produces a ring of keys from her belt, then shoves the door open to reveal a small round room. The large guard, hardly even winded from the climb, carries me inside.

I expected to be standing in a cell, but instead I find myself in a bedroom. There's a large four-poster bed with a golden canopy and several shelves of books. A wardrobe stands between two large windows, and there's even a small adjoining bathing room. In spite of everything, my eyes land on the bathtub, and a wave of relief washes over me.

"I can take it from here," the female soldier tells the large guard.

"What?" he asks again.

"Of for the love of—" She looks furious as she shoves him out of the room and closes the door behind him, leaving us alone. I square my shoulders and back up, eyeing her warily.

She glares at me with hatred on her face. "The king wants to see you."

"Oh, goody."

Her glower intensifies. "You should be thrilled because otherwise I'd fuck up your face."

"I'd still be prettier than you."

Her cheeks redden behind the blood, and she looks, if possible, even angrier. "Go in there and take a bath. You're disgusting."

"Yeah, well, being kidnapped twice in 72 hours will do that."

She scoffs. "You stupid bitch, you don't even realize how lucky you are. Take a bath, but don't take too long. I'll find you something else to wear."

I want to argue with her just out of spite, but a large part of me wants the bath more. "Are you going to untie my hands first?"

She looks at me, and I know she's thinking about saying no, but apparently common sense wins out. The soldier unties me, and I stumble into the bathing room. The door closes, and I immediately rush to the window.

As I look outside, my heart sinks.

It's clear why the soldier wasn't worried about leaving me in here alone. We're hundreds of feet off the ground, probably in one of the towers. Below, I can see the edge of the garden and a familiar iron fence. Beyond it is a rocky cliff and a small beach, then nothing but water as far as the eye can see.

I've never wished I could fly more than I do right now.

ODESSA, PRESENT

I leave the bathroom an hour later, clean, but no less miserable.

The dress the soldier left on the floor just inside the door is a bright blood-red, which feels like something of a bad omen. *Ugh, this is no time for superstition.*

I tug the dress over my head and step out of the bathroom, only to stop short. My eyes fly wide.

The soldier is gone. In her place, a tall, blonde man stands at the window, his back to me. I open my mouth, but before I can get a word out, he turns and smiles at me. "Odessa. You're somehow even more beautiful now than you were the last time we met."

A shiver of fear and revulsion travels down my spine.

Magnus Von Bargen looks almost exactly the same as I remember him, except now I'm fully aware of what kind of man he is and he looks all the more disgusting because of it.

Magnus must be from Thermia originally, because he's tall and blonde like most Thermians, with flinty blue-gray eyes that look harsh no matter his expression. Like all Fae, his face is smooth and young-looking, but his features are unmemorable—neither handsome, nor ugly. Most importantly, he doesn't have any cotton in his ears. *Arrogant idiot.*

"I'm surprised you didn't take any precautions to prevent me from compelling you, especially after being so careful with your guards."

"Is that a threat?"

"Did it not sound like one? Perhaps I wasn't clear enough."

To my surprise, Magnus laughs. "Age has been good to you. I can tell you're going to be everything I hoped for."

My eyes narrow. The way he's talking, you'd think we had met before, but we never did. I know he saw me because I heard him talking about it, but Magnus and I have never actually been introduced. Strange.

I shake off my confusion—it's not important right now—and take a large step closer. I look directly into his cold eyes, letting the note of persuasion infect my tone. "Take me to Kastian."

Magnus's eyes remain focused. "Not right now. You and I have so much to discuss."

I try again, pushing even more persuasiveness into my voice until I'm almost singing. "You want to take me to Kastian and then set both of us free. Nothing would make you happier."

He yawns. *Yawns!* "You may keep trying if you like. I can wait however long it takes for you to understand that you're powerless against me."

I set my jaw. I suppose Magnus might have the strongest will of any man in Ellender, but I doubt it. "How is this possible?"

Magnus smiles. "I'll tell you if you sit down and have something to eat. I had the servants bring up some food and wine."

My eyes land on the tray of fruit and pastries on the bed, which I hadn't noticed until now. My stomach growls loudly, but I don't move.

It's probably poisoned.

Clearly aware of where my mind has gone, Magnus reaches

for the tray himself and snatches a grape, popping it into his mouth. Then he takes the large decanter of wine and pours himself a goblet.

"To you." He toasts me. "And to our upcoming union."

I scowl. "What union? You can't honestly think I was ever going to marry you."

"We'll see," he says ominously. "Please sit down. You eat, and I'll talk."

My eyes dart to the tray again, and finally the growling in my stomach makes me relent. I sit on the edge of the bed and take a jam tart. It's delicious, and I hate myself for giving in so easily.

Magnus smiles, watching me with a hungry look in his eye. "I'm sorry that this is your welcome back to Hydratta. I'd planned for it to be more elaborate than this."

Oh, I'm sure he did.

"How did you know where to find me?" I ask.

"We got word that some mercenaries from Solistine had attacked your train within hours of the incident. Of course, I immediately sent ships out to look for you. One of them spotted the ship from Solistine sinking, and a group flying away toward the mainland. I had all my guards mobilized within hours. I must admit I was surprised to realize who you were traveling with. What happened to my emissary?"

I pause with another bite of pastry halfway to my mouth. Magnus's face is a neutral mask of innocence, but I'm not fooled. Even if Connell hadn't told us that Magnus orchestrated my first kidnapping, and I didn't already know exactly what sort of man he is, I would have known immediately that there was something off about Magnus from his eyes alone. They're cold and emotionless even when he's smiling.

I put another pastry in my mouth and chew slowly, giving myself a second to think. Then, making the split-second decision not to reveal that I know he planned my abduction, I swallow and clear my throat. "He was killed on the train...unfortunately."

"Oh my." Magnus's face falls. "I'm sorry to hear that."

He's not sorry. I don't know why or how, but I'm certain that Magnus wanted his emissary removed and decided to kill two birds with one stone by having the pirates murder him during my abduction.

"Well, what's done is done. "He shrugs, putting on an expression of false humility. "I'd rather focus on happier things, now. I've brought you here, as I'm sure you know, because I want you to be my queen."

I choke on my pastry. Good gods, this man is insane! He's trying to ignore the fact that his soldiers kidnapped me and he won't tell me where Kastian is, and move straight into wedding planning? "You're out of your mind. I was never going to marry you, and I certainly wouldn't now."

"See, I think you will. You're not the only one who knows how to persuade someone, and you've conveniently already told me whom I need to threaten to ensure your cooperation."

My heartbeat pounds against my chest, and the pastry falls from my hand onto the bed. "You can't. Forget about me, if you hurt Kastian, then Daemon will never agree to ally with you."

"I don't know about that. I think he still might, once I'm married to his cousin."

"If you believe that then you don't know anything about him or about me. You're going to be in for a rude awakening."

"I think your cousin could be persuaded when he learns how happy you are here, but if not, then it's no great loss."

My brow furrows. "I thought you were only doing this for the alliance."

"Actually, I think you misunderstand. The alliance would be an added benefit, but this is really about you. I've had you in the back of my mind for many years now."

I look up. "What? Why?"

"Because you're a land-born siren; the first one I've ever seen outside of historical accounts and portraits. You have no idea how useful you could be to me."

Nausea washes over me and my chest burns with an odd

combination of disgust and anger. Of course it's only because I'm a siren. He's like a collector—like every other vile man that taught me to hate how I looked from far too young an age. Who taught me to flinch every time someone called me beautiful.

Magnus takes advantage of my silence, walking over to the bed to look down his nose at me. "I'm not a monster, Odessa," he continues. "I don't want to force you into this. I'd rather have an obedient queen. Someone who knows how to keep the peace—someone who understands what's at stake and that you sometimes have to do unpleasant things for the greater good. I believe that person could be you."

I make a noise in the back of my throat somewhere between a growl and a scoff. "You don't *want* to force me, but you will."

He looks sad, like I'm the problem here—I'm the one being difficult and putting him in a position he doesn't like. "Unfortunately, I want this too much to let you ruin it."

"I'm ruining your plan because I won't just bend over and happily let you rape me?"

His nose wrinkles and his lip tips up in a sneer. "I think you'll find you're very happy to obey me when the alternative is watching your precious prince bleed out on the stones in front of this castle. Or perhaps you'd like to see what I'll do to your cousin when he arrives?"

I bare my teeth. "That's not much of a threat when I know either one of them could kill you without even trying."

"Would you like to test it? Do you really want to know where Kastian is now? He's in my dungeon, waiting for me to decide what to do with him. If you like, I could have him brought up here right now and we can fight it out, but I'll warn you, he's already been fed enough sedatives to knock out a dozen trolls. I doubt he'll be in the best condition to fight."

I swallow, trying to force my heart back down from my throat. My voice shakes with anger, but I push past it, infusing my tone with more persuasion than I've ever used before. "Throw yourself off this tower."

Magnus shakes his head wearily. "Let's not do this again, Odessa. Your powers cannot affect me, and the sooner you realize that, the sooner we can focus on what's really important."

"How is that possible?" I demand.

"Surely you know there are some exceptions to the siren powers. Like so many other things in nature, the siren song is really only intended to carry on the species. It's no different from a ram growing horns to fight off other males, or the Fae's wings appearing around their bonds, to warn anyone else to stay away."

"What's your point?"

"Siren compulsion doesn't work on women or children, non-compatible species, like trolls or dragons, direct relatives of sirens, or anyone who is soul-bonded—since they would be physically unable to betray their bond."

"So you're bonded? Then why would you want to marry me, you shouldn't be able to—"

I break off mid-sentence. What I was going to say was: "you shouldn't be able to consummate it," but I can't make myself say it. Even thinking about that is revolting.

Actually, come to think of it, I can't consummate a marriage either—it's said that to betray a soul-bond is painful enough to kill you. Would that still be true if he forced me? Probably. That might be painful enough to kill me regardless.

"You misunderstand," Magnus says, invading my increasingly panicked thoughts. "I'm not bonded, I just can't have children. It's one of the reasons I've felt no need to take a wife before now. I have no concerns about having an heir."

My brow furrows. I've never heard about siren magic not working on infertile men, but I guess it makes sense since all of those other exceptions are true. Only, Magnus has a daughter—Lyra—so what's going on here? "If you never wanted a wife before and can't have an heir; and it's not about the alliance with Vernallis, why would you suddenly want to marry me now?"

"Are you familiar with the history of land-born sirens?"

I blink, startled by his suddenly businesslike tone. "No."

"Allow me to educate you. Many years ago, before you or I were born, this continent was one large kingdom. The king lived in the north, in what is now Thermia, and didn't often worry about what was happening in the south, so eventually the people of what is now Hydratta wanted to break off from the rest of the kingdom and govern themselves."

"That's nice," I hiss, "but I don't really have time for a history lesson."

"You have time for whatever I want from you. You're not leaving this tower any time soon," he snaps, his true personality showing for just a moment before he covers it with a saccharine smile. "As I was saying, Hydratta decided to become its own kingdom, but then suddenly the king who ignored them didn't want to let them go, so he sent soldiers from the capital to force Hydratta to surrender. What the soldiers didn't know was that the new rulers of the island had anticipated this and they had a secret weapon. Their new queen was the daughter of a siren who was captured by a fisherman."

My stomach lurches as if I might be sick. I think it's the word "imprisonment" that's getting to me. I always assumed that my mother stayed on land because she chose to, but this other ancient siren was obviously not given the same choice.

It seems like, if Magnus has his way, I won't get a choice either.

Magnus carries on with his story, unbothered by my darkening expression. "Due to her mother's imprisonment, the siren queen was born on land and raised to be loyal to the Fae. So, when the soldiers marched on Hydratta, she used her powers of persuasion to send them all marching into the sea."

"That's horrible," I snap. "And it has nothing to do with me."

"I disagree. See, over the years, there were many attempts to breed landlocked sirens for their powers, but the practice was difficult and dangerous. Most who tried it ended up becoming obsessed with the sirens they tried to hold prisoner and dying. Eventually, history forgot about what the sirens could do, until I saw you, and I knew that the legendary first Queen of Hydratta could be reborn."

"You're insane," I bite out, "and whatever you're imagining isn't going to happen. I'm not staying here. Maybe I can't compel you, but there's a hell of a lot of people in this castle I can affect."

"You could, but you won't, because you know if you do that I'll murder Kastian and make you watch."

I suck in a breath, unable to hide my horror, and Magnus pounces on my reaction. "But it doesn't have to be that way, Odessa. We could work together, you and I. Just think about it for a moment. Can you imagine the possibilities of a ruler with the ability to influence anyone and everyone? Picture a queen who could ask her subjects for anything and they would be happy to oblige. There would be no unrest in the kingdoms, no need for wars, no pointless diplomatic arguments."

"There would be no independent thought, you mean," I bite out. "But there's an obvious flaw in your fantasy. What about the women and men like you? They wouldn't be affected."

"I've read accounts from men who believed that with enough selective breeding and training from an early age, a siren could be taught to influence women as well as men."

"You're talking about us like prized racehorses bred for speed."

"That's not an unreasonable comparison," he says thoughtfully.

I shake my head. *No. No, this cannot be happening.*

"I'll never do it. I won't marry you, and I won't influence anyone on your behalf. I'd rather die."

"You're not going to die," he says dismissively. "But Kastian will if you don't come around."

A lead ball drops into my stomach—cold, dense, final. Magnus is right: I would do almost anything to keep him from hurting Kastian. Except, will what I do even matter?

Magnus had planned to kill Kastian as early as a hundred years ago. He killed his family. Clearly, no matter what I do, he's not going to let Kastian walk free.

Daemon is coming, I remind myself.

If they don't hear from me, then Daemon and Alix will know something is wrong. They'll come to rescue us. I just need to make sure Magnus doesn't kill Kastian before then.

"If I marry you, will you let him go?" I ask, hating how my voice shakes but unable to stop it.

Magnus doesn't answer right away. He just stares at me, eyes cold and flat.

I grit my teeth behind my closed lips, trying not to betray my anxiety. I don't even need him to agree to let Kastian go—he'd be lying anyway—I just want him to have a reason to keep him alive until Daemon gets here.

"Yes," he says finally, lip curling. "After the wedding, and after you've written to your family in Vernallis to tell them it was your idea, I'll let Kastian go. I expect you to make your loyalty obvious. If you don't, you can watch him die through the windows of your new palace."

I let out a long breath. I know that's what I wanted to hear, but it didn't do much to alleviate my anxiety. I also know that I'll never actually marry Magnus. I would walk straight into the sea before I'd ever let him touch me. Still, agreeing out loud feels like a defeat.

"Fine," I say. The word comes out raw, gutted.

"Good girl." He flashes me a genuine smile and reaches out and pats my cheek. "Don't look so sad. You're going to make such a beautiful queen."

KASTIAN, AGE 18

Hundreds of masked nobles crowd around me, and though I don't know who anyone is, I despise them all.

I loathe their happy chattering voices and their pointless conversations. I hate them for forcing me to socialize when I would rather lock myself in my room and rot.

I hate them because I can't hate the person I'm really mad at.

I'm standing near the bow of my ship, leaning against the railing, and watching the last straggling groups of courtiers walking up the ramp to the deck. We're still docked in the harbor, but not for much longer. As soon as the last of the courtiers make their way down from the castle, we'll be setting sail.

It was my mother's brilliant plan to have this ball on the deck of a ship sailing around the harbor rather than in our standard ballroom. Admittedly, it wasn't a bad idea. The ship looks nice covered in decorations and lights, and the excited crowd is enchanted by doing something slightly unusual. They'll be talking about this party for years.

And they'll have a hell of a lot more to talk about if I fling myself over the side of the boat.

Not that I really would, but the idea has crossed my mind.

Just this morning, I'd been looking forward to this evening. I envisioned introducing Odessa to my parents, but now I'm torn between a desperation to see her and silent prayers that she doesn't show up.

Odessa isn't here yet—I'd know, as I've been obsessively watching the ramp up to the ship for the last half an hour, searching the eyes behind every mask for a hint of violet. I assume she wouldn't want to come, not after the scene in the garden this morning—not after she told me so clearly that she never wants to speak to me again—but I'm not sure. I haven't seen Daemon either, so maybe their whole family is just running late.

Waiting is torture.

"Ugh, I'm already ready to go home!" a frustrated voice says behind me.

I turn around and come face to face with my sister, Serena. Or, almost face to face, considering she's over a foot shorter than me even in her tall heels. She's wearing an emerald green ballgown and matching mask, and has a white flower in her dark hair, clearly reminiscent of the colors of the Hydrattan flag.

I slide over to make room for her next to me, and she leans against the railing.

"You look nice," I say out of brotherly obligation.

She scoffs. "I look tired, which is what I am. I almost made Dellanore or Avaline pretend to be me."

I crack a smile. "Don't you think Prince Thorne would notice?"

"Not at all." She scowls. "He's awful. Even worse than I expected, and my hopes weren't high."

"So I take it you won't be announcing an engagement tonight," I joke, cracking a smile for the first time all day.

She shakes her head, her scowl growing deeper. "No, but it wasn't even my choice."

I raise an eyebrow. "Excuse me?"

"He doesn't want to marry me," she says incredulously. "Can you believe that?"

My brow furrows. "Actually, no, I can't. What happened?"

Serena lets out another frustrated huff, then immediately smiles a wide fake smile, waving to a few courtiers behind us. "Wait for them to move along," she says out of the corner of her mouth.

I nod, still shocked. Not that I wanted Serena to marry Prince Thorne, but I can't imagine why he would be the one to reject the engagement. My sister is a princess, wealthy in her own right and objectively beautiful, whereas Thorne is a fucking asshole. She's far too good for him. So, what's the problem?

The courtiers move on, and Serena's smile slides back off her face. "Sorry." She sighs. "Anyway, Thorne isn't looking for just any princess; he wants a sorceress."

My eyebrows raise. "A human, you mean?"

Fae rarely use the word "sorceress." That, along with "witch," is a word almost exclusively reserved for humans with magic who somehow find their way into Ellender.

"No idea, I didn't ask for clarification," she huffs. "Apparently my magic isn't strong enough for whatever precious magical babies he's planning."

I shake my head. "Fucking idiot. Maybe he's just shallow and wants a human wife?"

She cracks a smile. "Are you saying I'm not as pretty as a human?"

"Of course that's not what I'm saying," I blurt out. "You can do far better than Prince Thorne."

"Oh, I know that." She rolls her eyes. "I'm offended, obviously, but at least now I won't have to marry him."

"You wouldn't have had to anyway. Father never would have made you go through with it."

"I don't know," she says dubiously. "Magnus has been in his

ear lately about what a benefit to us it would be to have an alliance with Vernallis."

I gesture aimlessly toward where the Vernalli and Hydrattan nobles are happily mingling. "Is this not friendly enough?"

Serena shrugs. "Don't ask me."

My brow furrows again. "It seems like Magnus has been in Father's ear a lot as of late."

Serena purses her lips. "I know. I'm honestly just glad he's delegating to someone. You know how controlling he can be."

"Oh, I know, believe me."

We fall silent, and I adjust my black mask on my nose before my gaze falls back on the ramp up to the ship. Still no Odessa...

"Speaking of 'pretty...'" Serena says, drawing my attention back to her.

I raise my eyebrows. "Were we speaking of that?"

She waves a hand in the air. "Before. Whatever. I just wondered if you were going to tell me about the girl."

"What girl?" I grind out, purposefully misunderstanding.

"The Vernalli girl you've been spending all your time with the last few days. The entire court is talking about it. I wondered if there would be an engagement announced tonight, after all."

I scowl. "She's no one. Nothing is happening, the court just likes to talk."

Suddenly, as if punctuating my point, a ripple of whispers passes over the ship. Serena looks past me and smiles smugly. "That's odd, because *no one* just arrived."

I whip around so fast I have to catch myself against the railing. Fortunately no one notices, except perhaps Serena, because every single person has stopped to watch as Odessa makes her way up the ramp to the ship.

She's wearing a silver mask that covers her eyes and nose, but there's still absolutely no question that it's her. She looks perfect. Her hair is long and loose, her cheeks are flushed, and she's wearing a silver dress that looks like it was painted onto her body.

I can't move. I'm rooted in place, watching the way the lights reflect off her dress and her huge violet eyes scan the crowd, looking for someone. Me? Or someone else?

I'm overwhelmed in a way that's hard to describe. Not just by her beauty—though, honestly, yes, that's part of it—but by the realization of how well she fits in here. She would make a perfect princess, but she doesn't want to be. She doesn't want *me*.

I yank my eyes away and turn my back.

My sister looks away too, refocusing on me. She cocks her head. "You certainly seem agitated if she really is no one."

"I'm not agitated," I snap.

Serena smiles. "Right, of course you're not."

I glower at her. "She's attractive, sure, but that's all it is."

Serena's smile falters. "I don't want to hear that! I'd like to think you were raised to be a better man than that."

Serena is so much older than me it's almost like being scolded by my mother, and I duck my head, suitably ashamed. "Fine. Sorry."

She scoffs. "I'd be angrier if I thought you really meant it. You like her, I can tell. Why don't you introduce me?"

"No!" I say so fast her face falls. I clear my throat. "I mean, no, that's not a good idea. I'm already betrothed, remember."

"Right, and where is Lyra this evening?" Serena asks in a tone of mock concern. "Shouldn't she be with you if you're so interested in her?"

I grit my teeth. "Good point. I think I'll go find her now. Excuse me."

I walk pointedly away from Serena, nudging the crowd out of the way. I couldn't care less about finding Lyra, but I suppose she's not the worst person I could get stuck spending this evening with. At least if I'm with Lyra, I'll have a good excuse to avoid Odessa.

It takes me a bit longer to find Lyra than I would have expected. Usually I can always find her exactly where she's supposed to be, whether that's standing with her father, or following my sisters around like a lost dog. Tonight, though, everything seems to be going wrong.

I loop around the ship several times, wishing I'd worn a larger mask that covered more of my face. Finally, when I pass the bar for the third time, I spot her. Lyra is standing off to the side of the bar wearing a periwinkle dress and looking nervous.

I walk up to her. "Good evening."

Lyra glances at me, swinging her long curtain of dark hair around. "Oh, of course it's you," she says, sounding both annoyed and distracted at the same time.

I stop and stare at her, startled enough to forget for a moment what I'm doing. It's not what she said, it's who said it. Lyra is always polite—too polite, if I'm honest. She usually curtseys and greets me formally as if we've never met, but for some reason tonight she looks like she'd rather be talking to anyone else.

"Are you feeling alright?" I ask, genuinely confused.

"Obviously," she says acidly, then looks back at me and startles. Seeming to pull herself together, she shifts her posture and fixes me with a simpering smile. "Oh, of course. I'm sorry, Your Highness."

I roll my eyes. "I've told you that you don't have to call me that."

"Right..." she says again, still sounding odd. Her eyes dart from me, to the crowd, to the bartender. She's clearly still nervous.

Before I can ask what's wrong, the bartender turns around and hands her two drinks.

"Who's the other one for?" I ask.

"You, actually. I was going to come find you."

"Really?"

"Yes." She hands me a glass, still looking anxious.

I sniff the drink. "What is this?"

"Something strong." She laughs lightly. "I'm not much of a

fan of ships. I thought it might help to take the edge off, so to speak."

"Cheers to that," I mutter, thinking of Odessa again. Taking the edge off seems like exactly what I need.

"Cheers," Lyra echoes, clinking her glass with mine.

I tilt my head back and drink the entire thing in one gulp.

KASTIAN, PRESENT

I wake up disoriented, with no idea where I am.

My head is pounding. There's a needle of pain stabbing between my eyes, and I hear—no, feel—a high-pitched ringing in my ears that pulses with the beat of my heart.

My throat is dry, and my tongue is thick against my teeth. I force my eyes open and stare up at a ceiling ribbed with dark, uneven stones. Torchlight flickers in the periphery of my vision, reflecting off the glistening veins of water trickling down the heavy stone walls. Then, the smell hits me; sharp and briny with a sickly overlay of rot.

Where the fuck am I? What happened?

I try to sit up and can't, which sends a jolt of panic through me. Something pins my wrists and ankles to whatever I'm lying on, and I can't free them no matter how hard I pull.

Breathe. Don't panic.

Deep breath in...

I choke. The horrible stench of the room breaks my usual

calming ritual and sends my panic rocking even higher. I squeeze my eyes shut, trying not to lose my shit.

When I open my eyes again, I'm focused. Alert.

I shift my weight as much as I can, flexing my fingers, testing the range of movement in my shoulders.

I'm lying on some sort of table, my wrists and ankles strapped down. The table is cold under my back, but the air is wet and heavy, clinging to my skin. The straps bite into the bone, and no matter how many times I arch my hips and kick, twist, and struggle, the cuffs refuse to move.

I can't use magic unless I can get my hands free. I try anyway, waving my fingers, but without the full use of my hands, nothing happens.

Someone's gone to a lot of fucking trouble to keep me here.

I close my eyes again and try to remember something leading up to this moment. Anything.

The last thing I remember is Odessa; her beautiful face looking up at me as I came apart inside her. Then, the soldiers streaming out of the swamp and Dessa begging me to go along with it and not get myself killed.

I remember realizing that, while I could probably fight my way out of the circle of guards, I wouldn't be able to do it before one of them grabbed her. I thought I'd have a better chance of both of us escaping if I waited until we were back in a part of Hydratta I was familiar with, so I let them put me on a horse, and waited. I was working on getting my wrists untied and my gag off, when something cracked against the back of my head.

After that, nothing. Everything is dark.

The soldiers obviously knocked me out and brought me here. That must mean that I'm somewhere in the capital of Hydratta. Under the castle, maybe?

I twist my head to the side and try to get a better sense of my surroundings. The chamber is bigger than I thought—at least fifteen paces wide. The walls are shot through with mineral stains and barnacles. I don't see a door or any windows, but if I strain my ears, I think I can hear distant voices.

Maybe if I can get just one hand free—

A door creaks somewhere out of sight, and quick footsteps echo on the stone floor. I freeze, every muscle locked. A shadow grows closer, and falls across the table, just before a figure steps into the light. "Don't struggle. You'll only hurt yourself."

My back goes straight, and I recoil in shock. "Magnus."

He's taller than I remember, but otherwise the same. Blonde hair, cold eyes, and an almost kind smile that hides what an evil bastard he is.

"That's King Magnus, now," he says, walking closer. "It's been a long time, Kastian. I admit I was surprised to hear you escaped Dyaspora and even more surprised to learn you risked crossing my border. You should have stayed in Vernallis. I might never have realized you were there."

I grit my teeth and sneer at him. "Where is she?"

"Who?"

"Don't play dumb. Tell me where Odessa is!"

He looks annoyed—tired, even—and clicks his tongue impatiently. "Both of you are so annoyingly single-minded. Shouldn't you be more concerned with *yourself* at the moment?"

"Tell me where she is."

He rolls his eyes. "Where's Kastian? Take me to Kastian," he mimics Odessa's high voice, then drops his voice low in some gravelly imitation of me. "Take me to Odessa. Tell me where she is!"

"I didn't realize you were interested in theater," I snap.

"You're both so painfully boring and predictable. You know, at first, I couldn't understand it. I didn't remember you being stupid—a little naïve maybe, but not as much of a fucking imbecile as your father was. I kept asking myself why you would ever risk coming back here, but then I remembered how obsessed you were with the little siren, and suddenly it all made sense."

Anger burns in my chest, but I don't rise to the bait. One

thing I remember about Magnus is that he always liked to hear himself talk. "What the fuck are you talking about?" I grind out.

He scoffs. "There's no need to try to protect her. I already have Odessa taken care of upstairs."

Upstairs. So she's in the castle, and I'm beneath it—or at least close by. Not that knowing that does shit to help me.

"No more questions?" Magnus asks, interrupting my thoughts. "Have you given up on her already? That's probably for the best." He stoops low, his mouth near my ear. "Do you think she'll wonder if you're still looking for her when I'm fucking her tonight? Or do you think she's already accepted that you're dead?"

White, fiery rage blurs my vision, and I try again to sit up, yanking my wrists so hard that the bindings slice through my skin. "If you fucking touch her—"

Magnus snorts. "Oh, I'm going to touch her, but that's not what you should be worried about. You should ask yourself why you're still alive and what I'm going to make her do to keep you that way."

The blinding fury inside me seems to burn even hotter, and a blue haze clouds my mind. I force myself to keep my face blank, but inside, I'm burning alive.

I'm not scared of Magnus—never have been—but the thought of what he could force Odessa to do, who he'd make her become just to keep me alive, chills my bones.

Magnus paces around to the foot of the table and stops. He pulls something out of the pocket of his green velvet jacket and twirls it between his fingers. For a moment I think it's a knife, but then he leans further into the torchlight, and I see that it's a glass syringe with clear liquid inside.

"What the fuck is that?" I demand.

He rolls his eyes again. "So direct, like you just expect answers to all your questions without even having to work for it. Your father was the same way."

Since leaving Dyaspora, I learned my father didn't die along with my mother and sisters. Magnus kept him alive, and allegedly tortured him for months—years, maybe—as a warning to anyone who opposed the coup.

I stiffen, and a cold certainty washes over me. Whatever Magnus is about to do to me is likely the exact thing that killed my father.

Magnus holds up his long needle, flicking the barrel of the syringe so a bead of liquid stands at the tip. He tilts his head as if considering a painting, then finds a vein on my arm and presses with his thumb, hard enough to leave a bruise. "I wish I could say this won't hurt..."

The needle slides into my skin, and for a brief, foolish second I think it's not working, but then the fire starts. First it burns within my arm, then races up through my shoulder into my chest. I try to keep my mouth closed, try to stay silent, but almost immediately a shout breaks free. I yell in agony as my body arches of its own accord, jerking against the table so hard, I wonder for a moment if the restraints on my arms and legs will break.

I pass out before I get a chance to find out.

When I wake up for the second time, all I'm aware of is *pain*.

My head pounds, and all my limbs ache, unlike anything I've experienced before. Even back in Dyaspora when I spent all day mining for ice and all night freezing half to death, nothing hurt like this. It's like I was lit on fire from the inside out, and all that's left is my charred remains.

Slowly, and with enormous effort, I pry my eyes open. I'm still in the dark cave-like room, still strapped to the table...still unable to reach Odessa.

I look up and my eyes find Magnus again through the haze of

pain. He's frowning, looking between me and a large gold pocket watch. "Barely five minutes. Disappointing."

Was it only that long? I would have sworn the pain went on for days.

I cough, my voice sounding ragged to my own ears. "What the fuck did you do?"

He smiles. "Oh, hardly anything yet, just a hint of poison. I'm told it feels like every vein in your body is burning, but that's merely a side effect. The real purpose is sedation."

"Keeping me strapped down isn't enough? Are you such a fucking coward you need to sedate me too?"

His lips twist in an ugly grimace, but he seems unable to ignore my question. Even now, he can't resist the urge to lecture me. "There's this strange thing about magic: even if you've trained your entire life to use it one way, under some circumstances, you'll be able to use it another way...your father taught me that. Once, without even using his hands, he spontaneously conjured a wave to knock me over during one of our sessions. I can't have you doing the same, so really, you can thank him for everything that's about to happen to you."

He pulls out another long needle and stabs it into my other arm and the burning begins all over again. He watches and waits until I've been burning for over an hour, then reaches into the folds of his coat and produces a knife. Not the surgical kind I half-expected, but a wicked-looking, old-fashioned hunting blade. My heart rate triples.

Without a word, Magnus brandishes the knife with a lazy little flourish. I try to jerk away as he reaches for me, but the straps bite into my wrists, cutting off circulation.

He presses one hand into the table by my head, and raises the blade above my chest. The knife tip hovers for a moment as he steadies his aim, then he plunges the blade down, cutting deep gashes into the tattoo of Odessa on my chest.

He doesn't cut deep enough to reach my heart, but he may as well have.

The pain is instant and total. It's a white-hot spike that shoots up to my shoulder and explodes behind my eyes. I scream and the sound scrapes my throat raw. Blood seeps out around the blade, mixing with the sweat and salt already pooling on my skin. I thrash and yell in agony, while Magnus looks on with blank curiosity.

And so it goes, for what feels like days.

I fall in and out of consciousness. Sometimes I awake to find Magnus there, and he injects more burning poison into my arms, other times the room is empty and I drive myself half-insane trying and failing to pull myself free.

At one point, I'm awake long enough that I try to use magic, but the burning sedative makes it impossible.

I keep thinking about how my father must have died right where I'm lying now. He had more magic even than I do and was hundreds of years older, but he died anyway, and so will I.

I black out and lose track of time.

Magnus returns again and again, injects me with more poison, and then stabs knives through various parts of me. Once, he drives a blade all the way through my wrist, pinning my arm to the table.

He doesn't seem to want to kill me, just to cause pain. I don't know what he's waiting for—if anything. He never asks me questions or tries to get any information from me, which makes the torture feel almost arbitrary. I don't know if he's motivated by hatred for my family, even after all these years, or if he just enjoys torturing. After a while, I stop caring either way.

When I'm conscious, I try to think about Odessa, because her face keeps me grounded in reality. She reminds me that there's a reason I want to survive this, and wouldn't be better off just closing my eyes and willing the pain to stop.

I remember her dancing at the Ashwater estate on Alix's thirtieth birthday, hair and dress twirling, and catching my eye before glancing away. I remember arguing with her when she wanted to fight during the battle in Thorne's castle. Glaring at each other, while I wrestled with this overwhelming protective urge I didn't know how to explain, and I remember her kneeling on my bed in my dark room, looking up at me with fire in her eyes.

I remember other things, too. Or maybe I'm imagining them? In my head, we're walking down the hallway in my palace in Hydratta. We're sitting in the sun watching a race. She's standing on the deck of a ship, smiling at me. We're lying on a beach together, and she's bending over me, crying.

A part of me knows these visions never happened, while another part is sure they're real.

"Oh my gods!" Odessa yells in my head. "Kastian, can you hear me?"

I try to blink up at her. She's crying, and her tears keep splashing my face.

"Kastian!" Odessa says again, sharply. "Wake up!"

More tears hit me. I blink again and stare up into her face, then frown, confused. It's not Odessa, and she's not crying. A strange, dark-haired woman is leaning over me, splashing water on my face.

"Fuck!" the woman curses under her breath. "Hang on, I'll get more water."

She leaves, and I try to call after her, but can't make my mouth work. I must fall into unconsciousness again, but wake up again a short time later to more water splashing my face.

"Sorry," the woman says again, "I don't know how to do this if you can't sit up. Can you open your mouth at all?"

I don't know why I feel the urge to obey this strange, disembodied female voice, but I try to open my mouth. It burns, like the bones in my jaw are scraping against each other, and I groan.

"Good, that's enough!" the woman says.

I feel a splash of water hitting my face again. Some of it gets into my mouth, and I swallow a few times, then force my eyes open, blinking rapidly. I try to focus, and a vaguely familiar set of green eyes swims in front of me. "Lyra?"

"Oh, thank gods!" Lyra says frantically. "I thought you were dead."

Confusion overwhelms me. I haven't thought about Lyra Von Bargen in over a century, so why is she here in my hallucination? Bring back Odessa.

"Dessa?" I croak.

"She's in the castle," Lyra says quickly, tipping more water into my mouth. "She's fine, I think. Well, she's locked up, but she's not hurt."

Good. That's good.

I swallow a few more mouthfuls of water and blink again. I'm starting to realize that this isn't a hallucination. Magnus's daughter really is leaning over me, pouring water into my mouth. Maybe I should be concerned that she's working with her father, but I can't find the energy.

How long have I been here?

"It's been three days," Lyra says, as if reading my mind.

Only three days? I would have sworn it had been an eternity.

"I don't know what to do to help," Lyra hisses, almost like she's angry with me. "I can try to get a message to Odessa's family in Vernallis, but it would take days to get there, and my father will force her to marry him before then. The wedding is supposed to be tomorrow."

I try to force my mind to focus. *Three days. Wedding tomorrow. Odessa.*

It takes a long moment for that idea to sink in. When it finally does, rage floods me. I try to make my mouth move, but nothing comes out except another painful moan.

"Is there anyone closer I can contact?" Lyra asks. "Do you have friends nearby?"

My mind is sluggish, slow to connect her words to meaning, but I force myself to focus.

"Jett," I croak.

Lyra's eyes go wide with anxiety, and she looms over me, swaying in and out of focus. "Is that a person? Where do I find them?"

My eyes flutter closed again, and Lyra splashes a large amount of water on my face. "Focus, Kastian! Who is Jett? Where do I find him?"

"Border town," I manage. "By the river."

"Border town by the river," she echoes, "...that must be the village near the Weeping Quagmire. Alright. I'll try, just don't die before I get back."

I try to thank her, but the words get caught in my throat. Before I can make another sound, the vision of Lyra shifts again.

I must really be hallucinating, because I swear that Lyra morphs into a tall, bearded man right in front of me.

Lyra doesn't come back, and the next time I wake up, I wonder if she was ever really here at all.

ODESSA, AGE 16

Dear gods, where is he?

I push through the teeming crowd on the deck of the ship, eyes scanning every face for Kastian. I thought I saw him when I first arrived, but now I'm not so sure.

Of course this would have to be a masked ball. *Of course*, the one time that finding someone could mean life or death I'm forced to search every single masked face for a glimpse of familiar eyes.

The ship has been transformed into a floating palace. Strings of tiny, star-bright lanterns traced every rail and spar, illuminating the upper deck with a warm, almost ethereal light. Under the clear night sky, hundreds of finely dressed lords and ladies spill across the deck, laughing and dancing. The court orchestra, imported for the occasion, sits on a raised platform near the stern, playing a hauntingly beautiful melody.

But I'm not here to enjoy any of it.

My heart beats an erratic tempo, and my hands practically

shake with anxiety. What if it already happened? What if Kastian is already dead?

Earlier, after escaping Magnus's office undetected, I went searching for Kastian to warn him what the advisor was planning, but I couldn't find him anywhere. He wasn't where I left him in the garden or in any of the long winding halls. I didn't know exactly where his room in the palace was, so I went to lunch in the dining hall hoping to see him there. He didn't show up.

And of course, that was my fault.

I told him to stay away from me, and he did.

I didn't want to attend the ball this evening, but it was the only place I could think of that Kastian was guaranteed to be... except now I can't find him anywhere.

What if I'm too late?

A tall, unfamiliar man steps in front of me and holds out his hand. "Would you care to dance?"

I don't have time for this! "No," I say, rather rudely, shoving past the man.

Kastian could be already dead, or being murdered below deck, or—

Wait a second.

I spot a tall figure standing on the opposite side of the ship leaning on the railing. He's wearing all black, and his back is to me, but I still recognize his posture and the swirling black tattoos on his right forearm. Even more incriminating, Lyra Von Bargen stands beside him wearing a long periwinkle gown and a purple and black mask.

At the sight of her, anger surges through my veins. Is she here to kill him? I've never wanted to seriously hurt anyone in my life, but I suddenly feel like I could easily commit murder.

I grit my teeth and push my way through the rest of the crowd. "Kastian!"

I reach them, and Kastian swivels around to face me. I'm relieved the moment I see him still breathing, but the relief is short-lived.

Kastian is wearing a simple black mask that covers only his eyes and the bridge of his nose. Underneath it, his dark eyes, normally sharp and attentive, are now clouded and glassy. They seem distant and unfocused, as if his mind is somewhere else.

His unfocused eyes land on me. "You."

His voice sounds off, and I stiffen, alarm shooting through me. "What's wrong with you?"

"You," he mutters again. "What are you doing here, Princess?"

Princess? Ugh. At any other time, I'd demand to know what he means by that, but not right now. I ignore the comment and reach frantically for his arm. "I need to talk to you right now. Please!"

"I thought you never wanted to talk to me again," he scoffs and turns away from me, swaying slightly.

"I know, but this is important."

He chuckles, which only makes my panic shoot higher. He seems drunk, but I've seen Daemon drunk dozens of times and he never looked quite this...vacant. Like he's been drugged.

I spin furiously toward Lyra. "What the hell did you do to him?"

I falter as I come face to face with a woman I've never seen before. It's definitely the same person who's been standing here this entire time—the same periwinkle dress, the same dark hair —but behind the black and purple mask her eyes are unfamiliar.

"Excuse me?" the strange woman asks. "Who are you?"

I blink in confusion and I look back and forth between Kastian, who is swaying slightly, to the strange dark-haired girl in the purple gown. I swore a moment ago I saw Lyra standing here...I'm losing my mind.

"Um, sorry." I shake my head, turning back to Kastian. "Please, you have to come with me! I really need to talk to you."

There's clearly something wrong with him. He's not just drunk, it's something else. I'm never going to be able to reason with him like this, but maybe if I just get him below deck we can hide until the ball ends, or he's sober enough to tell his parents what Magnus was planning.

He blinks at me again, dazedly as I grip his arm and try to haul him away from the strange girl. Except he won't budge, not even an inch, and he's far too big for me to drag.

"Kastian!" I say again, sharper this time, sinking my nails into his forearm. I want to cry with frustration. "I said, it's important." My voice cracks. "If you ever trusted me, please—"

And then the world explodes around me.

A blast thunders from the direction of the bow, rattling the entire ship. Kastian nearly topples into me, and I instinctively grab onto the railing, anchoring us both as a flicker of green and gold light bursts overhead.

For half a second, I think it's an attack, or a signal, but then the next explosion is followed by a thousand gasps.

Fireworks.

People swarm to the rails, necks craned, faces tipped up to the sky. They push and shove to get the best view, and in the mayhem I lose my grip on Kastian and in a split second he disappears, swallowed up by the shoving crowd.

A lump rises in my throat and my eyes burn—more out of frustration than anything else.

I lurch back through the mass of people, elbowing aside a pair of tipsy noblewomen who shriek in delight at the fireworks and in disgust at my shoving. I scan faces, desperate, searching for his eyes behind every black mask.

Finally, I spot him for a second time—he's reached the far end of the ship, still weaving unsteadily with each step.

I break into a run, but my foot catches on the hem of my elaborate gown, nearly sending me sprawling.

Suddenly, a pair of masked courtiers sweep in front of me, laughing and tossing handfuls of confetti. The glitter blinds me; I cough and frantically wave the sparkling cloud away, but as my vision clears, my heart sinks.

Kastian stands against the railing, alone for the briefest

instant, before a masked figure emerges from the shadows behind a stack of empty crates. The man is tall and broad-shouldered, his mask a wickedly grinning fox, golden in the spray of fireworks.

I can't tell whether it's Magnus or someone else, but it hardly matters as the next moments unfold with a sickening slowness: the man lunges, grabs Kastian by the back of the collar, and wrenches him against the rail. Still unsteady on his feet, Kastian's arms pinwheel, his mouth opens in a silent cry—but the music and the fireworks swallow every sound.

He falls backwards and disappears over the edge of the ship, plummeting down toward the dark water. I scream his name, but no one hears it over the booms echoing over the water.

I don't think, don't hesitate. I sprint.

My body moves before my brain has finished processing what just happened.

I reach the rail and, without breaking stride, vault onto it, barely gripping the slick, salt-sticky wood as I throw myself over the edge.

There's a single heartbeat of freefall. The sound of fireworks and laughter and music all vanishes, replaced by the roar of blood in my ears and the whistling of wind past my face.

Then, I hit the water. The cold air is gone in an instant, and the ocean embraces me.

KASTIAN, PRESENT

Lyra doesn't come back, and the next time I wake up, I wonder if she was ever really here at all.

Magnus returns, and there are more sedatives; more knives; more pain.

Sometimes I think I hear footsteps, hushed whispers, but then they fade into the rest of my fever dreams: Odessa laughing in a rowboat. Odessa lying by the lake; and again and again, we're on the beach and she's crying.

Once, I catch the scent of salt water, and for a brief, delirious second, I'm back on my ship and Dessa is asking me why I don't want to be the king—but by the time I blink, she and the ship are gone, dissolved into the shadows.

At least the pain is consistent—burning, stabbing, blinding.

Maybe that's why the next time I open my eyes and the pain feels slightly less extreme, I think I must be dead.

I blink up at the stone ceiling above me, my eyes suspiciously clear for the first time in...days, I think?

I try to sit up and can't, which sends my mind reeling. If I were dead, surely I wouldn't still be bound to this table.

I blink again, harder.

My wrists are still bound tight, crusted with blood from old wounds and fresh ones reopening. My tongue tastes like iron. Surely, that must mean I'm not dead—but then, why has the pain abandoned me?

Heavy footsteps stomp across the floor. My stomach clenches, and I refuse to turn my head to look, already knowing it's Magnus. The stomping footsteps are always Magnus.

He comes to stand in front of me, and his hair is slicked back, his face clean and expressionless. He sets a mug down on the table beside my head, then sits on a stool and regards me with an air of cool detachment. "Welcome back."

I open my mouth to speak, but my throat is too dry, and nothing but a raw gurgling sound comes out.

Unbothered, Magnus reaches for the mug and, with a slow, careful motion, lifts it to my mouth.

I don't bother resisting. He can't possibly feed me anything worse than the sedatives he's been shooting into my arms, and if he wanted me dead, I would be. Maybe he's only keeping me alive for entertainment.

Or maybe he's waiting for something else.

The first sip of tea scalds my tongue, but I force it down, the warmth spreading through my chest. I cough, then clear my throat. "No torture today?" I ask, my voice hoarse from screaming. "What happened? Are you getting bored?"

Magnus sets the mug down, wipes my mouth for me, then leans forward, elbows on the table like we're old friends catching up over drinks. "Not at all," he says conversationally. "It's only that I have something to tell you, and the sedatives can cause severe confusion as well as pain."

I glare at him. He doesn't need to tell me that—I'm not sure what's real and what isn't. Honestly, this conversation could be happening in my head and I would never know the difference.

In case this is real, I grit my teeth and stare at the ceiling, determined not to give Magnus the satisfaction of eye contact. The stalactite overhead is still there, fanged and dripping; if I could reach it, I'd break it off and drive it into Magnus's heart.

"I wanted to make sure you were lucid enough to understand my news," Magnus says lightly. "Today is my wedding day."

I blink at him, the words not fully penetrating my sluggish brain. Wedding. Today.

He steeples his fingers, the picture of calm. "I wanted to be sure you understood when I told you that I'm marrying your siren this afternoon. She's going to be my queen."

A stab of pain shoots through my chest, worse than anything Magnus has been able to inflict.

Magnus keeps talking, but I can't hear him.

The bond that I've been ignoring for decades ignites, exploding inside me. It's not a gentle burn, but a bloody inferno. It's as if the bond has a mind of its own and would rather kill me than tolerate the idea of Odessa being forced to marry someone else.

I think back to that day so many years ago when I woke up on a beach near the castle, unsure what had happened the night before. My memory was hazy, but there was this overwhelming feeling in my chest. It was like a second heartbeat, but I had no idea who it beat for.

Now, I suddenly know that it was always for her.

I don't understand how it's possible, but I've never been more certain of anything in my life.

Every time my chest throbbed when I thought of her, and I assumed it was because she was a threat to the bond, it was really the bond trying to tell me she was mine.

When the oracle inked her likeness on my skin, it wasn't a mistake; it was a prophecy.

When I begged her to understand that I didn't want anyone else—couldn't want anyone else—even though everyone knows that it's impossible to betray your soul-bond, I should have realized what was happening. I wasn't a fluke, and the bond wasn't wrong—it was, in fact, doing exactly what it was supposed to do, because even the idea of some hypothetical other person could never compare with Odessa.

And now, I understand why it's impossible to betray your bond, because hearing that she's going to be forced to marry someone else is physical torture. The sedative is nothing compared to the sensation of a living bond being slowly, methodically torn apart.

Magnus pulls out another syringe. I barely even notice when he stabs it through my skin, then stands, adjusting his cuffs, and with a final, satisfied glance at my shaking body, he leaves. He's gone back to find Odessa, while all I can do is lie here, staring up at the stone ceiling.

My body burns and burns until my vision blurs.

I'm burning alive, and for the first time in all this agony, I want to die

ODESSA, AGE 16

I'm barely aware of my body changing as I dive beneath the frothing waves. I almost don't notice the scales coating my legs and torso or the webbing stretching between my elongating fingers. My body knows this is where I belong in a way that my racing mind cannot, will not, comprehend.

Not now, while my only focus is on finding Kastian before it's too late.

I plunge deeper into the shadowy ocean, the water cool and heavy around me. My head swivels from side to side as I squint against the sting of salt that nips at my eyes, making my vision blur.

He must be here somewhere. *He has to be.*

I propel myself further down, my webbed fingers slicing through the water. It's strange and unsettling to look at, but I can't afford to think about it right now. I can't think about how monstrous I must look, or the frightening "rightness" of the ocean around me.

I dive deeper, the unfamiliar pressure building in my ears, until a sudden glint catches my eye.

There, far below me, I finally spot a tattooed forearm and the sleeve of a black shirt billowing like a ghostly flag.

My heart races and I kick my tail, propelling myself deeper into the dark. *Down, down, down.*

Along the sandy ocean floor, hundreds of fish of every size and color dart out of my way. Crabs scuttle beneath rocks, and squids blend seamlessly into the swaying seaweed. I ignore them, concentrating on the unconscious prince bobbing just above the sand.

Kastian's body is limp, his dark curly hair forming a weightless halo around him. His eyes are shut, and bubbles drift from his parted lips. A heavy iron chain, anchored at the end, is fastened around his ankle.

My eyes widen. I didn't even see the masked man attach the chain, and I don't know how I'm going to break it.

A spark of panicked anger shoots through me as I grip the chain in both hands, pulling with all my strength.

To my utter shock, the iron links snap as easily as twine, and I drop them onto the sand.

My heart races with hope as I wrap my webbed fingers around Kastian's arms and pull upward toward the surface. I'm amazed at how he's not heavy, and how fast I can swim. Only moments ago, I couldn't have dragged Kastian across the deck if my life depended on it, but now, when his life really hangs in the balance, I'm different. I'm stronger.

Without warning, something moves out of the corner of my vision.

I jerk as a creeping dread crawls up my spine, and I turn toward the feeling of eyes boring into my back.

Out of the swirling water, three ethereal figures emerge, and I recoil, as the hope in my chest stutters and dies.

The sirens look nothing like the beautiful woman from the

beach. They have the torsos of women and the bottom half of ocean predators. Each of their faces is angular with enormous pupil-less eyes and tight, greenish-gray skin that appears to be pulled tight over their skulls with no flesh between skin and bone. Their hair flows like ropes of swaying seaweed, and rows of needle-like teeth fill their wide mouths. The two in the back have sleek and powerful fish tails, while the leader's hip bones end above a mass of writhing black tentacles.

A whirlwind of fear and fascination churns within me. I open my own mouth and run my tongue over my teeth, and jolt at the sharp prick of fangs. Looking down, I see my own powerful, glittering tail.

Absurdly, the only thought that passes through my numb mind is that at least I don't have tentacles.

Like she somehow read my mind, the squid-like siren floats toward me, her tentacles undulating. She opens her horrific jaws and gives me something like a smile. My eyes land on a familiar crown of coral and pearls atop her green hair.

I open my mouth to try to speak. I'm not sure what I mean to say, but it doesn't matter because no words escape me. The water distorts my voice into a chilling blend of melody and anguish, echoing like a song entwined with a scream.

The tentacled queen stiffens at the sound of my voice rippling through the water. She raises a hand to her companions, and they fall back, swimming in wide circles around us like sharks stalking prey.

The queen glides through the water with effortless grace. Her mesmerizing, fathomless eyes lock onto me with unsettling intensity. Her lips don't move, but her ghostly voice whispers in the back of my mind: *You're back far sooner than I expected.*

I shake my head vigorously and try once again to speak. *No, I'm not. I'm not here for you.*

She looks at Kastian's floating body, and in my head her tone is slightly sarcastic. Mocking. *What's this? Another man, lost to a siren's lure. Unfortunate...and tragically predictable.*

I shake my head. *No, that's not what this is. I've already seen that happen once. I won't let it happen again.*

The queen drifts closer, and her voice in my mind answers as if she can hear my thoughts. She sounds almost amused. *You already let it happen. He's already dead. I warned you this would happen. You don't belong on land, and the longer you stay the more people you'll destroy.*

No! I try to shout, even as I know she's right. The bubbles have stopped rising from Kastian's mouth, and his body feels heavier in the water. *I can still help him.*

The siren responds as if the thought was intended for her. *You can't. You won't reach the surface in time.*

I can't keep my thoughts from leaking out for the siren to hear. *Please, help me.*

The siren's expression does not change. She doesn't blink, or even open her mouth, but somehow I know she's laughing at me. *Help you? Why would you assume I can do anything?*

Can you? I think desperately.

She gives me another wide, terrifying smile. *Perhaps, but what would you give me in exchange?*

Anything.

She drifts even closer—so close I can see the faint shimmer of luminescent patterns undulating beneath her skin, casting sickly green shadows across Kastian's slack face. Around us, the other sirens circle, watching the drama unfold with idle, predatory fascination. I clutch Kastian closer, his body growing heavier, colder, every second. The queen's power presses at my thoughts, relentless and insistent. *I'll save him for you, but when I do he won't remember you. It will be as if you never existed.*

I reel back. *He won't remember me? Why?*

The song of her mind seeps into mine, cool and unhurried, rolling over my panic like the tide erasing footprints in the sand. *That's just how it is. Would you rather he die, clutching the memory of you to his drowning chest?*

My eyes narrow, and my thoughts whip out of me before I can

contain them, frantic and stinging. *But why would you do that? What good does stealing his memory do for you?*

The siren queen's eyes narrow, her long tentacles curling in a lazy spiral. *Oh, dear, this isn't for me. We haven't even gotten to my payment yet. This is just the price of magic. Large rewards require large sacrifices, and this, my dear, is a very large reward.*

My teeth clench. I won't let him die. I won't.

Fine, then I'll tell him. I'll make him understand.

I wouldn't do that if I were you. There's a slow, syrupy amusement in the way her gaze lingers on me, as if she's savoring a delicate morsel. *Magic doesn't look kindly on loopholes, and there's no telling what could happen if you try to evade our bargain. Until the day your prince dies, he will never remember you and you will never be able to speak of your past together.*

My head pounds, my thoughts hammering in time with the beat of my heat. *My voice and his memories?*

Yes. That is the price of his life...I believe you said you'd be willing to give up anything.

Anger and grief hit me so hard it nearly drowns me. For a moment, I'm paralyzed in the water, clutching Kastian's arm, staring into the horror of what I've just agreed to, and what I'm about to lose.

Fine. I think bitterly. *Save him.*

A cold, predatory satisfaction glimmers in the siren queen's bottomless eyes. She drifts in closer, and I am trapped, nose to nose with her. *We haven't yet discussed my payment,* she hisses in my mind. *If I do this for you, in exchange you will return to the sea where you belong and serve me.*

Serve her? As what? Some monstrous creature, haunting shipwrecks and luring sailors to their doom?

My eyes flick desperately to the other sirens, the ones circling us like sharks, their hungry stares so intent I can almost feel them on my back.

In my mind, I see myself among them, my skin grey and stretched tight over bones, my teeth monstrous, my eyes gone flat and glassy, a predator stripped of memory or hope. Is that what waits for me on the other side of this bargain?

When would I have to come back? I think desperately. *Will I have time to say goodbye to my family?*

They're not your family! Her angry thoughts whip out as if to sting. *We are your family. This is where you belong.*

I shake my head. *No, no it isn't.*

The siren queen's face shifts, and for a moment I think I see pity in her—then it's gone, replaced by a predatory glee. *Fine, then I'll grant you this one more gift: There is no time limit for when you must return. You may spend centuries lying to yourself if you wish, but all sirens return to the sea eventually. One day, you'll realize you are no exception. You won't be able to resist the call of the sea, and you'll return. On that day, we'll find you. Wherever you are in the world, we'll know, and we'll come to collect.*

I'll just never return, I think in a panic, almost believing it.

The queen's mouth stretches wide, and she laughs, a soundless shriek that shudders the water. The circling sirens join in, their voices braiding together in a discordant, predatory chorus that makes every muscle in my body want to flee.

You may try, the queen says, her thoughts curling around mine like a promise and a curse. *But it is your nature, Odessa. You cannot choose what you are.*

I want to scream at her that she's wrong, that I belong to myself, not to any queen or curse or ocean. But the words dissolve in the water before I can even form them.

I look down at Kastian's limp body, his features growing gaunt, almost translucent, as the thin last shreds of life leak from him. Something inside me breaks.

If I have to become a monster to save him, then fine—I'll be the worst monster this ocean has ever seen.

I grit my teeth and glare at the queen. *I accept. Save him.*

KASTIAN, PRESENT

"He's in here!" A distant female voice shouts. *"Quickly, before someone sees us!"*

There's pounding footsteps, the creak of a door, and then a man swears. *"Fuck! Kas? Kas, can you hear me?"*

I hear the question, but it slips through my brain like water over sand.

"We're too late!" the woman hisses.

"No, we're not," the man replies. *"He's still breathing. Kas, come on, wake up."*

"I'm sorry, mate," chimes in another man. *"If he's not dead yet, he's most of the way there. I don't think—"*

"Don't you fucking finish that thought," the first man snaps. His voice is more familiar than the others, but I can't place it.

My sluggish brain struggles and fails to give meaning to all the yelling; to connect names to these vaguely familiar voices. I want to open my eyes, but I can't. I'm trapped in some strange place between sleeping and waking; between life and death. It feels as if a thousand tons of water is pressing down on me, and I'm not sure if I'm drowning or burning.

"What the fuck did they do to him?" the familiar man asks.

"Not they, he. *My father did this,"* the woman says grimly.

Her father did this?...who?

And then, it comes back to me. All at once, I remember where I am—*who* I am—and the realization causes an avalanche of emotions.

I'm overjoyed and relieved that I now recognize the voices around me. Lyra is back, and she brought Jett with her. The other man must be Connell.

At the same time, all the pain in my body returns at once. It's as if it was suppressed while I was floating half out of my mind, but now it's returned with a vengeance.

I don't care—I can tolerate it for just a bit longer now that help has arrived.

"If Kastian isn't dead yet, he's heavily sedated," Lyra says. "The problem is that those drugs build up, and after a while he'll be too paralyzed to breathe."

"You say that like you've seen this before," Jett says dangerously.

"I have," Lyra replies flatly.

I immediately try to take a deep breath and discover that Lyra is right. I can't move an inch, not just because of the restraints on my arms and legs, but it's as if my muscles have fused together. I feel my shallow breathing beneath a chest that refuses to rise, and a fresh wave of panic grips me.

"Someone needs to tell Odessa," Lyra says.

"Are you out of your mind? I'm not telling Dessa anything until there's absolutely no choice left."

If I could, I would shout in agreement. They can't tell Odessa that I'm dying, because I'm not. I won't. I'm going to get off this table and go find her.

"We're there, mate—there *is* no choice left," Connell says grimly. "I'm telling you, he's bloody—"

"What the fuck did I just say?" Jett barks. "Do not finish that sentence!"

"Stop yelling," the woman says. "Odessa thinks she's marrying my father so he'll set Kastian free, but if he's already dead, someone needs to stop her."

A lead weight lands on my already strangled chest. She's going through with the wedding willingly? For me?

I both love and hate her for that, and I can't decide which emotion is stronger.

"Go," Jett says. "We'll stay here and wake him up."

Lyra mumbles something I can't catch, but I hear the door close and assume she's left. A hand lands on my shoulder, and someone leans over me. "Fucking hell," Jett breathes. "Pull that damn knife out of his arm."

"You sure? The bleeding might make it worse," Connell says.

"Just fucking do it! We need to get him up and to a healer."

"If you say so, but I have to tell you, as something of an expert on death myself, he's not going to recover."

"Yes, he will. We didn't survive decades in frozen fucking hell for him to die now."

I've never appreciated Jett more; if only I could make myself sit up and tell him so.

Pain burns in my arm and I feel the blade I didn't even realize was still there being extracted from my wrist.

"I'm not a good healer," Jett mutters, "The great fucking irony is, Kastian is the only one I know who can use that kind of magic."

"This is Hydratta, mate. You can't swing a dead fish without hitting a healer, but I don't know how much good it will do."

"Fine," Jett barks. His tone keeps rising, clearly growing angrier by the second. I've never heard him so upset, not even in prison. "If not a healer, then I'll find a sorceress or a djinn or... something." He trails off, grunting with effort as he seems to try to undo the binding around my ankles.

"You'd need more than a djinn for this. You'd need a miracle," Connell grumbles.

"Then I'll get a fucking miracle! I am not going to be the one who has to tell Odessa or Daemon that I let Kastian die. It's not happening." His voice changes, growing curious, and I get the feeling he's looking over at Connell. "Wait, you're immortal. That's a damn miracle, right?"

"That's different."

"How?"

Jett's tone is so dangerous that Connell must realize he's on thin ice. He answers frankly, without any of his usual idiotic comments. "I'm immortal because I'm cursed to captain *The Sea Witch*."

"Sounds great!" Jett yells in exasperation. "How do we get another curse?"

If I could, I would go stiff. A curse doesn't sound ideal, but then again, I know there aren't a lot of options. I'm weak from blood loss and lack of food and water. That burning sedative has been building up for days, and I can tell I'm not breathing normally.

"It's not that simple, mate," Connell says.

"Can it be done or not?"

"Maybe, but I wouldn't recommend it. Your friend might not thank you if he wakes up cursed. It's not pleasant. I'm not even sure I'm really alive."

"You look pretty fucking alive to me!" Jett nearly yells. "He can be pissed at me later once he's alive again. How do you curse him?"

Connell doesn't answer Jett. Instead, his voice grows louder, and I can feel him leaning over me. "Hey, can you hear me, mate?"

He pauses like he's expecting me to answer him. My frustration rises, if I could just open my mouth... My entire body feels heavy and useless, and I can't force my lips to move.

Like he can read my mind, Jett cuts in. "Kas, if you're in there, blink." His palm slaps my cheek—a gentle one, by his standards—

and I work every last ounce of will to drag my eyelids up and down.

Jett's exhale stutters, almost a laugh, but it's broken at the edges. "He heard me!"

"That's something, at least," Connell mutters, sounding dubious. "I don't feel right trapping a man into this without even asking."

"Now you're growing a conscience?" Jett asks, incredulous. "What about not feeling right about letting him die?"

"Alright, alright," Connell grumbles, leaning close to me again. "Do you want to live? Blink once for yes, twice for no."

I'm surprised to find that I have to think about that for a second. Of course I want to live, but not like this. The worst hell I can think of would be to not die, and just be trapped like this; aware, but unable to move or speak. Unable to do anything while Magnus keeps stabbing me and holds Odessa prisoner.

If I'm trapped like this for the rest of time, it would be a far worse curse than anything Connell could put on me. Nothing could be worse than this. If I'm doomed to be trapped on this table, just waiting to die, I'd rather end it now.

"Blink!" Jett shouts near my ear. He reaches out and lifts one of my eyelids for me, and I get a blurry glimpse of his face and the ceiling beyond before he drops it closed again. "Come on, Kas. Dessa is here somewhere, and she needs you."

I gather far more strength than should be necessary and focus on opening my eyes again, just for a second. It takes an enormous effort, but my eyes finally flutter open.

I hope it's enough, and it must be, because Connell continues. "Alright, listen carefully because once it's done there's no going back. *The Sea Witch* is no ordinary ship. As long as she sails, she needs a captain, and that captain can't leave his post until another one is chosen. Not even death will end your service to the ship. Once you take command, the ship will be your entire life, and you must sail at least six months of every year until the end of time or another captain takes your place. This has to be your choice. I can't force it, but if you're willing, the ship will do the rest."

He lets his words hang heavy in the air.

I feel like there must be more to this—there must be a reason that Connell is the way he is, and why he calls his immortality a curse. Maybe it's just that being trapped eats away at you, and leaves you changed. Maybe it will be like Dyaspora, where hopelessness bleeds you dry, chipping away piece by piece, until you're not the same man who first arrived.

There's a moment where I see a vision of myself, drained and haggard, eyes gone white with salt, standing on the deck of a ship made of bones and teeth. I see the horizon, always just out of reach, eternity strung out like a noose. I see myself returning, year after year, to a world that forgot my name.

But then I see Dessa, violet eyes furious and alive. I see her laugh, and I know that I'll never get enough of that sound, no matter how many centuries I serve. I see her future—a future without me, maybe, but one where she's free.

If I have to become something monstrous to save her, then I'll do it. I die for her a thousand times over, so what's different about living for her?

Before I even have the chance to blink my acceptance, I feel something shift.

A cold wind seems to pass over me, raising every hair on my body. My heart beat turns erratic, thundering faster and faster until it finally stops. A long beat passes where my pulse doesn't pound, but my chest doesn't feel empty. The bond is still there, pulsing and alive.

My heart starts again, a single pulse, and I gasp and open my eyes.

ODESSA, PRESENT

The ocean is calling to me.

I'm standing at the window, looking out over the sea. The waves crash against the small, rocky beach beside the castle in time with my breathing. It feels as if the water is reaching out to me. Like it knows that there's no other option for me but to sink beneath the waves.

It's been four days since I was locked in the tower. I know that there's still a chance of getting out of this—of Daemon arriving in time to find Kastian and keep me from being forced into a marriage, but everyday my hope dwindles a little more and the call of the sea grows louder.

Magnus hasn't returned to the tower since the first day, except once to ask me to write a letter to Daemon and Alix telling them that I'm safe.

I wrote it, but only because I was sure that they'd be able to read between the lines and know that we're in trouble. I'm sure they'll come to help, with or without their budding army, but I don't know how long it will take the letter to reach them. By the time they get it, it might be too late.

I could be married and Kastian could be dead.

He might be dead already.

I try not to have that thought; try to shove it firmly from my mind every time it pops into my head, but it's becoming harder and harder with each passing day.

I try to remind myself that I'd know if he died because we're bonded, but that thought is only more terrifying. It's not as if I have years of experience of how a bond is supposed to feel. Apparently, I wasn't even aware of it for over a century, so how can I be sure that I would know if he was hurt?

Even now, when I focus, I can't feel anything. Kastian seems distant and unreachable.

A sharp knock sounds at the door. I don't even bother to look away from the window. I know that whomever it is—servant or soldier—will come in anyway no matter what I say. Sure enough, the doorknob turns and the hinges creak.

"Odessa?"

I glance over my shoulder. There's an unfamiliar servant girl standing there wearing a slightly too large dress. She's holding a bundle of white silk.

"Whatever that is, put it on the bed," I say without inflection.

The girl shuts the door behind her, but doesn't move to release the bundle of fabric.

I look over my shoulder again at her. Her face is screwed up, as if in concentration.

"Didn't you hear me? Put it on the bed."

"Shut up for a minute, I'm trying to concentrate," the servant says sharply.

My eyes go wide in surprise—it's probably the most emotion I've shown in days, but that barely registers. "What did you say?"

The girl says nothing, then before my eyes, she changes.

Her limbs grow longer and she shoots up several inches, her body shifting to fill out the too-large dress. Her dishwater blonde hair darkens and lengthens, and her small eyes grow larger in her skull.

I step back against the wall, alarmed. "What the—"

"Shh!" Lyra Von Bargen says, shaking out her arms. "Don't scream or anything, then they'll know I'm in here."

I gape at her, and it takes me a long moment to find words.

"You're a doppler," I finally blurt out the first thing that comes to mind.

She raises her eyebrows. "Obviously. I wouldn't have been able to come up here as myself. My father has a dozen guards on the stairs making sure you don't escape."

I shake my head in complete and utter disbelief, then blink at her a few more times, trying to pull myself together.

The last time I saw Lyra was from beneath Magnus's desk in his former office, and before that it was when she was threatening me in the hall outside my guest room. That feels like an entire lifetime ago—no, it *was* an entire lifetime ago.

"What are you doing here?" I demand.

"I came to help," she says. "This is your wedding dress—" she holds out the bundle of white fabric. "—put it on, and I'll walk you out of here pretending to be a guard."

"Why would you help me? We were never friends."

"I know," she says flatly. "Maybe I feel guilty about that."

I scoff. "Doubtful."

"Believe whatever you want," she says dismissively. "But you're not going to find anyone else willing to help you so you'd better decide now if you can live with trusting me."

I shake my head as if to clear it. I need a second to think.

Perhaps I'm feeling a bit numb at the moment, because the shock of seeing Lyra after all this time is quickly dissipating. Even watching her change her appearance right in front of me isn't as surprising as it feels like it should be. What does shock me, though, is that Lyra would ever want to help me. "I'm not going anywhere with you until you explain yourself."

"Oh sure, it's not like we're in a hurry or anything. Shall I let you braid my hair while we pour our hearts out to each other?"

I scowl. Even as she's offering to help she sounds a bit aggressive—spiteful, even. "You're Magnus's daughter. Why would I believe this isn't a trap?"

Her face twists in disgust and her eyes flick away from me. She lets out a long sigh. "Fine. You're the one on the short timeline, not me. What do you want to know?"

My mouth gapes open like a fish. What do I want to know? *Everything.*

"Where's Kastian?" I ask.

She winces. "Please don't ask me that first. I promise I'll tell you, I just think you should get out of this tower first."

My heartbeat speeds up, thumping relentlessly against my ribs. "Why?"

"Because where he is won't change where you are, and in less than an hour a real guard is going to come in here and take you downstairs to marry my father, and then I won't be able to help you anymore."

My heart starts pounding faster. Less than an hour? I hadn't realized this was all happening so soon. I hadn't realized that it was already too late.

I glance at the window, where the water is still just visible on the horizon, then turn back to Lyra. "I don't trust you."

"I wouldn't expect you to, but I'm not here to hurt you. If I were, I would have done it already, and I would have done it using someone else's face."

That's not a bad point.

"Why would you want to help me?"

She takes a deep breath. "Because Magnus cannot gain more power. It would be catastrophic to all of Ellender, and using you he would have nearly unlimited influence."

I raise an eyebrow. "You don't want your father to gain more power? That doesn't sound like you."

"Magnus isn't really my father," she snaps, noticeably not commenting on whether or not she's behaving like herself.

Remembering that Magnus already told me he can't have children, I look over Lyra, scanning her face. She's tall and willowy, with olive skin, green eyes, and long brown—almost black—hair. In short, she doesn't look anything like her supposed father. Magnus is pale and blonde with grey eyes. More importantly, though, Magnus's features are painfully ordinary. For whatever else can be said about Lyra, no one could deny she's striking.

"You're adopted?" I guess.

She scoffs. "'Adopted' is a strong word for what he did. He bought me."

"Excuse me?" I blurt out, instantly alert. "He *bought* you? What does that mean?"

Lyra crosses her arms over her chest and glares at a point slightly over my right shoulder. When she speaks, it comes out monotone. "My parents were extremely poor and I had many siblings. I was one of six or seven, I think, it's hard to remember now." She frowns, her eyes growing distant for a moment. "Anyway, Magnus learned of my shapeshifting abilities when I was very young. I don't know how he found out, but he went to my parents and offered to buy me from them and take me back to Hydratta."

I gasp, horrified. "And they just sold you?"

"They had half a dozen other children to feed." She shrugs as if it doesn't bother her, but her expression is tight. Clearly, this bothers her very much.

"Why would he want you?" I ask.

"He thinks long-term and always wanted power. He thought I'd be useful." She scowls again. "It was similar to how he's kept you in the back of his mind all these years."

I shudder. "He's delusional if he thinks I'll ever let myself be useful to him. I'd rather die first."

She frowns. "I wish I could say the same. For years I sought his approval and did all sorts of horrible things just because he asked me to. Just spying at first. I'd turn into someone else and walk around the castle, then report back what I'd heard. Later, when I got older, he'd sometimes send me on more complex missions. I'd have to steal things, or sometimes plant evidence to be found later. For a long time I drew the line at killing anyone myself, but I certainly helped orchestrate murders even if I didn't lift the knife."

"How old were you when you went to live with Magnus?" I ask, frowning.

"Five. Why?"

"Then whatever you did, it's not your fault. You were too young to know better and your parent was telling you what to do and praising you if you did it right."

"I know," she says briskly. "I don't blame myself, I blame him."

We share a dark look.

"I'm sorry," I say after a moment, knowing that words aren't nearly enough.

"It's fine," she waves me off. "Aside from the occasional times he'd ask me to transform into someone else to spy on the court, I wasn't treated badly. Magnus wanted others to believe that I was his daughter so he treated me like I was. I was raised here at court and had the best of everything. Tutors, clothes, jewelry. In many ways my life was probably better than it would have been with my family."

Again she sounds bitter, but this time I get it. I'd be more than just bitter if this had happened to me—I'd want revenge.

"I don't know what Magnus told King Sebastian and Queen Marbella about how I came to be there, because he'd already been working for them for decades at that point and was high up among the advisors and obviously couldn't suddenly have a five-year-old child with no explanation. He probably said that my mother was dead and he just learned I existed, or something like that. Magnus is very good at weaving stories."

It dawns on me that she's calling him "Magnus" and not

"Father." That seems significant, but I don't want to derail her and ask why—or rather, when—she stopped thinking of him as her parent.

"Magnus was convinced that the best way to gain power for himself would be to tie me to the existing royal family. I was betrothed to Prince Kastian more or less as soon as Magnus brought me to court, when I was five and he was three. By the time I was nine, I was being trained to be the perfect royal bride."

"Perfect for whom?" I ask.

She laughs without humor. "That's a good question, honestly. Kastian and I never really liked each other much. I was taught to be completely subservient and obedient, which never interested him."

I raise an eyebrow. "I know."

"Right, I suppose you do." She frowns, looking pensive. "Anyway, the plan was that I would marry Kastian, his parents would meet a sudden and unfortunate end, and I'd be queen. Then, as my father and the former top advisor, Magnus would swoop in to help rule the kingdom."

"And eventually Kastian would die too, right?"

"Exactly, but of course then you came and ruined everything." She almost smiles, and I get the feeling she's joking. Or at least, isn't all that bothered by my "ruining" her plans.

"I heard you talking about it once," I tell her.

She narrows her eyes. "You heard me talking about what?"

"Your betrothal...and your father's plans."

I hope she picks up the story from here because I don't know how much I can say out loud. I've never wanted to test the boundaries of the vow I made to the sirens in case I accidentally crossed the line and something horrible happened as a result.

Thankfully, Lyra grasps what I'm getting at. "I wish you hadn't heard that. Though, I suppose, it makes things easier. Obviously that plan failed too—Kastian didn't die while you were all visiting Vernallis."

"I know," I say stonily.

I want to add, "because I wouldn't let him," but I can't. Lyra doesn't seem to notice my internal battle.

"As I'm sure you know, it took several years after that for Magnus to work out a new plan to take the kingdom, but eventually he did it. By then he'd decided that it would be simpler to take the kingdom outright rather than through my marriage or some doomed war. He spent years bringing courtiers and soldiers over to his side, until finally he had enough support to ambush the royal family in their beds. I helped him do it." She gives me a challenging look, as if expecting me to condemn her.

I'm uncertain how I should feel. On the one hand, I sympathize with Lyra, but on the other hand, she was enmeshed in multiple plots to murder Kastian and his family.

"Did you kill anyone directly?" I ask.

She shakes her head. "I guess it's a good thing Kastian and I knew each other, because without me he wouldn't have lived any longer than his mother and sisters."

"What do you mean?"

"I was the one who my father sent to kill Kastian the night of the coup. By forcing me to wear his face, Magnus could give the impression of being in many places at once, which added to his mysticism as a ruler. I'm sure you've noticed how loyal his soldiers are?"

I nod, thinking of the guard who slapped me. "Yes."

"That's because he's got many of them convinced that he can be in multiple places at once. They think he's omniscient, that he knows and sees everything they do and judges them even when they're alone."

I shake my head in disgust. I wasn't that far off when I said the guard must have thought her king was a god.

This information is exactly the kind of thing I wanted to learn by coming here in the first place. Whether Hydratta became an ally or enemy of Vernallis, Alix and Daemon need to know that the Hydrattan citizens won't simply accept the removal of a king they've been brainwashed into worshiping.

It's too bad that now I may never get the chance to warn them.

"So why did you spare Kastian?" I ask.

Her eyes dart to the side, like she'd also been lost in thought and forgotten what we were talking about. It takes her a moment to return to her story. "On the night of the coup, Magnus wanted to capture King Sebastian himself, so he sent me after Kastian. When I got to his room I must have closed the door too loudly because he woke up and looked right at me. After that, I just couldn't do it. Stabbing him in their sleep was one thing, but I didn't want to fight it out or watch him die. Kastian and I might never have liked each other much, but we'd still known each other practically our whole lives. I didn't want to kill him—I didn't want to kill *anyone*."

"Thank you," I say hollowly. "For not killing him."

She laughs harshly. "Would you still thank me if I told you I wondered for years if I did the right thing? My father called me a coward and punished me for decades over it, and in the end I don't think I really helped Kastian at all because he got sent to Dyaspora instead, and I've heard that's worse than death."

I stare blankly at her. This is all so desperately sad and twisted, I'm not sure what I should think. I just feel numb.

"Why are you really here, Lyra?" I ask finally. "Why tell me all this?"

She sits up straighter, rolling her shoulders. "Because I want to help."

I assess her. "Why?"

"Because my father is the definition of evil."

I choke. "On that we can agree."

She scowls. "He can't be allowed to control the kingdom any longer. There's so much more that I know that I could tell you... why he's been obsessed with allying with Vernallis, what he wants to do with Ellender..."

"It's for precisely that reason that I wanted to come here in the first place. I never had any intention of getting married, but we—Vernallis, I mean—needed information. I know Magnus can't be allowed to simply exist beside Vernallis, and our court will need to do something about him, even if Kastian never wants to take his throne back."

Lyra winces. "He won't be taking his throne back."

"I know, he doesn't want to—"

"No, that's not what I mean." She looks pained. "Shit, I meant to get you out of the tower first before talking about this."

"About what?" I ask dangerously.

She closes her eyes. "I came up here to help, yes, but also to tell you that you don't have to marry my father to try and save Kastian...because he's already dead."

I hear her, but the words don't penetrate.

The world reels. I hear her say it—hear the syllables, register the words—but my mind simply refuses to shape them into a reality that can exist.

That's impossible. It can't be dead, because I can still feel the bond pulsing in my chest. He can't be dead, because most people don't survive the severing of a bond.

"You're lying," I hiss. I shake my head, still not fully comprehending. "I don't believe you. That's impossible. I would have felt it."

Lyra's brow wrinkles. "Felt what?"

"The bond," I say, clutching my chest, as if I can dig through bone and muscle and find the evidence Lyra has missed. "It—it's still here." I press my palm harder, expecting to feel blood or maybe a name seared into my skin, but there's nothing except the anxious, frantic beat of my heart. "I would have known."

Lyra looks away. "Maybe you haven't processed it yet. Maybe it takes time."

"It doesn't take time," I shoot back, too sharp. "Bonds don't just linger after death. They snap. They shatter. People have—" I falter. "Some people die from it. If he were dead, I would know."

"I'm not lying. I knew he would be in the dungeon where my father always keeps prisoners. I got to him a few days ago, then I went and found some people to help...but when we got back he wasn't responsive."

"Wasn't responsive?" I ask sharply. "That's not the same as dead."

"In this case it is—or, it will be. My father likes to use this sedative on his victims. It paralyzes your entire body while causing extreme pain."

She shudders, and I'm suddenly certain beyond a shred of doubt that Magnus has used it on her before. I remember like it was yesterday, hiding under the desk while Lyra tried to say she didn't want to kill anyone and Magnus warned her what would happen if she disobeyed.

Lyra swallows thickly. "If you use enough sedatives over time, or too much at once, the body forgets how to breathe and you suffocate, all the while fully aware of what's going on. That's the point Kastian was at right before I came up here, and there's no antidote to the sedative, so even if he's not dead yet, it's only a matter of hours. I'm sorry."

My ears ring and I stare blankly into space.

Maybe that's why I didn't feel the bond break? Or maybe it's just that I don't know what I'm supposed to feel. Maybe I'm defective and our bond is broken, and now I'll never get a chance to fix it. It's too late.

"I'm sorry," Lyra says again. "Really, I am. I didn't want to be the one to tell you, but I thought you deserved to know. You shouldn't get married because you think my father will let him go...that would never happen anyway."

What am I supposed to do now?

I feel numb—distant—as if I'm someone else standing off to the side and watching myself sitting on the bed. I nod, or at least try to, but my head is too heavy, as if it might snap off my neck.

If Kastian is dead, then what's the point of any of this?

My eyes land on the ocean, and I swear, it's as if the water calls out to me, begging me to go home.

KASTIAN, PRESENT

"Maybe you should take it easy for a minute," Jett says, without even a hint of his usual smile.

I've been awake for barely five minutes, and already the pain of the last several days is starting to feel like a distant memory. Like a nightmare that happened to someone else, rather than the thing that nearly killed me.

The thing that did kill me-—at least, I think it did. I don't know what else it could mean that my heart felt as if it stopped beating.

"You nearly died," Jett adds, clearly thinking along the same lines that I am. "Just wait a second before you run off and try to die again."

His eyes widen and he seems to remember at the same time as I do that's not going to happen. I'm not going to die again...ever.

Thinking about it is too much, so I don't. I shove the idea to the back of my mind and turn to look around the dungeon. "Where are we?"

"Under the castle," Jett answers.

"I knew it. But then, how did you find me?"

"That woman came and found us."

"Lyra?"

"Yeah," Jett says, still frowning. I'm not sure if his expression is due to worry over me, or something to do with Lyra.

"I thought she was mad," Connell interjects. "If it had been up to me we wouldn't have come after you...no offense, mate."

I look over, narrowing my eyes at the pirate, who is leaning against the wall looking slightly winded. As I watch, he slides down the dark stone wall to sit on the floor, and I notice for the first time that he's not bound with the belt anymore. When did that happen?

I turn to Jett. "You let him go?"

Jett shakes his head. "Not exactly, but we've come to an understanding."

My brow furrows, but I don't ask. There are more pressing questions on my mind. "So Lyra found you? I can't believe she cared. Why did you trust her?"

Jett digs in his pocket and pulls out a piece of paper, thrusting it at me. "She had this letter that Dessa must have written—or been forced to write—to Daemon and Alix. She refers to Magnus as 'just as wonderful a ruler as King Thorne.'"

I take it and scan it quickly. It's exactly as he said, Odessa was trying to write something that Magnus would allow to be sent to Daemon that would still alert him she was in trouble. It's so smart, and so very her. "Where is Odessa now?"

"She's in the castle," Jett answers.

"I have to go get her."

"Obviously," Jett agrees, a hint of his usual smile returning. "But you won't be able to do anything for Dessa if you collapse. At least have some water. When was the last time you ate?"

"*I'm fine,*" I say again, more pointedly.

Actually, "Fine" doesn't even begin to explain it. I feel entirely reborn. Alive. Perhaps better than I ever have before...although, all my sudden energy seems to have come at a cost.

"Are you alright?" I ask, glancing back at Connell.

The pirate looks up, and flashes a shaky grin. "I'm better than fine. Right as bloody rain, don't worry."

Jett and I exchange dubious glances. There wasn't a lot of time for Connell to explain exactly what I agreed to, and I'm not sure if my life comes at the expense of his, or if he's merely weakened by the ordeal.

As callous as it is, I'm not entirely sure I want to know right now. I don't want to think about what I might have done to myself, I want to go find Odessa. If I can't get to her, then what was the fucking point?

I take another large step toward the door. "I'm going to find her."

Connell looks up at me, and winces slightly. "You two go on ahead. I'll catch up."

Jett glances at the pirate again, and looks more conflicted than I would have expected, before turning back to me. "Fine. We'll come back for him later. You and I have a wedding to crash."

I take the lead, running out of the dungeon and into the long corridor outside.

We run down the rough-walled hallway to a door at the end and shove it open, stepping through, I stop short, taking in the familiar white stone hallway. My heart pangs and my stomach turns uncomfortably.

"What's wrong?" Jett hisses, skidding to a stop before he runs into me.

"Nothing," I mutter, shaking my head. "I just didn't expect to care."

"Care about what?"

"This was where I lived. It's just familiar, that's all."

"That's a good thing if you ask me. If you didn't know where we were going we'd be fucked. This place is huge."

I nod and sprint down another white-walled corridor, then another. We reach a winding set of white marble stairs, and run up them, two at a time.

"He doesn't post a lot of guards," I comment. "Maybe they're all posted outside the wedding."

"There were guards on our way in here," Jett says, panting a little from all the running. "That woman from before—"

"Lyra?"

"Yeah. She turned into someone who must have been important, because she just kept telling the guards she was bringing Connell and me down to the dungeon as prisoners and no one looked twice at her."

My eyes narrow. "What do you mean she turned into someone important."

"She's a shapeshifter. Didn't you know?"

I shake my head, pressing my lips together in a flat line.

Lyra Von Bargen is a doppler, and she just helped save my life —and Odessa's life too, maybe. Of all the fucking shocking things that have happened today, that might be the most unbelievable.

We barrel down the corridor, sprinting through the castle until the white corridors bleed into each other, and the only marker I have left is the gathering sense of dread—the certainty that every second we spend running in place is another second Magnus is closing in around Odessa.

Lyra said they were keeping Dessa in the tower. There are a dozen fucking towers in this palace, but I have to assume—have to hope—she meant the tallest one. Otherwise, it might take hours to check every single turret, and by then, it might be too late.

I'm not worried about the wedding—not exactly. There's no legal wedding in Ellender that would supersede a soul-bond, and I'm positive that's what Dessa and I have. It's not the wedding, it's after. It's what Magnus might do to her, or it's her believing I'm not coming to rescue her and whatever reckless thing she might do to try and save herself.

"How long was I down there?" I ask Jett as we cross the entrance hall and I lead the way through a door and up more and more stairs.

"I don't know exactly, why?"

"I remember Magnus coming to tell me he was going to force Dessa to marry him, but I don't know if that was today or yesterday or if it even happened at all. I hallucinated all sorts of shit."

Jett's expression turns dark. "Fuck, man, I'm sorry."

I blink at him, confused. It's not his fault Magnus is a sadistic psychopath. He's the one who came to help me, so why—

All at once, I get it.

Jett is Daemon's spymaster. It was an easy role for him to assume when all of us suddenly found ourselves helping to run Vernallis alongside Daemon and Alix. Jett is personable, a good liar, and great at getting out of tough situations...he's also fairly good at torturing people.

None of us really know what his life was like before Dyaspora. We've only ever heard the rose-colored stories, but I'm sure it wasn't all so wonderful. He was poor to the point of starving in a way that I never understood until these last few days. He was sent to prison for life for stealing a single loaf of bread, and somewhere along the line he clearly learned how to hurt people who hurt him. Now, I get the impression that he's waiting for the other shoe to drop—for me to realize that what he does for Vernallis is too similar to what Magnus did to me.

"It's not the same," I say shortly.

Jett looks confused. "What do you mean?"

"Magnus likes causing pain. It's different."

His black eyes widen for a second then his face blanks, which for him means returning to his usual grin. He laughs. "I know that, of course. Who knows, maybe one day I'll get a chance to take a crack at old Magnus and we can find out who's got a steadier hand."

"Mmm," I mumble, still not entirely sure he believes I don't blame him for any of this. "So, what day is it? When did Magnus last visit?"

Jett shakes his head as if to clear it. "If he told you about the wedding, then that was earlier today," he says, as he climbs the stairs behind me. "Lyra said Odessa was going along with it because Magnus told her he would kill you."

"Dessa's not stupid, she had to know he'd kill me anyway, eventually."

Jett swallows thickly. "Yeah, she probably did know. I think she was holding out for her letter to get to Daemon, but obviously it never did."

"It got to you," I say roughly. "I'm only standing here because of you."

Rather than smiling, his face falls slightly. "I don't really know what Connell did to you; soon you might not be thanking me."

"I agreed to it. It's on me, and I don't care what it was as long as I can get Odessa back from Magnus."

"You love her, then?" he asks—though it's more of a statement than a question. "What about your soul-bond?"

I open my mouth to tell him it's her—it's always been her, but then stop. That feels like the kind of thing I should say to Odessa before I say it to anyone else, and only once we're safe. I won't be able to breathe again until Magnus is dead and we're miles away from Hydratta.

We reach the top of the tower and stop in front of the door. Dread washes over me when I see that there are no guards posted here either. If Dessa were truly inside, there should be soldiers stationed outside, even if most have abandoned their posts in the hallways, or sent elsewhere for some reason.

Jett strides up to the door, his boots thumping against the ground. With a swift, forceful kick, he sends the door swinging open.

We step inside and my eyes scan the room, frantic, mapping the overturned chair, the untouched platter of food, the window thrown wide.

She's not here.

I expected it, and still the realization is like a cold fist closing around my gut. I run to the window, pressing my hands to the stone sill. The drop below is dizzying, sheer white walls plunging into jagged rocks. No rope, no marks, no sign anyone left this way.

"Fuck!" I roar, smacking the frame with my open palm. "Where is she?"

Jett circles the perimeter of the room, eyes narrowed. "Are you sure she was even here?"

I nod. Not only do I somehow just know she was here, I can smell her. Her scent lingers: ocean and wildflowers, a memory of her that clings to the air, mocking me.

Some small, sadistic part of me wonders if she left willingly. It would be a very Odessa thing to do to go through with the wedding if she thought it might save me. I can't even fault her for it.

Jett leans out the window, scanning the grounds below "They must have taken her somewhere else."

"We need to check the throne room. If they've already started the wedding, that's where it would be."

Jett nods and follows me back out the door. I take the stairs back down two at a time, heart thudding so loud it drowns out the world.

Then, before I've even reached the bottom, the echo of slow, deliberate footfalls on the stairs reverberates through the dimly lit corridor. Jett and I freeze, our breaths catching in our throats.

As Magnus comes into view, I'm not at all surprised. Over the last several days, I've become intimately familiar with those footsteps, but now, I'm excited to hear them.

Magnus stops short several stairs down from me. For a second, we lock eyes. His face contorts. His mouth opens slightly, yet nothing comes out. His face is locked in a slack-jawed grimace of disbelief, as though he can't quite process what he's seeing. Can't grasp that I'm here, and somehow made it out of the dungeon alive.

My lips tip up in a sneer. "Shit, I don't think I've ever seen you speechless before. For once in your fucking life you don't have anything to say."

Magnus doesn't answer me. His complexion turns ashen, and he cranes his head over his shoulder, shouting backwards down the stairs. "Guards!"

The stairwell echoes with the slap of boots and the metallic clatter of weapons. Jett grins and reaches for the short sword in his belt, but I'm not even planning to let them get close enough to cut.

With a flick of my hand, I draw the moisture from the air, the condensation beading on the cold walls, and shape it into a whip-thin ribbon of water that hovers, quivering, at my fingertips. I unleash it in a tidal wave that rises, growing wider and wider as it tears down the steps.

The soldiers' screams echo off the walls and Magnus's eyes go wider. He stands rooted in place, his face gone corpse-pale. Then, to my absolute satisfaction, his pale brown wings flicker into view behind him.

A laugh tears from my throat, loud and slightly hysterical. "You fucking coward."

Magnus spins on his heel, panic etched on his face, and bolts toward the stairs. I laugh, and lunge after him. My fingers curl around the fabric of his jacket, halting his escape.

Instinct takes over. The blood rushes hot in my veins, drowning out every other sensation. I grab him by the lapels, hoist him off the ground, and slam him into the closest wall. The impact echoes like a thunderclap. Magnus's head snaps backward, colliding with the stone. His jaw works open and closed, but nothing comes out except a thin, pathetic wheeze.

"Look at you," I hiss. "You know you're fucked, don't you."

"Don't you...dare—" he wheezes.

I laugh again. "You weak, pathetic, coward. You were only able to kill my family while they were sleeping. You could only keep me subdued while I was drugged, and now you need your guards to save you because you know that I can kill you without even breaking a sweat.

He chokes, trying to get words out as I shift my grip to Magnus's throat, pinning him against the wall with one hand. His eyes bulge, the blue irises ringed in frantic white. He claws at my hand. I let him flail for a few seconds longer, just to make sure he understands that he's powerless. "You're lucky I don't get off on causing pain, and I'd rather just kill you now. It won't even be hard, like squashing a bug."

I slam him backwards again and again until his head cracks against the hard stone wall and his body goes boneless. I release Magnus's limp body, watching as it crumples to the floor with a heavy thud.

"Is he dead?" Jett asks, more curious than anything

Kneeling beside him, I shake my head. "No. That would be far too fucking easy."

I rifle through the pockets of Magnus's jacket, turning them inside out.

"What are you looking for?" Jett asks.

I don't answer until my hand closes around a cool, metallic object in his pocket. I extract a syringe, its needle glinting under the dim light. "This."

"What is it?" Jett asks.

I smile slightly, then shove the syringe at Jett. "Here. It's a new tool for you to try. Just because I don't enjoy causing pain doesn't mean you should miss out."

Jett's black eyes flash with interest and his lip curls in a smile.

I leave Jett to handle Magnus. I hope that by suggesting he exercise his talents he realizes that I'm not bothered by them, but I make a mental note to have a longer conversation about it at a later date.

Then, I sprint down the wet stairs, leaping over several unconscious guards.

I'm not worried about the wedding now, just Odessa. Maybe Lyra got to her and helped her escape? Maybe she got out on her own? I have to—need to—find her.

I run down the hall, past the closed dining room doors and the stone pillars along the balcony railing that open up onto the gardens below. I pause, panting, and look out over the grounds.

Beyond the colorful garden and low iron fence, the ocean is wild, and the sky stained gray as if it might rain. I sweep my gaze over the rocky cliffs, searching for movement on the small beach. There's nothing, and I'm about to turn back when—*there!*

My heart thunders in my chest as I spot a redheaded figure in a white dress. She's alone, standing right at the edge of the water, staring out over the waves. Relief and excitement wash over me and I grip the railing, leaning over to shout her name. "Odessa!"

She doesn't hear me and I watch, helpless, as Dessa steps into the surf. My relief shifts into confusion and then dread so fast I can barely keep up with my own wild emotions.

Dessa wades up to her knees, but doesn't stop there, walking straight out, into the freezing, churning water. Her white dress is suddenly translucent, clinging to her skin, and her hair whips behind her in wild, streaming ribbons.

Cold panic slices through me, and for a second my body freezes on the balcony, paralyzed by the realization of what she's about to do.

I launch myself down the stairs, taking them three at a time. I burst out into the gardens and sprint toward the iron fence. My boots sink into the mud, and I nearly trip on the uneven stones, but I don't slow down.

The ocean is louder here, pounding the rocks in a sick, relentless rhythm. I reach the fence and vault over it, nearly tumbling down the rocky cliff.

Odessa is already thirty yards offshore, the water at her waist. Her face appears unchanged, but even at this distance I can see the scales crawling up her arms. The waves crash around her, salt spray flying, her head bowed against the wind. I skid to a halt on the sand, and cup my hands around my mouth and scream again. "Dessa!"

Finally, she stops, the water now nearly at her throat. She turns toward me, a question in her eyes, and the shock and recognition is so pure on her beautiful face that it steals my breath.

And then, right before my eyes, a long, dark tentacle snakes out of the water and pulls her beneath the waves.

I shout—half surprise, half agony—and before I've thought about what I'm doing, I pull my shirt over my head and toss it away, and step into the surf.

The cold water licks at my skin, but I don't feel it. Following in the footsteps of thousands of men before me, I dive beneath the dark waves, chasing after a siren, prepared to drown rather than lose her to the sea.

ODESSA, PRESENT

That was Kastian on the beach. Alive. I saw him!

My breath catches in my throat, and I don't get a chance to breathe before I'm suddenly pulled beneath the rolling waves. It's an odd sensation to gasp and take in water instead of air, and even stranger when I don't choke.

I feel the last of the change ripple through my body—feel my bones shifting and skin stretching beneath the water. The last shreds of the enormous wedding dress I was wearing tear and float away.

The last and only time I transformed into the other me, it had been so quick and seamless that I hardly felt it. This time, it was drawn out, slow, and uncomfortable to change bit by bit as I walked slowly into the water, unsure if I wanted to commit fully to the ocean.

I should have realized that I never really had a choice.

The siren queen grips me tight in her writhing tentacle, reminding me uncontrollably of the sea monster that destroyed Captain Connell's ship. I struggle, but it's impossible to escape.

I have to, though. I have to get back to the surface. I need to know for sure...

The tentacle circles my waist and even with my increased strength I can't pull free. The queen pulls me down, down, down into the dark until we're face to face. *I told you that you'd return someday.*

No! I think frantically. *Wait! I'm not ready.*

Her ethereal voice sneaks into my mind, soft and gentle as a lullaby. *Not ready? You've had decades, my dear. What else could you possibly want?*

I stare into the queen's black, inky gaze. She appears unchanged, as if it was only yesterday I last saw her. Only yesterday that I bargained away Kastian's memories and my voice to save his life.

Beyond the queen's writhing tentacles, there are dozens, perhaps even hundreds, of sirens—far more than I ever saw at one time or even realized existed.

Stop thrashing, the queen's ghostly voice scolds me. *You chose this.*

I don't stop, kicking my tail and pushing against her tentacle winding tighter and tighter around my torso. *Let me go!*

I will once you've convinced me that you're here to fulfill our bargain. Look at the others, Odessa. In the water, we are as one.

I look beyond her terrifying face toward the others. Most of the sirens possess tails akin to fish, shimmering with iridescent scales that catch the light and dance with every subtle movement. Some have more dolphin-like features, their sleek bodies gliding with an effortless grace. Some are holding tridents or rough-hewn clubs, while still others are wearing decorative veils woven from fishing nets. They're all gazing at me in unison, their glassy eyes vacant and unblinking, like toy soldiers waiting for a command.

Is that what will happen to me? How long until I'm just another set of vacant eyes?

As if the question was meant for her, the queen answers me. *Only the queen may give orders or act of her own free will, and there cannot be two of us. I told you many years ago that there is no room in the ocean for a siren who refuses to join the pack. You knew what would happen if you entered the water.*

I'm at a loss for words, because deep down, she's right.

I should have known that stalling wasn't an option; that the second I dipped so much as a toe in the sea, I wouldn't have any choice.

I did know, actually. I was fully aware of the consequences when I returned to the water, yet I went through with it. Just moments ago, it felt like my sole path to freedom.

With Kastian gone and no help from Vernallis before I'd be forced to marry Magnus, an eternity beneath the ocean hadn't seemed so bad.

Except, Kastian *isn't* gone—I just saw him—and now I need to get back to the surface no matter what it takes.

Forgetting for a moment that I can't speak out loud, I open my mouth and a desperate, haunting cry escapes, a warbling, guttural shriek that vibrates not just the water but the bones in my skull.

As one, the vacant eyed sirens turn to look at me. A few even shift, as if to reach toward me.

In the same instant, the queen's glassy eyes widen and her grip slackens, her tentacle slipping from my waist. I twist and pull with all my strength, feeling the cool, slick surface of her tentacle slide away as I finally break free. *Yes!*

For a dizzying, glorious moment, I'm free.

Victory swells in my chest and I throw myself upward through the water, my new limbs propelling me in a frantic spiral, every muscle straining toward the barely-there shimmer of the surface.

Then, my heart stops. I freeze in place, as I see a familiar silhouette, strong and tall, plunging toward me through the blue-green haze.

For one wild heartbeat I think it's a trick, a hallucination, some echo of my own longing. But then he grows clearer, unmistakable. My heart pounds in my chest as I spot Kastian slicing through the water with powerful strokes, his gaze locked onto mine, the distance between us closing alarmingly fast.

My heart stutters and my vision darkens around the edges. I knew I saw him, but I'm not entirely sure I believed it until now.

Kastian is alive, and he's *here.*

His face is set in a kind of desperate focus, but there's unmistakable fear there too, a terror I've never seen him wear before. He's not looking at the queen, or the writhing mob of sirens, or even the black abyss below—he's looking only at me, as if the rest of the ocean is just background noise.

Just like I can hear the siren queen, I can hear Kastian's thoughts, erratic and loud, like he's screaming over himself, every single thought broadcasted at once. *Need to find her. What is that fucking thing? Can't breathe. Not leaving you, Odessa.*

I hear my own name through the din of jumbled thoughts, and latch onto it.

Kastian, no! Go back! I shout in my mind, trying desperately to make him hear me.

Evidently, he can't, because his erratic internal monologue doesn't slow for even a second. *Lungs burning, can't breathe. Should be dead. Don't fucking touch her.*

He clearly can't communicate in his head, and doesn't realize that I—we—can hear his every thought. I don't understand how he hasn't had to go back up for air yet—why isn't he drowning? How much longer until he does? Or, will the other sirens attack him first?

I kick my tail harder, new, unused muscles burning as I slice through the water, eyes locked on his distant silhouette. If I can just reach him before the sirens pull us both back down, maybe we can both return to the surface.

It's a desperate, naïve hope, a fragile thread, but I hold onto it with every ounce of strength I have.

We're only feet apart when the current shifts. Two sirens appear on either side of me. Their vice-like hands hold both my arms, tugging me back like the undertow. I thrash against their grip, blind panic surging through me, but their hands—webbed, inhuman, merciless—hold me fast.

I scream, and another unearthly wail escapes my mouth. The sound vibrates through the water, and the sirens holding me stop moving. They don't release my arms, but it's almost as if they've been stunned into inaction.

The screams upset them...or maybe it's a command?

I open my mouth again, but before I can do anything another ghostly wail comes reverberating up from the deep.

The queen's scream is different from mine—full of rage rather than terror. Kastian hears the scream too, and his body jerks as if he's just been stabbed. He stops swimming, treading water with desperate kicks, his whole focus zeroed in on me.

Behind me, the siren queen's scream turns into something like a laugh; a hollow, bubbling sound that starts in her chest and seems to echo from every direction. The other sirens join in until it's a ghostly, horrifying chorus of sound.

The queen's voice breaks through the chorus, clear in my mind. *Like every other siren before you, you must sever all ties to the land. If you are too weak, then I'll do it for you.*

The sirens restraining me tighten their hold, their cold fingers biting into my arms to keep me in place as the siren queen glides by, her tentacles undulating in deliberate, menacing circles.

A thick, sucker-lined tentacle snaps around Kastian's ankle with the speed of a whip. He hardly has a moment to realize what's happening before she pulls him down, twisting him in a disorienting whirl. He fights back, thrashing and kicking, but the queen is so much stronger. She drags him down into the black water, out of sight.

My heart jumps into my throat and I act on instinct. I rake the ragged edges of my nails across the nearest siren's face.

Her flesh shreds like kelp, releasing a torrent of inky-black blood that clouds the water around us. The pain stuns her, and she reels back, but still, she doesn't let go of me. After a second, it's as if I never hurt her at all. Her glassy eyes stare at me, unphased, even as her own blood fills the water around her.

I don't understand it and I don't have time to think. Panic wells up in me and I scream again in frustration, a raw, shredding note of rage and terror.

For a single heartbeat, all the sirens freeze. The two sirens holding me falter, their grip slacking.

And all at once, I get it.

It's not that the noise upsets them, it's that they react to it. In the water, the sirens are of one mind—only the queen can give the orders, and there can only be one queen.

I don't waste the chance—I pull free from the sirens and I kick my tail, propelling myself after the queen and Kastian.

From somewhere down below, a reverberating musical note floats toward us. At the sound, the siren closest to me recovers, sharp fingers reaching for me. I evade her fingers, swimming as fast as I can past the other glassy-eyed sirens.

Except, they're not so glassy-eyed anymore.

Some are still frozen, but others are moving, waking up. As I pass, one hurls a trident at me—one of those ancient, three-pronged ones, built from bone and coral and flecked with rust.

I see it spinning toward my heart and time slows. My hand moves before I can think to command it. I catch the trident mid-spin, momentum nearly wrenching my arm from the socket. The impact vibrates all the way into my jaw.

Far below me, I see the queen. She's dragging Kastian deeper, nearly reaching the very bottom of the ocean.

It seems as if he's still moving, struggling to free himself. I have no idea how he's not drowning. Maybe it's his magic? He did something because this time he knew he was going into the water? Maybe it's something else, but at the moment I don't care.

I tear after them, still clutching the trident, and behind me, I can feel rather than see the other sirens hunger and anticipation. The pack is feverish—starving—their bloodlust electrifying the water.

The queen wraps two of her tentacles around Kastian's chest, one around his throat, and another coils about his ankle, pulling him in a corkscrewing spiral. He claws at the tentacles, but the queen is too strong. The more he fights, the tighter she squeezes. He's being crushed alive.

My chest spasms with a panic so deep it seems to reverberate outward. I feel the sirens behind me grow nervous, some of them let out ghostly wails of their own, adding to the collective panic.

Stop! I shout—half in my head and half out loud, the sound coming out in a long, keening wail.

Kastian looks up and his eyes lock onto mine. His gaze burns and I feel the bond throbbing warm in my chest.

In the same instance, the queen turns to look at me too and her lips peel back in a hideous grin. *You pitiful, insolent child. Can't you see that I'm doing this to help you?*

I don't answer—don't hesitate. I draw the trident back and slash, aiming for her torso.

The queen's eyes widen, and for a moment I see pure shock on her face. Somehow, even now, she didn't believe I'd want to hurt her.

Her tentacles whip around, catching me hard across the cheek. *You'll destroy anyone you care about. I'm helping you!*

Her blow sends a shockwave through my head, but I barely feel it.

I drive the trident forward with every ounce of fury and fear and love I have ever known. The barbs pierce her side, ripping through cartilage and muscle and bone.

Her body convulses in a spasm so violent that she drops Kastian entirely. Dark inky blood flows out of her body, turning the water black. And for a heartbeat her thoughts flash through me—an electric jolt of agony and rage and something like pride.

I scream, a triumphant, guttural howl, and the sound ignites the sirens. Some scatter, some dart toward me to help, while still others let out screams of their own, the ghostly cries ringing through the water so loud that I'm sure they can be heard up above.

ODESSA, PRESENT

Kastian and I erupt from the sea, gasping.

I cling to him, and he to me. For a moment, we just hang there, suspended, both of us too exhausted to move.

Below us, the sea is still roiling. I can feel the rioting chaos of the sirens awakening. I can hear their tangled voices roaring over each other, screaming, wailing, their thoughts now fractured and disjointed. A thousand hungry voices with no conductor.

It's so loud I can't think. I can barely swim, Kastian grips my waist and pulls me toward shore, until at last, we collapse onto the rocky beach.

The moment we touch land, everything goes silent.

"Dessa?" Kastian asks, voice strangled. "Are you alright?"

Am I alright? I don't know. I can't speak. I can't even find words to describe what I am right now.

Overwhelmed.

Exhausted.

Alive.

Dazed and silent, I push myself up, bracing my arms against the damp sand, and look around.

The beach is empty. The air smells of rain, and the sun has shifted behind a cloud, turning the sky a strange blue-grey, like a storm is coming.

When I glance down at my fingers, they're normal—not webbed or elongated into claws. That's a relief.

That is, until, Kastian's dark eyes dart toward something behind me and widen. I turn my head to look, and I'm startled to realize that we haven't made it that far out of the sea. We're lying on the sand, just barely beyond where the waves are lapping at the shore. His feet are still in the water, and mine...aren't there at all.

"Fuck," I blurt out, suddenly finding my voice again.

I pull my tail in, trying to scramble further onto the sand. Scrambling with a tail isn't all that graceful, and I flop forward, nearly falling face-first into the sand, before catching myself against Kastian's shoulder. He laughs, in an exhausted, humorless sort of way.

I toss my hair back to glower, the image of the terrifying, hideous sirens flashing in my mind. "How can you laugh? I'm sure I look monstrous right now."

"You don't."

My frown deepens. "Don't lie."

"I'm not. All this—" He gestures toward my face and chest, "—is normal. It's just your, uh, tail. Here." He bends down and picks me up, tail and all, and carries me further up the beach. By the time he sets me down again, the tail has shrunk back into two legs—albeit with an impression of scales along my feet and calves.

I sit on the sand and pull my knees up to my chest, wrapping both arms around them. Kastian sits next to me and we're silent for a moment, watching the waves crashing against the beach.

I don't know what to do—what to think. Kastian is alive, I'm alive, the siren queen is dead, and I don't really understand any of it.

Kastian reaches over and his fingers curl into my hair. He turns my head, forcing me to look at him. "Say something."

I exhale a long breath. "You're an idiot."

He blinks rapidly. "Excuse me?"

"You heard me! What were you thinking?

I only realize that I'm yelling when he shouts back, matching my tone. "What was *I* thinking?" he roars, "*You* threw yourself into the fucking ocean. I was *thinking* I had to find you."

"You could have—no, you *should* have drowned. How were you breathing? Any man should have died ten times over."

"I keep telling you, Princess, I'm not just any man."

"Arrogant prick. I—" My voice cracks. "I thought you were dead!"

"And you thought that meant you could leave me?" He grips my hair harder, squeezing painfully. "Nothing is going to take you away from me, not even death."

Emotion explodes in my chest. The bond and my pulse fall into sync, making me hyper aware of my own thundering heartbeat. I'm not really sure if we're arguing, or just processing all the pent up emotions of the last several days—the last several decades, really.

I want to believe him. I want everything to be alright now that neither of us died and I can feel the bond strong between us. I want this to be the beginning of something rather than the end; Except...

"Could you hear what the siren said?" I ask, no longer yelling.

He shakes his head. "No, just a lot of screaming."

"She said it's in our nature to destroy anyone we care about. I could still end up hurting you, we don't know—"

He shakes his head, cutting me off. "I'm not worried about it."

"Why?"

"Do you know where we are?" Kastian asks, by way of answering me.

I frown. "Of course, what—"

Kastian sits up and looks me dead in the eyes. "This is the same beach where you left me,"

My breath catches in my chest. "Where I left you, when?"

He doesn't answer immediately, glancing out over the water as if seeing far more there than I can. My racing heart thunders with anxiety, and finally, I can't take the silence any longer. "When?" I ask again, louder.

"You know, it's the strangest thing." He says slowly. "When Magnus was torturing me I thought I was dying. I was sure I died, actually, but then Connell woke me up."

"Connell?" I demand, "What—"

"I'll explain everything in a minute, just listen. When I woke up I had all these memories I'd never had before...of you."

I gape at him. "What do you mean?"

"I mean, I remember you. I remember everything."

My mouth falls open with shock, and I can only stare at him, a thousand questions racing through my head.

And then, all at once, I understand.

Until the day he dies he'll never remember you and will never be able to speak of it.

"You died."

"Maybe only for a moment." He grins. "Apparently it's not even the first time. Maybe all sirens really do kill the men who love them, but I already died twice for you. I think that's enough."

His words pound in my head. *The men who love them.*

A smile spreads across my face and I let out a startled laugh.

We're both alive. We're here. And he remembers me.

I launch myself at him, and he raises both hands instinctively to catch me, both of us tumbling backwards in the sand.

I press my lips to his and for an instant, the kiss is a gentle collision—relief turned physical—but then Kastian's mouth slants over mine with a sudden, reckless hunger, and it shifts into something else. Something hot and greedy.

He pulls me closer and I slide my hands up his bare chest, fingers brushing against the tattoo of my face.

I pull back, abruptly, breaking our kiss long enough to look down at the tattoo. "You realize what this means, now, right?"

He nods, the tip of his nose nearly brushing my cheek. "Honestly, even before the memories came back, I think I was half certain what it meant already. I knew I loved you when I was eighteen years old. There was never a world where you weren't going to be mine."

I grin, at a loss for words, and he rolls me so I'm straddling his lap, knees digging into the sand. I clutch his shoulders, digging my nails into his skin, and I'm suddenly all too aware of my nakedness, and I realize, somewhat belatedly, that we're out in the open, fully visible from the windows of the castle.

I could not possibly care less.

I feel reckless, invincible. Maybe it's the knowledge that we both died a little to get here.

I lower my mouth to his for another kiss, harder this time, teeth clashing and lips bruising. His hands slide down my sides and over the backs of my thighs. Delicious anticipation blooms in my belly and I roll my hips.

My movement draws a raw, involuntary groan from deep in Kastian's chest. He pins me with his dark gaze, before pressing his mouth to my breast, hot and wet against my skin, tongue circling my nipple, laving and biting in perfect, merciless rhythm.

I arch my back, and Kastian digs his fingers into my ass, yanking me closer.

I let out a little gasp as my sensitive core comes in contact with his belt buckle, and I reach between us with fumbling fingers and undo his trousers. He moves his mouth to my other breast as I reach beneath his waistband to wrap my fingers around his hard cock. He hisses, hips jerking, and his teeth graze my nipple, just enough to sting.

I stroke him, marveling at the heat and weight in my palm, the way his breath stutters when I squeeze just a little harder.

I tighten my grip around the base of him, feeling the heat pulse through my palm. I let my thumb slide over the ridges and veins of his cock, delighting in how his whole body arches up into my touch, desperate and ragged. The muscles in his stomach flex as he tries to keep from thrusting into my hand, and for a moment, I savor the way he lets me take the lead.

I drag the head of his cock slowly between my legs, just barely letting it graze where I want him most, savoring the slick, throbbing ache there. His dark eyes never leave mine, and he looks almost angry with need. His hands are braced hard against my waist, fingers trembling as he fights the urge to just flip me over and fuck me into the sand.

"Dessa," he rasps, voice strained and shredded. "Stop fucking teasing."

I give him a wicked, lopsided smile. "What? You're not enjoying yourself?"

"I'm dying," he growls, and the way he says it, half-joking and half-furious, makes me laugh.

I lower my mouth to his neck and bite softly, which sends a full-body shudder through him. I rise a little higher on my knees and let the tip of him push past my entrance, just the barest inch before pulling back.

I glance down, watching the way my body takes him in, and the sight makes my whole stomach flutter. I lean forward and trap his bottom lip between both of mine, sucking on it as I let myself sink down further, impaling myself on his cock.

He groans, low and obscene and utterly helpless, but the sound is lost as at that moment, thunder rips across the sky and lightning flashes making the hair on my arms stand up.

Kastian tilts his head back and looks up at the darkening sky. His brow furrows, but before he can say anything I reach for his face, clamping my hands on either side of his rough, stubble-covered cheeks, and pull his attention back to me. Our eyes lock as I rise, sliding him nearly out of me, and come back down filling myself once more.

My hands fall to his shoulders and my nails dig into his skin as I ride him, grinding my hips in slow circles and feeling him twitch and throb inside me. With every thrust, my breath catches and my muscles clench tighter, drawing him in even further.

The sky flashes bright again, and raindrops begin to fall, cooling my burning skin.

Kastian starts moving his hips, shallow at first, matching my slow, rocking rhythm. Then, he curses under his breath and grabs my hips in both hands, finally losing enough composure to thrust upward hard and fast.

I cry out, burying my face in his shoulder, biting down to keep from screaming out loud as the beginnings of an orgasm begin to grow in my belly, sending little sparks of pleasure over me. I roll my hips, taking him deeper, losing myself in the desperate, punishing pressure.

"Fuck," Kastian says, an honest, broken sound, and I smile, drunk on the power of it. "You feel—"

"I know," I gasp, bracing my hands on his chest and rising up, then sinking back down, hard, until I see stars.

The rain falls faster, coating our skin and soaking my already wet hair. Kastian lets out a sound that's half growl, half groan, and when I tilt my hips in just the right way, he nearly doubles over, forehead pressed to my shoulder, teeth grazing the curve between my neck and collarbone. It sends a jolt of electricity straight down my spine, and I shudder, clenching around him, savoring the way his composure unravels thread by thread.

The next time I rise up on my knees, Kastian's hands clamp down on my hips. For a split second, I'm suspended—weightless, raw with anticipation. Then he wrenches me up and off him in one fluid motion.

I make a noise that's somewhere between a moan and a whimper, reaching for him instinctively, but before I can even form the words to complain, he's already flipping me around.

My back hits Kastian's chest and I stare out at the stormy ocean. The waves churn and lightning streaks across the dark sky, as Kastian's arm wraps around my middle, holding me up and guiding me back down on his cock. My knees nearly buckle, legs trembling as I try to stay upright

His left arm anchors me against his torso, and the right slides around my hip, tracing a line up my body. He palms my breast, fingers rough, then drifts back down, over my quivering stomach, and lower still.

His fingers brush my clit, gently at first, then harder, rubbing slow, perfect circles, each one syncing with the relentless rhythm of his thrusts.

My head falls back against his shoulder, a strangled cry escaping my lips. The pleasure is so immediate, so overwhelming, I can barely breathe.

I claw at his forearm, fingers digging in as the pressure builds to an impossible height. I am nothing but need—raw, feral, desperate.

Kastian buries his face in the side of my neck. "You're mine," he says, voice ragged. "You've always been mine.

I whimper and my legs shake violently, toes curling in the sand, and I can feel myself about to shatter. Kastian's hand works me faster, harder, never letting up, and soon I'm writhing in his lap, clawing at him. All I can do is ride the sensation, the sharp edge of pleasure building and building until it's too much and I cry out, the force of my orgasm racking through me. My vision whites out, my whole body going limp.

The sensation is too much—so intense I nearly pass out, and maybe I do, for a heartbeat, because suddenly I'm on my back in the sand, Kastian above me, his face flushed and wild.

He slides back inside me with a slow, punishing thrust, and the aftershocks are so sharp I almost sob. He's careful, though, slower now, letting me set the pace as I cling to his shoulders, nails raking down his back.

I wrap my legs around his hips, pulling him closer, deeper, and our bodies slide together slick and easy, like we were designed to fit this way. The storm is ripping the sky open above us, but it's nothing compared with the storm inside my chest.

Just when I think I can't take any more, he tenses above me. His muscles go rigid, every line of his body straining and shuddering, and then he's spilling into me with a groan that's equal parts pleasure and pain.

He moans my name, voice cracking, and I feel my own orgasm flare up again, smaller but just as sharp, rippling up my spine and making my toes curl in the wet sand.

He collapses on top of me, chest crushing mine, and for a long time neither of us moves. The rain hammers down, soaking us to the bone, but neither of us lets go.

He buries his face in my neck and I close my eyes and listen to the thunder, the rush of the rain, the wild pounding of his heart against mine. For the first time in forever, I feel safe.

Eventually, Kastian props himself up on his elbows and looks down at me, his expression soft and searching. He brushes the pads of his thumbs across my cheeks, wiping away the tears I didn't know I was still crying.

"You okay?" he asks, voice hoarse and threaded with concern.

I nod, letting a shaky laugh escape. "Better than okay." And I mean it. My body is spent, but every piece of me feels knit together, as though something broken in me finally set right.

He grins, wide and a little smug, and kisses my forehead before rolling off to collapse beside me in the sand.

The sea is a wild, frothing thing just a few feet away, and the air tastes like salt and electricity. I stare up at the sky, watching the lightning fork across the clouds, and realize that every part of me is still humming from the aftershocks.

"Did you ever think," I murmur, "that it would be like this?"

He snorts, a genuine and unguarded sound. "No. I hoped, but... no."

Kastian reaches over and twines our fingers together, giving my hand a reassuring squeeze. I turn my face to his, and he's already watching me, eyes dark and warm.

"We should probably get dressed and go inside," he says, though he makes no move to do so.

I close my eyes and sigh, content to let the rain wash over me a while longer. "We could stay like this. Just for a few more minutes."

He laughs. "As you wish, Princess. I'm not going anywhere."

And for the first time in my life, I believe him.

ODESSA, PRESENT

Finally, the rain slows and reality creeps back in.

Kastian explains briefly that Jett and Connell are here, and that we don't need to worry about Magnus anymore. I've said before that I don't like torture, but after what happened to Kastian, I hope Jett enjoys himself.

I stand up and go in search of something to cover myself with, finding the shreds of the discarded wedding dress tangled in the rocks along the water, and drape the ruined fabric around myself like a dress, securing them with a bit of discarded rope.

"You look ridiculous," Kastian laughs, eyeing my makeshift dress up and down. "No other woman on the continent could pull off wearing that."

I grin and spin around to show him the back. "So what you're saying is I'm pulling it off?"

He laughs again, and picks me up, spinning us both around before he lowers me back down to the ground, letting my body slide down his chest, and pressing his lips to the side of my throat, nipping at my pulse.

I grin, but shove him away. "Stop. We have forever for that, we need to go inside."

"We don't *need* to do anything. At least, not immediately."

"We should find Jett, and Lyra, I suppose. Is she on our side?"

Kastian shakes his head. "No idea. If I wasn't so focused on you I'm sure I'd be more shocked to see her again after so long. Did you know she's a doppler?"

I nod. "She's the one who helped me escape the tower— although it sounds like if I'd just waited a little longer for you to find me we could have avoided a lot of this."

Kastian looks toward the ocean. "What do you think will happen to them now?"

"To whom? The sirens?"

He nods. "It's ironic, but it was Magnus of all people who told me nearly everything I know about sirens. They have the capacity for independent thought, obviously," he nods to me, "but they don't use it. They're a hive mind controlled by a single queen."

I bite my lip, thinking of how the sirens reacted when I screamed—how the tentacled queen warned me over and over that there could be only one ruler of the sea. "I think..." I clear my throat. "I think I could lead them if I wanted to. I can't hear them now that we're on land, but I still feel them I think. They're awake for the first time in who knows how long."

It's one of the many things I love about Kastian that he doesn't immediately tell me what he thinks I should do. Instead, he just asks: "Do you want that? To be their queen?"

I laugh. "No. All I've ever wanted was to be right here with you...but I suppose it's good to know the sirens are there if we ever need them."

He cocks his head. "What would we need them for?"

I shrug. "I don't know. Why do Daemon and Alix have an army when we're not at war? It's always good to be prepared."

"Fair enough."

"We can all discuss it at the next council meeting back in

Vernallis. There's so much we're going to have to explain, and even if Magnus is subdued I still think—"

"Wait," Kastian interrupts. His eyes shift, suddenly darkening, and his face falls. "Shit. I have to tell you something."

His tone is serious and I pull back again, alarmed. "What's wrong?"

"We can't go back to Vernallis. At least, I can't...not right now."

"Did you want to stay here? That's fine. I assumed you still didn't want the crown, but it's rightfully yours so—"

"No," he interrupts again. "I definitely don't want to rule Hydratta, but that's not what I'm talking about. I can't stay here with you. I can't stay in *Ellender*. At least, not all the time."

My eyes narrow and I drop his hand. "What the hell are you talking about?"

"In order to survive and come after you I had to make a deal."

"What kind of deal?"

"A permanent one. Connell offered me a way to live and I accepted it. He gave me his ship."

"What do you mean he gave you his ship?"

"*The Sea Witch* needs a captain, and now that captain is me. According to Connell, I have to spend at least six months out of the year on the ship. He didn't have a lot of time to explain the details."

My eyes grow wide, and I turn to stare out at the stormy water in disbelief. On the horizon, I see a large ship I swear wasn't there before. I shiver. "I assume I can't go with you or you wouldn't sound like this was so dire."

Kastian straightens. "What?"

My eyebrows furrow in confusion. "You're saying you're going to be gone six months out of every year and I can't go with you, right?"

"Would you want to go with me?"

My eyes widen and for a long second I fail to speak, then words come flooding back all at once.

"You fucking idiot!" I screech. "Come in the water with me, I need to hit you so you can feel it."

"What? No." Kastian's eyes widen and he yanks his hand away before I can drag him toward the water.

"You're immortal, you can take it," I snap. "You deserve it if you didn't think I'd want to go with you?"

"It would be a long time away from Vernallis," he says. "I wasn't sure—"

I grab his face and pull it down so he's looking me directly in the eye. "Listen to me. I don't care about anything else, wherever you go, I go."

His answers is when I pull his mouth back down to mine.

"Wait!" A harsh voice yells across the courtyard. "Stop right there!"

Kastian and I look at each other, then pivot slowly toward the green-jacketed guard rushing toward us across the castle courtyard.

"Yes?" Kastian says, mildly.

The guard skids to a halt, looking equal parts indignant and confused. "You're not supposed to be here," he blurts out.

I raise my eyebrows. "We're not? On whose orders."

The guard's eyebrows furrow. "The king, he—"

"—doesn't need you to speak on his behalf!"

I stiffen, but don't move an inch as King Magnus walks out of the palace. Beside him, walks Jett, smiling his usual mischievous smile.

I feel Kastian stiffen beside me as my mouth falls open.

Jett catches my eye and grins wider. "*Nice dress,*" he mouths.

I look at Magnus again, and understanding dawns. I grip Kastian's hand, squeezing hard.

The guard looks as confused as Kastian, looking to his king, then back to us. Finally, he takes a step back. "Oh, my mistake."

"Get out," Magnus snaps.

The guard turns on his heel and scampers away, while Magnus moves into his place in front of Kastian and I. My shoulders tense, my muscles coiling with a nervous energy that I can't quite shake, despite the fact that I keep reminding myself there's no real threat. Kastian senses my unease and gently clasps my hand, his fingers warm and reassuring against my skin.

"Your tone is off," Kastian says.

I let out a relieved sigh. I should have known that if I realized this wasn't really Magnus, then Kastian would too.

As if to emphasize the point, Magnus cocks a hip and rolls his eyes. "I know it is. I can do the voice right if I really have to, but it feels wrong."

"Fair enough," I reply. "It must feel strange to use his body. Where did you put the real Magnus?"

Magnus's eyes widen in a pointed way, and I swear I see Lyra's expression bleeding though. "Come on, let's go into one of the offices so we can talk. There are spies all over this damn castle and I don't want to be overheard."

I smile slightly, thinking that just because we lock ourselves in an office doesn't necessarily mean we'll be safe from spies.

I'll have to check under the desk.

We follow Lyra in the shape of Magnus back into the castle and into the very same office I once hid in. Jett closes the door behind us and Kastian turns in a circle, eyes darting over the bookshelves, the arched windows and the dark oak desk. "It looks exactly the same. I'm surprised he didn't use my father's office."

"He never touched any of your rooms," Magnus says in Lyra's voice. They let out a frustrated breath. "Hang on a moment."

Before our eyes, Magnus's skin ripples, bubbling as if overheated. His body shrinks, and Lyra stands before us in too-large clothing, shaking out her arms. "That's better," she says in her normal voice.

Jett gapes at her. "That is the most amazing fucking thing I've ever seen."

Lyra gives him a hint of a smile, then looks back at Kastian. "Sorry, I was saying that my father never touched any of your rooms."

"Why?"

"I don't know, but as far as I know, your bedroom, your sister's rooms, your parent's offices...they're all still there."

I glance up at Kastian trying to read his feelings about that, but his face remains stonily unchanged. He doesn't say anything and finally I cut into the uncomfortable silence. "So, where's the real Magnus?"

"Under the castle," Jett answers darkly.

"Alive?"

"For now," Jett nods, then exchanges a meaningful look with Lyra of all people. "He's sedated, but still breathing. I figured we might need him. Daemon might want to question him, or...what about you, Kas?"

"What about me?" Kastian asks.

"I don't know. If it were me, I'd want revenge."

Kastian looks pensive. "I have revenge. I'm free and he's locked in his own dungeon."

"But did you want to do anything specific to him? Ask him anything?" Jett asks, incredulous.

"I want to never think about him again," Kastian says flatly. "But I don't know...maybe I'll have some other ideas when we come back in six months. Keep him alive just in case."

I glance at Lyra, wondering if she'll have any issue with that, but she says nothing. Apparently she doesn't care one bit about her adoptive father...and I can't say I blame her.

"Alright, that's settled for now," I say slowly. "What about Connell?"

"What about him?" Jett asks.

I shrug. Kastian's mention of our returning in six months just made me realize that he isn't here. "Well, for one, where is he?"

"Lying down in one of the guest suites," Lyra answers. "He doesn't look like he's feeling too well."

"Did giving up the ship hurt him?"

Kastian frowns. "It must have. Is he going to live?"

"He'll be fine," Jett grumbles. "I'll handle him."

I raise my eyebrows, and open my mouth to comment, but Kastian beats me to it. He laughs. "Don't tell me the pirate is growing on you?"

"I wouldn't go that far," Jett grumbles. "But he's not...horrible. He saved your life."

"True," Kastian says, sobering instantly.

"I'll have our healer take a look at him," Lyra says. "I think it's possible that he's just experiencing how it feels to be mortal for the first time in decades."

"So does that mean you're staying here?" I ask Jett.

"Maybe for a little while, but I need to go back to Vernallis and talk to Daemon and Alix as soon as possible. I assumed you'd be going with me?"

"I'm not sure." I glance sideways at Kastian. "How long before we need to return to the ship?"

"No idea," Kastian says. "Maybe Connell can tell me after the healer sees him."

"The only question left is what to do about Hydratta," Jett says.

All eyes turn to Kastian who takes a step back. "Whatever you're all thinking, stop. I haven't thought of this as my kingdom for over a century...and maybe even before that."

"The people wouldn't take a change in leadership well even if you did want the throne," Lyra says flatly with no apology in her voice—as if it's just a fact. "It's been far too long since your family was in power and things have moved on."

"Didn't you say the people view Magnus as a god?" I ask.

Her nose wrinkles. "Not all of them, but essentially yes. In my opinion it will be too much for them to experience a sudden shift. They won't bow to Daemon, or whatever your Vernalli king's name is. They don't know him and he's not from here."

"Just for the sake of argument, Magnus isn't from Hydratta either," I remind her. "He's Thermian."

"True, but that's not a bad thing right now. Thermia is the entire reason why an alliance with Vernallis was a good move for Hydratta."

I press the heels of my hands to my eyes. "I'm too exhausted for a political discussion. I need a bath, and a real dress," I gesture loosely at my toga-style rags.

Jett snickers, but quiets when Kastian shoots him a look.

"Alright," Kastian says with finality in his tone. "We don't need to solve all of the problems on the continent this afternoon. All I want to know is who's in charge until Daemon and Alix get here and can weigh in?"

"Me," Lyra says flatly, as if it brokers no argument. "Obviously."

We all look at her.

"No offense, but we don't know much about you," Jett says after a long moment.

"And?" she snaps. "You don't have to trust me. If anything, *you* need *me* to trust *you*. You're only in here because I let you be —I found you to save Kastian, I got Odessa out of the tower, I didn't stop you from torturing my father or tell the guards to seize you the moment you walked through the door."

"Yeah, but you're not the rightful ruler," Jett argues.

She glares sideways at Kastian. "Without me, the *rightful ruler* would have died years ago."

"I agree with her," Kastian cuts in. "Lyra should hold on to the crown, but I have a suggestion."

"What?" Lyra barks.

"Don't tell anyone what happened to Magnus. At least, not yet. That way, you can be him sometimes and make the transition smoother."

She blinks, startled, then her expression turns pensive.

I sigh. I know I've thought it before, but Lady Lyra Von Bargen is not a meek girl, she's a calculating woman who is clearly much more than she appears.

When Kastian and I leave the office, Jett is still inside with Lyra, helping to draft a letter to Daemon and Alix. It seems as if Hydratta and Vernallis will be forging an alliance after all, but I doubt Kastian and I will be on land long enough to see it happen. At least, not right away. We'll have to see how things are going when we return in six months.

"I wish I had a chance to pack before we have to leave," I comment.

Kastian looks sideways at me. "I don't think it's like a prison sentence," Kastian says. "Connell clearly came to shore for long stretches of time. We can stop in the harbors to buy things."

I grin. "But that's so dangerous."

He rolls his eyes. "You could find danger alone in an empty room, Princess. I doubt it matters much where we go."

"Now you mention it, where are we going right now?"

He's leading me up a flight of white marble stairs and I followed without question, trusting that he's leading me wherever I need to go. Still, I'm curious.

"I'm taking you to my room," he says. "My old room."

I raise my eyebrows. "Why? Wasn't once enough to hold you over for a few hours?"

His eyes heat. "Let's agree that you'll take that word out of your vocabulary."

"What word?"

"*Once.*"

I laugh. "Touched a nerve, did I?"

"Absolutely. Once is offensive when every day for the rest of my life will never be enough of you...but actually, that's not what I was thinking about. I want to see if I can find something."

He takes my hand and tugs me faster up the stairs and down the hall until I'm practically running to keep up. A laugh bubbles up in my throat, and I'm grinning ear to ear when we finally stop in front of a closed door.

Kastian pushes the door open and my eyes go wide as I look around. "Wow."

"Wow what?" he asks, walking deliberately across the room.

"Wow...I thought your room at the Ashwater Estate was strangely impersonal, but no. I see you've always been exactly the same."

He scowls at me and I grin.

The room is dusty from lack of use, but underneath that I can tell that nothing is out of place. The bed is made, there's barely any art on the walls, and not a single drawer has been left open. I wonder how Kastian is going to handle living with me...maybe it's lucky that I didn't have a chance to pack. It will take longer for a new mess to accumulate, and by then he'll already be in too deep. I smile at the thought.

Kastian stands over a desk in front of a large window and starts opening drawers one by one. I walk over to stand behind him, looking over his shoulder.

"Ah, there it is," he says triumphantly, reaching for something in the very smallest drawer.

"What?"

He holds his hand out, fist closed, and drops something into my palm. My breath catches when I stare down at an ancient brass key.

I hold it up to the light from the window, and it glimmers. "You still have this?"

"Apparently," he says. "I forgot about it—I guess I thought I lost it years ago, but I just remembered it's been here all along."

I glance up, my chest constricting. I'm not entirely sure we're talking about the key anymore—Maybe we never really were.

"My father told me this opens some treasure buried somewhere off the coast of Solistine. Who knows, maybe we can go find it now. It seems like we'll certainly have enough time."

As if he heard his name called, he suddenly glances sideways out the window. I follow his gaze and spot the outline of a dark ship bobbing on the horizon. A shiver travels up my spine.

Kastian looks back down at me, his brow furrowed. "You're really sure about this? I don't want you to be cursed along with me."

"What about this is a curse?" I scoff. "You can never die? That seems perfect. And I also feel like you're forgetting that I grew up on a ship. I love ships. And if you're the captain now you'll need to learn to do every single job on board. Fortunately for you, I'd be willing to teach you."

He grins. "What about Vernallis, though? What about all our friends and family?"

I shrug. "Six months isn't forever. We'll come back, it'll just give them enough time to miss us. If we leave soon, we could be back by yule. Belle is visiting again this year and I don't want to miss it."

Kastian grins. "As you wish."

KASTIAN, FIVE MONTHS LATER

I wake up to the sound of singing.

It's not normal singing—there are no words, and hardly any melody, but nevertheless I recognize the horrible screechy sound. It's mind-numbingly painful to listen to, so I roll over and pull my pillow over my head to drown it out. When that doesn't help, I grab Odessa's pillow too and pile them on top of each other.

Of course, Dessa isn't in bed.

I knew the moment I heard the wailing, which I can't understand but she swears has meaning, that Dessa was outside *"talking"* to her sisters...or subjects? I'm not entirely sure what the sirens are to her. She doesn't know yet either, and until she decides we're living in this strange limbo.

The *"pack"* are used to following their queen across the ocean, and they like to swim alongside our ship. Most of them have regained their independence now that the last queen has lost her hold on them, but they still remain close. Occasionally, when we sail into a harbor, the pack will transform into their other shapes and sit on the rocks waiting for us—or, rather, waiting for Odessa. The appearance of so many sirens in broad daylight has caused the sort of chaos and rumors that I'm sure have already made their way back to Vernallis.

I'm sure everyone will have a lot to say about it when we see them again in a few weeks. We've already changed course, and are heading back in the direction of Vernallis. We should arrive by yule, and when we arrive, we have a lot of questions for them as well.

The horrible shrieking sound continues and I groan, burrowing my face further into the mattress.

If I didn't already know I was bonded to Odessa, I would have known instantly the moment I heard that grating, excruciating sound. It's like metal on metal, and it's hard to imagine how it could possibly be hypnotic or beautiful. At least, it's hard to believe until I hear Odessa answer.

Whichever siren was shrieking stops and Odessa replies in a tone so persuasive and hypnotic I find myself climbing out of bed. Not because I have to—she's not compelling me—but just because I want to.

I pull on pants, but don't bother with a shirt. The tattoo of Odessa's face that Magnus sliced open has healed as if nothing ever happened, and I know Dessa likes seeing it. I like it too, and go out of my way to make sure it's visible whenever possible.

I climb the wooden stairs from the captain's quarters and step out onto the sunny deck. A few crewmen nod at me. "Morning Captain." "Nice day, isn't it Captain?"

I nod back, not speaking as I know they can't hear me. They've all got cotton shoved in their ears, and at the moment I envy them.

I'd thought Odessa and I would sail the ship on our own—between her knowledge of ships and my water magic, it hadn't seemed so hard. She quickly dispelled me of that notion, and we hired a small crew in the first port we stopped at.

Having the crew is an adjustment, especially for me who

would prefer to do every single job myself, but I'm growing used to them. The unpredictability of the sea has quickly taught me that no one man can be an island.

Granted, right now, I'd prefer the crew to disappear.

I reach for the nearest sailor and spin him toward me, then tap my ear for him to take the cotton out. He eyes me dubiously, and shake his head. "I can't. Sorry sir. I'd rather miss Odessa not have to jump after me again."

Oh, right. This is the man who heard the sirens a few months ago and flung himself overboard, forcing Odessa to go after him. We were more careful after that.

"Go inside," I mouth, pointing toward the door leading to below the deck. "All of you, go inside."

To my relief, he understands, and gathers the other men, all of them disappearing below deck. Only when I'm sure they're all gone do I finally approach Odessa.

She's wearing tight trousers and what looks to be my shirt, and leaning over the railing of the ship, her hair blowing in the wind.

I come up behind her and put a hand on her lower back to alert her that I'm there.

She looks up. "Oh, morning, Captain."

I shake my head. "Please, I'm begging you to stop calling me that."

"No," she says pointedly, then jerks her head toward the sea. "They told me the wind is shifting, we should change course or we'll blow too far south."

"Could they have told you that without all the screaming?"

She scowls and blows her hair out of her face. "They're trying to help. I feel responsible for them, it's my fault they're all adrift."

In my opinion she's looking at this all wrong. It's not her fault the sirens are disorganized, they should be thanking her that they can all think for themselves now...but this isn't the time to talk about that.

"Can you send them away?"

Her eyes narrow. "Why?"

I reach around and grip her ass to pull her closer, her hands falling flat on my chest. I press my face into the side of her neck, my answer getting lost in her hair. "Because I heard you singing and now I can't think of anything else but making you scream for me."

She sucks in a sharp breath, her fingers curling against my skin.

I trail my lips down her throat, and at the same time Dessa cranes her neck, singing something over her shoulder to the sirens.

Her voice catches, the sound coming out choked, when I reach between us to stroke her tight nipples through the thin fabric of my shirt.

I shove her—my—shirt up, and find she's not wearing anything underneath. Her bare breasts tighten when exposed to the air and I groan, pressing my already painfully hard cock into her stomach.

She leans back against the railing, hands braced on the wood, and tips her face up to meet mine, her eyes gone dark and hungry. "Here?" she teases. "You realize the crew could come back any second."

I smirk, nuzzling into her neck. "I told them to go inside. They know better than to interrupt me when I'm busy."

Odessa snorts, biting back a laugh as I run my tongue up her throat. "So I'm a distraction now, am I?"

"You're the only thing I want to be distracted by."

Odessa doesn't need more encouragement than that. She likes being out in the open air, and I've discovered I like it too. Ever since that rowboat in the swamp, and later on the beach, it's just not the same in a bed—not that we haven't tried that too.

She lets her head fall back, exposing more of her throat, and I take gentle advantage, kissing the delicate skin until she squirms. With one hand, I grip her hip to steady her, while the other roams down to undo her belt. "I miss when you wore dresses."

She chuckles. "No you don't, because when I wore dresses I wore underwear too."

"True."

She's right, of course. She always is. I growl—a real, involuntary sound—and slide my hand down to her waistband, fingers dipping beneath the fabric. She's already wet, and I draw my fingers slowly through her, savoring the heat and slickness, before lifting them to my lips and licking them clean. She watches, transfixed.

"I want to feel you come on my tongue," I growl, and it's not a suggestion or a request. It's a promise.

I drop to my knees without hesitation, ignoring the hard planks digging into my shins. I push her trousers down her hips, and she steps out of them with practiced grace, leaving her standing there in nothing.

I wrap my arms around her thighs and pull her close, burying my face between her legs. I lap at her slowly at first, relishing every gasp and stifled moan, but soon she's writhing, gripping my shoulders with desperate fingers.

She leans back even further over the railing, her legs shaking. I suck on her clit and she cries out, her legs shaking. "Enough. I can't...it's too much."

"Once is never enough." I say, kissing a trail along her thigh. "I want you to drown me."

She lets out a breathless gasp as I move my mouth back to her core, and her answer comes out strangled. "As you wish."

ABOUT THE AUTHOR

USA Today and International bestselling author Kate King loves sassy heroines, crazy magic, and alpha-hole heroes.

An avid reader and writer from a young age, she has been telling stories her whole life. Ever a fan of the dramatic, she lives in an 18th century church with her husband and two cats, and often writes in cemeteries.